STORIES OF CRIME AND DETECTION

STORIES OF CRIME AND DETECTION

Edited by

Joan D. Berbrich

G 64

McGRAW-HILL BOOK COMPANY

New York   St. Louis   Dallas   San Francisco   Atlanta

ACKNOWLEDGMENTS

Baskervilles Investments Limited for permission to reprint "The Reigate Puzzle" by Sir Arthur Conan Doyle.
Brandt & Brandt for permission to reprint "Aunt Minnie and the Accessory After the Fact" by Samuel Hopkins Adams. Copyright, 1945 by Liberty Weekly Incorporated; "The Old Barn on the Pond" by Ursula Curtiss, © 1965 by Davis Publications, Inc. First published in *Ellery Queen's Mystery Magazine;* and "The Possibility of Evil" by Shirley Jackson, © 1965 by Stanley Edgar Hyman. All reprinted by permission of Brandt & Brandt.
John Cushman Associates for permission to reprint "The Dove and the Hawk" by Anthony Gilbert. Reprinted by permission of John Cushman Associates, Inc., copyright © 1966 by Davis Publications, Inc. First published in *Ellery Queen's Mystery Magazine.*
Miriam Allen deFord for permission to reprint "A Case for the UN" by Miriam Allen deFord. Reprinted by permission of the author. First published in *Ellery Queen's Mystery Magazine.*
Dodd, Mead & Company, Inc. for permission to reprint "The Absence of Mr. Glass" by Gilbert K. Chesterton. Reprinted by permission of Dodd, Mead & Company, Inc. from *The Father Brown Omnibus* by G. K. Chesterton. Copyright 1914 by Dodd, Mead & Company, Inc. Copyright renewed 1942 by Gilbert K. Chesterton; "The Dream" by Agatha Christie. Reprinted by permission of Dodd, Mead & Company, Inc. from *The Regatta Mystery* by Agatha Christie. Copyright 1932, 1934, 1935, 1936, 1939 by Agatha Christie Mallowan. Copyright renewed 1967 by Agatha Christie Mallowan.
Robert L. Geiser for permission to reprint "Project Murder" by Steven Peters. Reprinted by permission of the author. First published in *Ellery Queen's Mystery Magazine.*

(continued on facing page)

Library of Congress Cataloging in Publication Data

Berbrich, Joan D   comp.
   Stories of crime and detection.

   (Patterns in literary art, 13)
   CONTENTS: All in the family: Coates, R. M. The net. Curtiss, U. The old barn on the pond. Poe, E. A. The oval portrait. Millar, M. The couple next door. [etc.]
   1. Detective and mystery stories. [1. Detective stories. 2. Crime and criminals—Fiction] I. Title.
PZ5.B418St   [Fic]   73-8832
ISBN   0-07-004826-6

Editorial Development, Susan Gelles; Editing and Styling, Vickie Woodruff; Design, Cathy Gallagher; Production, Renee Laniado

Mrs. Florence Kersh for permission to reprint "Murderer's Eye" by Gerald Kersh. Reprinted by permission of the Estate of Gerald Kersh, Mrs. Florence Kersh, executrix.

The Sterling Lord Agency, Inc. for permission to reprint "Carrot for a Chestnut" by Dick Francis. Reprinted by permission of The Sterling Lord Agency, Inc. Copyright © 1970 by Dick Francis. Also reprinted from *Sports Illustrated*, Jan. 5, 1970, by permission of the author.

Margaret B. Maron for permission to reprint "A Very Special Talent" by Margaret E. Brown. Copyright 1970 by H.S.D. Publications, Inc. From *Alfred Hitchcock's Mystery Magazine*, by permission of the author.

Harold Matson Company, Inc. for permission to reprint "The Green Elephant" by Dashiell Hammett. Copyright 1923, 1951 by Dashiell Hammett. Reprinted by permission of Harold Matson Company, Inc.

Scott Meredith Literary Agency, Inc. for permission to reprint "The President's Half Disme" by Ellery Queen. Reprinted by permission of the author and the author's agents, Scott Meredith Literary Agency, Inc., 580 Fifth Avenue, New York, N.Y. 10036. First published in *Ellery Queen's Mystery Magazine*; "D as in Detail" by Lawrence Treat. Reprinted by permission of the author and the author's agents, Scott Meredith Literary Agency, Inc., 580 Fifth Avenue, New York, N.Y. 10036. First printed in *Ellery Queen's Mystery Magazine*, October, 1964.

The New Yorker Magazine, Inc. for permission to reprint "The Net" by Robert M. Coates. Reprinted by permission; copr. © 1940, 1968 The New Yorker Magazine, Inc.

Harold Ober Associates, Inc. for permission to reprint "The Couple Next Door" by Margaret Millar. Reprinted by permission of Harold Ober Associates, Incorporated; copyright 1954 by Mercury Publications, Inc. First published in *Ellery Queen's Mystery Magazine*.

G. P. Putnam's Sons for permission to reprint "The Nine Mile Walk" by Harry Kemelman. Reprinted by permission of G. P. Putnam's Sons from *The Nine Mile Walk* by Harry Kemelman. Copyright 1947 by The American Mercury, Inc., and © 1967 by Harry Kemelman.

Paul R. Reynolds, Inc. for permission to reprint "Bubble Bath No. 3" by Margery Allingham. Copyright © 1967. Reprinted by permission of Paul R. Reynolds, Inc., 599 Fifth Avenue, New York, N.Y. 10017.

Walker & Company, Inc. for permission to reprint "The Red Silk Scarf" by Maurice Leblanc. From the book *The Confessions of Arsène Lupin* by Maurice Leblanc. Published by Walker & Company, Inc., New York, N.Y. © 1967 by Walker & Company, Inc.

A. Watkins, Inc. for permission to reprint "The Professor's Manuscript" by Dorothy L. Sayers. Reprinted from *In The Teeth of the Evidence* © by Dorothy L. Sayers 1939; originally published by William Collins, Sons, Ltd. Reprinted by permission of A. Watkins, Inc.

Acknowledgments v

CONTENTS

GENERAL INTRODUCTION

The mystery story is the single most popular kind of reading in the English-speaking world. To prove this statement for yourself, wander through the corridors of a hospital and notice what books most of the patients are reading. Or stroll down the aisle of a commuter train and glance at the titles of the paperbacks being absorbed.

What is the appeal? Why is this love for the mystery story so nearly universal? The answer probably lies first of all in our childhood. Almost all children play cops and robbers, or cowboys and Indians. They hardly care which side they are on—the important thing is the pursuit and the excitement that pursuit generates.

Next the adolescent. To the horror of parents and surgeons, teenagers play "chicken," turning automobiles into lethal weapons, playing on each other's fears, trying to overcome their own fears. News stories tell of dreadful statistics of teen-age drivers who, followed by a police car, step on the gas pushing their vehicles to 90, 100, 110 miles an hour—accepting the possibility of violent death rather than a summons. Fear of the law? A little. But also, surely, a momentary cessation of reason as the excitement of the chase obsesses them.

Nor does maturity end this absurd need. A short time ago a newspaper came into existence dedicated to the printing of only *good* news. It quickly went into bankruptcy; no one was interested in reading only good news. It is the bad news—the violent news, the news of multiple murders and widespread corruption—that claim readers' interest. People seem to experience a vicarious pleasure in reading about, or viewing at a distance, crime and violence. Yet these same people who seem to be simultaneously attracted and repulsed by crime and violence will flee the moment they feel personally confronted with the actuality of it.

This paradoxical love-hate, attraction-repulsion movement operates in all crime stories, but it is less true of the pure detective story. In many detective stories one scarcely sees the violence though one knows that murder has been committed. The mood is thoughtful; the suspense is intellectual. Why, then, the appeal?

The answer this time seems to lie in the adjectives just used—"thoughtful" and "intellectual." The individual, alone and sovereign, grasps a problem, observes and interprets clues, and solves the problem. Whether the reader is a plumber, a lawyer, a scientist, or a president makes little difference; for the time being, he is Sherlock Holmes or Gideon or even Hercule Poirot, masterfully controlling the labyrinthine search for order. Sometimes the reader even discerns the solution before the famous detective does, and what a lovely feeling of superiority *that* provides!

There are other theories that explain the popularity of the detective story. Some critics have suggested that it enables us to merge our own guilt with that of a suspect, and to find our guilt erased as the suspect is cleared and the true criminal identified. Some have suggested that the detective story appeals to our innate desire for law and order, as we help to track down the criminal and protect the innocent. And some have suggested that it permits us to identify with the criminal, releasing some of our anger and frustration at the society against which we fear to rebel.

But probably there is also some truth in the simplest theory of all: that mysteries are short, easy to read, and hold our interest, and so we read them just for fun—just to relax—just to forget our real problems. And perhaps that is the best reason in the world for reading mysteries.

History

The crime story is as old as man. In the Old Testament, Cain killed Abel; in Greek myths, parent killed child, and brother killed sister; in every civilization, from the most ancient to the present, crime has existed.

But the detective story is different. Some scholars, like Dorothy Sayers, trace the detective story also to the Old Testament, and certainly a case can be made for doing so. But the detective story *as we know it today* is not very old at all. It couldn't exist until police forces and detectives did; and it was only in the early nineteenth century that the Sûreté in France and Scotland Yard in England, were established.

In America the police had not even gotten off to a proper start before Edgar Allan Poe, after studying with interest the work of the Sûreté in Paris, wrote the first detective story: "The Murders in the Rue Morgue." The year was 1841, and the story was published in *Graham's Magazine* in Philadelphia. Its hero was the first modern detective: C. Auguste Dupin—a man who solved crimes by thinking about them, by organizing known data, and by drawing conclusions from them. His major talent was a calculating insight into the way his fellow human beings acted and thought. This first detective story also used for the first time the "locked room" approach. This approach refers to a mystery in which a dead body is found in a room locked from the inside, and the cause of death is not suicide.

Poe quickly followed this story with "The Mystery of Marie Roget," the first detective story based on a real case and the first example of armchair detection. In a third story, "The Purloined Letter," Poe used for the first time the technique of the most unlikely solution. In a less well-known story, "Thou Art the Man," Poe captured a few more firsts: the first use of the most unlikely suspect; the first use of ballistics; the first use of an anonymous sleuth; the first use of the laying of a false trail by the real criminal; the first use of a psychological third degree to extort a confession. By the time Poe finished his small group of detective stories, almost all of the "firsts" had been tried. For the next century and a half, mystery writers would be kept busy elaborating, refining, and developing Poe's ideas.

By comparison, the detective *novel* was a bit of a laggard. In 1866 Gaboriau's *L'Affaire Lerouge* was published in France. Just twelve years later in America Anna Katharine Green wrote *The Leavenworth Case* about a detective who used many of the techniques Poe had introduced to solve criminal problems.

Before Green and even before Gaboriau, the novel of espionage had made its debut with a work called *The Spy* written by James Fenimore Cooper in 1821. Based on historical notes from the American Revolution, *The Spy* contained all of the elements that later made the modern novel of espionage a success: coded messages, disguises, flight and pursuit, use of famous personages, and mercenary motives.

Few "firsts" remained. Mark Twain found one when he used fingerprints to help identify a criminal in *The Tragedy of Pudd'nhead Wilson* in 1894. After that, mystery writers concocted new methods of killing, new methods of deception, new methods of detection; yet they were not really new, just replays. Only in our own time has it become possible once again to come up with a "first." And this is the result of the development of forensic science. Whether the modern laboratory will expand the field for the detective story or destroy the field by making it the subject of routine inquiry remains to be seen. The detective story may be entering its finest period, or it may be already facing its own "death by unnatural means."

Types of Mystery Stories

Since life itself is a mystery and death is an even greater one, properly speaking every story ever written might be called a "mystery." This is especially true of a novel like *Jane Eyre*, yet Charlotte Brontë's novel is never included on any list of mysteries. For, by definition a mystery story or novel must, first and last, concentrate on the mystery to be solved, not on a life story or the mores of an age or a setting. Even this definition is broad, so broad that it covers a half dozen very different kinds of stories and novels.

1. *The Crime Story.* This is the most general type. It embraces any kind of crime committed by a professional criminal or an amateur. The emphasis may be on the planning or the commission of the crime, or on the solution. If the latter, the problem may be solved by an ordinary person, by a detective, or even by official law officers.

Related to the crime story is the story of true crime, a narration of a crime actually committed. Again, emphasis varies. Several favorites are told over and over: the Lizzie Borden murders, the disappearance of Dr. Parkman, the Leopold-Loeb kidnapping.

Newer to the field is the non-fiction novel, defined and popularized by Truman Capote. The non-fiction novel takes an actual crime, uses all of the known data, then adds dialogue and a little description to turn non-fiction into a novel. The outstanding example, of course, is Capote's best seller, *In Cold Blood*.

2. *The Detective Story*. This type emphasizes the art of detection—the finding of clues, the interpretation of clues, the application of deduction or psychology, and finally the determining of the solution. The detective story, as it is known today, started with Edgar Allan Poe in the mid-nineteenth century. Poe's detective C. Auguste Dupin is intellectually astute, marvelously observant, sensitive to human nature, perceptive, and idiosyncratic. As such, he is the true ancestor of nine-tenths of the detectives who have followed him and who carry faithfully these inherited characteristics. Note especially Ellery Queen (Ellery Queen), Hercule Poirot (Agatha Christie), and Nero Wolfe (Rex Stout).

Although the three detectives mentioned above are "favorite sleuths" —that is, they appear in a series of novels and short stories—the detective story does not demand such a personage. The detective may be a much humbler, mundane individual such as the schoolteacher aunt in "Aunt Minnie and the Accessory After the Fact" or the traveling salesman in "The Professor's Manuscript." The important thing is that the emphasis be clearly on the *solution* of a crime, and that the solution be based on a recognition and interpretation of clues.

3. *The Police Procedural Story*. The emphasis here, once again, is on the solution of a crime, but the solver is now a member of an official police system. That system may be Scotland Yard, a New York City police precinct, or a small town sheriff's office. But the solver is official, has access to scientific equipment, to a laboratory, and must cope with the red tape that accompanies official routine. The police procedural can be exciting and varied, but it can also become thoroughly dull if the writer forces us to trail a police detective on door-to-door inquiries or through long nightly reports. An intriguing byproduct of the police procedural novel is the great wealth of information that is given about current police methods of detection. With Dell Shannon (the Los Angeles police), Ed McBain (the 87th precinct) or Lawrence Treat (Homicide Squad, some city), the serious reader can learn much about fingerprinting, hair and blood analysis, tire treads, moulages, and computer identification.

4. *The Gothic Mystery*. Horace Walpole is usually given credit for starting this enduring type of mystery with his *Castle of Otranto*. In

this novel written two centuries ago the following elements are present: the lonely castle, the supernatural happenings, the gory murders, the damsel in distress, the handsome young man who comes to the rescue. The American Gothic changes the castle to a large family home in the country, but it retains most of the other trappings so dear to the hearts of Gothic readers. Love plays a major role in this type of mystery. The woman is almost always young and beautiful and helpless; indeed, she is often rather stupid, scarcely aware of the danger surrounding her until several people have been killed. Her innocence and her naive trust are exactly the traits that appeal to the hero who is always good (though occasionally in the beginning of the narrative he *seems* to be evil). The Gothic is rejected contemptuously by most critics, but many continue to be published each year to satisfy their loyal readers. Among the best of the Gothic writers are Mary Stewart, Victoria Holt, and Georgette Heyer.

5. *The Spy Story.* The story of espionage goes in and out of popular favor with unusual regularity. A small but fervent school of readers keeps spy stories alive at all times, but some added impetus is necessary to send them to the top of the best-seller list of mysteries. James Bond (Ian Fleming) and his incredible exploits started one high period; LeCarre's *The Spy Who Came In from the Cold* started another. The story of espionage is, almost always, international with the action rushing the reader from country to country. Trains were the favorite vehicle for years, though planes have been gaining steadily. Exotic settings are preferred, and the major enemy depends on the current political situation. Perhaps it is the latter that makes spy stories seem dated faster than other types of mysteries. The spy who comes into conflict with Hitler's henchmen simply means less to us today than does the quiet little man down the block who murders his wife and three children. The first is part of history; the second is part of daily life. Even so, the spy story has already had a long existence and shows no signs of disappearing.

Who's Who in the World of Sleuths

Most readers of mysteries have a couple of sleuths they favor above all others. It makes little difference to the real mystery buff if the favored sleuth appears unchanging in novel after novel; if he always looks the same and talks the same; if he solves cases in an astonishingly similar fashion. Part of the fun of having a favorite sleuth is that one grows accustomed to his way of thinking as well as to his idiosyncrasies. The first provides a head start in solving the mystery; the second, like comic irony, offers the reader the opportunity to feel indulgent and superior.

Fortunately writers have a penchant for the quirks and headwhirling touches that distinguish one human being from another. Below is a small "Who's Who of Favorite Sleuths." Each entry gives vital information—not statistical, but human—the small details that bestow on each detective a special and distinctive personality.

Holmes, Sherlock. (Sir Arthur Conan Doyle). Moody; plays the violin and sports a deer-stalker cap; observes, reasons, and deduces; is given to enigmatic utterances.

Dupin, C. Auguste. (Edgar Allan Poe). Of an illustrious family and given to ratiocination; devoted to "meditation and a meerschaum"; has a passion for darkness, which he believes is essential to reflection.

Brown, Father. (G. K. Chesterton). Short and chubby; a priest; usually seen carrying an umbrella (which he drops frequently) and wearing a round hat; possesses a simple goodness and a not-so-simple insight; shares Chesterton's love for the paradoxical.

Queen, Ellery. (Ellery Queen). Lean and long; has a probing inquisitive brain; is fascinated by off-beat mysteries and odd bits of information; concentrates by prowling and scowling, likes Duesenbergs and tweeds.

Poirot, Hercule. (Agatha Christie). Small Belgian with an egg-shaped head and a Dali-like mustache; is famous for his "little grey cells;" raises vegetable marrows; is aware of his own superiority and often speaks of it.

Wolfe, Nero. (Rex Stout). Fat, astute, and raises 10,000 orchids; fond of money and of himself; dislikes movement of any kind but has a trusted assistant, Archie Goodwin, who runs, snoops, and fights.

Mason, Perry. (Erle Stanley Gardner). Plays punchball with words in courtrooms; instinctively chooses clients who are *always* innocent; revels in the care and admiration of his secretary, Della Street; tops in forensic medicine and law.

Maigret. (Georges Simenon). An Inspector with the French police; has a tendency to stand in the rain a great deal; often thinks morosely of his health, his neglected dinners, and the evil ways of the world.

Marlowe, Philip. (Raymond Chandler). Tough and sardonic; "a common man and yet an unusual man ... a man of honor"; known for sharp dialogue and memorable wisecracks; always low in funds; capable of absorbing and inflicting huge quantities of physical punishment.

Gideon, George. (J. J. Marric). A Commander in the C.I.D., London, England; is big-shouldered and just; juggles several cases at one time with great dexterity; projects a nice, fatherly image.

Campion, Albert. (Margery Allingham). A gifted amateur detective; sports horn-rimmed glasses; is aesthetic; sees all and understands more.

Alleyn, Roderick. (Ngaio Marsh). A Chief Inspector; witty, intellectual, and aphoristic; likes to travel; is married to Troy, a gifted painter and a fair-to-middling detective herself when husband is away.

Bond, James. (Ian Fleming). Explosive and ruthless; sees women as objects; probably remembered best for *Goldfinger;* prefers exotic sadism and "soul-erosion."

Marple, Jane. (Agatha Christie). A sweet old lady of St. Mary's Mead, a charming English village; knits as she sleuths; works by drawing analogies to people and incidents she has known; eyes tend to twinkle quite a lot.

Fell, Gideon (Dr.). (John Dickson Carr). Omniscient; of great bulk usually swaddled in a box-pleated cape; capable of Gargantuan mirth and Gargantuan distress; twirls alternately a bandit's mustache and a crutch-handled stick; plays chess, smokes cigars, and has several chins.

Fansler, Kate. (Amanda Cross). Literate, scholarly university professor; kind but can be caustic; often found in library stacks and college classrooms although she is also at home in rural surroundings.

Wimsey, Lord Peter. (Dorothy Sayers). An eccentric aristocrat with a taste for vintage port and a curiosity that is dazzlingly versatile; too "cute" for many readers, but totally captivating to others; one of the earliest of the egghead charmers who now abound.

Opara, Christie. (Dorothy Uhnak). First-grade police detective; can slam a gangster under the jaw while breaking up a narcotics ring; attractive to look at (says Casey Reardon) and also to watch in operation; tough and gentle as she proves herself in what used to be a man's world.

Templar, Simon. (Leslie Charteris). Also known as "The Saint"; the Robin Hood of modern crime; is physically daring, a sort of cultured Batman; knows about everything from fine paintings to thief-proof locks; possesses total invincibility.

Lupin, Arsène. (Maurice Leblanc). Brilliant and conceited thief; alternately torments and assists the Paris police; is concerned with real justice rather than with court justice; a skillful acrobat, both physically and mentally.

All in the Family

CHAPTER ONE

Most murderers are ordinary people. They eat, sleep, and dress as ordinary people do. They may have nine-to-five jobs in offices or stores, or they may be housewives or plumbers. But what most of them have in common is that they're members of a family, both loved and loving.

This is not so strange as it at first seems. Only those we truly care about can disappoint and infuriate and enrage us. Only those we live with daily can needle us to the point of violence or frustrate us to the point of despair. Only those we love can—through disillusionment—become those we hate. It is the stress of the intensity of personal relations and the thinness of the line between love and hate that from time to time cause people to murder.

The tradition of murder within the family is an old one—as old as man.

Consider the biblical tradition. God created Adam and Eve, and Eve bore two sons, Cain and Abel. Both sons offered gifts to God: Abel, a shepherd, offered a lamb; Cain, a farmer, offered vegetables. God smiled on Abel's gift, and praised him, and Cain grew exceeding angry. He, the elder brother, had been slighted. His pride hurt, his eyes blinded by jealousy, Cain led the trusting Abel into the fields and there slew him— *the first murder.*

Later the Lord asked Cain, "Where is thy brother Abel?" and Cain replied, "I know not. Am I my brother's keeper?"—*the first interrogation and the first act of perjury through evasion.* Then the Lord found Cain guilty and placed upon his forehead a brand—the mark of Cain—and sent him away, east of Eden—*the first verdict* and *the first sentence.*

Consider the Greek mythological tradition. The leader of the gods, Cronus, had gained his position by rebelling against his father. Now legend claimed that one of *his* children would, in turn, overthrow him. Cronus tried to avert the threat by swallowing each child as it was born —infanticide. When Zeus came along, his mother—tired of losing her children to her cannibalistic spouse—gave Cronus a stone to swallow in place of the new baby. Zeus lived, grew to maturity, and marshaled forces against his father. Cronus was defeated, and Zeus became the supreme god, using his power to maim, punish, and destroy. His thunderbolts were aimed most often at his brothers and sisters, his wives and children—all members of the Olympian family.

Consider the newspaper printed this morning. The subject matter is the same: a husband kills his wife, a mother strangles her children, a youth slays his lover and then himself.

The conclusion is clear: violence occurs most often *within* a family, or between two people who know each other well. The answer to the question why this happens is also clear, but it demands a little thought.

Police know that in order for a murder to be committed, three conditions are usually necessary: motive, opportunity, and means. Unfortunately, all three are available in most homes.

Motive. One partner in a marriage may be jealous of the other; if affection wanes or eyes wander, love turns to hate and violence erupts. The result can be anticipated, and the motive—in terms of human fallibility—is comprehensible. But there are other times when the motive seems trivial, even absurd. A husband's sloppiness or a wife's nagging hardly merits a violent reaction, yet given the right conditions—daily pressure, mounting frustration, inability to escape—the trivial act, the minor habit, can unexpectedly escalate into a motive for murder.

Opportunity. Members of a family are with each other much of the time. Sometimes they are sleeping and hence especially vulnerable. Sometimes they travel together, on a winding road or over a poorly built bridge. Sometimes they eat together. The opportunity is there, not occasionally, but half a dozen times daily.

Means. Motive and opportunity count for little unless the "means" is at hand. No problem. The average household is a veritable storehouse of deadly weapons. There are plastic bags, sharp-edged knives, the gas in the kitchen range, a hammer, an ice pick, electricity, the front stairs, and the bathtub filled with water. One of Hitchcock's most memorable television thrillers showed a frozen leg of lamb used as a club for murder, then cooked and eaten—a disappearing weapon, indeed!

2

The most easily available weapon, though, is human strength. Powered by anger, a pair of clutching hands will suffice.

Motive, opportunity, and *means*—small wonder that, when a murder does take place, the police first investigate the immediate family, then friends, and last of all, strangers. The poet and playwright Oscar Wilde understood this. A prison inmate himself, he described in "The Ballad of Reading Gaol" a fellow prisoner who was a murderer and was about to be executed. Wilde brooded about murder until he began to understand *why* one human robs another of that one precious, irreplaceable gift—*life:*

> And all men kill the thing they love,
> By all let this be heard,
> Some do it with a bitter look,
> Some with a flattering word,
> The coward does it with a kiss,
> The brave man with a sword!

INTRODUCTION: The Net

The net used to catch fish is a material thing, made in factories or by hand. The net used to catch criminals is nonmaterial and is often woven by the criminal himself, or by the victim. Such a net may be made of the words and actions, the fears and emotions, of the humans involved.

In this story there is a net of this type, woven by Walter and Ann; but there is also a second net, made by Ann's family. The old Greek playwrights knew that no individual stands alone, that each of us is a combination of what we think we are and of what others think us to be. The author, sensitive to both kinds of nets, subtly blends them. The result is a sharp study of the ambiguity of guilt.

The Net

Robert M. Coates

Walter had just turned the corner of Charles Street into Seventh when he saw her. She was standing a little way up the block talking to a fellow in a black overcoat and a black felt hat, and just the way they were standing—the fellow leaning back against the wall of the building there and she crowded close against him, looking up at him—was enough to let Walter know the kind of talk they were having. Almost without thinking, he stopped and stepped back a pace down Charles, out of sight around the corner.

This was the way things went, then; this was what she had left him for. He had known it, but this was the first time he had ever had sight of it, and it sent a queer feeling through him, as if more air than he could breathe had been forced into him. He was a tall man, with a pale, solemn, heavy-jawed face and a slow, slightly awkward manner of movement. He placed himself against the railing of an areaway and stood there, looking down Seventh Avenue, waiting. He knew she would have to come around the corner when she started home, and whether she was alone or the fellow was still with her, he would have a right to speak to her then. Till then he would wait. He had time.

It was growing late and the evening had been cold; there were few people walking. Down by Christopher Street there was a cluster of bright signs and illuminated buildings, but up where he was the houses were mostly dark, and the only sound was the rough, shuffling whir of

4

the tires on pavement as the cars went flying by. Then the traffic lights changed and the cars stopped, at Charles, at Tenth, at Christopher; at Charles, a black truck crawled out across the avenue and went slowly on down the street past Walter, toward Hudson.

That was all the cross traffic there was, but for a few seconds longer the avenue was still. Then the lights went green and the headlights moved forward, sifting past each other as the cars took up their varying speeds. A moment later, Walter heard the tap of her heels on the sidewalk, coming around the corner, and she passed him.

"Hello, Ann," he said softly.

She hadn't noticed him till then; he could tell that from the way her head snapped around and the look that came over her face. Then she turned her head away. She kept on walking. "Hello, Walter," she said wearily.

He was walking along beside her. "Where you been, Ann?" he asked. "I was at your people's house and they said you'd went to the movies."

"I did."

"Yeah. The movies."

She glanced up at him, and he could see her face pinching up in the way it did when she got angry. But she didn't say anything; she just turned her face forward again, tucked her chin down in the fur collar of her coat, and walked on. He kept pace with her. "I saw you talking to that fellow back there, Ann," he went on in his slow, insistent voice. "I saw you."

"Well," she said. "So you saw me. Can't a girl meet a friend on the street?"

"Yeah. But the movies."

He knew she didn't like to be prodded like that about things, even when she was telling the truth, and he half expected her to burst out with something then and there. He could feel his chest tightening already, in that mixture of fear and excitement and stubbornness that always came over him when they got into an argument. But she just kept on walking. After a few steps she turned to him again. "You was up to the folks'?" she asked, her voice very innocent and offhand. "Who'd you see? Was Ma there?"

"Yes, your mother was there," he said. "As you doubtless know. I know what you're thinking, Ann, but I didn't think it would give you pleasure. She didn't give me no nice reception. But that don't bother me, either; that I expected. I'm not blind, and I know who it was that turned you against me and broke up our marriage. But there's an old saying, Ann, that marriages are made in heaven, and I believe it, and I believe she will get her punishment, too, for what she's done—turning a man's wife against her lawful husband. If not now, then she'll surely get it in the hereafter. But it's not her I'm worried about; I leave her to her own devices. It's you, Ann. Listen," he said. "What you don't get is, I'd take you back tomorrow. Like that. I don't care who you been with, what you done—even that fellow back there, Ann, whoever he is. I don't ask. But a fellow you got to meet on street corners, can't even show to your folks—but even him, Ann; I'd forget everything. Just so long as you'd tell me, come clean about things. But this lying and hiding. Listen, Ann—" He had thought a good deal about this meeting and had planned for it, and this was one of the things he had figured on saying, so he found himself talking faster and faster. But just then a crazy thing happened.

They were passing a series of old-fashioned houses with high-stooped entrances, and the steps running down from them made the sidewalk narrow. And there was a couple, a man and a girl, walking up the street toward them; in his excitement, Walter didn't notice them until he was upon them, and then there wasn't room for them all to pass. The man bumped him, and Walter stumbled, trying to sidestep them, but all the time his eyes were on Ann. She had walked on, never varying her pace, as if she had nothing to do with him at all, and at the sight of her tan-stockinged legs flicking briskly away beneath her black coat a kind of panic took hold of him. "I'm your husband, Ann!" he yelled suddenly. He could see both the man's and the girl's faces turned toward him, but for the moment he didn't care. He shoved past them and ran after Ann, grabbing at her arm. "I'm your husband," he repeated, his voice still loud. "Don't that mean anything to you? For better or for worse." Then he saw that she was laughing, and he let go of her arm.

It was only a little way farther on to her family's apartment house. When they reached it, she ran up the three or four steps to the entrance. Walter followed her, letting the street door swing shut behind him. They were alone in the dim vestibule. She bent her head for a moment, fumbling in her bag for the key, then she glanced up. "Well, Walter," she said. She wasn't laughing now, but she might just as well have been; he could tell from the look on her face that she was only waiting to get on upstairs to start in again. "Well, it's been a enjoyable little walk."

He could feel the air crowding into his lungs again, so hard that it made his whole chest feel hot inside. "Maybe it ain't finished yet," he said.

"Well, it is for me. I'm going up."

"I'm coming up too."

"No you won't."

"Why won't I?" Without his meaning it to, he could hear his voice getting louder. "What you got to conceal up there?"

"Oh, Walter! It ain't that and you know it. But you know what'll happen. You and Ma." He hadn't realized that he had moved closer to her, but he must have, for suddenly she stepped back a pace and stared up at him. "Walter," she said. "You been drinking?"

"I have not been drinking," he said, and he let his voice go louder still when he said it. Let her scare a little, he was thinking; at least she wasn't laughing at him any more. She was paying attention to him now. "Well, then," she said, and she began talking faster. "Listen, Walter. This kind of chasing around ain't getting us anywhere, you hiding around corners and laying for me and all that. Why don't we get together some other way, sometime? I could come up to your place sometime, even. You still got the apartment, haven't you? We could talk."

"You come up there," he said, "and maybe you wouldn't never leave it again." He hadn't meant to put it like that; what he'd meant was that if she came up, it would have to be because she wanted to stay there and be with him again, but the way it came out it sounded threatening, even to him, and she must have thought so too, for she stared at him blankly a moment. Then, suddenly, she made a kind of a dive out of the corner where he had crowded her. "Then go home then! Get out of here!" he heard her cry, and she began pushing with both hands against his chest. He grabbed her wrists and she screamed. When she screamed, his hands went directly to her throat.

He had only intended to stop her screaming, but as soon as he touched her a strange kind of strength flowed into his hands, a strength that came from somewhere inside him and that once released could not be recalled, so that he couldn't have let go if he'd tried. For a while she struggled, jerking her body this way and that and pulling at his arms with her hands. It didn't bother him. He had shoved her back against the wall, so hard that her head bumped against it and her hat tipped over sidewise. He just stiffened his legs and stood there, his hands locked hard in the flesh of her throat; he was surprised at how strongly he stood there, meeting and conquering every move she made. "Laugh now," he said once, not loud, but almost gently.

Her knee worked up somehow between them until it was pressing against his thigh, but there was no strength in it; the strength was all in him, and soon the knee slipped harmlessly down again. Then her body lashed back and forth once or twice, fast and violently, and stopped, and her eyelids, which had been tight shut, opened so that he could see through her lashes the blue of her eyes, glittering in the dim light overhead. A kind of shudder ran through her. It was some time after that before he realized that she wasn't struggling any more.

It was the strain on his arms that told him of the change. Her body was just so much weight now, almost more than he could hold, and he let her slide slowly down along the wall until she was sitting on the floor, her back propped against the corner of the vestibule. Well, I did it, he thought, I did it; and for a moment he stood looking down at her uncertainly, not knowing what he ought to do next. One leg was crooked awkwardly sidewise, he noticed, so that the skirt was pulled up above the stocking top, and he bent down and pulled the hem over the knee. Then he turned and went out the door.

At the top of the steps he stopped and looked up and down the street. At first glance it seemed there was no one in sight at all, not a soul; then he noticed a couple of people standing in front of a house farther down the block—a man and a girl, he thought, though he couldn't be sure; about all he could see was their faces, and these were no more than pale spots in the shadows where they were standing. Farther still, down almost to Hudson, he sighted two others, two men, dark against the light from a shop window on the corner. And now there was a girl clipping quickly along on the opposite sidewalk; it was amazing how silently they all moved, and how easy it was not to notice them in the darkness. He stood where he was for a while, watching them, trying to determine if there was any sign of a concerted scheme in their actions. He had a feeling that they were only moving as they did in order to set a trap for him; at a signal they might all turn and begin running to surround him.

But none of them paid any attention to him. The couple down the block just stood there, the two men walked onward, the girl hurried around the corner and disappeared. Walter went down the steps and turned up toward Seventh Avenue. Well, I did it, he thought again, and as before, the thought carried no emotion with it except relief. It had to be done, it was coming to her; that was the way his thoughts ran, and what little guilt he had was submerged in a kind of careless irresponsibility, the feeling that a drunken man has when he knows he has done something wrong, admits it and doesn't care. The emotion was so close to that of drunkenness that even Walter recognized it. I could say I was drunk, he thought, his mind momentarily occupied with stratagems. But as soon as the idea came to him, he rejected it. I've got better reasons than that, he decided: her laughing at me, cheating on me, chasing at every corner. As he neared Fourth Street, another man, a new one, sprang up suddenly before him, a short, heavy-set fellow stepping out of the shadows and striding directly toward him.

The man passed without giving him a second glance, but after the man had gone by, Walter stopped and stepped back against a house wall, watching his progress down the street; suppose he was headed for *her* house, he was thinking, and the fear became so strong that he almost set out in pursuit of the stranger. I could ask him for a match, get him talking, lead him on past the door, he thought. As he hesitated, the man went by; he went three or four doors farther before he turned in.

Walter walked on. He didn't hurry, and when he reached the end of the block he even stopped for a moment, glancing, as if idly, up and down before crossing the street. The night was a net, he realized, with its streets and its people walking this way and that along them; what he had to do was to find his way out without disturbing anything or anyone. The thing that worried him most now was his breathing; he discovered that it had been bothering him for some time. He would find himself breathing fast and hard, so hard that it hurt his chest, and then he would take a deep breath, so long and so deep that when he let it out he could feel the flesh of his body shrinking away from his clothes, leaving the skin damp and prickly and cool. Then the hard, quick breathing would begin again.

Like a man that's been running, he thought. That was one thing he mustn't do; without even thinking about it, he knew he mustn't run. Or talk. For a while he had had the notion of going up to his brother-in-law's place. It was just a notion, or really it was more like a picture that had come into his mind; somehow, he didn't want to go home, and suddenly he had seen himself sitting with Frank and Ethel in their warm apartment, and then he had thought how pleasant it would be, it would rest him; they'd send out for some beer even, maybe. But he saw now that it wouldn't do. He'd get to talking, and there was no way of knowing how they'd take it. At the thought, the picture in his mind changed in a way that made him go cold all over; from seeing their faces smiling at him, friendly and companionable, he had seen them go white and staring, and hard with horror as they looked at him.

It was an awful thing he had done, all right, and the funny part was that he hadn't meant to. "God sakes!" he said. For the moment he was arguing with Frank and Ethel, and he found himself talking out loud. "If I'd meant to do it, wouldn't I have planned the thing different? Me here with no more than a couple bucks in my pocket." If it had been Friday, even, when his pay came through at the shop; then he'd have had a matter of thirty-five dollars in his hand, enough to start out with, anyway. But maybe Frank would lend him some money; he'd done as much for him on occasion.

"I swear, Frank, it's the first time I ever even laid hands on her. I never meant to harm a hair of her head." He had stopped talking out loud, but he was still arguing to himself when he remembered that Frank was Ann's brother; he had had an idea all along that his mind was running too fast for him, sort of, so that he was overlooking things. And maybe important things. This proved it. If Frank was Ann's brother, that left him out, of course; he was the last man to turn to now. It was late, too. His mind had been racing ahead, full of confidence, but now it was swarming with doubts and uncertainties: how could he expect to burst in on them now, at this hour, asking for money, without them asking questions? And even if he did get some money, where would he go?

It would mean quitting his job, leaving everyone he knew, everything. Me a man that's near forty, he thought.

It was just that Frank was the only one in the family that had ever had a decent word for him.

And the thing was, he hadn't meant to do it. All the time back there in the vestibule it had seemed like all the dozen of times in the past when he and Ann would have arguments; and she'd slump down in a chair or a sofa, so mad that she couldn't keep from crying but still trying to hide it; and he'd shout something, slam the door and go out. And then, like as not, she'd get up, slam the door too, and go off to see one of her girl friends or something. But not now. Now she would lie where she was, in the dim hallway, until someone came in from the street or down from the apartments above, and stumbled over her.

It would happen any minute now, if it hadn't happened already, and at the thought a vast sorrow rose up slowly inside him and filled him—sorrow for himself and for Ann, but mostly for himself. What I've got myself in for, he kept thinking. A whole group of people, men and women all talking and laughing, were coming down the steps of a house ahead of him, and he slowed his pace so as not to get tangled up with them on the sidewalk. But they just stood there, and finally he had to brush past them. As he did so, he shoved one of the men and gave the whole group such a fierce look that they must have noticed it; he was sure he saw their faces change.

I could tell you something that would stop your giggling, he thought, and this time, when he thought of the terror he could bring to their faces, he felt an odd sort of satisfaction; it would serve them right, he thought. When he had gone a few paces farther on, he looked back. They were all trailing off down the street, and on an impulse he stopped and leaned against an areaway railing, watching them. It would happen any minute now, he thought.

How long he stood there he didn't know, but it couldn't have been long, and the thing that made him conscious of time again was a thin knife sound like a scream or a siren; then a car's headlights turned into the street from away down at Hudson. He watched them, and it was some seconds before he realized what was the matter with them: the car was heading up the wrong way, against traffic.

Only a police car would do that, he thought, and as if in confirmation he saw it swing in toward the curb and stop, just about where the entrance to Ann's house would be. Well, then, the police were coming, he thought; that was right, it was proper, and if the old woman—he realized that one of the things he had been worrying about was Ann's mother; he'd known she'd be mixed up in the scene down there some way. But if the police were there and she started her ranting and screaming—well, they'd know how to stop her. Slowly he pushed himself away from the railing.

He'd go on up to Frank's, he thought, but it was only when he started walking on up the street, toward Seventh, that he realized how tired he was. So maybe, after all, he'd go home. It's too much, he thought. It's too much to expect of a man. He was still arguing about this question of packing up and leaving town for good. But he was almost too tired, and too lonely to bother about it. Unexpectedly, as he walked, a picture came into his mind of the couple he had bumped into when Ann and he were walking home. Down this very block, it had been, and he could see them again, their faces turning in surprise as he shoved past them shouting; somehow, the recollection only added to his feeling of lonely helplessness.

If he could only talk to them, he thought, he could explain everything; they were the only people in the world, perhaps, who would understand. But they had gone, and the thought vanished too, almost as soon as it had come to him. He walked on up to Seventh and then turned north, toward the subway. Maybe he'd go up to Frank and Ethel's after all; if there had been a reason against going there, he had forgotten it, and anyway it wasn't worth bothering about now. Most of all, now, he felt tired.

FOR DISCUSSION: The Net

1. Jealousy of a husband or of a wife is not unusual, but why might this jealousy continue even after a couple are separated? Under what conditions might jealousy even be intensified after separation?
2. In this story Ann's laugh infuriates her husband. How can something as simple and human as laughter stimulate violence? Is the trivial act of laughter in itself the cause of the murder, or is it indirectly the cause, a symbol of Ann's attitude or of Walter's feeling of inferiority?
3. The behavior of Ann's mother is one strand in the net that closes around Walter. Describe two ways in which her attitude unwittingly helps to establish a background for the murder.
4. Walter is slow and determined. Neither his brain nor his body can operate with speed and precision. How might the slowness of his thinking have contributed to the breakup of his marriage? How did it influence his actions, both before and after the murder?
5. In the last paragraph Walter wishes he could talk to the young couple "he had bumped into when Ann and he were walking home." He had never seen the couple before that. Why then did he feel that perhaps only they might understand why he had killed Ann?

INTRODUCTION: The Old Barn on the Pond

Irony, a major element in many mystery stories, is difficult to define. If you use words in such a way that they convey the opposite of their literal meaning, this is irony. If, for example, someone breaks a new vase and you compliment him on his dexterity, you are being ironic. But irony also results if there is incongruity between what is expected to happen and what actually does happen. If you spend all summer working on an old car and you can't make it work, and then your little brother, who has been warned not to touch the car, twists something and it starts to work, that's irony.

In this story the author uses irony in several different ways. Her topic —the portrayal of a man with an inflated ego—is complex and subtle, and irony permits both writer and reader to cut through the shadows to the truth. Howard Hildreth is an intelligent man and a professional playwright. He—more than most people—should have realized that irony exists in life as well as in fiction.

The Old Barn on the Pond
Ursula Curtiss

He came back on a raw, darkly glistening day in March, but it was not at all the triumphant return he had planned. It was a hasty, off-balance thing, like being pushed rudely onto a stage before the raised trumpets had blown a single note.

Conlon's letter—the letter that had brought him tumbling up from New York to this inhospitable part of the New England countryside—was still in his pocket. He had never liked Conlon, but the architect was Marian's cousin and it would have looked odd, when he had the old barn remodeled, to have given the job to someone else. And now here was Conlon writing "... have been approached by friends about the possibility of renting your property here for the summer, with an option to buy. As they have a young child, they would like to drain the pond, and although I told them I was certain you would not permit this—"

For a moment the typed lines had blurred before Howard Hildreth's eyes—except for that one staring phrase.

Drain the pond.

"Not yet," he thought lucidly—"not after only six months." Anonymous in the Forty-second Street Library, he had read up on the subject, and learned that under certain conditions—depth of water, amount of rainfall, and other climatic factors—this kind of soil might have sucked its secret under at the end of a year, provided there was no extensive digging.

But not yet. He had sat down at once to write a brief note of refusal, but another phrase struck up at him from Conlon's letter. "... I was certain you would not permit this—"

A deliberate challenge? Bill Conlon was Marian's cousin, remember, and had been away at the time. Better go up there, stay a week or two, establish the impression of keeping the place as a country retreat upon which he might descend at any time. It was only necessary for Conlon; the townspeople, he was sure, accepted his remodeling of the barn as proof of his faith that his missing wife would some day return.

At that thought, alone in his comfortable apartment, Howard Hildreth shuddered ...

On the station platform there were gratifying little whispers and stirs of recognition—"Isn't that Howard Hildreth, the playwright? I'm sure it is"—and a turning of heads which he pretended not to see. He could hardly pretend not to see Conlon, striding across the platform toward him with his fair head a little cocked. Conlon had Marian's eyes, light gray with a peculiar curl of lid; but that was the only physical resemblance between them.

Hildreth put out a hand and said with an air of geniality, "Well, this is kind. I hope you haven't been meeting trains all day?"

Conlon sent one of his roving glances around the platform. "Matter of fact, a fellow in our office was supposed to catch this one but he seems to have missed it. Come on, I'll give you a lift."

After his first annoyance at Conlon's balloon-pricking, Hildreth was pleased; this would give him a chance to demonstrate his calm. He said as they got into the car, "I can see how you thought I wouldn't be using the place this summer. I'd have been in touch with you sooner about coming up but we've had a little trouble in the cast."

He waited for Conlon to show interest, but the other man only said, "Too bad. Play still going well?"

"Very, thanks."

"I particularly liked"—Conlon turned a sharp corner with care—"the third act. It packs quite a wallop. Are you working on a new play?"

"I am, as a matter of fact, and I thought a little peace and quiet ... You know New York," said Hildreth resignedly. In his tone were autograph hunters, sheaves of fan mail, a telephone carrying an invitation with each ring.

And part of it was true. *The Far Cry* was that rarest of things, a hit first play, and the playbill's revelation that it had been eight years in the writing had given an additional fillip. Eight years—what constancy! No wonder that superb third act expertly shivered like a diamond. Here was no glib young creature with a gift for bubbling out dialogue but a major talent who cut his work like a precious stone.

So the critics said, and the important hostesses, and Howard Hildreth, who had been laughed at in this little town, and had his credit refused and his electric light turned off, found his champagne all the winier and forgot those few hours of frantic typing . . .

". . . not a word," Conlon was saying, and Hildreth wrenched his attention from his play, his other self. They were out of the town now, rising into little hills and woodland, puddled and glinted yellowly by a sky which, having rained earlier, was now gloating over it.

Hildreth's mind spun back and recaptured the sense of his companion's words. He said, "Nor I. But I refuse to believe . . . you knew Marian—"

"I think she's dead," said Conlon bluntly without turning his head. "I think she was dead all the time the police were out looking for her."

"But . . . where—?" said Hildreth in a shocked voice.

Conlon waved a hand at the dimming landscape. "There's almost as much water as there is land around here," he said. "Lake, marshes, even quicksand. She had such a horror of things eaten up in the water, remember?"

"Stop!" said Hildreth with genuine violence. "You mustn't talk about her as though—Besides, Marian was happy, she would never have—"

"Committed suicide, or disappeared on purpose?" said Conlon when it was apparent that Hildreth was not going to finish. "Oh, I never thought she had. As you say, I knew Marian . . . here we are."

The car had descended a gentle twisting curve. At the bottom, opposite a stand of birches and set perhaps a hundred feet in from the road, was the pond, as round and clear as a wondering eye, lashed by willows that looked lamplit in the approaching dusk.

On the far side of it, on a slight rise, stood the creamy new structure, the remodeled barn, which six months ago had been weather-beaten planks and a wobbly brown-painted door. There was no breath of wind; the house and reflection met themselves in a mirror stillness.

Howard Hildreth gazed, and his heart raced with such horror that he wondered if he was about to have a stroke. He wrenched at his horn-rimmed glasses with a trembling hand, and heard Conlon say curiously, "Are you all right, Howard?"

"Yes. These damned glasses—the doctor warned me that I needed new ones." Even the effort of speaking calmly seemed to put a nut-cracker pressure on his heart. "You've done a beautiful job of remodeling the barn, Bill. The photographs you sent didn't do it justice. Shall we go on in?"

The drive up to the house itself was screened by willows. By the time Conlon had helped him inside with his bags, Hildreth was able to say almost normally, "Well, here we are. You'll have a drink, won't you?"

Conlon shook his head. He said with a hand on the doorknob, "Sarah —Sarah Wilde, you know—ordered a few essentials for the kitchen, so you ought to get through the night without starving. Well—"

Hildreth did not press him to stay. He said, standing in the open doorway, "These friends of yours that I had to disappoint—do I know them? What's their name?"

"Pocock," said Conlon promptly, and it was so unlikely a name that Hildreth had to believe him. Or was it meant to be a shortened version of poppycock?

He did not even look around at the long studio that took up most of the lower front of the house. He waited tensely for the final retreat of Conlon's motor, and when even the echoes were gone he opened the door and walked the length of the driveway in the lonely frog-sounding dusk.

And there was light enough—just enough—to show him the same sickening apparition. On the far side of the pond stood the new barn, radiantly pale, bearing no resemblance to its former weather-beaten brown. But at his feet, glassily etched on the surface of the water, lay the old barn, with its knotholes and weather stains and the wide brown-painted door.

Hildreth drew a long uneven breath. There was no one to see him step squashily to the reed-grown edge of the pond and dip a hand in the icy water. The old barn quaked under the willows, and shook and was presently still again—but it was still the old barn . . .

He did not drink—Marian had—but he took a tranquilizer and headed for his reviews like a child to its mother's skirts. The *Times, Tribune, Daily News*, the out-of-town papers. "Last night at the Odeon Theatre this critic was refreshingly jolted . . ."

"*The Far Cry* is just that in a season so far noted for its weary offer-ings . . ." "Let us hope we do not have to wait another eight years for the next Hildreth play . . ."

And presently he knew what had happened to him out there at the pond's edge. Autosuggestion, hallucination—at any rate, there was an accepted term for it; if beauty lay in the beholder's eye, so did other things. He knew what was under that pleasant and pastoral surface, and at the subconscious tension of his mind, because Conlon had been with him, his retina had produced the appropriate setting.

But not for Conlon, with all his suspicions—and in retrospect, the man had exuded suspicion. Conlon had looked at the pond and seen nothing amiss; for him, the still water had reflected only his personal creation of shored-up beams and plaster and creamy paint and whatever else went into his remodeling of an old structure. The thought gave Hildreth a satisfaction that, keyed up as he was, bordered on triumph.

What a joke on them all, he mused as he broiled the steak Sarah Wilde had left in the refrigerator, if only he, Hildreth, could see this watery witness, gaze at it in their presence, say casually, "Lovely day, isn't it?"— and stand there calmly and casually in the midst of their blindness.

Not that the reflection would be on the pond in the morning. Tonight it had simply been a product of nerves and fatigue, and a good night's sleep would erase it. Still, he was shaken, and he prudently avoided his after-dinner coffee. He darkened the downstairs, flipped on the staircase switch, and went up to his bedroom.

And came face to face with a portrait of Marian which he never knew had been taken.

As the blood came and went from his heart more slowly, he realized that the matted and mounted photograph on the bureau was not a portrait but an enlarged snapshot; on closer inspection it bore a telltale grain and blurriness. It was in color and it showed Marian laughing. There was a halo of sunlight on the close curls that scrambled over her beautifully shaped head, and the same light picked out the comma of mirth beside her mouth although her short, soft, full white throat was in shadow.

Marian laughing . . .

. . . laughing at his play, which she was not supposed to have seen at all until he had written the final word—*Curtain*. Managing to say through the laughter, "My dear playwright, you don't mean to say you've been muddling around with this thing for eight years and missed the whole *point*? It ought to be satire at the end, don't you see, and you fox the audience in the third act instead of this heavy Russian gloom going on and on? It would have such a wonderful, final crack-the-whip effect, and you could get rid of Anna coming in and saying"—she draggled at her hair, which was much too short and curly for draggling—"whatever that long lugubrious speech is."

Her face was brilliant with excited laughter. "Oh, *wait* till I tell Bill and Sarah we've found a way to finish the Odyssey at last! They'll be so —Howard, for heaven's sake, I'm only—*Howar*—"

For such a full throat, it was as soft and weak as a child's . . .

In the morning Hildreth looked at the pond, and the old weather-beaten barn was still there, shaken and distorted under a gently falling rain. Disturbingly, he was not terrified or shocked or even very surprised; it was as though, at some point during his sleep, his brain had accepted this phenomenon as readily as the pond had accepted Marian.

After breakfast he made arrangements for renting a car, and then he called Sarah Wilde.

It was through Sarah, who also had an apartment in the building on East Tenth Street, that he had met Marian Guest. Sarah and Marian were copywriters in the same advertising agency, and although Hildreth had a sober loathing of advertising copy and all the people who wrote it —there was a flippancy about them that appalled him—Sarah was well connected. An aunt of hers was a best-selling novelist, and it had never harmed any hopeful playwright to have even a hearsay acquaintance with a publisher. He had cultivated Sarah in the elevator, lent her an umbrella one day, and ultimately wound up at a party in her apartment.

And there was Marian, sitting on the floor although there were chairs available. She wore black slacks and an expensive-looking white silk shirt with a safety pin where a button should have been, and, profile tilted in the lamplight, she was explaining with zest how she had come by her black eye and scraped cheekbone. She had been walking her dog George and had fallen over a sheep on a leash. "The man said it was a Bedlington but he was obviously trying to cover up his own confusion. Poor George bit him, not the man, and I think he's got a hair ball."

Although there were two or three other girls present, all with a just-unboxed Madison Avenue attractiveness, the attention seemed to cluster about Marian. She said presently to Howard Hildreth in her boyish and uninhibited voice, "You look terribly broody. What are you hatching?"

"A play," he told her distantly, and it might have been the very distance that attracted her, as it was the attention focused on her that attracted him. At any rate, he ended up taking her home to her apartment on Barrow Street, drinking innumerable cups of black coffee, and telling her about his play. He began challengingly, prepared for amusement when she learned that he had already been working on it for three years; but she listened, her light clear eyes as wide and sober as a child's.

She said, "What do you do—for an income, I mean?"

When he said flatly, "I'm a shoe clerk," she stared past him with a kind of wondering sadness.

"How marvelous," she had said, "to give that much of a damn about anything."

There was Marian, summed up in a single sentence; even after they were married she never told him anything as self-revelatory as that. And under the influence of her respect for his dedication, his work, which had always been his Work to him, was able to come out in the open with its capital letter. Until she had defected—

But Hildreth had learned to discipline his mind, and he did it now.

He said into the telephone, "Sarah? I'm an ingrate for not calling you last night to tell you how much I like the way you've done the place—as well as providing my dinner—but . . ."

Sarah Wilde cut him off easily. "Do you like it? I'm glad. It's rather a lot of lavender, but you did specify—"

"Yes," Hildreth gazed, secretly entertained, at the lavender draperies, the lavender cushions, round and square and triangular, piled on the black tweed couch. Lavender—Marian's favorite color. Any doubters close to Marian could not help saying to themselves, "Well, if he can live with that..."

"It's very soothing," he said to Sarah with the defensive air of a husband standing up for his wife's vagaries. "Very restful. I like the picture on my bureau, by the way."

It was as though the telephone cord had been pulled taut between them. "It is a good one, isn't it? I took it—oh, some time last summer, I think, and I'd forgotten all about it until Bill Conlon happened to see it and thought you'd like an enlargement."

"It was very thoughtful of you both," said Hildreth with perfect evenness. "That's the way I think of her, you know. Laughing. I suppose Bill's told you that I haven't given up hope."

"Of course you haven't," said Sarah, bright and artificial.

Between them, in the small silence that followed, lay the many trips that he and Conlon had taken to view unidentified female bodies which corresponded even roughly with Marian's age and height. It was grim work, which helped; he was always a thoroughly pale and shaken man. And with each fruitless trip, because of the very nature of such an errand, the official belief that Marian Hildreth was dead had grown. Hildreth could tell that Sarah believed it too—in which, of course, she was quite right.

She was veering quickly away from the subject now, saying something about dinner this week. Hildreth accepted for Thursday evening, adding with a deprecating little laugh that he trusted it wouldn't be an Occasion; he'd come up here to get started on his new play.

"No, just two or three people," Sarah assured him. "I did tell you, didn't I, how much I liked *The Far Cry*? I thought I knew what was coming in the third act, but it was one time I loved being made a fool of."

Hildreth thanked her, a trifle aloofly, and there was not the smallest alarm along his nerves. He suspected that Sarah and Conlon, mere acquaintances six months ago, would be married before the year was out, but the fact that they had undoubtedly seen the play together didn't matter. They could not say, "That last act sounds like Marian," because as far as they knew Marian had never laid eyes on the script—she had said wryly, in fact, two or three days before that last night, "Howard thinks I'll mark his baby, like a gypsy..."

(What a very tellable joke it would have been, what an irresistible

18

nugget for gossip columns, because Marian's was not a secret-keeping nature: that Howard Hildreth had toiled unremittingly over his play for eight years, and in the space of a single hour his wife, who had never written anything but tongue-in-cheek praise of vinyl tile and slide fasteners, had offhandedly supplied the satirical twist that made it a success.)

Even at the thought Hildreth felt a qualm of nausea. Although his portable typewriter stood ready on the desk at the far end of the studio, with a fresh ream of yellow paper beside it, he let himself out the front door into the falling rain and walked to the pond's edge. There was the old barn, shaking dimly under the falling drops, and he knew that in some terrible way he was drawing strength from this private vision, locked under the willows for his eyes, and apparently for his alone . . .

A notion of incipient madness slid across his mind, but he looked quickly about him and everything else was sane and clear. If Marian thought to retaliate after death . . .

He drew himself up sharply.

In the afternoon he was gracious to the editor of the local newspaper, with the result that his favorite publicity picture appeared in the next morning's issue. He was holding his horn-rimmed glasses with one ear-piece casually collapsed, and the three-quarter turn of his head almost concealed the double chin developed since those lean days.

". . . seeking inspiration for his new play," said the account below, proudly, and, "Residents will recall the still-unresolved disappearance of Mrs. Marian Hildreth six months ago. Mrs. Hildreth, 38, told her husband late on the evening of October 4, 1963, that she was going out for a walk. She did not return, and no trace of her has since been found. Mr. Hildreth maintains his staunch belief that his wife is still alive, possibly suffering from a loss of memory . . ."

Hildreth read with calm pleasure the rest of the telling—how the pond on the property had been dragged without result. The police had indeed dragged it over his demurs—"Oh, come now, she wouldn't fall into a pond she's lived beside for five years"—and then came the heavily tactful, "Mr. Hildreth, your wife wasn't—er . . . ?"

Because Marian's more madcap exploits were not unknown to the local police. They viewed her with a tolerant and even an indulgent eye—that was the effect she had on people; but under the circumstances they could not rule out a tragic and alcoholic whim.

"No," Hildreth had said with transparent stoutness. "Oh, she may have had a highball or two after dinner . . ."

He knew, he had known at the moment of her death, that the marital partner was usually Suspect Number One. But that had not actually held true in little Ixton, Connecticut. If there had been any whisper of discord, any suggestion of dalliance by either party, any prospect of inheriting money—or even if Marian's life had been insured—the police might have looked deeper than they did. As it was, they walked past the burlaped yew, the burlaped roses, Marian's burlaped body, and then announced that they would drag the pond.

This procedure netted them two ancient inner tubes, a rotted and hinged object which had once been the hood of a convertible, and a rust-fretted oil drum which seemed to have spawned a great many beer cans. If the police had returned at just after dark, when one particular piece of burlap among the yews had been lifted free of its stiffened secret, and the secret transferred to the now officially blameless water ... but, predictably, they had not.

They could have no further reason for dragging the pond now—indeed, thought Hildreth, they would need a warrant. And for a warrant they would need evidence.

That was the safety element in a spur-of-the-moment murder. The cleverest planners—Hildreth rejected the word *killers*—had come to grief over elaborate timetables, unsuspected correspondence, a hint of fear dropped somewhere. There could be none of that in this case. Neither he nor Marian had known what was coming until that moment of her crowing laughter, that intolerable tearing-down of the secrecy and seriousness of his Work.

It was not so much that Marian had burst the bonds of curiosity and somehow contrived to unlock the desk drawer which housed his script, nor even that she had slipped at least temporarily into the ranks of the people who found him clownishly amusing. It was that she was right. Like someone engaged on a painstaking tapestry, he had been following stitch after stitch and lost sight of the pattern, which had leaped at once to Marian's unbothered and mischievous eye.

It was as if ... he could not say at the time, because his logic had smoked away like cellophane in a flame. Later, more calmly, he could compare himself to a woman who, after a long and difficult labor, watches the doctor merrily bearing the infant off to his own home.

But there was no evidence, and he would not be tricked or trapped. His visit here—the first since the five weeks or so after he had reported Marian missing—would proclaim his innocence. Not to the police—he wasn't worried about them—but to Bill Conlon and Sarah Wilde, the only people who, close to Marian, might just possibly ...

Hildreth arranged yellow paper beside his uncovered typewriter in the white-walled lavender-and-black studio, but he did not, that morning or the next or the one after that, commence even the roughest work on a new play.

He told himself defensively that he had spent several months under considerable strain; a man didn't bounce back from that right away. And critical success was paralyzing in itself: there was the inevitable re-studying of the first work in search of the magic ingredient, and the equally inevitable fear of comparison with a second.

At no time did he allow it to cross his mind that there were one-play playwrights as there were one-book novelists, and that his one play would still be in various stages of rewriting except for Marian's unruly wit. But there was a moment when, seated blankly at the typewriter, he thought, *Do I look like the pond?* and got up and crossed the room to examine himself in a mirror.

But no; he hadn't changed at all in spite of his damp little tremor of fright. And if he could see the truth on the pond's surface, surely he could see it on his own? There was the gained weight, granted, but his dark eyes gave back their old serious look, his eyebrows were forbiddingly level, a lock of hair—now pampered by his New York barber—still hung with dedication.

But when he stared long enough and hard enough, moving his face to within an inch or two of the mirror, tiny little Howard Hildreths peeked out of the pupils, and behind them—

Ah, behind *them* . . .

He developed a kind of triumphant passion for the pond. He watched it ballooned with clouds, or covered with nervous little wrinkles under a sudden wind. He saw the weather-beaten planks and the brown door warp and fly to pieces under the miniature tidal waves caused by water bugs or perhaps frogs. Pretending to enjoy a cigarette in the course of a stroll, he took note of the passing cars that slowed for an admiring view of the clean creamy little house behind the willowed pond, and no car jerked to a shocked halt, no one screamed.

Hildreth had a Polaroid camera, and one afternoon, in a fascinated test, he took a picture of the pond. Conlon's photographs had shown no abnormality, but this time it was he who was pressing the shutter. The day warranted color film—the willows dripped and candled about the round eye of water, enameled so perfectly that it might have been a brooch.

Wouldn't it be odd, thought Hildreth, counting excitedly to sixty, if only the camera and I—?

He was peeling the paper shield away when Sarah Wilde's voice said at his shoulder, "Oh, may I see?"

The print and its fluttering attachment dropped to the ground.

Hildreth got only a swinging glimpse of Sarah's slanted white cheek, caught only the beginning of the rueful, "I'm sorry, I didn't mean—" before he bent, barely circumventing her; if necessary he would have put his shoe on the print.

As it was, he snatched it up and turned away, manufacturing a cough, while he finished stripping the shield. He said a second later, turning back, "Not bad, is it?" and handed the innocent color print to Sarah. No, not the camera and himself—only himself.

Sarah, he thought watchfully, was a remarkably beautiful young woman. Her dropped lashes were a thick unretouched silver-brown, her polished hair a slightly deeper brown; her gaze, when she lifted it, would be gray. With the suave red lipstick to counterpoint the water-color effect, she was quietly startling in any gathering.

"Very good indeed," she said, handing the print back by its edges. "The pond's so pretty, isn't it? Especially now."

She glanced at the circle of water and then back at Hildreth, who following her gaze had still seen the placidly mirrored old barn. A tremble of nerves ran along his throat. To control a wild impulse toward laughter he said in a considering, landownerish way, "It seems quite full, but you've had heavy rains this month, haven't you?" and he slid the print casually into his coat pocket.

"Yes, it is full," said Sarah in his own considering tone, and there was no doubt about it; the eyes that moved from the pond to his face held some kind of—doubt? Challenge? Hildreth said coolly, "Well, if you'll excuse me, it's back to the typewriter," and he took a step away.

"Wait, I almost forgot what I came for." Sarah was dipping into her calf handbag. "Here—the mailman put this in my box instead of yours. Wonderful to get fan mail. Don't forget about dinner tonight—cocktails at six thirty."

It wasn't fan mail which Hildreth opened when the red Volkswagen had disappeared over the hill, but one of the many letters which the police had told him, always arrived in the wake of a disappearance. This one was from "Someone Who Can Help," and in exchange for two hundred dollars mailed to an enclosed box number in Vermont the writer would put him in touch with his missing wife.

The maddening part of these communications was that they could not be ignored—at least, not by a man in whom hope supposedly sprang eternal. Hildreth, sitting down to write the form reply that thanked the writer and said he was turning the letter over to the officers in charge of the investigation, thought angrily that there ought to be a law.

The afternoon passed slowly. Conlon telephoned to say that there would be a plumber coming over to do something to the downstairs bath, and Hildreth said pettishly, "Really, Bill, forgive me, but I thought all that had been taken care of. One doesn't greet plumbers in the middle of Scene One, you know."

He was mollified a little later by a delegation from the local high-school magazine, asking humbly for a "Best Wishes from Howard Hildreth" to be photostated for the graduation issue. One of the shiny-haired, wide-eyed girls ventured close to his typewriter, in which Hildreth fore-sightedly kept a typed yellow sheet—the opening scene of *The Far Cry* —and he said at once, austerely, "Please don't—I have a 'thing' about work in progress."

It only added to their awe. But he had had it, thought Hildreth, pres-ently seeing them to the door; he had had all the local adulation he wanted. Imperiously buying delicacies at the only market that carried them, he had seen the fawning face of the manager who only a year ago had told him that if his bill wasn't settled promptly he would find him-self in the small-claims court.

He had been pointed out respectfully on the main street, and had de-clined invitations from the town's reigning hostess. More importantly, he had been accepted everywhere without a trace of suspicion; if there was any sentiment in the air, it was one of embarrassed pity for a man who so courageously continued to hope.

In a day or two he could go back to New York, having established to Bill Conlon and Sarah Wilde and everybody else that there was no ques-tion of his selling or even renting the property with its pretty, deadly pond.

He was all the more shocked, in the midst of these comfortable reflec-tions, when at a little after three he had a call from a Sergeant Fisk at the police station. Some little girls looking for pussy willows in a field on the outskirts of the town had discovered a woman's leather handbag and part of a dress with some suggestive stains; would Hildreth please come down and see if he could identify them?

"Certainly," said Hildreth, staring angrily out the window. "Of course, being out in the weather, I imagine they're pretty well—?"

"No, sir, they were stuffed in the remains of an old stone wall and they're still in fair condition. Recognizable, anyway."

"I'll leave right away," said Hildreth, tempering his eagerness with the right amount of dread.

At the police station he was asked to wait—Sergeant Fisk would be right with him.

By four o'clock Sergeant Fisk still was not with him; at four thirty, fuming, Hildreth walked up to the uniformed man at the switchboard and said sharply, "I came here at the request of Sergeant Fisk to look at some objects for identification, and I cannot wait any longer. Please leave a message—"

"Just a minute, sir," said the policeman unruffledly, and slipped a plug into its socket and inquired for Sergeant Fisk. "There's a Mr. Hildreth here, been waiting since—okay, I'll tell him to go right in."

But the handbag and dress fragment, when Hildreth reached Sergeant Fisk's office, had been transferred to Lieutenant Martin's office, where there was some question as to their possible connection with the vanishing of a Colorado couple making a cross-country tour four months ago. Hildreth contained his temper as he went with the sergeant to Martin's office; he was, he remembered, a man who would do anything to find a clue to his wife's fate.

He was badly tempted when, at after five o'clock, he surveyed a rotted and mildewed navy calf handbag, empty, and the sleeve and half the bodice of what had once been a yellow wool dress. Why not say, "Yes, they're my wife's," and bury his face in his hands and be done with it?

Because, he thought with a feeling of having stepped back from the edge of a cliff, Marian had never worn yellow—she said it made her look like a two-legged hangover; and there was a suggestion of something on the leather lining of the bag that could easily be a nearly obliterated name or monogram. Hildreth had read what modern police laboratories could do with things like that. So he shook his head and said, "They're not my wife's," and with a shudder at the stains on the rotting yellow wool, "Thank God."

Three hours, he thought as he drove home seething in the rainy dusk; three hours on a fool's errand which he could not have risked refusing. Just barely time to dress for dinner at Sarah Wilde's—and then get out of here, tomorrow.

He was restored at the thought, and at the glimpse of the old barn quivering on the pond in the last of the light as he drove to Sarah's. His temper was further improved by Sarah's big, casually gay living room—two rooms thrown together in a very old saltbox—and the contrast between an open fire and a cold rattling rain on the windows.

The other guests were already established with drinks—Conlon, a Mr. and Mrs. Slater, and Mrs. Slater's decorative visiting sister.

Hildreth thawed, physically and temperamentally. He felt a slight jar of recognition when he was introduced to the Slaters, but he had undoubtedly encountered them on the station platform at some forgotten time, or in a local store. He noted with approval that Sarah had obviously got someone in for the evening, because there were sounds of kitchen activity while Sarah sat on the couch, in black and pearls, beside Conlon.

On the rare occasions when he and Marian had entertained, Marian had charged in and out like a demented puppy, crying, "My God, who's been watching the beans? Nobody!" Or, abashedly, "We all like nutmeg instead of pepper in our mashed potatoes, don't we?"

Sarah had turned her head and was gazing at him; somebody had clearly asked a question. Hildreth used a handkerchief on his suddenly damp forehead and temples and said, "I got wetter than I thought—that's really quite a downpour," and he got up to stand by the fire.

And the bad moment was gone, further wiped out by Sarah's "You said you mightn't be here long on this visit, Howard, so we're having your favorite dinner—you know, what you won't eat in restaurants."

"Don't tell me . . . ?" said Hildreth, delighted, but it was: trout, a crisp deep-gold outside, succulent white within, delicately enhanced by herbs that only hinted at themselves. He ate with deliberate pleasure, not succumbing until close to the end of dinner to his habit of providing backgrounds for people.

The extraordinarily good-looking sister from New Haven—her name was Vivian Hughes—seemed the kind of young woman who, convinced in her teens that she could have any man she wanted, had ended up with none; there was a kind of forced grace to the frequent turn of her head, and lines of discontent around her really striking green eyes.

Mrs. Slater wasn't a fair test, because she had ticketed herself earlier by a reference to the young twins they had left with a baby-sitter, and by her very casualness she had given herself away. She was the new and on the whole the best breed of mother, thought Hildreth approvingly; slender, amiable, intelligent, she kept her maternal dotings strictly for hearth and home.

Slater? Hildreth gazed obliquely through candlelight at the other man, perhaps a year or two younger than his own forty. The lean, polished, ruddy face suggested an outdoorsman, but everything else pointed to an executive. He went on gazing, and like an exposed print washed gently back and forth in developer, outlines began to emerge.

A desk, not executive grain, but scarred oak. Two telephones on it. A uniformed man in a far doorway saying, "Yes, sir, right away," then disappearing down one of a warren of corridors.

Yes, Slater was a police officer of some sort, or a detective, glimpsed or perhaps even talked to in the first stages of the investigation six months ago. And Sarah and Conlon hoped that he would be terrified by this recognition, and go to pieces. That was the whole point of this friendly little gathering.

How very disappointed they must be. Hildreth stirred his coffee tranquilly, because no motive for murder had existed until sixty seconds before Marian died, and there wasn't a single clue. In an enjoyment of the attention he now knew to be trained on him he said in a well-fed voice, "Marvelous dinner, Sarah. I don't know when I've had trout like that," and Sarah said, "As a matter of fact, you never have."

She was leaning forward a little in the candlelight, her gaze cool and removed. "The trout were from your pond, Howard, and they were caught this afternoon while you were down at the police station. You didn't know that Marian had had the pond stocked for you, as a birthday present, just before she—disappeared, because you love trout but never trust it in restaurants. We didn't know about it either until the friend who did it for her stopped by to see Bill a couple of weeks ago."

Hildreth's neck felt caught in one of those high white collars you saw on injured people; he could not turn it even when he heard Conlon's, "Nice fat trout, I thought, but lazy. They bit at anything." ... while he had sat in the police station, decoyed there by a telephone call.

"You all ate it," said Hildreth triumphantly, in a candlelight that had begun to tremble and dampen his face. "You all—"

"No. Ours was perch from the Old Town Fish Market," said Sarah, and although she continued to hold his gaze, her forehead had a cold glimmer and her mouth seemed clenched against a scream.

Hildreth lost them all then. He dropped his eyes, but instead of his dessert cup he saw his dinner plate, with the neat spiny bones from which all the succulent white flesh had been forked away. Marian's soft white throat, and the busy, inquisitive, nibbling mouths at the bottom of the pond, and the plump things placed on his plate—

He heard his chair go crashing back, and the gagging cry of horror that issued from his own throat as he plunged blindly for somewhere to be sick; and, from a mist, Slater's voice saying, "... looks like it. Very definitely. We'll get at it first thing in the morning..."

FOR DISCUSSION: The Old Barn on the Pond

1. Howard Hildreth's outstanding characteristic is pride. Beginning in the first sentence with "the triumphant return he [Hildreth] had planned," Ursula Curtiss skillfully plants many phrases that indicate his monstrous ego. Play the detective for a bit, and see if you can identify a dozen of these phrases.

2. Hildreth's ego *is* Hildreth. It affects every phase of his life—as a dramatist, as a suitor, as a husband, as a murderer. Exactly how, in each case, did his ego influence his actions?

3. Explain why each of the following is ironic:
   a. Marian's suggestion for the last act of Hildreth's play;
   b. the attitudes of the villagers toward Hildreth;
   c. Marian's stocking of the pond with trout shortly before her death;
   d. the final dinner scene.

4. Among readers of mysteries, Curtiss is known for her ability to create an almost intolerable suspense. In this story the point of focus is the pond. How does the author first make the reader conscious of the importance of the pond? What other incidents transform the pond from inanimate nature to personal enemy? How is this transformation related to the steady growth of suspense?

INTRODUCTION: The Oval Portrait

Humans have a way of equating love and possession. The small boy who clutches a beautiful butterfly in his fist soon learns the awful consequences. But the husband-artist who obsessively clutches his wife's beauty learns a far more bitter lesson.

In this short story, first published in 1842, Edgar Allan Poe describes a situation that any modern psychologist would recognize: an excess of love, misdirected, can destroy. This is no ordinary short story about murder. There is no deadly weapon, no anger, no homicidal intent. Yet there is a murder.

The Oval Portrait
Edgar Allan Poe

The chateau into which my valet had ventured to make forcible entrance, rather than permit me, in my desperately wounded condition, to pass a night in the open air, was one of those piles of commingled gloom and grandeur which have so long frowned among the Appennines, not less in fact than in the fancy of Mrs. Radcliffe. To all appearances it had been temporarily and very lately abandoned. We established ourselves in one of the smallest and least sumptuously furnished apartments. It lay in a remote turret of the building. Its decorations were rich, yet tattered and antique. Its walls were hung with tapestry and bedecked with manifold and multiform armorial trophies, together with an unusually great number of very spirited modern paintings in frames of rich golden arabesque. In these paintings, which depended from the walls not only in their main surfaces, but in very many nooks which the bizarre architecture of the chateau rendered necessary—in these paintings my incipient delirium, perhaps, had caused me to take deep interest; so that I bade Pedro to close the heavy shutters of the room—since it was already night, —to light the tongues of a tall candelabrum which stood by the head of my bed, and to throw open far and wide the fringed curtains of black velvet which enveloped the bed itself. I wished all this done that I might resign myself, if not to sleep, at least alternately to the contemplation of these pictures, and the perusal of a small volume which had been found upon the pillow, and which purported to criticize and describe them.

Long, long I read—and devoutly, devoutly I gazed. Rapidly and gloriously the hours flew by and the deep midnight came. The position of the candelabrum displeased me, and outreaching my hand with difficulty, rather than disturb my slumbering valet, I placed it so as to throw its rays more fully upon the book.

But the action produced an effect altogether unanticipated. The rays of the numerous candles (for there were many) now fell within a niche of the room which had hitherto been thrown into deep shade by one of the bedposts. I thus saw in vivid light a picture all unnoticed before. It was the portrait of a young girl just ripening into womanhood. I glanced at the painting hurriedly, and then closed my eyes. Why I did this was not at first apparent even to my own perception. But while my lids remained thus shut, I ran over in my mind my reason for so shutting them. It was an impulsive movement to gain time for thought—to make sure that my vision had not deceived me—to calm and subdue my fancy for a more sober and more certain gaze. In a very few moments I again looked fixedly at the painting.

That I now saw aright I could not and would not doubt; for the first flashing of the candles upon that canvas had seemed to dissipate the dreamy stupor which was stealing over my senses, and to startle me at once into waking life.

The portrait, I have already said, was that of a young girl. It was a mere head and shoulders, done in what is technically termed a *vignette* manner; much in the style of the favorite heads of Sully. The arms, the bosom, and even the ends of the radiant hair melted imperceptibly into the vague yet deep shadow which formed the background of the whole. The frame was oval, richly gilded and filigreed in *Moresque*. As a thing of art nothing could be more admirable than the painting itself. But it could have been neither the execution of the work, nor the immortal beauty of the countenance, which had so suddenly and so vehemently moved me. Least of all, could it have been that my fancy, shaken from its half slumber, had mistaken the head for that of a living person. I saw at once that the peculiarities of the design, of the *vignetting*, and of the frame, must have instantly dispelled such idea—must have prevented even its momentary entertainment. Thinking earnestly upon these points, I remained, for an hour perhaps, half sitting, half reclining, with my vision riveted upon the portrait. At length, satisfied with the true secret of its effect, I fell back within the bed. I had found the spell of the picture in an absolute *life-likeness* of expression, which, at first startling, finally confounded, subdued, and appalled me. With deep and reverent awe I replaced the candelabrum in its former position. The cause of my deep agitation being thus shut from view, I sought eagerly the volume which discussed the paintings and their histories. Turning to the number which designated the oval portrait, I there read the vague and quaint words which follow:

"She was a maiden of rarest beauty, and not more lovely than full of glee. And evil was the hour when she saw, and loved, and wedded the painter. He, passionate, studious, austere, and having already a bride in his Art; she a maiden of rarest beauty, and not more lovely than full of glee; all light and smiles, and frolicsome as the young fawn; loving and cherishing all things; hating only the Art which was her rival; dreading only the pallet and brushes and other untoward instruments which deprived her of the countenance of her lover. It was thus a terrible thing for this lady to hear the painter speak of his desire to portray even his young bride. But she was humble and obedient, and sat meekly for many weeks in the dark, high turret-chamber where the light dripped upon the pale canvas only from overhead. But he, the painter, took glory in his work, which went on from hour to hour, and from day to day. And he was a passionate, and wild, and moody man, who became lost in reveries; so that he *would* not see that the light which fell so ghastly in that lone turret withered the health and the spirits of his bride, who pined visibly to all but him. Yet she smiled on and still on, uncomplainingly, because she saw that the painter (who had high renown) took a fervid and burning pleasure in his task, and wrought day and night to depict her who so loved him, yet who grew daily more dispirited and weak. And in sooth some who beheld the portrait spoke of its resemblance in low words, as of a mighty marvel, and a proof not less of the power of the painter than of his deep love for her whom he depicted so surpassingly well. But at length, as the labor drew nearer to its conclusion, there were admitted none into the turret; for the painter had grown wild with the ardor of his work, and turned his eyes from the canvas rarely, even to regard the countenance of his wife. And he *would* not see that the tints which he spread upon the canvas were drawn from the cheeks of her who sat beside him. And when many weeks had passed, and but little remained to do, save one brush upon the mouth and one tint upon the eye, the spirit of the lady again flickered up as the flame within the socket of the lamp. And then the brush was given, and then the tint was placed; and, for one moment, the painter stood entranced before the work which he had wrought; but in the next, while he yet gazed, he grew tremulous and very pallid, and aghast, and crying with a loud voice, 'This is indeed *Life* itself!' turned suddenly to regard his beloved:—*She was dead!*"

FOR DISCUSSION: The Oval Portrait

1. Poe uses about half of the text preparing the reader for the real story. This is an unusual technique, but the author knew exactly what he was doing. What is accomplished by this long introduction? Could you have accepted the rather startling ending without it? Why or why not?
2. Was the young wife aware of what was happening? Could she have prevented the tragedy? Explain.
3. Near the end of the story is this sentence—"And he *would* not see that the tints which he spread upon the canvas were drawn from the cheeks of her who sat beside him." The word *would* is italicized. What does this suggest about the painter? What is the real object of his love?
4. Like most of Poe's short stories, "The Oval Portrait" is permeated by the supernatural, but a psychological interpretation is possible. If you were a psychologist, how might you interpret the action? Which interpretation—the supernatural or the psychological—appeals more to you and why? Which best illuminates one kind of husband-wife relationship?

INTRODUCTION: The Couple Next Door

There are several classic plots dear to all mystery writers. One favorite deals with a marriage between a younger woman and an older man. That's what this story is about. But the Rackhams, of course, were different. They both delighted in a quiet life and in quiet pleasures. Each swore that life without the other would be unbearable. Caring for this idyllic couple were a sober family doctor, George Tracy, and a retired investigator, Mr. Sands.

Unfortunately even the most placid family life can be disrupted by a lie, and between them, the Rackhams told quite a few. Lies have a way of developing lives of their own—of catapulting simple events into catastrophes.

The Couple Next Door
Margaret Millar

It was by accident that they lived next door to each other, but by design that they became neighbors—Mr. Sands, who had retired to California after a life of crime investigation, and the Rackhams, Charles and Alma. Rackham was a big, innocent-looking man in his fifties. Except for the accumulation of a great deal of money, nothing much had ever happened to Rackham, and he liked to listen to Sands talk, while Alma sat with her knitting, plump and contented, unimpressed by any tale that had no direct bearing on her own life. She was half Rackham's age, but the fullness of her figure, and her air of having withdrawn from life quietly and without fuss, gave her the stamp of middle-age.

Two or three times a week Sands crossed the concrete driveway, skirted the eugenia hedge, and pressed the Rackhams' door chime. He stayed for tea or for dinner, to play gin or scrabble, or just to talk. "That reminds me of a case I had in Toronto," Sands would say, and Rackham would produce martinis and an expression of intense interest, and Alma would smile tolerantly, as if she didn't really believe a single thing Sands, or anyone else, ever said.

They made good neighbors: the Rackhams, Charles younger than his years, and Alma older than hers, and Sands who could be any age at all . . .

It was the last evening of August and through the open window of Sands' study came the scent of jasmine and the sound of a woman's harsh, wild weeping.

He thought at first that the Rackhams had a guest, a woman on a crying jag, perhaps, after a quarrel with her husband.

He went out into the front yard to listen, and Rackham came around the corner of the eugenia hedge, dressed in a bathrobe.

He said, sounding very surprised, "Alma's crying."

"I heard."

"I asked her to stop. I begged her. She won't tell me what's the matter."

"Women have cried before."

"Not Alma." Rackham stood on the damp grass, shivering, his forehead streaked with sweat. "What do you think we should do about it?"

The *I* had become *we*, because they were good neighbors, and along with the games and the dinners and the scent of jasmine, they shared the sound of a woman's grief.

"Perhaps you could talk to her," Rackham said.

"I'll try."

"I don't think there is anything physically the matter with her. We both had a check-up at the Tracy clinic last week. George Tracy is a good friend of mine—he'd have told me if there was anything wrong."

"I'm sure he would."

"If anything ever happened to Alma I'd kill myself."

Alma was crouched in a corner of the davenport in the living room, weeping rhythmically, methodically, as if she had accumulated a hoard of tears and must now spend them all in one night. Her fair skin was blotched with patches of red, like strawberry birthmarks, and her eyelids were blistered from the heat of her tears. She looked like a stranger to Sands, who had never seen her display any emotion stronger than ladylike distress over a broken teacup or an overdone roast.

Rackham went over and stroked her hair. "Alma, dear. What is the matter?"

"Nothing . . . nothing . . ."

"Mr. Sands is here, Alma. I thought he might be able—we might be able—"

But no one was able. With a long shuddering sob, Alma got up and lurched across the room, hiding her blotched face with her hands. They heard her stumble up the stairs.

Sands said, "I'd better be going."

"No, please don't. I—the fact is, I'm scared. I'm scared stiff. Alma's always been so quiet."

"I know that."

"You don't suppose—there's no chance she's losing her mind?"

If they had not been good neighbors Sands might have remarked that Alma had little mind to lose. As it was, he said cautiously, "She might have had bad news, family trouble of some kind."

"She has no family except me."

"If you're worried, perhaps you'd better call your doctor."

"I think I will."

George Tracy arrived within half an hour, a slight, fair-haired man in his early thirties, with a smooth unhurried manner that imparted confidence. He talked slowly, moved slowly, as if there was all the time in the world to minister to desperate women.

Rackham chafed with impatience while Tracy removed his coat, placed it carefully across the back of the chair, and discussed the weather with Sands.

"It's a beautiful evening," Tracy said, and Alma's moans sliding down the stairs distorted his words, altered their meaning: *a terrible evening, an awful evening.* "There's a touch of fall in the air. You live in these parts, Mr. Sands?"

"Next door."

"For heaven's sake, George," Rackham said, "will you hurry up? For all you know, Alma might be dying."

"That I doubt. People don't die as easily as you might imagine. She's in her room?"

"Yes. Now will you *please—*"

"Take it easy, old man."

Tracy picked up his medical bag and went towards the stairs, leisurely, benign.

"He's always like that." Rackham turned to Sands scowling. "Exasperating son-of-a-gun. You can bet that if he had a wife in Alma's condition he'd be taking those steps three at a time."

"Who knows?—perhaps he has."

"*I* know," Rackham said crisply. "He's not even married. Never had time for it, he told me. He doesn't look it but he's very ambitious."

"Most doctors are."

"Tracy is, anyway."

Rackham mixed a pitcher of martinis, and the two men sat in front of the unlit fire, waiting and listening. The noises from upstairs gradually ceased, and pretty soon the doctor came down again.

Rackham rushed across the room to meet him. "How is she?"

"Sleeping. I gave her a hypo."

"Did you talk to her? Did you ask her what was the matter?"

"She was in no condition to answer questions."

"Did you find anything wrong with her?"

"Not physically. She's a healthy young woman."

"Not *physically*. Does that mean—?"

"Take it easy, old man."

Rackham was too concerned with Alma to notice Tracy's choice of words, but Sands noticed, and wondered if it had been conscious or unconscious: Alma's a healthy young woman... Take it easy, old man.

"If she's still depressed in the morning," Tracy said, "bring her down to the clinic with you when you come in for your X-rays. We have a good neurologist on our staff." He reached for his coat and hat. "By the way, I hope you followed the instructions."

Rackham looked at him stupidly. "What instructions?"

"Before we can take specific X-rays, certain medication is necessary."

"I don't know what you're talking about."

"I made it very clear to Alma," Tracy said, sounding annoyed. "You were to take one ounce of sodium phosphate after dinner tonight, and report to the X-ray department at 8 o'clock tomorrow morning without breakfast."

"She didn't tell me."

"Oh."

"It must have slipped her mind."

"Yes. Obviously. Well, it's too late now." He put on his coat, moving quickly for the first time, as if he were in a rush to get away. The change made Sands curious. He wondered why Tracy was suddenly so anxious to leave, and whether there was any connection between Alma's hysteria and her lapse of memory about Rackham's X-rays. He looked at Rackham and guessed, from his pallor and his worried eyes, that Rackham had already made a connection in his mind.

"I understood," Rackham said carefully, "that I was all through at the clinic. My heart, lungs, metabolism—everything fit as a fiddle."

"People," Tracy said, "are not fiddles. Their tone doesn't improve with age. I will make another appointment for you and send you specific instructions by mail. Is that all right with you?"

"I guess it will have to be."

"Well, good night, Mr. Sands, pleasant meeting you." And to Rackham, "Good night, old man."

When he had gone, Rackham leaned against the wall, breathing hard. Sweat crawled down the sides of his face like worms and hid in the collar of his bathrobe. "You'll have to forgive me, Sands. I feel—I'm not feeling very well."

"Is there anything I can do?"

"Yes," Rackham said. "Turn back the clock."

"Beyond my powers, I'm afraid."

"Yes ... Yes, I'm afraid."

34

"Good night, Rackham." *Good night, old man.*

"Good night, Sands." *Good night old man to you, too.*

Sands shuffled across the concrete driveway, his head bent. It was a dark night, with no moon at all.

From his study Sands could see the lighted windows of Rackham's bedroom. Rackham's shadow moved back and forth behind the blinds as if seeking escape from the very light that gave it existence. Back and forth, in search of nirvana.

Sands read until far into the night. It was one of the solaces of growing old—if the hours were numbered, at least fewer of them need be wasted in sleep. When he went to bed, Rackham's bedroom light was still on.

They had become good neighbors by design; now, also by design, they became strangers. Whose design it was, Alma's or Rackham's, Sands didn't know.

There was no definite break, no unpleasantness. But the eugenia hedge seemed to have grown taller and thicker, and the concrete driveway a mile wide. He saw the Rackhams occasionally; they waved or smiled or said, "Lovely weather," over the backyard fence. But Rackham's smile was thin and painful, Alma waved with a leaden arm, and neither of them cared about the weather. They stayed indoors most of the time, and when they did come out they were always together, arm in arm, walking slowly and in step. It was impossible to tell whose step led, and whose followed.

At the end of the first week in September, Sands met Alma by accident in a drug store downtown. It was the first time since the night of the doctor's visit that he'd seen either of the Rackhams alone.

She was waiting at the prescription counter wearing a flowery print dress that emphasized the fullness of her figure and the bovine expression of her face. A drug-store length away, she looked like a rather dull, badly dressed young woman with a passion for starchy foods, and it was hard to understand what Rackham had seen in her. But then Rackham had never stood a drug-store length away from Alma; he saw her only in close-up, the surprising, intense blue of her eyes, and the color and texture of her skin, like whipped cream. Sands wondered whether it was her skin and eyes, or her quality of serenity which had appealed most to Rackham, who was quick and nervous and excitable.

She said, placidly, "Why, hello there."

"Hello, Alma."

"Lovely weather, isn't it?"

"Yes. . . . How is Charles?"

"You must come over for dinner one of these nights."

"I'd like to."

"Next week, perhaps. I'll give you a call—I must run now, Charles is waiting for me. See you next week."

But she did not run, she walked; and Charles was not waiting for her, he was waiting for Sands. He had let himself into Sands' house and was pacing the floor of the study, smoking a cigarette. His color was bad, and he had lost weight, but he seemed to have acquired an inner calm. Sands could not tell whether it was the calm of a man who had come to an important decision, or that of a man who had reached the end of his rope and had stopped struggling.

They shook hands, firmly, pressing the past week back into shape.

Rackham said, "Nice to see you again, old man."

"I've been here all along."

"Yes. Yes, I know. . . . I had things to do, a lot of thinking to do."

"Sit down. I'll make you a drink."

"No, thanks. Alma will be home shortly, I must be there."

Like a Siamese twin, Sands thought, *separated by a miracle, but returning voluntarily to the fusion—because the fusion was in a vital organ.*

"I understand," Sands said.

Rackham shook his head. "No one can understand, really, but you come very close sometimes, Sands. Very close." His cheeks flushed, like a boy's. "I'm not good at words or expressing my emotions, but I wanted to thank you before we leave, and tell you how much Alma and I have enjoyed your companionship."

"You're taking a trip?"

"Yes. Quite a long one."

"When are you leaving?"

"Today."

"You must let me see you off at the station."

"No, no," Rackham said quickly. "I couldn't think of it. I hate last-minute depot farewells. That's why I came over this afternoon to say goodbye."

"Tell me something of your plans."

"I would if I had any. Everything is rather indefinite. I'm not sure where we'll end up."

"I'd like to hear from you now and then."

"Oh, you'll hear from me, of course." Rackham turned away with an impatient twitch of his shoulders as if he was anxious to leave, anxious to start the trip right now before anything happened to prevent it.

"I'll miss you both," Sands said. "We've had a lot of laughs together."

Rackham scowled out of the window. "Please, no farewell speeches. They might shake my decision. My mind is already made up, I want no second thoughts."

"Very well."

"I must go now.   Alma will be wondering—"

"I saw Alma earlier this afternoon," Sands said.

"Oh?"

"She invited me for dinner next week."

Outside the open window two hummingbirds fought and fussed, darting with crazy accuracy in and out of the bougainvillea vine.

"Alma," Rackham said carefully, "can be very forgetful sometimes."

"Not that forgetful.   She doesn't know about this trip you've planned, does she? . . .   Does she, Rackham?"

"I wanted it to be a surprise.   She's always had a desire to see the world.   She's still young enough to believe that one place is different from any other place. . . .   You and I know better."

"Do we?"

"Goodbye, Sands."

At the front door they shook hands again, and Rackham again promised to write, and Sands promised to answer his letters.   Then Rackham crossed the lawn and the concrete driveway, head bent, shoulders hunched.   He didn't look back as he turned the corner of the eugenia hedge.

Sands went over to his desk, looked up a number in the telephone directory, and dialed.

A girl's voice answered, "Tracy clinic, X-ray department."

"This is Charles Rackham," Sands said.

"Yes, Mr. Rackham."

"I'm leaving town unexpectedly.   If you'll tell me the amount of my bill I'll send you a check before I go."

"The bill hasn't gone through, but the standard price for a lower gastrointestinal is twenty-five dollars."

"Let's see, I had that done on the—"

"The fifth.   Yesterday."

"But my original appointment was for the first, wasn't it?"

The girl gave a does-it-really-matter sigh.   "Just a moment, sir, and I'll check."   Half a minute later she was back on the line.

"We have no record of an appointment for you on the first, sir."

"You're sure of that?"

"Even without the record book, I'd be sure.   The first was a Monday. We do only gall bladders on Monday."

"Oh.   Thank you."

Sands went out and got into his car.   Before he pulled away from the curb he looked over at Rackham's house and saw Rackham pacing up and down the veranda, waiting for Alma.

The Tracy clinic was less impressive than Sands had expected, a converted two-story stucco house with a red tile roof. Some of the tiles were broken and the whole building needed paint, but the furnishings inside were smart and expensive.

At the reception desk a nurse wearing a crew cut and a professional smile told Sands that Dr. Tracy was booked solid for the entire afternoon. The only chance of seeing him was to sit in the second-floor waiting room and catch him between patients.

Sands went upstairs and took a chair in a little alcove at the end of the hall, near Tracy's door. He sat with his face half hidden behind an open magazine. After a while the door of Tracy's office opened and over the top of his magazine Sands saw a woman silhouetted in the door frame—a plump, fair-haired young woman in a flowery print dress.

Tracy followed her into the hall and the two of them stood looking at each other in silence. Then Alma turned and walked away, passing Sands without seeing him because her eyes were blind with tears.

Sands stood up. "Dr. Tracy?"

Tracy turned sharply, surprise and annoyance pinching the corners of his mouth. "Well? Oh, it's Mr. Sands."

"May I see you a moment?"

"I have quite a full schedule this afternoon."

"This is an emergency."

"Very well. Come in."

They sat facing each other across Tracy's desk.

"You look pretty fit," Tracy said with a wry smile, "for an emergency case."

"The emergency is not mine. It may be yours."

"If it's mine, I'll handle it alone, without the help of a poli—I'll handle it myself."

Sands leaned forward. "Alma has told you, then, that I used to be a policeman."

"She mentioned it in passing."

"I saw Alma leave a few minutes ago. . . . She'd be quite a nice-looking woman if she learned to dress properly."

"Clothes are not important in a woman," Tracy said, with a slight flush. "Besides, I don't care to discuss my patients."

"Alma is a patient of yours?"

"Yes."

"Since the night Rackham called you when she was having hysterics?"

"Before then."

Sands got up, went to the window, and looked down at the street.

People were passing, children were playing on the sidewalk, the sun shone, the palm trees rustled with wind—everything outside seemed normal and human and real. By contrast, the shape of the idea that was forming in the back of his mind was so grotesque and ugly that he wanted to run out of the office, to join the normal people passing on the street below. But he knew he could not escape by running. The idea would follow him, pursue him until he turned around and faced it.

It moved inside his brain like a vast wheel, and in the middle of the wheel, impassive, immobile, was Alma.

Tracy's harsh voice interrupted the turning of the wheel. "Did you come here to inspect my view, Mr. Sands?"

"Let's say, instead, your viewpoint."

"I'm a busy man. You're wasting my time."

"No. I'm giving you time."

"To do what?"

"Think things over."

"If you don't leave my office immediately, I'll have you thrown out." Tracy glanced at the telephone but he didn't reach for it, and there was no conviction in his voice.

"Perhaps you shouldn't have let me in. Why did you?"

"I thought you might make a fuss if I didn't."

"Fusses aren't in my line." Sands turned from the window. "Liars are, though."

"What are you implying?"

"I've thought a great deal about that night you came to the Rackhams' house. In retrospect, the whole thing appeared too pat, too contrived: Alma had hysterics and you were called in to treat her. Natural enough, so far."

Tracy stirred but didn't speak.

"The interesting part came later. You mentioned casually to Rackham that he had an appointment for some X-rays to be taken the following day, September the first. It was assumed that Alma had forgotten to tell him. Only Alma *hadn't* forgotten. There was nothing to forget. I checked with your X-ray department half an hour ago. They have no record of any appointment for Rackham on September the first."

"Records get lost."

"This record wasn't lost. It never existed. You lied to Rackham. The lie itself wasn't important, it was the *kind* of lie. I could have understood a lie of vanity, or one to avoid punishment or to gain profit. But this seemed such a silly, senseless, little lie. It worried me. I began to wonder about Alma's part in the scene that night. Her crying was most unusual for a woman of Alma's inert nature. What if her crying was also a lie? And what was to be gained by it?"

"Nothing," Tracy said wearily. "Nothing was gained."

"But something was *intended*—and I think I know what it was. The scene was played to worry Rackham, to set him up for an even bigger

All in the Family 39

scene. If that next scene has already been played, I am wasting my time here. Has it?"

"You have a vivid imagination."

"No. The plan was yours—I only figured it out."

"Very poor figuring, Mr. Sands." But Tracy's face was gray, as if mold had grown over his skin.

"I wish it were. I had become quite fond of the Rackhams."

He looked down at the street again, seeing nothing but the wheel turning inside his head. Alma was no longer in the middle of the wheel, passive and immobile; she was revolving with the others—Alma and Tracy and Rackham, turning as the wheel turned, clinging to its perimeter.

Alma, devoted wife, a little on the dull side. . . . What sudden passion of hate or love had made her capable of such consummate deceit? Sands imagined the scene the morning after Tracy's visit to the house. Rackham, worried and exhausted after a sleepless night: *"Are you feeling better now, Alma?"*

"Yes."

"What made you cry like that?"

"I was worried."

"About me?"

"Yes."

"Why didn't you tell me about my X-ray appointment?"

"I couldn't. I was frightened. I was afraid they would discover something serious the matter with you."

"Did Tracy give you any reason to think that?"

"He mentioned something about a blockage. Oh, Charles, I'm scared! If anything ever happened to you, I'd die. I couldn't live without you!"

For an emotional and sensitive man like Rackham, it was a perfect set-up: his devoted wife was frightened to the point of hysterics, his good friend and physician had given her reason to be frightened. Rackham was ready for the next step. . . .

"According to the records in your X-ray department," Sands said, "Rackham had a lower gastrointestinal X-ray yesterday morning. What was the result?"

"Medical ethics forbid me to—"

"You can't hide behind a wall of medical ethics that's already full of holes. What was the result?"

There was a long silence before Tracy spoke. "Nothing."

"You found nothing the matter with him?"

"That's right."

"Have you told Rackham that?"

"He came in earlier this afternoon, alone."

"Why alone?"

"I didn't want Alma to hear what I had to say."

"Very considerate of you."

"No, it was not considerate," Tracy said dully. "I had decided to back out of our—our agreement—and I didn't want her to know just yet."

"The agreement was to lie to Rackham, convince him that he had a fatal disease?"

"Yes."

"Did you?"

"No. I showed him the X-rays, I made it clear that there was nothing wrong with him. . . . I tried. I tried my best. It was no use."

"What do you mean?"

"He wouldn't believe me! He thought I was trying to keep the real truth from him." Tracy drew in his breath, sharply. "It's funny, isn't it? —after days of indecision and torment I made up my mind to do the right thing. But it was too late. Alma had played her role too well. She's the only one Rackham will believe."

The telephone on Tracy's desk began to ring but he made no move to answer it, and pretty soon the ringing stopped and the room was quiet again.

Sands said, "Have you asked Alma to tell him the truth?"

"Yes, just before you came in."

"She refused?"

Tracy didn't answer.

"She wants him to think he is fatally ill?"

"I—yes."

"In the hope that he'll kill himself, perhaps?"

Once again Tracy was silent. But no reply was necessary.

"I think Alma miscalculated," Sands said quietly. "Instead of planning suicide, Rackham is planning a trip. But before he leaves, he's going to hear the truth—from you and from Alma." Sands went towards the door. "Come on, Tracy. You have a house call to make."

"No. I can't." Tracy grasped the desk with both hands, like a child resisting the physical force of removal by a parent. "I won't go."

"You have to."

"No! Rackham will ruin me if he finds out. That's how this whole thing started. We were afraid, Alma and I, afraid of what Rackham would do if she asked him for a divorce. He's crazy in love with her, he's obsessed!"

"And so are you?"

"Not the way he is. Alma and I both want the same things—a little peace, a little quiet together. We are alike in many ways."

"That I can believe," Sands said grimly. "You wanted the same things, a little peace, a little quiet—and a little of Rackham's money?"

"The money was secondary."

"A very close second. How did you plan on getting it?"

Tracy shook his head from side to side, like an animal in pain. "You keep referring to plans, ideas, schemes. We didn't start out with plans or schemes. We just fell in love. We've been in love for nearly a year, not daring to do anything about it because I knew how Rackham would react if we told him. I have worked hard to build up this clinic; Rackham could destroy it, and me, within a month."

"That's a chance you'll have to take. Come on, Tracy."

Sands opened the door and the two men walked down the hall, slowly and in step, as if they were handcuffed together.

A nurse in uniform met them at the top of the stairs. "Dr. Tracy, are you ready for your next—?"

"Cancel all my appointments, Miss Leroy."

"But that's imposs—"

"I have a very important house call to make."

"Will it take long?"

"I don't know."

The two men went down the stairs, past the reception desk, and out into the summer afternoon. Before he got into Sands' car, Tracy looked back at the clinic, as if he never expected to see it again.

Sands turned on the ignition and the car sprang forward like an eager pup.

After a time Tracy said, "Of all the people in the world who could have been at the Rackhams' that night, it had to be an ex-policeman."

"It's lucky for you that I was there."

"Lucky." Tracy let out a harsh little laugh. "What's lucky about financial ruin?"

"It's better than some other kinds of ruin. If your plan had gone through, you could never have felt like a decent man again."

"You think I will anyway?"

"Perhaps, as the years go by."

"The years." Tracy turned, with a sigh. "What are you going to tell Rackham?"

"Nothing. You will tell him yourself."

"I can't. You don't understand, I'm quite fond of Rackham, and so is Alma. We—it's hard to explain."

"Even harder to understand." Sands thought back to all the times he had seen the Rackhams together and envied their companionship, their mutual devotion. Never, by the slightest glance or gesture of impatience or slip of the tongue, had Alma indicated that she was passionately in love with another man. He recalled the games of scrabble, the dinners, the endless conversations with Rackham, while Alma sat with her knitting, her face reposeful, content. Rackham would ask, "Don't you want to play too, Alma?" And she would reply, "No, thank you, dear, I'm quite happy with my thoughts."

Alma, happy with her thoughts of violent delights and violent ends.

Sands said, "Alma is equally in love with you?"

"Yes." He sounded absolutely convinced. "No matter what Rackham says or does, we intend to have each other."

"I see."

"I wish you did."

The blinds of the Rackham house were closed against the sun. Sands led the way up the veranda steps and pressed the door chime, while Tracy stood, stony-faced and erect, like a bill collector or a process server.

Sands could hear the chimes pealing inside the house and feel their vibrations beating under his feet.

He said, "They may have gone already."

"Gone where?"

"Rackham wouldn't tell me. He just said he was planning the trip as a surprise for Alma."

"He can't take her away! He can't force her to leave if she doesn't want to go!"

Sands pressed the door chime again, and called out, "Rackham? Alma?" But there was no response.

He wiped the sudden moisture off his forehead with his coat sleeve. "I'm going in."

"I'm coming with you."

"No."

The door was unlocked. He stepped into the empty hall and shouted up the staircase, "Alma? Rackham? Are you there?"

The echo of his own voice teased him from the dim corners.

Tracy had come into the hall. "They've left, then?"

"Perhaps not. They might have just gone out for a drive. It's a nice day for a drive."

"Is it?"

"Go around to the back and see if their car's in the garage."

When Tracy had gone, Sands closed the door behind him and shot the bolt. He stood for a moment listening to Tracy's nervous footsteps on the concrete driveway. Then he turned and walked slowly into the living room, knowing the car would be in the garage, no matter how nice a day it was for a drive.

The drapes were pulled tight across the windows and the room was cool and dark, but alive with images and noisy with the past:

"I wanted to thank you before we leave, Sands."

"You're taking a trip?"
"Yes, quite a long one."
"When are you leaving?"
"Today."
"You must let me see you off at the station. . . ."

But no station had been necessary for Rackham's trip. He lay in front of the fireplace in a pool of blood, and beside him was his companion on the journey, her left arm curving around his waist.

Rackham had kept his promise to write. The note was on the mantel, addressed not to Sands, but to Tracy.

> *"Dear George:*
>
> *You did your best to foil me but I got the truth from Alma. She could never hide anything from me; we are too close to each other. This is the easiest way out. I am sorry that I must take Alma along, but she told me so often that she could not live without me. I cannot leave her behind to grieve.*
>
> *Think of us now and then, and try not to judge me too harshly.*
>
> *Charles Rackham."*

Sands put the note back on the mantel. He stood quietly, his heart pierced by the final splinter of irony: before Rackham had used the gun on himself, he had lain down on the floor beside Alma and placed her dead arm lovingly around his waist.

From outside came the sound of Tracy's footsteps returning along the driveway, and then the pounding of his fists on the front door.

"Sands, I'm locked out. Open the door. Let me in! Sands, do you hear me? Open this door!"

Sands went and opened the door.

FOR DISCUSSION: The Couple Next Door

1. In this story the author attempts to do two things simultaneously: to give accurate information about the ages of all of the characters and at the same time to convey the seeming unimportance of the differences in their ages. Exactly *how* does she achieve each of these aims? Why is this emphasis on age important to the story?

2. At one point Dr. Tracy tells Sands that he can't bring himself to tell Rackham the truth. Then he adds: "You don't understand, I'm quite fond of Rackham, and so is Alma. We—it's hard to explain." Do you think Tracy is telling the truth? Is it possible to be fond of someone and yet plan his death? If Tracy and Alma truly cared

about Rackham, why didn't they just leave him and go away together?

3. Throughout the entire story Alma had consistently appeared to Sands as a devoted and thoroughly contented wife. Yet by the end of the story we know this was just an act. Could a supposedly not-very-bright person like Alma fool a trained investigator over a fairly long period of time? Is this realistic?

4. The irony in this story is not nearly so sharp as it is in "The Old Barn on the Pond," but it is considerably more poignant. How does the author use irony to create a final scene that is both touching and bitter?

The Mind
of a
Criminal

CHAPTER TWO

One of the most difficult questions to answer is: what is the mind of a criminal like? How does a criminal think? During the last few centuries there have been all sorts of hypotheses. Phrenologists have claimed that you can recognize a criminal by the shape of his head or by the number of bumps on it; graphologists have claimed that you can recognize him by his handwriting; sociologists have claimed that you can recognize him by his family background and environment; psychologists have claimed that you can recognize him by his early childhood experiences. All to some extent are right, and, to an equal extent, all are wrong. Indeed, a major part of the problem is that we keep trying to generalize—to find one explanation for all criminals.

Every generalization about criminals is doomed to failure, just as almost every generalization about human beings is doomed to failure. It might be better, then, to ask a more limited question: what makes a criminal different from the majority of law-abiding citizens?

The answer seems to be implicit in the question: the average citizen abides by the law, while the criminal does not. But this isn't quite true. Most of us accept the law as a necessary substructure of society, but we have little hesitation about disliking parts of it or bending the rules when it is convenient. We cheat, just a bit, on our income tax returns; we run a red light late at night when no other cars (or policemen) are around;

we take a few pencils from the office for use at home. The "criminal" does the same thing ... only he does it on a larger scale. Instead of a few pencils, he snatches a few diamonds; he cheats by manipulating account books or arranging bribes; and, sometimes, he murders.

Is crime then a matter of *degree?* Is an inch below the law acceptable, while a foot is not? But that's overly simple. Stealing a few pencils from a blind man is criminal; taking them from the office is not. (Notice how the verb changes: the criminal *steals;* we *borrow* or *take!*)

Crime is not, then, merely a matter of degree. Is it intent perhaps? When we take a few pencils, we harm no one—nor do we intend to. The office budget is large. Here the criminal varies. Sometimes he, too, intends no harm. Will a bank be endangered by the loss of a few thousand dollars? More often, however, he *does* intend harm, or not intending it, simply does not care if it results. He needs the money, he wants the money. If someone suffers, so be it. So intent does play a part.

Is it also perhaps a matter of intent of another kind? Those ubiquitous pencils will never cause my neighbor to call me a criminal. No policeman will be interested in them. Taken to court, any judge will laugh and dismiss the case. In other words, though taking the pencils is illegal *by statute,* it is condoned by the laws *of our society.* The criminal, on the other hand, knows that his acts will be considered illegal not only by the courts, but also by himself and by the society of which he is a part. Even his peers in criminal practice, though they may envy or admire his daring, will agree that what he has done is unlawful, wrong, criminal.

In the final analysis it is not the written law of the land that determines the *rightness* of our acts; it is the unwritten law, the customs, the mores.

Some people will argue that a criminal can be identified by being caught, a criminal act can be defined by being discovered, but this is not really true, either. Although the person who commits a criminal act may not be labeled a criminal if he has not been arrested, most of us would agree that a murderer, or a person who robs a bank, or a person who steals cars, is a criminal, nevertheless. This loophole, too, we reserve for ourselves, the "law-abiding" public. Cheating on one's income tax is an *American* thing to do, but being caught at cheating, especially being arrested for cheating, arouses disapproval. It suggests blatant cheating rather than the extra business deduction or the slightly inflated contribution. The first is frowned upon by our society; the second is (enviously) applauded.

A more striking characteristic of the criminal that is *not* shared by the average citizen is his willingness to commit violence in order to achieve his ends. This is not true of all criminals, of course, but it is true of many; conversely, it is not generally true of noncriminals.

What, then, is the mind of a criminal like?

He is an anarchist, less interested in a stable society than in his own desires.

He is an extremist, bored with moderation and requiring large doses of excitement and even violence.

He is an egotist, with an intemperate confidence that he is the cleverest and most deserving fellow in the world.

And sometimes he is a masochist, needing punishment from authority-figures in order to survive.

Even this is only a beginning. Perhaps we can learn more from the hundreds of mystery writers who have tried to understand the criminal mind and have tried to depict it. From their works it may be possible to gain an insight into the minds of individual criminals until eventually, through a process of accumulation, one begins to understand, just a little, the mind of a criminal.

INTRODUCTION: The Green Elephant

A white elephant is a possession too valuable to throw away and too expensive and/or embarrassing to maintain or keep. In this story the nonspecific *white* changes to *green,* for a pretty obvious reason.

Joe Shupe would like to be a successful criminal, but he's a flabby, unorganized, unthinking blob of a man, and $250,000 worth of "hot" money is a very green elephant, indeed. Joe has the desire to be a criminal, but he lacks the ruthlessness and the confidence of the "professional."

Dashiell Hammett, one of the greats in mystery writing, here studies the foggy mind of Joe Shupe, a petty criminal who has stumbled into large-scale crime. The story emphasizes, as few others do, the differences rather than the similarities among criminals.

The Green Elephant
Dashiell Hammett

Joe Shupe stood in the doorway of the square-faced office building—his body tilted slantwise so that one thin shoulder, lodged against the gray stone, helped his crossed legs hold him up—looking without interest into the street.

He had stepped into the vestibule to roll a cigarette out of reach of the boisterous wind that romped along Riverside Avenue, and he had remained there because he had nothing better to do. In fact, he had nothing else to do just now. Tomorrow he would revisit the employment offices—a matter of a few blocks' walk along Main and Trent Avenues, with brief digressions into one or two of the interesting streets—for the fifth consecutive day; perhaps to be rewarded by a job, perhaps to hear reiterations of the now familiar "nothing in your line today." But the time for that next pilgrimage to the shrines of Industry, through which he might reach the comparative paradise of employment, was still some twenty hours away; so Joe Shupe loitered in the doorway, and dull thoughts began to crawl around in his little round head.

He thought of the Swede first, with distaste. The Swede—he was a Dane, but the distinction was too subtle for Joe—had come down to the city from a Lost Creek lumber camp with money in his pockets and faith in his fellows. When the men came together and formed their brief friendship only fifty dollars remained of the Swede's tangible wealth. Joe got that by a crude and hoary subterfuge with which even a timber-beast from Lost Creek should have been familiar. What became of the swindled Swede's faith is not a matter of record. Joe had not given that a thought; and had his attention been called to it he probably would have been unable to see in it anything but further evidence of the Swede's unfitness for the possession of money.

But what was vital to Joe Shupe was that, inspired by the ease with which he had gained the fifty dollars, he had deserted the polished counter over which for eight hours each day he had shoved pies and sandwiches and coffee, and had set out to live by his wits. But the fifty dollars had soon dribbled away, the Swede had had no successors; and now Joe Shupe was beset with the necessity of finding employment again.

Joe's fault, as Doc Haire had once pointed out, was that he was an unskilled laborer in the world of crime, and therefore had to content himself with stealing whatever came to hand—a slipshod and generally unsatisfactory method. As the same authority had often declared: "Making a living on the mace ain't duck soup! Take half these guys you hear telling the world what wonders they are at puffing boxes, knocking over joints, and the rest of the lays—not a half of 'em makes three meals a day at it! Then what chance has a guy that ain't got no regular racket, but's got to trust to luck, got? Huh?"

But Joe Shupe had disregarded this advice, and even the oracle's own example. For Doc Haire, although priding himself upon being the most altogether efficient house-burglar in the Northwest, was not above shipping out into the Couer d'Alenes now and then to repair his finances by a few weeks' work in the mines. Joe realized that Doc had been right; that he himself was not equipped to dig through the protecting surfaces with which mankind armored its wealth; that the Swede's advent had been a fortuitous episode, and a recurrence could not be expected. He blamed the Swede now. . . .

A commotion in the street interrupted Joe Shupe's unaccustomed introspection.

Across the street two automobiles were twisting and turning, backing and halting, in clumsy dance figures. Men began to run back and forth between them. A tall man in a black overcoat stood up in one of the cars and began shooting with a small-caliber pistol at indeterminate targets. Weapons appeared in the other automobiles, and in the hands of men in the street between the two machines. Spectators scrambled into doorways. From down the street a policeman was running heavily, tugging at his hip, and trying to free his wrist from an entangling coat-tail. A man was running across the street toward Joe's doorway, a black gladstone bag swinging at his side. As the man's foot touched the curb he fell forward, sprawling half in the gutter half on the sidewalk. The bag left his hand and slid across the pavement—balancing itself as nicely as a boy on skates—to Joe's feet.

The wisdom of Doc Haire went for nothing. With no thought for the economics of thievery, the amenities or specialization, Joe Shupe followed his bent. He picked up the bag, passed through the revolving door into the lobby of the building, turned a corner, followed a corridor, and at length came to a smaller door, through which he reached an alley. The alley gave to another street and a street-car that had paused to avoid a truck. Joe climbed into the car and found a seat.

Thus far Joe Shupe had been guided by pure instinct, and—granting that to touch the bag at all were judicious—had acted deftly and with beautiful precision. But now his conscious brain caught up with him as it were, and resumed its dominion over him. He began to wonder what he had let himself in for, whether his prize were worth the risk its possession had entailed, just how great that risk might be. He became excited, his pulse throbbed, singing in his temples, and his mouth went dry. He had a vision of innumerable policemen, packed in taxicabs like pullets in crates, racing dizzily to intercept him.

He got to the street four blocks from where he had boarded the street car, and only a suspicion that the conductor was watching him persuaded him to cling to the bag. He would have preferred leaving it inconspicuously between the seats, to be found in the car barn. He walked rapidly away from the car line, turning thankfully each corner the city put in his path, until he came to another row of car tracks. He stayed on the second car for six blocks, and then wound circuitously through the streets again, finally coming to the hotel in which he had his room.

A towel covering the keyhole, the blind down over the one narrow window, Joe Shupe put the bag on his bed and set about opening it. It was securely locked, but with his knife he attacked a leather side, making a ragged slit through which he looked into depths of green paper.

"Holy hell!" his gaping mouth exclaimed. "All the money in the world!"

He straightened abruptly, listening, while his small brown eyes looked suspiciously around the room. Tiptoeing to the door, he listened again; unlocked the door quickly and flung it open; searched the dark hall. Then he returned to the black bag. Enlarging the opening, he dumped and raked his spoils out on the bed; a mound of grey-green paper—a bushel of it—neatly divided into little soft, paper-gartered bricks. Thousands, hundreds, tens, twenties, fifties! For a long minute he stood open-mouthed, spellbound, panting; then he hastily covered the pile of currency with one of the shabby grey blankets on the bed, and dropped weakly down beside it.

Presently the desire to know the amount of his loot penetrated Joe's stupefaction and he set about counting the money. He counted slowly and with difficulty, taking one package of bills out of its hiding place at a time and stowing it under another blanket when he had finished with it. He counted each package he handled, bill by bill, ignoring the figures printed on the manilla wrappers. At fifty thousand he stopped, estimating that he had handled one-third of the pile. The emotional seething within him, together with the effort the unaccustomed addition required of his brain, had by then driven his curiosity away.

His mind, freed of its mathematical burden, was attacked by an alarming thought. The manager of the hotel, who was his own clerk, had seen Joe come in with the bag; and while the bag was not unusual in appearance, nevertheless, any black bag would attract both eyes and speculation after the evening papers were read. Joe decided that he would have to get out of the hotel, after which the bag would have to be disposed of.

Laboriously, and at the cost of two large blisters, he hacked at the bag with his dull knife and bent it until, wrapped in an old newspaper, it made a small and unassuming bundle. Then he distributed the money about his person, stuffing his pockets and even putting some of the bills inside his shirt. He looked at his reflection in the mirror when he had finished, and the result was very unsatisfactory: he presented a decidedly and humorously padded appearance.

That would not do. He dragged his battered valise from under the bed and put the money into it, under his few clothes.

There was no delay about his departure from the hotel; it was of the type where all bills are payable in advance. He passed four rubbish cans before he could summon the courage to get rid of the fragments of the bag, but he boldly dropped them into the fifth; after which he walked— almost scuttled—for ten minutes, turning corners and slipping through alleys, until he was positive he was not being watched.

At a hotel across the city from his last home he secured a room and went up to it immediately. Behind drawn blinds, masked keyhole, and closed transom, he took the money out again. He had intended finishing his counting—the flight across the city having rekindled his desire to know the extent of his wealth—but when he found that he had bunched it, had put already counted with uncounted, and thought of the immensity of the task, he gave it up. Counting was a "tough job," and the afternoon papers would tell him how much he had.

He wanted to look at the money, to feast his eyes upon it, to caress his fingers with it, but its abundance made him uneasy, frightened him even, notwithstanding that it was safe here from prying eyes. There was too much of it. It unnerved him. A thousand dollars, or perhaps even ten thousand, would have filled him with wild joy, but this bale.... Furtively, he put it back in the valise.

For the first time now he thought of it not as money,—a thing in itself, —but as money—potential women, cards, liquor, idleness, everything! It took his breath for the instant—the thought of the things the world held for him now! And he realized that he was wasting time, that these things were abroad, beckoning, while he stood in his room dreaming of them. He opened the valise and took out a double handful of the bills, cramming them into his pockets.

On the steps descending from the office to the street he halted abruptly. A hotel of this sort—or any other—was certainly no place to leave a hundred and fifty thousand dollars unguarded. A fine chump he would be to leave it behind and have it stolen!

He hurried back to his room and, scarcely pausing to renew his former precautions, sprang to the valise. The money was still there. Then he sat down and tried to think of some way by which the money could be protected during his absence. He was hungry—he had not eaten since morning—but he could not leave the money. He found a piece of heavy paper, wrapped the money in it and lashed it securely, making a large but inconspicuous bundle—laundry, perhaps.

On the street newsboys were shouting extras. Joe bought a paper, folded it carefully so that its headlines were out of sight, and went to a restaurant on First Avenue. He sat at a table back in one corner, with his bundle on the floor and his feet on the bundle. Then with elaborate nonchalance he spread the paper before him and read of the daylight hold-up in which $250,000 had been taken from an automobile belonging to the Fourth National Bank. $250,000! He grabbed the bundle from the floor, knocking his forehead noisily against the table in his haste, and put it in his lap. Then he reddened with swift self-consciousness, paled apprehensively, and yawned exaggeratedly. After assuring himself that none of the other men in the restaurant had noted his peculiar behavior, he turned his attention to the newspaper again, and read the story of the robbery.

Five of the bandits had been caught in the very act, the paper said, and two of them were seriously wounded. The bandits, who, according to the paper, must have had information concerning the unusually large shipment from some friend on the inside, had bungled their approach, bringing their own automobile to rest too far from their victim's for the greatest efficiency. Nevertheless, the sixth bandit had made away with the money. As was to be expected, the bandits denied that there was a sixth, but the disappearance of the money testified irrefragably to his existence.

From the restaurant Joe went to a saloon on Howard Street, bought two bottles of white liquor, and took them to his room. He had decided that he would have to remain indoors that night; he couldn't walk around with $250,000 under his arm. Suppose some flaw in the paper should suddenly succumb to the strain upon it? Or he should drop the bundle? Or someone should bump heavily into it?

He fidgeted about the room for hours, pondering his problem with all the concentration of which his dull mind was capable. He opened one of the bottles that he had bought, but he set it aside untasted: he could not risk drinking until he had safeguarded the money. It was too great a responsibility to be mixed with alcohol. The temptations of women and cards and the rest did not bother him now; time enough for them when the money was safe. He couldn't leave the money in his room, and he couldn't carry it to any of the places he knew, or to any place at all, for that matter.

He slept little that night, and by morning had made no headway against his problem. He thought of banking the money, but dismissed the thought as absurd: he couldn't walk into a bank a day or so after a widely advertised robbery and open an account with a bale of currency. He even thought of finding some secluded spot where he could bury it; but that seemed still more ridiculous. A few shovels of dirt was not sufficient protection. He might buy or rent a house and conceal the money on his own premises; but there were fires to consider, and what might serve as a hiding place for a few hundred dollars wouldn't do for many thousands: he must have an absolutely safe plan, one that would be safe in every respect and would admit of no possible loophole through which the money could vanish. He knew half a dozen men who could have told him what to do; but which of them could he trust where $250,000 was concerned?

When he was giddy from too much smoking on an empty stomach, he packed his valise again and left the hotel. A day of uneasiness and restlessness, with the valise ever in his hand or under his foot, brought no counsel. The grey-green incubus that his battered bag housed benumbed him, handicapped by his never-agile imagination. His nerves began to send little fluttering messages—forerunners of panic—to his brain.

Leaving a restaurant that evening he encountered Doc Haire himself.

"Hullo, Joe! Going away?"

Joe looked down at the valise in his hand.

"Yes," he said.

That was it! Why hadn't he thought of it before! In another city, at some distance from the scene of the robbery, none of the restrictions that oppressed him in Spokane would be present. Seattle, Portland, San Francisco, Los Angeles, the East!

Although he had paid for a berth, Joe Shupe did not occupy it; but sat all night in a day coach. At the last moment he had realized that the ways of sleeping-cars were unknown to him—perhaps one was required to surrender one's hand baggage. Joe did not know, but he did know that the money in his valise was not going to leave his hands until he had found a securer place for it. So he dozed uncomfortably through the ride over the Cascades, sprawled over two seats in the smoking-car, leaning against the valise.

In Seattle he gained no more liberty than he had had in Spokane. He had purposed to open an account with each bank in the city, distributing his wealth widely in cautious amounts: and for two days he tried to carry out his plan. But his nervous legs simply would not carry him through the door of a bank. There was something too austere, too official, too all-knowing, about the very architecture of these financial institutions, and there was no telling what complications, what questioning, awaited a man inside.

A fear of being bereft of his wealth by more cunning thieves—and he admitted frankly now that there might be many such—began to obsess him, and kept him out of dance-hall, pool-room, gambling-house, and saloon. From anyone who addressed even the most casual of sentences to him he fled headlong. On his first day in Seattle he bought a complete equipment of bright and gaudy clothes, but he wore them for only half an hour. He felt that they gave him an altogether too affluent appearance, and would certainly attract the attention of thieves in droves; so he put them away in his valise, and thereafter wore his old clothes.

At night now he slept with the valise in bed beside him, one of his arms bent over it in a protecting embrace that was not unlike a bridegroom's, waking now and then with the fear that someone was tugging at it. And every night it was a different hotel. He changed his lodgings each day, afraid of the curiosity his habit of always carrying the valise might arouse if he stayed too long in any one hotel.

Such intelligence as he was ordinarily in possession of was by this time completely submerged beneath the panic in which he lived. He went aimlessly about the city, a shabby man with the look of a harried rabbit in his furtive eyes, destinationless, without purpose, filled with forebodings that were now powerless except to deepen the torper in his head.

A senseless routine filled his days. At eight or eight-thirty in the morning he would leave the hotel where he had slept, eat his breakfast at a nearby lunch-room, and then walk—down Second to Yessler Way, to Fourth, to Pike—or perhaps as far as Stewart—to Second, to Yessler

Way, to Fourth. . . . Sometimes he would desert his beat to sit for an hour or more on one of the green iron benches around the totem in Pioneer Square, staring vacantly at the street, his valise either at his side or beneath his feet. Presently, goaded by an obscure disquietude, he would get up abruptly and go back to his promenade along Yessler Way to Fourth, to Pike, to Second, to Yessler Way, to . . . . When he thought of food he ate meagerly at the nearest restaurant, but often he forgot to eat all day.

His nights were more vivid; with darkness his brain shook off some of its numbness and became sensitive to pain. Lying in the dark, always in a strange room, he would be filled with wild fears whose anarchic chaos amounted to delirium. Only in his dreams did he see things clearly. His brief and widely spaced naps brought him distinct, sharply etched pictures in which invariably he was robbed of his money, usually to the accompaniment of physical violence in its most unlovely forms.

The end was inevitable. In a larger city Joe Shupe might have gone on until his mentality had wasted away entirely and he collapsed. But Seattle is not large enough to smother the identities of its inhabitants: strangers' faces become familiar; one becomes accustomed to meeting the man in the brown derby somewhere in the vicinity of the post office, and the red-haired girl with the grapes on her hat somewhere along Pine Street between noon and one o'clock; and looks for the slim youth with the remarkable moustache, expecting to pass him on the street at least twice during the course of the day. And so it was that two Prohibition enforcement officers came to recognize Joe Shupe and his battered valise and his air of dazed fear.

They didn't take him very seriously at first, until, quite by accident, they grew aware of his custom of changing his address each night. Then one day, when they had nothing special on hand and when the memory of reprimands they had received from their superiors for not frequently enough "showing results" was fresh, they met Joe on the street. For two hours they shadowed him—up Fourth to Pike, to Second, to Yessler Way. . . . On the third round-trip confusion and chagrin sent the officers to accost Joe.

"I ain't done nothing!" Joe told them, hugging the valise to his wasted body with both arms. "You leave me be!"

One of the officers said something that Joe did not understand—he was beyond comprehending anything by now—but tears came from his red-rimmed eyes and ran down the hollows of his cheeks.

"You leave me be!" he repeated.

Then, still clasping the valise to his bosom, he turned and ran down the street. The officers easily overtook him.

Joe Shupe's story of how he had come into possession of the stolen quarter-million was received by everyone—police, press and public—with a great deal of merriment. But, now that the responsibility for the money's safety rested with the Seattle police, he slept soundly that night, as well as those that followed; and when he appeared in the courtroom in Spokane two weeks later, to plead futilely that he was not one of the men who had held up the Fourth National Bank's automobile, he was his normal self again, both physically and mentally.

FOR DISCUSSION: The Green Elephant

1. According to Doc Haire, what is Joe Shupe's major weakness as a criminal? Is this weakness evident in the noncriminal aspects of Joe's life? Did it play any part in Shupe's turning toward crime?
2. The scene of the robbery begins with the sentence: "Across the street two automobiles were twisting and turning, backing and halting, in clumsy dance figures." The entire scene is reminiscent of the jerkiness and air of unreality of a marionette show. What does this suggest about Joe's angle of vision and about the relationship between him and the robbery?
3. Shakespeare once wrote: "The fault, dear Brutus, is not in our stars, but in ourselves, that we are underlings." The "stars"—or Fate—gave Joe Shupe the one big chance he had always coveted, and he muffed it. Shakespeare had one explanation. How might modern psychology explain Joe's actions?
4. Which haunted Joe more: the statute laws or the laws of society? Explain the significance of your answer.
5. There is a deep and poignant irony in the last paragraph of this story —an irony that clarifies Joe's basic personality. What was his real need? His most pervasive fear? Was his real need in conflict with his conscious desires? Explain.

Most criminals who commit more than one crime develop a *modus operandi*—a regular pattern or procedure of operation. Among police this is known as an "M.O.," and it can be exceedingly helpful in tracking down the perpetrator of a crime.

The fact that a *modus operandi* is recognized does not guarantee that the criminal will be caught quickly, but it certainly decreases the number of suspects and facilitates investigation. Knowing this, why do criminals still adhere to a *modus operandi?* Because it is human nature to do so. If something works once, we are tempted to try again and again. We are creatures of habit, and past success makes us feel secure. It is a human need that criminals share with the rest of us.

Bubble Bath No. 3
Margery Allingham

At five o'clock on a September afternoon Ronald Fredrick Torbay was making preparations for his third murder. He was being wary because he was well aware of the dangers of carelessness.

He knew, 'way back before his first marriage, that a career of homicide got more chancy as one went on. Also, he realized, success was liable to go to a man's head.

For an instant he paused and regarded himself thoughtfully in the shaving glass of the bathroom in the new cottage he had hired so recently.

The face which looked back at him was thin, middle-aged, and pallid. Sparse dark hair receded from its high narrow forehead and the eyes were blue and prominent. Only the mouth was really unusual. That narrow slit, quite straight, was almost lipless and, unconsciously, he persuaded it to relax into a half smile. Even Ronald Torbay did not like his own mouth.

A sound in the kitchen below disturbed him and he straightened up hastily. It might be Edyth coming up to take her long discussed bubble bath before he had prepared it for her, and that would never do.

He waited, holding his breath, but it was all right; she was going out of the back door. He looked out the window to see her disappearing round the side of the house into the small square yard which was so exactly like all the other square yards in the long suburban street. He knew she was going to hang some linen on the line to air, and although the maneuver gave him the time he needed, still it irritated him.

Of the three homely, middle-aged women whom he had persuaded to marry him and then to will him their modest possessions, Edyth was proving easily the most annoying. In their six weeks of marriage he had told her a dozen times not to spend so much time in the yard. He hated her being out of doors alone. She was shy and reserved, but now that new people had moved in next door there was always the danger of some overfriendly woman starting up an acquaintance with her, and that was the last thing to be tolerated at this juncture.

Each of his former wives had been shy. He had been very careful to choose the right type and felt he owed much of his success to it. Mary, the first of them, had met her fatal "accident" almost unnoticed in the bungalow of a housing development very like the present one he had chosen, but in the north instead of the south of England.

At the time it had been a growing place, the Coroner had been hurried, the police sympathetic but busy, and the neighbors scarcely curious— except that one of them, a junior reporter on a local paper whose story was picked up by the wire services, had written a flowery paragraph about the nearness of tragedy in the midst of joy, published a wedding-day snapshot, and had titled the article with typical northern understatement, *Honeymoon Mishap*.

Dorothy's brief excursion into his life and abrupt exit from it had given him a little more bother. She had deceived him when she told him she was quite alone in the world. An interfering brother had turned up after the funeral to ask awkward questions about her small fortune. He might have been a nuisance if Ronald had not been very firm with him. There had been a brief court case duly recorded in a small item in newsprint. However, Ronald had won his case handsomely, and the insurance company had paid up without a murmur.

All that was four years ago. Now, with a new name and a newly invented background, he felt remarkably safe.

From the moment he had first seen Edyth, sitting alone at a little table under the window in a seaside hotel dining room, he had known that she was to be his next subject. He always thought of his wives as "subjects."

Edyth had sat there looking stiff and neat and a trifle severe, but there had been a secret timidity in her face, an unsatisfied, half-frightened expression in her nearsighted eyes. She was also wearing a genuine diamond brooch.

He had spoken to her that evening, had weathered the initial snub, and finally got her to talk. After that the acquaintance had progressed just as he had expected. His methods were old-fashioned and heavily romantic, and within a week she was hopelessly infatuated.

From Ronald's point of view her history was ideal. She had taught in a girls' boarding school during her twenties before being summoned home to look after a demanding father, whose long illness had monopolized her life; now at forty-three she was alone, comparatively well off, and as much at sea as a ship without a rudder.

Ronald was careful not to let her toes touch the ground. He devoted his entire attention to her, and in exactly five weeks he married her at the registry office of the town where they were both strangers. The same afternoon they each made a will in the other's favor and moved into the villa which he had been able to hire cheaply because the holiday season was at an end.

Two things signed her death warrant earlier than had been Ronald's original intention. One was her obstinate reticence over her monetary affairs and the other was her embarrassing interest in his job.

Ronald had told her that he was a junior partner in a firm of cosmetic manufacturers who were giving him a very generous leave of absence. Edyth accepted the statement without question, but almost at once she had begun to plan a visit to the office and the factory and said she must buy some new clothes so as not to "disgrace" him. At the same time she kept all her business papers locked in an old writing case and steadfastly refused to discuss them, however cautiously he raised the subject. Ronald had given up feeling angry with her and had decided to act.

He turned from the window and began to run the bath.

The bathroom was the one room they had repainted. Ronald had done it himself and had put up the little shelf over the bath to hold a small electric heater of the old-fashioned type. He switched it on now and stood looking at it until the two bars of glowing warmth appeared. Then he went out onto the landing, leaving the heater alight.

The fuse box which controlled all the electricity in the house was concealed in the bottom of the linen cupboard at the head of the stairs. Ronald opened the door carefully and, using his handkerchief so that his fingerprints should leave no trace, pulled the main switch.

Back in the bathroom the heater's glow died away; the bars were almost black again by the time he returned. He eyed the heater approvingly and then, still using the handkerchief, he lowered it carefully into the water. It lay close to the foot of the tub where it took up practically no room at all. The white cord of the heater ran up over the porcelain side of the bath, along the baseboard, under the door, and into a wall socket just outside on the landing.

When he had first installed the heater, Edyth had demurred at this somewhat slipshod arrangement. But he had explained that the local Council was stupid and fussy about fitting wall sockets in bathrooms since water was said to be a conductor, and she had agreed to let him run the cord under the linoleum.

At the moment the heater was perfectly visible in the bath. It certainly looked as if it had fallen into its odd position accidentally, but no one in his senses could have stepped into the water without seeing it. Ronald paused, his ugly mouth narrower than ever. The beautiful simplicity of the main plan, so swiftly fatal and, above all, so safe as far as he was concerned, gave him a thrill of pleasure—as it always did.

He turned off the faucet and waited, listening. Edyth was coming back. He could hear her moving something on the concrete outside the back door below and he took a paper sachet from his jacket pocket.

He was reading the directions on the back of it when a slight sound made him turn his head, and he saw, to his horror, the woman herself not five feet away. Her neat head had appeared suddenly just above the flat roof of the scullery, outside the bathroom window. She was clearing the dead leaves from the gutters and must, he guessed, be standing on a stepladder.

It was typical of the man that he did not panic. Still holding the sachet lightly, he stepped between her and the bath and spoke mildly.

"What on earth are you doing there, darling?"

Edyth started so violently that she almost fell off the ladder. "Oh, how you startled me! I thought I'd just do this little job before I came up to change. If it rains, the gutter floods all over the back step."

"Very thoughtful of you, my dear." He spoke with that slightly acid amusement with which he had found he could best destroy her slender vein of self-assurance. "But not terribly clever when you knew I'd come up to prepare your beauty bath for you. Or was it?"

The slight intonation on the word "beauty" was not lost on her. He saw her swallow.

"Perhaps it wasn't," she said without looking at him. "It's very good of you to take all this trouble, Ronald."

"Not at all," he said with just the right amount of masculine, offhand insensitivity. "I'm taking you out tonight and I want you to look as nice as possible. Hurry up, there's a good girl. The foam doesn't last indefinitely, and like all very high-class beauty treatments, it's expensive. Undress in the bedroom, put on your gown, and come along."

"Very well, dear." She began to descend while he turned and shook the contents of the sachet into the water. The crystals, smelling strongly of roses, floated on the tide and then when he turned the water on hard, they began to dissolve into thousands of iridescent bubbles. The bubbles grew into a fragrant feathery mass which obscured the bottom of the bath and overflowed the porcelain sides of the tub.

It was perfect.

He opened the door to call to her and just then she appeared. She came shrinking in, her blue dressing gown strained round her thin body, her hair thrust into an unbecoming bathing cap.

62

"Oh, Ronald!" she said staring at the display. "Won't it make an awful mess? Goodness! All over the floor!"

Her hesitation infuriated him.

"That won't matter," he said savagely. "You get in while the foam is still there. Hurry. Meanwhile I'll go and change myself. Get in, and lie down. It'll take the sallowness out of your skin."

He went out and paused, listening. She locked the door as he had known she would. The habits of a lifetime do not change with marriage. He heard the bolt slide home and forced himself to walk slowly.

He gave her sixty seconds—thirty to take off her things and thirty to hesitate on the brink of the rosy mass.

"How is it?" he shouted from the linen cupboard.

She did not answer at once and the sweat broke out on his forehead. Then he heard her.

"I don't know yet. I'm only just in. It smells lovely."

He did not wait for the final word; his hand wrapped in his handkerchief had found the main switch.

"One, two . . . three," he said with horrible prosaicness—and pulled.

From the wall socket behind him there was a single spluttering flare as the fuse went, and then silence.

All round Ronald it was so quiet that he could hear the pulses in his own body, and he could hear no sound at all from the bathroom.

After a while he crept back along the passage and tapped at the door. "Edyth? Are you there? Edyth?"

There was no response, no sound.

"Edyth?" he said again.

The silence was complete, and after a long minute he straightened his back and let out a deep sighing breath of relief.

Almost at once he was keyed up again in preparation for the second phase. As he well knew, this next was the tricky period. The discovery of the body must be made, but not too soon. He had made that mistake after Dorothy's "accident" and had actually been asked by the local police Inspector why he had become alarmed so soon; but he had kept his head that time, and the dangerous moment had passed.

This time he had decided to wait half an hour before he began to hammer loudly on the door, then to shout for a neighbor, and finally to force the lock. He had planned to stroll out to buy an evening paper, shouting his intention to do so to Edyth from the front step for any passer-by to hear; but as he walked back along the landing he knew there was something else he must do first.

Edyth's leather writing case in which she kept all her private papers was in the bottom of her hatbox. She had really believed he had not known of its existence, he reflected bitterly.

He went softly into the bedroom and opened the wardrobe door. The case was exactly where he had last seen it, plump and promising, and his hands closed over it gratefully. There were bundles of savings certificates, one or two thick envelopes whose red seals suggested the offices of lawyers, and, on top, ready for the taking, one of those familiar gray books which the Post Office issues to its savings-bank clients.

He opened it with shaking fingers and fluttered through the pages. The sum made him whistle. £7250! Then a drop as she had drawn out £50 for her trousseau.

£7200. He thought that was the final entry but on turning the page saw that there was one more recorded transaction. It was less than a week old. He remembered the book coming back through the mail and how clever she had thought she had been smuggling it in.

He glanced at the written words and figures idly at first, but then, as his heart jolted in sudden panic, stared at them, his eyes prominent and glazed.

She had taken almost all of it out. There it was in black and white: *September 4th: Withdrawal seven thousand one hundred and ninety-eight pounds.*

His first thought was that the money must still be there, in hundred-pound notes perhaps, in one of the envelopes. He tore through them hastily, forgetting all caution in his anxiety. Papers, letters, certificates fell on the floor in confusion.

The envelope, addressed to himself, pulled him up short. It was new and freshly blotted, the name inscribed in Edyth's own unexpectedly firm hand—*Ronald Torbay, Esquire.*

He wrenched it open and stared at the single sheet of bond paper within. The date, he noted in horrified amazement, was only two days old.

> Dear Ronald:
>
> If you ever get this I am afraid it will prove a dreadful shock to you. For a long time I have been hoping that it might not be necessary to write it, but now your behavior has forced me to face some very unpleasant possibilities.
>
> I am afraid, Ronald, that in some ways you are very old-fashioned. Has it not occurred to you that any homely, middle-aged woman who has been swept into a hasty marriage to a stranger must, unless she is a perfect idiot, be just a little suspicious on the subject of *baths?*
>
> You must know that I am a dedicated newspaper reader, and after reading about two women who had met with fatal accidents in bubble baths soon after their marriages, I rather began to wonder.

Frankly, I did not want to suspect you because for a long time I thought I was in love with you; but when you persuaded me to make my will on our wedding day, I could not help wondering. And then as soon as you started fussing about the bathroom in this house, I thought I had better do something about it rather quickly. I am old-fashioned, too, Ronald, so I went to the police.

Have you noticed that the people who have moved into the house next door have never tried to speak to you? We thought it best that I should merely talk to the woman over the garden wall, and it is she who looked up the newspaper items I told her about. She even went a little further and found some cuttings from local provincial newspapers, each of which contained a press snapshot of the husband taken at the funeral.

They are not very clear, but even so, as soon as I saw them I realized it was my duty to agree to the course suggested to me by the Inspector. He told me that he had been looking for a man answering that description for over three years, ever since the two photographs were brought to his notice by your poor second wife's brother.

What I am trying to say is this: if you should ever lose me, Ronald—out of the bathroom, I mean—you will find that I have gone out over the roof and am sitting in my dressing gown in the kitchen next door. I was a fool to marry you, but not quite such a fool as you assumed. Women may be silly but they are not so stupid as they used to be. We are picking up the idea, Ronald.

Yours,
Edyth

P.S. On reading this I see that in my nervousness I have forgotten to say that the new people next door are not a married couple but Inspector Batsford of the C.I.D. and his assistant, Policewoman Richards. They assure me that there cannot be sufficient evidence to convict if you are not permitted to attempt the crime again. That is why I am forcing myself to be brave and play my part, for I am very sorry for those other poor wives of yours, Ronald. They must have found you as fascinating as I did.

With his slit mouth twisted into an abominable O, Ronald Torbay raised haggard eyes from the letter.

The house was quiet, and even the whine of the mower next door had ceased. In the hush he heard a sudden clatter as the back door burst open and heavy footsteps raced through the hall, up the stairs toward him.

FOR DISCUSSION: Bubble Bath No. 3

1. Ronald Torbay had an unusual *modus operandi*. How did he establish the setting during the weeks preceding the planned murder? How did he plan to commit the murder? How did this fact (that he had an M.O.) lead to his discovery?

2. Unlike Joe Shupe in "The Green Elephant," Torbay is a sophisticated, experienced criminal. Find within the text of the story the following items:

   a. three things Torbay said or did that prove premeditation;

   b. three things Torbay said or did that prove his efficiency with regard to detail;

   c. three things Torbay said or did that turned out to be mistakes.

   In light of your answers, would you consider Torbay a "successful" criminal? Explain.

3. Usually the suspense in a mystery story comes from the reader's struggle to identify the criminal. How does Allingham create suspense even though she starts off by telling us that the main character is a murderer?

4. Edyth wrote: "Women may be silly but they are not so stupid as they used to be. We are picking up the idea, Ronald." What exactly did Edyth mean? What skills and abilities were available to her that would not have been available to a woman even a century ago?

INTRODUCTION: A Very Special Talent

Accidents can happen. In fact, accidents *do* happen all the time in this very human world. Someone leaves a basket at the top of a flight of stairs, or pours some leftover lye into an old, no-longer-used salt shaker, or neglects to mention that the steering wheel of the family car has turned uncooperative, especially on hairpin turns. Most of the mishaps that result are real accidents—and therefore tragic. But a few of them are not accidents at all.

Everyone knows that there are some unpleasant people one cannot warn; to them, a warning is a challenge. Is it wrong—is it criminal—to exploit that weakness to destroy them, or are they really destroying themselves? The answer demands rational analysis, not rationalization; but since rationalization is part of almost every human's mental equipment, it is difficult to answer the question honestly.

A Very Special Talent

Margaret E. Brown

"But he used to hit me," Angela explained, rubbing her shoulder in memory of past bruises. "What else could I do?"

"You could have divorced him," I said firmly.

"He wouldn't let me. You know what the grounds for divorce were in this state then. Don't you care that he beat me?"

Of course it enraged me that that brute had hit my lovely, fragile-looking wife, even if it had been before I'd met her. "Nevertheless," I said, "it's the principle of the thing. It just isn't done."

"It was his own fault," she insisted. "I told him it was dangerous to have the radio that close to the bathtub when he'd been drinking, but that was like waving a red flag at a bull. He would have done it then or died."

She giggled suddenly, remembering that he had, indeed, died.

I was appalled. What does a man do when, after seven blissful years of marriage and two lovely children, he discovers that his adorable little fluff of a wife is a cold-blooded murderess who goes around killing people who aren't nice to her?

"I am *not* a cold-blooded murderess," Angela flared indignantly, "and I would never, *never* kill anyone who wasn't nasty to a whole lot of other people, too."

At this point the back screen door banged and Sandy, my five-year-old replica right down to a cowlick of red hair and a faceful of freckles, burst into the room and angrily demanded, "What's the matter with you guys? Can't you hear Matt crying? Georgie hit him and he's all bloody!"

Angela whirled and followed Sandy from the room at a trot, with me just behind them.

Four-year-old Matt sat sobbing on the back doorstep. Blood trickled from a split on his lower lip onto his white T-shirt while Sandy's best friend, Chris Coffey, awkwardly patted his shoulder.

One of the things I love about Angela is her absolute cool whenever one of the boys is hurt. I tend to panic at the sight of their blood, but she remains calm and utterly soothing.

She swooped Matt up in her arms, assessed the damage and cheerfully assured him that he wouldn't need stitches. In the kitchen, she applied a cold cloth to his swollen lip and soon had him tentatively smiling again.

The screen door banged again and Jill Coffey, our next door neighbor and Angela's closest friend, came charging in. "That Georgie! I saw it all! Matt hadn't done a thing to him and Georgie just hauled off and socked him!"

"Yeah, Dad," Sandy chimed in. "He won't let us swing, and it's our jungle vine. Chris and me, we built it."

Matt started to cry again, Jill raged on, Angela began to shoot sparks, and Sandy's shrill indignation pierced the chaotic din.

"Hold it!" I shouted. "One at a time."

With many interruptions, a coherent story finally emerged.

When our development was built, the creek which used to cut through our back yards had been diverted, leaving an eight-foot gully overhung with huge old willows which the developers had mercifully spared. With so much of the area bulldozed into sterility, the gully lured kids from blocks around.

Depending on the degree of danger, various stretches of it attracted different age groups: the pre-adolescents usually congregated a block away, where the banks were somewhat steeper and the old creek rocks larger and more jagged. In the section between our house and the Coffeys', the bank was more of a gentle grassy slope and there were fewer rocks, so the pre-school set usually played there.

It seemed that Sandy and his cronies had tied a clothesline rope to one of the overhanging willow branches and had been playing Tarzan, swinging out over the gully as if on jungle vines, experiencing a thrill of danger more imaginary than real. Then Georgie Watson had come along and, as usual, destroyed their fun by taking over the rope swing and hitting Matt.

An overweight nine-year-old, Georgie was a classic neighborhood bully, afraid of boys his own age and a terror to everyone under six. No neighborhood gathering was complete without a twenty-minute discussion of Georgie's latest bit of maliciousness and a psychological dissection of his motives which usually ended with, "Well, what can you expect, with parents like that?"

I suppose every suburban neighborhood has its one obnoxious family; it seems to be written into the building code. At any rate, the Watsons were ours: loud, vulgar, self-righteous, and completely heedless of anyone else's rights and desires.

They gave boisterous mid-week parties which broke up noisily at one in the morning, or they would come roaring home at two from a Saturday night on the town and Mr. Watson would lean on the horn to bring the baby-sitter out.

After such a riotous night, you'd think the man would have the decency to sleep in on Sunday morning nursing a king-size hangover, but no. There he'd be, seven o'clock the next morning, cranking what must be the world's noisiest lawn mower and carrying on a shouted conversation with Mrs. Watson in the upstairs bedroom.

Mrs. Watson was just as bad. Georgie had been born after they had given up all hope of having children and she doted on him. Though quick enough to complain when any boy Georgie's age or older picked on him, she was completely blind to his faults.

If confronted by an angry parent and bleeding child, Mrs. Watson would look the enraged mother straight in the eye and say blandly, "Georgie said he didn't do it and I find Georgie to be very truthful. Besides, he *never* provokes a fight."

"That kid is a menace to the neighborhood!" Angela fumed, after the three boys had settled down in front of the TV with a pitcher of lemonade.

We had moved out to our screened back porch and Angela was still so angry that her paring knife sliced with wicked precision as she frenched the string beans for dinner.

"But the doctors must love him," Jill said wryly. "Five days into summer vacation and he's drawn blood at least four times that I know of."

She stopped helping Angela with the beans and ticked off the incidents on her fingers. "Dot's boy had to have three stitches after Georgie threw a rock at him; he pushed little Nancy Smith onto a broken bottle; my Chris got a cut on his chin when Georgie tripped him yesterday, and now your Matt. How we'll get through this summer without having all our kids put in the hospital, I don't know."

"Somebody ought to do something about him," Angela said, giving me a meaningful look.

"Not me," I protested. "The last time I complained to Watson about

Georgie, he waved a monkey wrench in my face and told me adults ought to let kids fight it out among themselves."

"I know!" Jill exclaimed brightly. "Let's hire a couple of twelve-year-olds to beat him up!"

"The Watsons would sue," said Angela glumly.

"Maybe they'll send him to camp or something this year," I offered hopefully.

"Not a chance," Angela said. "Mrs. Watson couldn't be separated from him that long."

She finished the beans, wiped the paring knife on the seat of her denim shorts, then gazed out through the early evening twilight toward the gully, absentmindedly thwacking the handle of the knife on the palm of her hand.

"Think positively," she said suddenly. "Maybe Georgie did us a favor just now."

Jill and I looked at each other blankly.

"Maybe that rope isn't safe to swing on," she said.

"But it's good and strong, Mrs. Barrett," Chris volunteered from the doorway. Their program over, the three boys had drifted out to the porch.

"Yeah, Mom," Sandy added. "I tied it with a square knot, just like Dad showed me."

"He did," echoed Matt with all the assurance of one who hadn't even mastered a granny knot yet.

Angela grinned at him and tousled his hair, a gesture he hated. "Just the same, I'd feel better if your father and I took a look at it."

So out we all went, across the already dew-dampened grass to the gully, and while I examined the rope for signs of fraying, Angela swung her lithe hundred pounds up into the willow tree with catlike grace. Naturally, Matt and Sandy are the envy of their peers with a mother who thinks nothing of dropping her work and her dignity to shinny up a tree for a tangled kite or to clamber onto a roof to get a ball lodged in the rain gutters.

"It seems strong enough," I said. "What about the knot, Angela?" Between the leaves and the fading light, I could barely see her.

She poked her neat little pointed face through the willow leaves. "I really don't think it's safe, Alex. Maybe you could pick up a stronger rope tomorrow."

She dropped to the ground, barely panting with the exertion. "It's a fine knot," she said to Sandy, "but the rope *is* old. Dad'll get you another tomorrow; but until he does, I want your solemn promise that you won't swing on it or let any of your friends swing on it."

"That goes for you, too, Chris," Jill said.

"Well it doesn't go for me!" sneered a juvenile voice.

We whirled, and there was dear old Georgie, cocky in the security of knowing that we were too civilized to smack the impertinence off his face.

"Oh, yes, it does," Angela contradicted coldly. "If it isn't strong enough to hold the little ones, it isn't strong enough to hold you."

Georgie flushed at this allusion to his weight. It seemed to be his only sensitive spot. "You're not my mother," he yelled, "and I don't have to mind you!"

I took a step toward him, my civility rapidly retreating before a barbarous desire to flatten him, but Angela restrained me.

"It's dangerous, Georgie, so you'll just have to stay off of it," she said, and took the end of the rope and tossed it up into the tree.

"I can still get it," Georgie taunted, but he showed no inclination to do so, with me blocking his path.

At that moment, Mrs. Watson called him in for the evening. Jill suddenly remembered that she'd forgotten to take a steak out of the freezer and headed for home with Chris, while Angela, Sandy and I gave Matt a head start before racing to our own back door.

The prospect of a long summer spent coping with Georgie Watson, together with the usual mayhem of feeding, tubbing and bedding our two young acrobats, blotted out the interrupted conversation I'd been having with Angela until we were in bed ourselves. I remembered it with a jolt.

"Didn't the police suspect anything?" I asked in the semidarkness of our bedroom.

"The police were very sympathetic and nice," Angela murmured sleepily. "They could see he had locked the bathroom door himself. Actually, all I had done was balance the radio too close to the edge of the shelf and hoped for the best." As if that ended it, she rolled over and put the pillow over her head.

"Oh, no, you don't!" I muttered, lifting the pillow, for I had just recalled something else. "What about 'The Perfect Example'?"

"Sh!" she whispered. "You'll wake the boys."

"Well, did you?" I whispered hoarsely.

In that city neighborhood where we had spent our first two years of marriage, home had been a second floor walkup in a converted brownstone. Its age, dinginess and general state of deterioration were somewhat ameliorated by the low rent and large, relatively soundproof rooms, and it attracted several other young couples.

We were all blithely green at life and marriage, determined to succeed in both, and that old house would have exuded happiness had it not been for the constantly disapproving eye of our landlady.

She lived on the third floor of the house, and every time the outer vestibule door opened she would appear on the landing, lean over the wobbly old mahogany railing and peer down the marble stairwell, hoping to catch someone sneaking in a forbidden pet or leaving a shopping cart in the vestibule.

She bullied her husband, tyrannized her three timorous daughters, and took a malicious delight in stirring up animosity among her tenants. "I don't care what that snip in 2-D says," she would confide to her innocent victim, "I think your clothes are very ladylike."

It was only after you had lived in the house a couple of months that you realized she was putting lies in your mouth, too. It was like an initiation to a fraternity, that first two months. Afterward, you would laugh with the more experienced tenants and compare the lies as they recalled, with amusing mimicry, how they knew by your icy expression exactly when she had slandered them to you.

She was such a perfect example of everything the young wives never wanted to become that we all called her "The Perfect Example" behind her back.

It was bad enough when she pitted couple against couple, but it stopped being funny when she managed to slip her knifed tongue into a shaky marriage, as happened twice while we lived there. The first marriage probably would have crumbled anyhow, but the second was a couple of teen-agers deeply in love but handicapped by parental opposition and the sheer inexperience of youth.

When she discovered what was happening, Angela broke the rule of silence and tried to make them understand how "The Perfect Example" was destroying them, but it was too late. The girl went home to her parents and the boy stormed off to California.

Never had I seen Angela so blazingly angry. "She's like a big fat spider, leaning on that railing, watching us flies walk in and out, spinning her web for the defenseless midges!" she raged, almost in tears. "Why aren't there laws against people like that?"

So it had seemed like divine vengeance when, two days later, the decrepit mahogany railing had finally pulled loose from the wall and collapsed under her weight, and "The Perfect Example" had plummeted to the marble tiles of the vestibule three floors below. As soon as the police had declared her death a regrettable accident, her husband had put the house up for sale and happily removed himself and the three dazed daughters back to the corn fields of his native Kansas.

"What about 'The Perfect Example'?" I repeated, shaking Angela.

"Oh, Alex," she pleaded, "it's after midnight."

"I want to know."

"She *knew* the house was old, but she was too miserly to spend a cent in repairs. That rail would have collapsed sooner or later—you heard the police say that—and I just helped it along a bit. And don't forget that I told her it wasn't safe to lean against all the time."

"That was sporting of you," I said bitterly. "Just because you warned those two—that *is* all, isn't it?—you think that justifies everything!"

"Tell me something, Angela—*Angela!* Boy, your parents had some sense of humor when they named *you!*—how do you see yourself? As an avenging angel or Little Mary Sunshine scattering rays of joy through oppressed lives?"

"I'll tell you how I see myself, Alex Barrett," she said in exasperation, propping herself up on one slim elbow. "I see myself as the very tired mother of two boys who are going to be awake and wanting their breakfasts in about five or six hours! I see myself as the wife of a man who wants to hash over every petty little incident that happened *years* ago when I am exhausted!"

She fell back upon the bed and plopped the pillow over her head again. I didn't think it prudent to take it off a second time; she might decide to tell me it wasn't safe. "Petty little incident," indeed!

The night was broken by restless dreams in which I defended Angela before massed benches of irate judges and policemen who demanded adequate reasons why she should not be taken out and hanged. They were unmoved when I argued that she was a perfect wife and tender mother, and it only seemed to infuriate them when I added that she in no way *looked* like a murderess. Through it all, a hooded hangman with a frayed clothesline rope looped around his shoulders swung back and forth on the chandelier chanting, "We're going to give her the rope! The rope! We're going to give her the rope! The rope!"

Shreds of the dream clung to me all day. I couldn't rid myself of a feeling of apprehension, and when I stopped at a hardware store after work to buy Sandy's new rope, it seemed as if I were somehow adding to Angela's guilt.

As I drove into the carport late that afternoon, I saw Sandy rummaging in the toolshed. "I got your Tarzan rope for you," I called.

"Thanks, Dad," he said, dragging out an old tarp, "but we're going to play army men. Can me and Chris and Matt have this for a tent in the gully?"

"O.K., but aren't you afraid Georgie will tear it down?"

"Oh, we don't have to worry about *him* anymore," Sandy said cheerfully, and disappeared around the corner of the house before I could find my voice.

Oh, no, I thought, and roared, *"Angela!"* as I tore into the house, nearly ripping the screen from its hinges. No answer.

"Surely Sandy would have thought it worth mentioning if the police had carted his mother off to jail," I jittered to myself, trying to look at the situation coolly. "Angela!"

Then I heard her voice: "Alex! I'm over here at Jill's. Come on over," she called.

"Hi, Alex!" Jill caroled as I pushed open their screen. "We're sort of celebrating. Want a drink?"

Women! Were they all so cold-blooded that they could murder a child, obnoxious as that child had been, without turning a hair? I sank down on the porch glider, unable to speak for the moment.

"Poor dear," said Angela solicitously. "Did you have a bad day? You look so drained."

"What happened to Georgie?" I demanded, glaring at Angela.

"Didn't Sandy tell you?" asked Jill as she handed me the tall cool drink that I so desperately needed. "He was swinging on the boys' Tarzan rope and it broke with him. He fractured both legs, one in two places," she added with satisfaction.

"He wasn't killed?" I croaked weakly.

"Of course not, Alex" said Angela. "How could he have been? There weren't any rocks under the rope and that stretch of gully is mostly grass."

"I hate to seem ghoulish," Jill said, "but it really does make the summer for us. By the time he gets out of those casts and off his crutches, school will be open again."

She grinned at Angela. "I just can't believe it! A whole summer without Georgie Watson beating up every little kid in sight!"

"Just a lucky break for everyone," I murmured sarcastically. There was no point in asking if the break had occurred up by the knot which Angela had examined last night.

"Well, it is," Jill insisted stoutly. "And as I told Mrs. Watson, it was his own fault. Angela very specifically warned him not to swing on that old rope till you could get a stronger one."

"Angela's very thoughtful that way," I observed.

At least she had the grace to blush.

The next day, a Saturday, even I was forced to admit that if it were any indication, it was going to be a very relaxed summer. The boys peacefully slaughtered the bad guys all day in the gully without once running in to us with tearful tales of Georgie's latest tyranny.

After all, I thought as I watched an afternoon baseball game undisturbed, *maybe a summer of enforced solitude will be good for Georgie's character.*

When I awoke early Sunday morning, my subconscious had completed the job of rationalizing the situation: don't some wives occasionally bring

tive child and an aggressively rebellious adolescent. The resulting snarling habit of mind was precisely what was now hindering his success as an adult. Not that Chick would have agreed, of course. Chick never agreed with anyone if he could help it. Always knew better, did Chick.

He was unprepared for the severity of the physical symptoms of fear. His usual attitude toward any form of authority was scorn (and authority had not so far actually belted him one across his sulky mouth). Horses had never scared him because he had been born to the saddle and had grown up mastering everything on four legs with contemptuous ease. He believed in his heart that no one could really ride better than he could. He was wrong.

He looked apprehensively over his shoulder, and the shifting pain in his stomach sharply intensified. That simply couldn't happen, he thought wildly. He'd heard about people getting sick with fear. He hadn't believed it. It couldn't happen. Now, all of a sudden, he feared it could. He tightened all his muscles desperately, and the spasm slowly passed. It left fresh sweat standing out all over his skin and no saliva in his mouth.

The house was dark. Upstairs, behind the black open window with the pale curtain flapping in the spartan air, slept Arthur Morrison, trainer of the 43 racehorses in the stables below. Morrison habitually slept lightly. His ears were sharper than half a dozen guard dogs', his stable hands said.

Chick forced himself to turn his head away, to walk in view of that window, to take the 10 exposed steps down to the chestnut's stall.

If the guv'nor woke up and saw him.... Gawd, he thought furiously, he hadn't expected it to be like this. Just a lousy walk down the yard to give a carrot to the gangly chestnut. Guilt and fear and treachery. They bypassed his sneering mind and erupted through his nerves instead.

He couldn't see anything wrong with the carrot. It hadn't been cut in half and hollowed out and packed with drugs and tied together again. He'd tried pulling the thick end out like a plug, and that hadn't worked either. The carrot just looked like any old carrot, any old carrot you'd watch your ma chop up to put in a stew. Any old carrot you'd give to any old horse. Not a very young, succulent carrot or a very aged carrot, knotted and woody. Just any old ordinary *carrot*.

But strangers didn't proposition you to give any old carrot to one special horse in the middle of the night. They didn't give you more than you earned in half a year when you said you'd do it. Any old carrot didn't come wrapped carefully alone in a polythene bag inside an empty cheese-cracker packet, given to you by a stranger in a car park after dark in a town six miles from the stables. You didn't give any old carrot in the middle of the night to a chestnut who was due to start favorite in a high-class steeplechase 11 hours later.

Chick was getting dizzy with holding his breath by the time he'd completed the 10 tiptoed steps to the chestnut's stall. Trying not to cough, not to groan, not to let out the strangling tension in a sob, he curled his sweating fingers around the bolt and began the job of easing it out, inch by frightening inch, from its socket.

By day he slammed the bolts open and shut with a smart practiced flick. His body shook in the darkness with the strain of moving by fractions.

The bolt came free with the tiniest of grating noises, and the top half of the split door swung slowly outward. No squeaks from the hinges, only the whisper of metal on metal. Chick drew in a long breath like a painful, trickling, smothered gasp and let it out between his clenched teeth. His stomach lurched again, threateningly. He took another quick, appalled grip on himself and thrust his arm in a panic through the dark, open space.

Inside the stall, the chestnut was asleep, dozing on his feet. The changing swirl of air from the opening door moved the sensitive hairs around his muzzle and raised his mental state from semiconsciousness to inquisitiveness. He could smell the carrot. He could also smell the man: smell the fear in the man's sweat.

"Come on," Chick whispered desperately. "Come on, then, boy."

The horse moved his nose around toward the carrot and finally, reluctantly, his feet. He took it indifferently from the man's trembling palm, whiffling it in with his black mobile lips, scrunching it languidly with large rotations of jaw. When he had swallowed all the pulped-up bits he poked his muzzle forward for more. But there was no more, just the lighter square of sky darkening again as the door swung shut, just the faint sounds of the bolt going back, just the fading smell of the man and the passing taste of carrot. Presently he forgot about it and turned slowly round again so that his hindquarters were toward the door, because he usually stood that way, and after a minute or two he blinked slowly, rested his near hind leg lazily on the point of the hoof and lapsed back into twilight mindlessness.

Down in his stomach the liquid narcotic compound with which the carrot had been injected to saturation gradually filtered out of the digesting carrot cells and began to be absorbed into the bloodstream. The process was slow and progressive. And it had started two hours late.

Arthur Morrison stood in his stable yard watching his men load the chestnut into the motor horse box that was to take him to the races. He was eyeing the proceedings with an expression that was critical from habit and bore little relation to the satisfaction in his mind. The chestnut was the best horse in his stable: a frequent winner, popular with the public, a source of prestige as well as revenue. The big steeplechase at

Cheltenham had been tailor-made for him from the day its conditions had been published, and Morrison was adept at producing a horse in peak condition for a particular race. No one seriously considered that the chestnut would be beaten. The newspapers had tipped it to a man, and the bookmakers were fighting shy at 6 to 4 on. Morrison allowed himself a glimmer of warmth in the eyes and a twitch of smile to the lips as the men clipped shut the heavy doors of the horse van and drove it out of the yard.

These physical signs were unusual. The face he normally wore was a compound of concentration and disapproval in roughly equal proportions. Both qualities contributed considerably to his success as a racehorse trainer and to his unpopularity as a person, a fact Morrison himself was well aware of. He didn't in the least care that almost no one liked him. He valued success and respect much more highly than love and held in incredulous contempt all those who did not.

Across the yard Chick was watching the horse van drive away, his usual scowl in place. Morrison frowned irritably. The boy was a pest, he thought. Always grousing, always impertinent, always trying to scrounge up more money. Morrison didn't believe in boys having life made too easy: a little hardship was good for the soul. Where Morrison and Chick radically differed was the point at which each thought hardship began.

Chick spotted the frown and watched Morrison fearfully, his guilt pressing on him like a rock. He couldn't know, he thought frantically. He couldn't even suspect there was anything wrong with the horse or he wouldn't have let him go off to the races. The horse had looked all right, too. Absolutely his normal self. Perhaps there had been nothing wrong with the carrot.... Perhaps it had been the wrong carrot, even.... Chick glanced around uneasily and knew very well he was fooling himself. The horse might look all right but he wasn't.

Arthur Morrison saddled up his horse at the races, and Chick watched him from 10 nervous paces away, trying to hide in the eager crowd that pushed forward for a close view of the favorite. There was a larger admiring crowd outside the chestnut's saddling stall than for any of the other seven runners, and the bookmakers had shortened their odds.

Behind Morrison's concentrated expression an itch of worry was growing insistent. He pulled the girth tight and adjusted the buckles automatically, acknowledging to himself that his former satisfaction had changed to anxiety. The horse was not himself. There were no lively stamping feet, no playful nips from the teeth, no response to the crowd; this was a horse that usually played to the public like a film star. He couldn't be feeling well, and if he wasn't feeling well he wouldn't win. Morrison tightened his mouth. If the horse were not well enough to win, he would prefer him not to run at all. To be beaten at odds-on would be a disgrace. A defeat on too large a scale. A loss of face. Particularly as Morrison's own eldest son Toddy was to be the jockey. The newspapers would tear them both to pieces.

Morrison came to a decision and sent for the vet.

The rules of jump racing in England stated quite clearly that if a horse had been declared a runner in a race, only the say-so of a veterinarian was sufficient grounds for withdrawing him during the last three-quarters of an hour before post time. The Cheltenham racecourse veterinarian came and looked at the chestnut and, after consulting with Morrison, led it off to a more private stall and took its temperature.

"His temperature's normal," the veterinarian assured Morrison.

"I don't like the look of him."

"I can't find anything wrong."

"He's not well," Morrison insisted.

The veterinarian pursed his lips and shook his head. There was nothing obviously wrong with the horse, and he knew he would be in trouble himself if he allowed Morrison to withdraw so hot a favorite on such slender grounds. Not only that, this was the third application for withdrawal he'd had to consider that afternoon. He had refused both the others, and the chestnut was certainly in no worse a state.

"He'll have to run," the veterinarian said positively, making up his mind.

Morrison was furious and went raging off to find a steward, who came and looked at the chestnut and listened to the vet and confirmed that the horse would have to run whether Morrison liked it or not. Unless, that was, Morrison cared to involve the horse's absent owner in paying a heavy fine?

With a face of granite Morrison resaddled the chestnut, and a stable lad led him out into the parade ring, where most of the waiting public cheered and a few wiser ones looked closely and hurried off to hedge their bets.

With a shiver of dismay, Chick saw the horse reappear and for the first time regretted what he'd done. That stupid vet, he thought violently. He can't see what's under his bloody nose, he couldn't see a barn at 10 paces. Anything that happened from then on was the vet's fault, Chick thought. The vet's responsibility, absolutely. The man was a criminal menace, letting a horse run in a steeplechase with dope coming out of its eyeballs.

Toddy Morrison had joined his father in the parade ring and together they were watching with worried expressions as the chestnut plodded lethargically around the oval walking track. Toddy was a strong, stocky professional jockey in his late 20's with an infectious grin and a generous view of life that represented a direct rejection of his father's. He had inherited the same strength of mind but had used it to leave home at 18 to ride races for other trainers, and had only consented to ride for his father when he could dictate his own terms. Arthur Morrison, in consequence, respected him deeply. Between them they had won a lot of races.

Chick didn't actually dislike Toddy Morrison, even though, as he saw it, Toddy stood in his way. Occasionally Arthur let Chick ride a race if Toddy had something better or couldn't make the weight. Chick had to share these scraps from Toddy's table with two or three other lads in the yard who were, though he didn't believe it, as good as he was in the saddle. But though the envy curdled around inside him and the snide remarks came out sharp and sour as vinegar, he had never actually come to hate Toddy. There was something about Toddy that you couldn't hate, however good the reason. Chick hadn't given a thought to the fact that it would be Toddy who would have to deal with the effects of the carrot. He had seen no farther than his own pocket. He wished now that it had been some other jockey. Anyone but Toddy.

The conviction suddenly crystalized in Chick's mind as he looked at Toddy and Morrison standing there worried in the parade ring that he had never believed the chestnut would actually start in the race. The stranger, Chick said to himself, had distinctly told him the horse would be too sick to start. I wouldn't have done it, else, Chick thought virtuously. I wouldn't have done it. It's bloody dangerous, riding a doped steeplechaser. I wouldn't have done that to Toddy. It's not my fault he's going to ride a doped steeplechaser, it's that vet's fault for not seeing. It's that stranger's fault, he told me distinctly the horse wouldn't be fit to start. . . .

Chick remembered with an unpleasant jerk that he'd been two hours late with the carrot. Maybe if he'd been on time the drug would have come out more and the vet would have seen. . . .

Chick jettisoned this unbearable theory instantly on the grounds that no one can tell how seriously any particular horse will react to a drug or how quickly it will work, and he repeated to himself the comforting self-delusion that the stranger had promised him the horse wouldn't ever start—though the stranger had not in fact said any such thing. The stranger, who was at the races, was entirely satisfied with the way things were going and was on the point of making a great deal of money.

The bell rang for the jockeys to mount. Chick clenched his hands in his pockets and tried not to visualize what could happen to a rider going over jumps at 30 miles an hour on a doped horse. Chick's body began playing him tricks again: he could feel the sweat pricking down his back and the pulse had come back in his ears.

Supposing he told them, he thought. Supposing he just ran out there into the ring and told Toddy not to ride the horse, it hadn't a chance of jumping properly, it was certain to fall, it could kill him bloody easily because its reactions would be all shot to bits.

Supposing he did. The way they'd look at him. His imagination blew a fuse and blanked out on that picture because such a blast of contempt didn't fit in with his overgrown self-esteem. He could not, could *not* face the fury they would feel. And it might not end there. Even if he told them and saved Toddy's life, they might tell the police. He wouldn't put it past them. And he could end up in the dock. Even in jail. They weren't going to do that to him, not to *him*. He wasn't going to give them the chance. He should have been paid more. Paid more because he was worth more. If he'd been paid more, he wouldn't have needed to take the stranger's money. Arthur Morrison had only himself to blame.

Toddy would have to risk it. After all, the horse didn't look too bad, and the vet had passed it, hadn't he, and maybe the carrot being two hours late was all to the good and it wouldn't have done its work properly yet, and in fact it was really thanks to Chick if it hadn't; only thanks to him that the drug was two hours late and that nothing much would happen, really, anyway. Nothing much would happen. Maybe the chestnut wouldn't actually *win*, but Toddy would come through all right. Of course he would.

The jockeys swung up into their saddles, Toddy among them. He saw Chick in the crowd, watching, and sketched an acknowledging wave. The urge to tell and the fear of telling tore Chick apart like the Chinese trees.

Toddy gathered up the reins and clicked his tongue and steered the chestnut indecisively out onto the track. He was disappointed that the horse wasn't feeling well but not in the least apprehensive. It hadn't occurred to him, or to Arthur Morrison, that the horse might be doped. He cantered down to the post standing in his stirrups, replanning his tactics mentally now that he couldn't rely on reserves in his mount. It would be a difficult race now to win. Pity.

Chick watched him go. He hadn't come to his decision, to tell or not to tell. The moment simply passed him by. When Toddy had gone he unstuck his leaden feet and plodded off to the stands to watch the race, and in every corner of his mind little self-justifications sprang up like nettles. A feeling of shame tried to creep in round the edges, but he kicked it out smartly. They should have paid him more. It was their fault, not his.

He thought about the wad of notes the stranger had given him with the carrot. Money in advance. The stranger had trusted him, which was more than most people seemed to. He'd locked himself into the bathroom and counted the notes, counted them twice, and they were all there, £300 just as the stranger had promised. He had never had so much money all at once in his life before. . . . Perhaps he never would again, he thought. And if he'd told Arthur Morrison and Toddy about the dope, he would have to give up that money, give up the money and more. . . .

Finding somewhere to hide the money had given him difficulty. Three hundred used £1 notes had turned out to be quite bulky, and he didn't want to risk his ma poking around among his things, like she did, and coming across them. He'd solved the problem temporarily by rolling them up and putting them in a brightly colored round tin which once held toffees but which he used for years for storing brushes and polish for cleaning his shoes. He had covered the money with a duster and jammed the brushes back in on top and put the tin back on the shelf in his bedroom where it always stood. He thought he would probably have to find somewhere safer, in the end. And he'd have to be careful how he spent the money—there would be too many questions asked if he just went out and bought a car. He'd always wanted a car . . . and now he had the money for one . . . and he still couldn't get the car. It wasn't fair. Not fair at all. If they'd paid him more. . . . Enough for a car. . . .

Up on the well-positioned area of stands set aside for trainers and jockeys, a small man with hot dark eyes put his hand on Chick's arm and spoke to him, though it was several seconds before Chick started to listen.

". . . I see you are here, and you're free, so will you ride it?"

"What?" said Chick vaguely.

"My horse in the Novice Hurdle," said the little man impatiently. "Of course, if you don't want to. . . ."

"Didn't say that," Chick mumbled. "Ask the guv'nor. If he says I can, well, I can."

The small trainer walked across the stand to where Arthur Morrison was watching the chestnut intently through the race glasses and asked the same question he'd put to Chick.

"Chick? Yes, he can ride it for you, if you want him." Morrison gave the other trainer two full seconds of his attention and glued himself back onto his race glasses.

"My jockey was hurt in a fall in the first race," explained the small man. "There are so many runners in the Novice Hurdle that there's a shortage of jockeys. I just saw that boy of yours, so I asked him on the spur of the moment, see?"

"Yes, yes," said Morrison, 90% uninterested. "He's moderately capable, but don't expect too much of him." There was no spring in the chestnut's stride. Morrison wondered in depression if he was sickening for the cough.

"My horse won't win. Just out for experience you might say."

"Yes. Well, fix it with Chick." Several other stables had the coughing epidemic, Morrison thought. The chestnut couldn't have picked a worse day to catch it.

Chick, who would normally have welcomed the offer of a ride with condescending complacency, was so preoccupied that the small trainer regretted having asked him. Chick's whole attention was riveted on the chestnut, who seemed to be lining up satisfactorily at the starting tape. Nothing wrong, Chick assured himself. Everything was going to be all right. Of course it was. Stupid getting into such a state.

The start was down the track to the left, with two fences to be jumped before the horses came past the stands and swung away again on the left-hand circuit. As it was a jumping race, they were using tapes instead of stalls, and as there was no draw either, Toddy had lined up against the inside rails, ready to take the shortest way home.

Down in the bookmakers' enclosure they were offering more generous odds now and some had gone boldly to evens. The chestnut had cantered past them on his way to the start looking not his brightest and best. The bookmakers in consequence were feeling more hopeful. They had expected a bad day, but if the chestnut lost, they would profit. One of them would profit terrifically—just as he would lose terrifically if the chestnut won.

Alexander McGrant (Est. 1898), real name Harry Buskins, had done this sort of thing once or twice before. He spread out his fingers and looked at them admiringly. Not a tremble in sight. And there was always a risk in these things that the boy he'd bribed would get cold feet at the last minute and not go through with the job. Always a gamble, it was. But this time, this boy, he was pretty sure of. You couldn't go wrong if you sorted out a vain little so-and-so with a big grudge. Knock-overs, that sort were. Every time.

Harry Buskins was a shrewd middle-aged East End Londoner for whom there had never been any clear demarcation between right and wrong and a man who thought that if you could rig a nice little swindle now and then, well, why not? The turnover tax was killing betting . . . you had to make a quick buck where you could . . . and there was nothing quite as sure or quick as raking in the dough on a red-hot favorite and knowing for certain that you weren't going to have to pay out.

Down at the post the starter put his hand on the lever and the tapes went up with a rush. Toddy kicked his chestnut smartly in the ribs. From his aerie on top of the stand the commentator moved smartly into his spiel, "They're off, and the first to show is the gray. . . ." Arthur Morrison and Chick watched with hearts thumping from different sorts of anxiety, and Harry Buskins shut his eyes and prayed.

Toddy drove forward at once into the first three, the chestnut beneath him galloping strongly, pulling at the bit, thudding his hooves into the ground. He seemed to be going well enough, Toddy thought. Strong. Like a train.

The first fence lay only 100 yards ahead now, coming nearer. With a practiced eye Toddy measured the distance, knew the chestnut's stride would meet it right, collected himself for the spring and gave the horse the signal to take off. There was no response. Nothing. The chestnut made no attempt to bunch his muscles, no attempt to gather himself onto his haunches, no attempt to waver or slow down or take any avoiding action whatsoever. For one incredulous second Toddy knew he was facing complete and imminent disaster.

The chestnut galloped straight into the three-foot-thick, chest-high solid birch fence with an impact that brought a groan of horror from the stands. He turned a somersault over the fence with a flurry of thrashing legs, threw Toddy off in front of him and fell down on top and rolled over him.

Chick felt as if the world were turning gray. The colors drained out of everything and he was halfway to fainting. Oh God, he thought. Oh God. *Toddy.*

The chestnut scrambled to his feet and galloped away. He followed the other horses toward the second fence, stretching out into a relentless stride, into a full-fledged thundering racing pace.

He hit the second fence as straight and hard as the first. The crowd gasped and cried out. Again the somersault, the spread-eagled legs, the crashing fall, the instant recovery. The chestnut surged up again and galloped on.

He came up past the stands, moving inexorably, the stirrups swinging out from the empty saddle, flecks of foam flying back now from his mouth, great dark patches of sweat staining his flanks. Where the track curved round to the left, the chestnut raced straight on. Straight on across the curve, to crash into the rail around the outside of the track. He took the solid timber across the chest and broke it in two. Again he fell in a thrashing heap and again he rocketed to his feet. But this time not to gallop away. This time he took three painful limping steps and stood still.

Back at the fence Toddy lay on the ground with first-aid men bending over him anxiously. Arthur Morrison ran down from the stands toward the track and didn't know which way to turn first, to his son or his horse. Chick's legs gave way and he sagged down in a daze onto the concrete steps. And down in the bookmakers' enclosure Harry Buskins' first reaction of delight was soured by wondering whether, if Toddy Morrison were badly injured, that stupid boy Chick would be scared enough to keep his mouth shut.

Arthur Morrison turned toward his son. Toddy had been knocked unconscious by the fall and had had all the breath squeezed out of him by the chestnut's weight, but by the time his father was within 100 yards he was beginning to come round. As soon as Arthur saw the supine figure move, he turned brusquely round and hurried off toward the horse: it would never do to show Toddy the concern he felt. Toddy would not respect him for it, he thought.

The chestnut stood patiently by the smashed rail, only dimly aware of the dull discomfort in the foreleg that wouldn't take his weight. Arthur Morrison and the veterinarian arrived beside him at the same time, and Arthur Morrison glared at the vet.

"You said he was fit to run. The owner is going to hit the roof when he hears about it." Morrison tried to keep a grip on a growing internal fury at the injustice of fate. The chestnut wasn't just any horse—it was the best he'd ever trained, had hoisted him higher up the stakes-won list than he was ever likely to go again.

"Well, he seemed all right," said the vet defensively.

"I want a dope test done," Morrison said truculently.

"He's broken his shoulder. He'll have to be put down."

"I know. I've got eyes. All the same, I want a dope test first. Just being ill wouldn't have made him act like that."

The veterinarian reluctantly agreed to take a blood sample, and after that he fitted the bolt into the humane killer and shot it into the chestnut's drug-dazed brain. The best horse in Arthur Morrison's stable became only a name in the record books. The digested carrot was dragged away with the carcass but its damage was by no means spent.

It took Chick 15 minutes to realize that it was Toddy who was alive and the horse that was dead, during which time he felt physically ill and mentally pulverized. It had seemed so small a thing, in the beginning, to give a carrot to the chestnut. He hadn't thought of it affecting him much. He'd never dreamed anything like that could make you really sick.

Once he found that Toddy had broken no bones, had recovered consciousness and would be on his feet in an hour or two, the bulk of his physical symptoms receded. When the small trainer appeared at his elbow to remind him sharply that he should be inside changing into colors to ride in the Novice Hurdle race, he felt fit enough to go and do it, though he wished in a way that he hadn't said he would.

In the changing room he forgot to tell his valet he needed a lightweight saddle and that the trainer had asked for a breast girth. He forgot to tie the stock round his neck and would have gone out to ride with the ends flapping. He forgot to take his watch off. His valet pointed everything out and thought that the jockey looked drunk.

The novice hurdler Chick was to ride wouldn't have finished within a mile of the chestnut if he'd started the day before. Young, green, sketchily schooled, he hadn't even the virtue of a gold streak waiting to be mined: this was one destined to run in the ruck until the owner tired of trying. Chick hadn't bothered to find out. He'd been much too preoccupied to look in the form book, where a consistent row of naughts might have made him cautious. As it was, he mounted the horse without attention and didn't listen to the riding orders the small trainer insistently gave him. As usual, he thought he knew better. Play it off the cuff, he thought scrappily. Play it off the cuff. How could he listen to fussy little instructions with all that he had on his mind?

On his way out from the weighing room he passed Arthur Morrison, who cast an inattentive eye over his racing colors and said, "Oh yes ... well, don't make too much of a mess of it. ..."

Morrison was still thinking about the difference the chestnut's death was going to make to his fortunes and he didn't notice the spasm of irritation that twisted Chick's petulant face.

There he goes, Chick thought. That's typical. *Typical.* Never thinks I can do a bloody thing. If he'd given me more chances ... and more money ... I wouldn't have given. ... Well, I wouldn't have. He cantered down to the post, concentrating on resenting that remark, "don't make too much of a mess of it," because it made him feel justified, obscurely, for having done what he'd done. The abyss of remorse opening beneath him was too painful. He clutched at every lie to keep himself out.

Harry Buskins had noticed that Chick had an unexpected mount in the Novice Hurdle and concluded that he himself was safe, the boy wasn't going to crack. All the same, he had shut his bag over its swollen takings and left his pitch for the day and gone home, explaining to his colleagues that he didn't feel well. And in truth he didn't. He couldn't get out of his mind the sight of the chestnut charging at those fences as if he couldn't see. Blind, the horse had been. A great racer who knew he was on a racetrack starting a race. Didn't understand there was anything wrong with him. Galloped because he was asked to gallop, because he knew it was the right place for it. A great horse, with a great racing heart.

Harry Buskins mopped the sweat off his forehead. They were bound to have tested the horse for dope, he thought, after something like that. None of the others he'd done in the past had reacted that way. Maybe he'd got the dose wrong or the timing wrong. You never knew how individual horses would be affected. Doping was always a bit unpredictable.

He poured himself half a tumbler of whiskey with fingers that were shaking after all, and when he felt calmer he decided that if he got away with it this time he would be satisfied with the cleanup he'd made, and he wouldn't fool around with any more carrots. He just wouldn't risk it again.

Chick lined up at the starting post in the center of the field, even though the trainer had advised him to start on the outside to give the inexperienced horse an easy passage over the first few hurdles. Chick didn't remember this instruction because he hadn't listened, and even if he had listened he would have done the same, driven by his habitual compulsion to disagree. He was thinking about Toddy lining up on this spot an hour ago, not knowing that his horse wouldn't see the jumps. Chick hadn't known dope could make a horse blind. How could anyone expect that? It didn't make sense. Perhaps it was just that the dope had confused the chestnut so much that although its eyes saw the fence, the message didn't get through that he was supposed to jump over it. The chestnut couldn't have been really blind.

Chick sweated at the thought and forgot to check that the girths were still tight after cantering down to the post. His mind was still on the inward horror when the starter let the tapes up, so that he was caught unawares and flatfooted and got away slowly. The small trainer on the stand clicked his mouth in annoyance, and Arthur Morrison raised his eyes to heaven.

The first hurdle lay side-by-side with the first fence, and all the way to it Chick was illogically scared that his horse wouldn't rise to it. He spent the attention he should have given to setting his horse right in desperately trying to convince himself that no one could have given it a carrot. He couldn't be riding a doped horse himself . . . it wouldn't be fair. Why wouldn't it be fair? Because . . . because. . . .

The hurdler scrambled over the jump, knocked himself hard on the timber frame, and landed almost at a standstill. The small trainer began to curse.

Chick tightened one loose rein and then the other, and the hurdler swung to and fro in wavering indecision. He needed to be ridden with care and confidence and to be taught balance and rhythm. He needed to be set right before the jumps and to be quickly collected afterward. He lacked experience, he lacked judgment and he badly needed a jockey who could contribute both.

Chick could have made a reasonable job of it if he'd been trying. Instead, with nausea and mental exhaustion draining what skill he had out of his muscles, he was busy proving that he'd never be much good.

At the second fence he saw in his mind's eye the chestnut somersaulting through the air, and going round the bend his gaze wavered across to the broken rail and the scuffed-up patches of turf in front of it. The chestnut had died there. Everyone in the stable would be poorer for it. He had killed the chestnut, there was no avoiding it anymore, he'd killed it with that carrot as surely as if he'd shot the bolt himself. Chick sobbed suddenly, and his eyes filled with tears.

He didn't see the next two hurdles. They passed beneath him in a flying blur. He stayed on his horse by instinct, and the tears ran down and were swept away as they trickled under the edge of his jockey's goggles.

The green hurdler was frightened and rudderless. Another jump lay close ahead, and the horses in front went clattering through it, knocking one section half over and leaving it there at an angle. The hurdler waited until the last minute for help or instructions from the man on his back and then in a muddled way dived for the leaning section, which looked lower to him and easier to jump than the other end.

From the stands it was clear to both the small trainer and Arthur Morrison that Chick had made no attempt to keep straight or to tell the horse when to take off. It landed with its forefeet tangled up in the sloping hurdle and catapulted Chick off over its head.

The instinct of self-preservation which should have made Chick curl into a rolling ball wasn't working. He fell through the air flat and straight, and his last thought before he hit was that that stupid little sod of a trainer hadn't schooled his horse properly. The animal hadn't a clue how to jump.

He woke up a long time later in a high bed in a small room. There was a dim light burning somewhere. He could feel no pain. He could feel nothing at all. His mind seemed to be floating in his head and his head was floating in space.

After a long time he began to believe that he was dead. He took the thought calmly and was proud of himself for his calm. A long time after that he began to realize that he wasn't dead. There was some sort of casing round his head, holding it cushioned. He couldn't move.

He blinked his eyes consciously and licked his lips to make sure that they at least were working. He couldn't think what had happened. His thoughts were a confused but peaceful fog.

Finally he remembered the carrot, and the whole complicated agony washed back into his consciousness. He cried out in protest and tried to move, to get up and away, to escape the impossible, unbearable guilt. People heard his voice and came into the room and stood around him. He looked at them uncomprehendingly. They were dressed in white.

"You're all right, now," they said. "Don't worry, young man, you're going to be all right."

"I can't move," he protested.

"You will," they said soothingly.

"I can't feel ... anything. I can't feel my feet." The panic rose suddenly in his voice. "I can't feel my hands. I can't ... move ... my hands." He was shouting, frightened, his eyes wide and stretched.

"Don't worry," they said. "You will in time. You're going to be all right. You're going to be all right."

He didn't believe them, and they pumped a sedative into his arm to quiet him. He couldn't feel the prick of the needle. He heard himself screaming because he could feel no pain.

When he woke up again he knew for certain that he'd broken his neck.

After four days Arthur Morrison came to see him, bringing six new-laid eggs and a bottle of fresh orange juice. He stood looking down at the immobile body with the plaster cast round its shoulders and head.

"Well, Chick," he said awkwardly. "It's not as bad as it could have been, eh?"

Chick said rudely, "I'm glad you think so."

"They say your spinal cord isn't severed, it's just crushed. They say in a year or so you'll get a lot of movement back. And they say you'll begin to feel things any day now."

"They say," said Chick sneeringly. "I don't believe them."

"You'll have to, in time," said Morrison impatiently.

Chick didn't answer, and Arthur Morrison cast uncomfortably around in his mind for something to say to pass away the minutes until he could decently leave. He couldn't visit the boy and just stand there in silence. He had to say *something*. So he began to talk about what was uppermost in his mind.

"We had the result of the dope test this morning. Did you know we had the chestnut tested? Well, you know we had to have it put down anyway. The results came this morning. They were positive.... *Positive*. The chestnut was full of some sort of narcotic drug, some long name. The owner is kicking up hell about it and so is the insurance company. They're trying to say it's my fault. My security arrangements aren't tight enough. It's ridiculous. And all this on top of losing the horse itself, losing that really great horse. I questioned everyone in the stable this morning as soon as I knew about the dope, but of course no one knew anything. God, if I knew who did it I'd strangle him myself." His voice shook with the fury which had been consuming him all day.

It occurred to him at this point that Chick being Chick, he would be exclusively concerned with his own state and wouldn't care a damn for anyone else's troubles. Arthur Morrison sighed deeply. Chick did have his own troubles now, right enough. He couldn't be expected to care all that much about the chestnut. And he was looking very weak, very pale.

The doctor who checked on Chick's condition 10 times a day came quietly into the small room and shook hands with Morrison.

"He's doing well," he said. "Getting on splendidly."

"Nuts," Chick said.

The doctor twisted his lips. He didn't say he had found Chick the worse-tempered patient in the hospital. He said, "Of course it's hard on him. But it could have been worse. It'll take time, he'll need to learn everything again, you see. It'll take time."

"Like a bloody baby," Chick said violently.

Arthur Morrison thought, a baby again. Well, perhaps second time around they could make a better job of him.

"He's lucky he's got good parents to look after him once he goes home," the doctor said.

Chick thought of his mother, forever chopping up carrots to put in the stew. He'd have to eat them. His throat closed convulsively. He knew he couldn't.

And then there was the money, rolled up in the shoe-cleaning tin on the shelf in his bedroom. He would be able to see the tin all the time when he was lying in his own bed. He would never be able to forget. Never. And there was always the danger his ma would look inside it. He couldn't face going home. He couldn't face it. And he knew he would have to. He had no choice. He wished he were dead.

Arthur Morrison sighed heavily and shouldered his new burden with his accustomed strength of mind. "Yes, he can come home to his mother and me as soon as he's well enough. He'll always have us to rely on."

Chick Morrison winced with despair and shut his eyes. His father tried to stifle a surge of irritation, and the doctor thought the boy an ungrateful little beast.

FOR DISCUSSION: Carrot for a Chestnut

1. Carefully, throughout the story, Dick Francis constructs a portrait of Chick. Near the beginning, he notes: "Chick always knew better than anyone else." Find four other comments that help us to understand the kind of person Chick is.

2. An interesting parallel can be drawn between Alexander McGrant and Chick. A second parallel can be drawn between Chick and the horse he rode in the Novice Hurdle race. How is Chick like McGrant? How is he like the "green" horse? How does each of these parallels contribute to our knowledge of Chick's character?

3. Chick never considered himself a criminal. Would you describe what he did as a criminal action? Who was responsible: McGrant, Chick's father, society, or Chick himself? Considering Chick's attitude *after* he regains consciousness, explain why you think he will either change his way *or* will continue deeper into a life of crime.

4. The ending of this story comes as a surprise to most readers, yet Dick Francis scrupulously planted several clues. Skim the story a second time and see how many of these clues you can find. How does Francis handle the clues so that they are completely honest yet do not give away the ending?

5. Now that you have had a glimpse into the minds of four very different criminals, can you decide even *one* characteristic that all criminals share?

Footprints
and
Fingerprints

CHAPTER THREE

By far the most challenging aspect of detective work is the accumulation and interpretation of evidence. It demands a sharp eye for observation, a knowledge both of scientific methods and of human nature, and the ability to think logically and, at the same time, intuitively.

Edgar Allan Poe was one of the first to write stories in this area, as can be seen in "The Purloined Letter" and "Murders in the Rue Morgue." But it was Arthur Conan Doyle, creator of the famous fictional detective Sherlock Holmes, who really turned the process of detection into a fine art. Holmes peered everywhere, pondered, and produced incredibly complex solutions to incredible problems.

Holmes's miraculous powers of observation and reasoning put to shame the simple policeman who had little else but his badge and nightstick to help him track down criminals. But changes were in the air as the nineteenth century yielded to the twentieth. The uniqueness of the human fingerprint was noted, analyzed, and classified, and within a few years, the fingerprinting of criminals for identification and conviction was commonly accepted by the police and by the courts.

Other developments quickly followed to give twentieth-century criminology a new look:

Patrol cars equipped with two-way radios make policemen mobile and provide them with a means for giving and receiving on-the-spot information.

Charts of dental characteristics make possible swift identifications of unclaimed bodies.

The significance of a *modus operandi* (method of operation) helps police to recognize patterns in crime and to apprehend perpetrators of multiple crimes.

The classification of photographs of known criminals provides mug-shot galleries where victims or witnesses, immediately after a crime, can "finger" the criminal.

Closed circuit TV and special "trip" cameras, installed in banks and jewelry shops, are excellent and permanent witnesses of crimes-in-progress.

The science of ballistics, by which a bullet can be traced to a particular weapon, makes convictions surer and faster.

Analysis of even one human hair—yielding information regarding age, sex, and nationality—gives the police vital information and usually a good head start.

Serology, the testing and identification of bloodstains, permits a positive statement that a crime has been committed and sometimes a positive identification of the criminal.

Laboratory analysis of the minutest traces of paint, lead, or other materials helps policemen to connect a victim with a locale, or a criminal with his victim.

Analysis of clothing fibers sometimes provides incontrovertible circumstantial evidence of the criminal's presence at the scene of the crime.

Handwriting analysis makes forgery more difficult and helps to solve kidnapping cases.

Moulages of footprints make clues permanent for prolonged study and permit an easy check on suspects over a period of time.

Ultraviolet light makes readable registration numbers and other markings that a criminal may confidently file off.

With the help of "identikits," the information provided by victims and/or witnesses can be used to sketch a composite picture of the criminal.

Lie detectors, while still fallible, can clear a suspect who is telling the truth or pile up additional suspicion against one who is not.

This list is already incomplete. Every week, every month, sees new discoveries, new inventions developed in forensic laboratories which make life harder for the criminal and easier for the police. Unfortunately some of these inventions are taken over by the criminals or simply become known to criminals. Fingerprinting, for example, has lost much of its effectiveness. Since every criminal knows about it, most are careful to wear gloves or to erase all possible prints before leaving the scene of the crime. Still, technology has, on the whole, been the friend and assistant of the lawman.

All these developments have changed the mystery story as well as the police precinct. The lone sleuth still operates, but he no longer monopolizes the field. Just as popular now is the police procedural story that shows the dozens of small steps performed in the lab which culminate in the apprehension of the criminal.

For most readers, though, whether the hero is an armchair detective, a man in blue, or a lab technician makes little difference. The fun lies in the pursuit—in noting each clue, in studying it from every angle, and finally in fitting it triumphantly into its proper place in the intellectual jigsaw puzzle.

INTRODUCTION: The Reigate Puzzle

Sir Arthur Conan Doyle was an eye specialist, a dramatist, a war correspondent, a whaler, an athlete, and a spiritualist. But he was, above all (note this with reverence), the creator of the one and only, the truly inimitable Sherlock Holmes.

Holmes is, without question, the world's best-known, least-fictitious, fictitious character. Organizations, beginning with the Baker Street Irregulars, have dedicated themselves to the study of his life and habits. (Christopher Morley, Elmer Davis, Gene Tunney, and Franklin Delano Roosevelt were all at one time members of one of these illustrious groups.) Holmes' residence—221B Baker Street—is more famous than most real buildings, and for a time the address was even used for the Secret Service quarters at FDR's Maryland White House.

Holmes captured the public imagination almost as soon as he appeared. When Conan Doyle tired of Holmes and tried to kill him off, the protest was so shrill and lasting that the reluctant author resurrected him and set him forth on another series of mystery-solving expeditions.

In this story Holmes proves to be a clever graphologist: one who analyzes handwriting, usually with the hope of gaining insight into the character of the writer. Otherwise, it is a typical Sherlock Holmes story showing the famous sleuth at his detecting best. As always, the well-known formula is apparent: Observation + Deduction = Solution.

The Reigate Puzzle
A. Conan Doyle

It was some time before the health of my friend Mr. Sherlock Holmes recovered from the strain caused by his immense exertions in the spring of '87. The whole question of the Netherland-Sumatra Company and of the colossal schemes of Baron Maupertuis are too recent in the minds of the public, and are too intimately concerned with politics and finance to be fitting subjects for this series of sketches. They led, however, in an indirect fashion to a singular and complex problem which gave my friend an opportunity of demonstrating the value of a fresh weapon among the many with which he waged his lifelong battle against crime.

On referring to my notes I see that it was upon the fourteenth of April that I received a telegram from Lyons which informed me that Holmes was lying ill in the Hotel Dulong. Within twenty-four hours I was in his sick-room and was relieved to find that there was nothing formidable in his symptoms. Even his iron constitution, however, had broken down under the strain of an investigation which had extended over two months, during which period he had never worked less than fifteen hours a day and had more than once, as he assured me, kept to his task for five days at a stretch. Even the triumphant issue of his labors could not save him from reaction after so terrible an exertion, and at a time when Europe was ringing with his name and when his room was literally ankle-deep with congratulatory telegrams I found him a prey to the blackest depression. Even the knowledge that he had succeeded where the police of three countries had failed, and that he had outmaneuvered at every point the most accomplished swindler in Europe, was insufficient to rouse him from his nervous prostration.

Three days later we were back in Baker Street together; but it was evident that my friend would be much the better for a change, and the thought of a week of springtime in the country was full of attractions to me also. My old friend, Colonel Hayter, who had come under my professional care in Afghanistan, had now taken a house near Reigate in Surrey and had frequently asked me to come down to him upon a visit. On the last occasion he had remarked that if my friend would only come with me he would be glad to extend his hospitality to him also. A little diplomacy was needed, but when Holmes understood that the establishment was a bachelor one, and that he would be allowed the fullest freedom, he fell in with my plans and a week after our return from Lyons we were under the colonel's roof. Hayter was a fine old soldier who had seen much of the world, and he soon found, as I had expected, that Holmes and he had much in common.

On the evening of our arrival we were sitting in the colonel's gunroom after dinner, Holmes stretched upon the sofa, while Hayter and I looked over his little armory of Eastern weapons.

"By the way," said he suddenly, "I think I'll take one of these pistols upstairs with me in case we have an alarm."

"An alarm!" said I.

"Yes, we've had a scare in this part lately. Old Acton, who is one of our county magnates, had his house broken into last Monday. No great damage done, but the fellows are still at large."

"No clue?" asked Holmes, cocking his eye at the colonel.

"None as yet. But the affair is a petty one, one of our little country crimes, which must seem too small for your attention, Mr. Holmes, after this great international affair."

Holmes waved away the compliment, though his smile showed that it had pleased him.

"Was there any feature of interest?"

"I fancy not. The thieves ransacked the library and got very little for their pains. The whole place was turned upside down, drawers burst open, and presses ransacked, with the result that an odd volume of Pope's *Homer,* two plated candlesticks, an ivory letter-weight, a small oak barometer, and a ball of twine are all that have vanished."

"What an extraordinary assortment!" I exclaimed.

"Oh, the fellows evidently grabbed hold of everything they could get." Holmes grunted from the sofa.

"The county police ought to make something of that," said he; "why, it is surely obvious that—"

But I held up a warning finger.

"You are here for a rest, my dear fellow. For heaven's sake don't get started on a new problem when your nerves are all in shreds."

Holmes shrugged his shoulders with a glance of comic resignation towards the colonel, and the talk drifted away into less dangerous channels.

It was destined, however, that all my professional caution should be wasted, for next morning the problem obtruded itself upon us in such a way that it was impossible to ignore it, and our country visit took a turn which neither of us could have anticipated. We were at breakfast when the colonel's butler rushed in with all his propriety shaken out of him.

"Have you heard the news, sir?" he gasped. "At the Cunningham's, sir!"

"Burglary!" cried the colonel, with his coffee-cup in mid-air.

"Murder!"

The colonel whistled. "By Jove!" said he. "Who's killed, then? The J. P. or his son?"

"Neither, sir. It was William, the coachman. Shot through the heart, sir, and never spoke again."

"Who shot him, then?"

"The burglar, sir. He was off like a shot and got clean away. He'd just broke in at the pantry window when William came on him and met his end in saving his master's property."

"What time?"

"It was last night, sir, somewhere about twelve."

"Ah, then, we'll step over afterwards," said the colonel, coolly settling down to his breakfast again. "It's a baddish business," he added when the butler had gone; "he's our leading man about here, is old Cunningham, and a very decent fellow too. He'll be cut up over this, for the man has been in his service for years and was a good servant. It's evidently the same villains who broke into Acton's."

"And stole that very singular collection," said Holmes thoughtfully.

"Precisely."

"Hum! It may prove the simplest matter in the world, but all the same at first glance this is just a little curious, is it not? A gang of burglars acting in the country might be expected to vary the scene of their operations, and not to crack two cribs in the same district within a few days. When you spoke last night of taking precautions I remember that it passed through my mind that this was probably the last parish in England to which the thief or thieves would be likely to turn their attention—which shows that I have still much to learn."

"I fancy it's some local practitioner," said the colonel. "In that case, of course, Acton's and Cunningham's are just the places he would go for, since they are far the largest about here."

"And richest?"

"Well, they ought to be, but they've had a lawsuit for some years which has sucked the blood out of both of them, I fancy. Old Acton has some claim on half Cunningham's estate, and the lawyers have been at it with both hands."

"If it's a local villain there should not be much difficulty in running him down," said Holmes with a yawn. "All right, Watson, I don't intend to meddle."

"Inspector Forrester, sir," said the butler, throwing open the door.

The official, a smart, keen-faced young fellow, stepped into the room. "Good-morning, Colonel," said he. "I hope I don't intrude, but we hear that Mr. Holmes of Baker Street is here."

The colonel waved his hand towards my friend, and the inspector bowed.

"We thought that perhaps you would care to step across, Mr. Holmes."

"The fates are against you, Watson," said he, laughing. "We were chatting about the matter when you came in, Inspector. Perhaps you can let us have a few details." As he leaned back in his chair in the familiar attitude I knew that the case was hopeless.

"We had no clue in the Acton affair. But here we have plenty to go on, and there's no doubt it is the same party in each case. The man was seen."

"Ah!"

"Yes, sir. But he was off like a deer after the shot that killed poor William Kirwan was fired. Mr. Cunningham saw him from the bedroom window, and Mr. Alec Cunningham saw him from the back passage. It was quarter to twelve when the alarm broke out. Mr. Cunningham had just got into bed, and Mr. Alec was smoking a pipe in his dressing-gown. They both heard William, the coachman, calling for help, and Mr. Alec ran down to see what was the matter. The back door was open, and as he came to the foot of the stairs he saw two men wrestling together outside. One of them fired a shot, the other dropped, and the murderer rushed across the garden and over the hedge. Mr. Cunningham, looking out of his bedroom, saw the fellow as he gained the road, but lost sight of him at once. Mr. Alec stopped to see if he could help the dying man, and so the villain got clean away. Beyond the fact that he was a middle-sized man and dressed in some dark stuff, we have no personal clue; but we are making energetic inquiries, and if he is a stranger we shall soon find him out."

"What was this William doing there? Did he say anything before he died?"

"Not a word. He lives at the lodge with his mother, and as he was a very faithful fellow we imagine that he walked up to the house with the intention of seeing that all was right there. Of course this Acton business has put everyone on their guard. The robber must have just burst open the door—the lock has been forced—when William came upon him."

"Did William say anything to his mother before going out?"

"She is very old and deaf, and we can get no information from her. The shock has made her half-witted, but I understand that she was never very bright. There is one very important circumstance, however. Look at this!"

He took a small piece of torn paper from a notebook and spread it out upon his knee.

"This was found between the finger and thumb of the dead man. It appears to be a fragment torn from a larger sheet. You will observe that the hour mentioned upon it is the very time at which the poor fellow met his fate. You see that his murderer might have torn the rest of the sheet from him or he might have taken this fragment from the murderer. It reads almost as though it were an appointment."

Holmes took up the scrap of paper, a facsimile of which is here reproduced.

at quarter to twelve learn what maybe

"Presuming that it is an appointment," continued the inspector, "it is of course a conceivable theory that this William Kirwan, though he had the reputation of being an honest man, may have been in league with the thief. He may have met him there, may even have helped him to break in the door, and then they may have fallen out between themselves."

"This writing is of extraordinary interest," said Holmes, who had been examining it with intense concentration. "These are much deeper waters than I had thought." He sank his head upon his hands, while the inspector smiled at the effect which his case had had upon the famous London specialist.

"Your last remark," said Holmes presently, "as to the possibility of there being an understanding between the burglar and the servant, and this being a note of appointment from one to the other, is an ingenious and not entirely impossible supposition. But this writing opens up—" He sank his head into his hands again and remained for some minutes in the deepest thought. When he raised his face again I was surprised to see that his cheek was tinged with color, and his eyes as bright as before his illness. He sprang to his feet with all his old energy.

"I'll tell you what," said he, "I should like to have a quiet little glance into the details of this case. There is something in it which fascinates me extremely. If you will permit me, Colonel, I will leave my friend Watson and you, and I will step round with the inspector to test the truth of one or two little fancies of mine. I will be with you again in half an hour."

An hour and a half had elapsed before the inspector returned alone.

"Mr. Holmes is walking up and down in the field outside," said he. "He wants us all four to go up to the house together."

"To Mr. Cunningham's?"

"Yes, sir."

"What for?"

The inspector shrugged his shoulders. "I don't quite know, sir. Between ourselves, I think Mr. Holmes has not quite got over his illness yet. He's been behaving very queerly, and he is very much excited."

"I don't think you need alarm yourself," said I. "I have usually found that there was method in his madness."

"Some folk might say there was madness in his method," muttered the inspector. "But he's all on fire to start, Colonel, so we had best go out if you are ready."

We found Holmes pacing up and down in the field, his chin sunk upon his breast, and his hands thrust into his trousers pockets.

"The matter grows in interest," said he. "Watson, your country trip has been a distinct success. I have had a charming morning."

"You have been up to the scene of the crime, I understand," said the colonel.

"Yes, the inspector and I have made quite a little reconnaissance together."

"Any success?"

"Well, we have seen some very interesting things. I'll tell you what we did as we walk. First of all, we saw the body of this unfortunate man. He certainly died from a revolver wound as reported."

"Had you doubted it, then?"

"Oh, it is as well to test everything. Our inspection was not wasted. We then had an interview with Mr. Cunningham and his son, who were able to point out the exact spot where the murderer had broken through the garden-hedge in his flight. That was of great interest."

"Naturally."

"Then we had a look at this poor fellow's mother. We could get no information from her, however, as she is very old and feeble."

"And what is the result of your investigations?"

"The conviction that the crime is a very peculiar one. Perhaps our visit now may do something to make it less obscure. I think that we are both agreed, Inspector, that the fragment of paper in the dead man's hand, bearing, as it does, the very hour of his death written upon it, is of extreme importance."

"It should give a clue, Mr. Holmes."

"It *does* give a clue. Whoever wrote that note was the man who brought William Kirwan out of his bed at that hour. But where is the rest of that sheet of paper?"

"I examined the ground carefully in the hope of finding it," said the inspector.

"It was torn out of the dead man's hand. Why was someone so anxious to get possession of it? Because it incriminated him. And what would he do with it? Thrust it into his pocket, most likely, never noticing that a corner of it had been left in the grip of the corpse. If we could get the rest of that sheet it is obvious that we should have gone a long way towards solving the mystery."

"Yes, but how can we get at the criminal's pocket before we catch the criminal?"

"Well, well, it was worth thinking over. Then there is another obvious point. The note was sent to William. The man who wrote it could not have taken it; otherwise, of course, he might have delivered his own message by word of mouth. Who brought the note, then? Or did it come through the post?"

"I have made inquiries," said the inspector. "William received a letter by the afternoon post yesterday. The envelope was destroyed by him."

"Excellent!" cried Holmes, clapping the inspector on the back. "You've seen the postman. It is a pleasure to work with you. Well, here is the lodge, and if you will come up, Colonel, I will show you the scene of the crime."

We passed the pretty cottage where the murdered man had lived and walked up an oak-lined avenue to the fine old Queen Anne house, which bears the date of Malplaquet upon the lintel of the door. Holmes and the inspector led us round it until we came to the side gate, which is separated by a stretch of garden from the hedge which lines the road. A constable was standing at the kitchen door.

"Throw the door open, officer," said Holmes. "Now, it was on those stairs that young Mr. Cunningham stood and saw the two men struggling just where we are. Old Mr. Cunningham was at that window—the second on the left—and he saw the fellow get away just to the left of that bush. So did the son. They are both sure of it on account of the bush. Then Mr. Alec ran out and knelt beside the wounded man. The ground is very hard, you see, and there are no marks to guide us." As he spoke two men came down the garden path, from round the angle of the house. The one was an elderly man, with a strong, deep-lined, heavy-eyed face; the other a dashing young fellow, whose bright, smiling expression and showy dress were in strange contrast with the business which had brought us there.

"Still at it, then?" said he to Holmes. "I thought you Londoners were never at fault. You don't seem to be so very quick, after all."

"Ah, you must give us a little time," said Holmes good-humoredly.

"You'll want it," said young Alec Cunningham. "Why, I don't see that we have any clue at all."

"There's only one," answered the inspector. "We thought that if we could only find— Good heavens, Mr. Holmes! what is the matter?"

My poor friend's face had suddenly assumed the most dreadful expression. His eyes rolled upward, his features writhed in agony, and with a suppressed groan he dropped on his face upon the ground. Horrified at the suddenness and severity of the attack, we carried him into the kitchen, where he lay back in a large chair and breathed heavily for some minutes. Finally, with a shamefaced apology for his weakness, he rose once more.

"Watson would tell you that I have only just recovered from a severe illness," he explained. "I am liable to these sudden nervous attacks."

"Shall I send you home in my trap?" asked old Cunningham.

"Well, since I am here, there is one point on which I should like to feel sure. We can very easily verify it."

"What was it?"

"Well, it seems to me that it is just possible that the arrival of this poor fellow William was not before, but after, the entrance of the burglar into the house. You appear to take it for granted that although the door was forced the robber never got in."

"I fancy that is quite obvious," said Mr. Cunningham gravely. "Why, my son Alec had not yet gone to bed, and he would certainly have heard anyone moving about."

"Where was he sitting?"

"I was smoking in my dressing-room."

"Which window is that?"

"The last on the left, next my father's."

"Both of your lamps were lit, of course?"

"Undoubtedly."

"There are some very singular points here," said Holmes, smiling. "Is is not extraordinary that a burglar—and a burglar who had some previous experience—should deliberately break into a house at a time when he could see from the lights that two of the family were still afoot?"

"He must have been a cool hand."

"Well, of course, if the case were not an odd one we should not have been driven to ask you for an explanation," said young Mr. Alec. "But as to your ideas that the man had robbed the house before William tackled him, I think it a most absurd notion. Wouldn't we have found the place disarranged and missed the things which he had taken?"

"It depends on what the things were," said Holmes. "You must remember that we are dealing with a burglar who is a very peculiar fellow, and who appears to work on lines of his own. Look, for example, at the queer lot of things which he took from Acton's—what was it?—a ball of string, a letter-weight, and I don't know what other odds and ends."

"Well, we are quite in your hands, Mr. Holmes," said old Cunningham. "Anything which you or the inspector may suggest will most certainly be done."

"In the first place," said Holmes, "I should like you to offer a reward—coming from yourself, for the officials may take a little time before they would agree upon the sum, and these things cannot be done too promptly. I have jotted down the form here, if you would not mind signing it. Fifty pounds was quite enough, I thought."

"I would willingly give five hundred," said the J. P., taking the slip of paper and the pencil which Holmes handed to him. "This is not quite correct, however," he added, glancing over the document.

"I wrote it rather hurriedly."

"You see you begin, 'Whereas, at about a quarter to one on Tuesday morning an attempt was made,' and so on. It was at a quarter to twelve, as a matter of fact."

I was pained at the mistake, for I knew how keenly Holmes would feel any slip of the kind. It was his specialty to be accurate as to fact, but his recent illness had shaken him, and this one little incident was enough to show me that he was still far from being himself. He was obviously embarrassed for an instant, while the inspector raised his eyebrows, and Alec Cunningham burst into a laugh. The old gentleman corrected the mistake, however, and handed the paper back to Holmes.

"Get it printed as soon as possible," he said; "I think your idea is an excellent one."

Holmes put the slip of paper carefully away into his pocketbook.

"And now," said he, "it really would be a good thing that we should all go over the house together and make certain that this rather erratic burglar did not, after all, carry anything away with him."

Before entering, Holmes made an examination of the door which had been forced. It was evident that a chisel or strong knife had been thrust in, and the lock forced back with it. We could see the marks in the wood where it had been pushed in.

"You don't use bars, then?" he asked.

"We have never found it necessary."

"You don't keep a dog?"

"Yes, but he is chained on the other side of the house."

"When do the servants go to bed?"

"About ten."

"I understand that William was usually in bed also at that hour?"

"Yes."

"It is singular that on this particular night he should have been up. Now, I should be very glad if you would have the kindness to show us over the house, Mr. Cunningham."

A stone-flagged passage, with the kitchen branching away from it, led by a wooden staircase directly to the first floor of the house. It came out upon the landing opposite to a second more ornamental stair which came up from the front hall. Out of this landing opened the drawing-room and several bedrooms, including those of Mr. Cunningham and his son. Holmes walked slowly, taking keen note of the architecture of the house. I could tell from his expression that he was on a hot scent, and yet I could not in the least imagine in what direction his inferences were leading him.

"My good sir," said Mr. Cunningham, with some impatience, "this is surely very unnecessary. That is my room at the end of the stairs, and my son's is the one beyond it. I leave it to your judgment whether it was possible for the thief to have come up here without disturbing us."

"You must try round and get on a fresh scent, I fancy," said the son with a rather malicious smile.

"Still, I must ask you to humor me a little further. I should like, for example, to see how far the windows of the bedrooms command the front. This, I understand, is your son's room"—he pushed open the door —"and that, I presume, is the dressing-room in which he sat smoking when the alarm was given. Where does the window of that look out to?" He stepped across the bedroom, pushed open the door, and glanced round the other chamber.

"I hope that you are satisfied now?" said Mr. Cunningham tartly.

"Thank you, I think I have seen all that I wished."

"Then if it is really necessary we can go into my room."

"If it is not too much trouble."

The J. P. shrugged his shoulders and led the way into his own chamber, which was a plainly furnished and commonplace room. As we moved across it in the direction of the window, Holmes fell back until he and I were the last of the group. Near the foot of the bed stood a dish of oranges and a carafe of water. As we passed it Holmes, to my unutterable astonishment, leaned over in front of me and deliberately knocked the whole thing over. The glass smashed into a thousand pieces and the fruit rolled about into every corner of the room.

"You've done it now, Watson," said he coolly. "A pretty mess you've made of the carpet."

I stooped in some confusion and began to pick up the fruit, understanding for some reason my companion desired me to take the blame upon myself. The others did the same and set the table on its legs again.

"Hullo!" cried the inspector, "where's he got to?"

Holmes had disappeared.

"Wait here an instant," said young Alec Cunningham. "The fellow is off his head, in my opinion. Come with me, father, and see where he has got to!"

They rushed out of the room, leaving the inspector, the colonel, and me staring at each other.

" 'Pon my word, I am inclined to agree with Master Alec," said the official. "It may be the effect of this illness, but it seems to me that—"

His words were cut short by a sudden scream of "Help! Help! Murder!" With a thrill I recognized the voice as that of my friend. I rushed madly from the room on to the landing. The cries, which had sunk down into a hoarse, inarticulate shouting, came from the room which we had first visited. I dashed in, and on into the dressing-room beyond. The two Cunninghams were bending over the prostrate figure of Sherlock Holmes, the younger clutching his throat with both hands, while the elder seemed to be twisting one of his wrists. In an instant the three of us had torn them away from him, and Holmes staggered to his feet, very pale and evidently greatly exhausted.

"Arrest these men, Inspector," he gasped.

"On what charge?"

"That of murdering their coachman, William Kirwan."

The inspector stared about him in bewilderment. "Oh, come now, Mr. Holmes," said he at last, "I'm sure you don't really mean to—"

"Tut, man, look at their faces!" cried Holmes curtly.

Never certainly have I seen a plainer confession of guilt upon human countenances. The older man seemed numbed and dazed, with a heavy, sullen expression upon his strongly marked face. The son, on the other hand, had dropped all that jaunty, dashing style which had characterized him, and the ferocity of a dangerous wild beast gleamed in his dark eyes and distorted his handsome features. The inspector said nothing, but, stepping to the door, he blew his whistle. Two of his constables came at the call.

"I have no alternative, Mr. Cunningham," said he. "I trust that this may all prove to be an absurd mistake, but you can see that— Ah, would you? Drop it!" He struck out with his hand, and a revolver which the younger man was in the act of cocking clattered down upon the floor.

"Keep that," said Holmes, quietly putting his foot upon it; "you will find it useful at the trial. But this is what we really wanted." He held up a little crumpled piece of paper.

"The remainder of the sheet!" cried the inspector.

"Precisely."

"And where was it?"

"Where I was sure it must be. I'll make the whole matter clear to you presently. I think, Colonel, that you and Watson might return now, and I will be with you again in an hour at the furthest. The inspector and I must have a word with the prisoners, but you will certainly see me back at luncheon time."

Sherlock Holmes was as good as his word, for about one o'clock he rejoined us in the colonel's smoking-room. He was accompanied by a little elderly gentleman, who was introduced to me as the Mr. Acton whose house had been the scene of the original burglary.

"I wished Mr. Acton to be present while I demonstrated this small matter to you," said Holmes, "for it is natural that he should take a keen interest in the details. I am afraid, my dear Colonel, that you must regret the hour that you took in such a stormy petrel as I am."

"On the contrary," answered the colonel warmly, "I consider it the greatest privilege to have been permitted to study your methods of working. I confess that they quite surpass my expectations, and that I am utterly unable to account for your result. I have not yet seen the vestige of a clue."

"I am afraid that my explanation may disillusion you, but it has always been my habit to hide none of my methods, either from my friend Watson or from anyone who might take an intelligent interest in them. But, first, as I am rather shaken by the knocking about which I had in the dressing-room, I think that I shall help myself to a dash of your brandy, Colonel. My strength has been rather tried of late."

"I trust you had no more of those nervous attacks."

Sherlock Holmes laughed heartily. "We will come to that in its turn," said he. "I will lay an account of the case before you in its due order, showing you the various points which guided me in my decision. Pray interrupt me if there is any inference which is not perfectly clear to you.

"It is of the highest importance in the art of detection to be able to recognize, out of a number of facts, which are incidental and which vital.

Otherwise your energy and attention must be dissipated instead of being concentrated. Now, in this case there was not the slightest doubt in my mind from the first that the key of the whole matter must be looked for in the scrap of paper in the dead man's hand.

"Before going into this, I would draw your attention to the fact that, if Alec Cunningham's narrative was correct, and if the assailant, after shooting William Kirwan, had *instantly* fled, then it obviously could not be he who tore the paper from the dead man's hand. But if it was not he, it must have been Alec Cunningham himself, for by the time that the old man had descended several servants were upon the scene. The point is a simple one, but the inspector had overlooked it because he had started with the supposition that these county magnates had had nothing to do with the matter. Now, I make a point of never having any prejudices, and of following docilely wherever fact may lead me, and so, in the very first stage of the investigation, I found myself looking a little askance at the part which had been played by Mr. Alec Cunningham.

"And now I made a very careful examination of the corner of paper which the inspector had submitted to us. It was at once clear to me that it formed part of a very remarkable document. Here it is. Do you not now observe something very suggestive about it?"

"It has a very irregular look," said the colonel.

"My dear sir," cried Holmes, "there cannot be the least doubt in the world that it has been written by two persons doing alternate words. When I draw your attention to the strong *t*'s of 'at' and 'to,' and ask you to compare them with the weak ones of 'quarter' and 'twelve,' you will instantly recognize the fact. A very brief analysis of these four words would enable you to say with the utmost confidence that the 'learn' and the 'maybe' are written in the stronger hand, and the 'what' in the weaker."

"By jove, it's as clear as day!" cried the colonel. "Why on earth should two men write a letter in such a fashion?"

"Obviously the business was a bad one, and one of the men who distrusted the other was determined that, whatever was done, each should have an equal hand in it. Now, of the two men, it is clear that the one who wrote the 'at' and 'to' was the ringleader."

"How do you get at that?"

"We might deduce it from the mere character of the one hand as compared with the other. But we have more assured reasons than that for supposing it. If you examine this scrap with attention you will come to the conclusion that the man with the stronger hand wrote all his words first, leaving blanks for the other to fill up. These blanks were not always sufficient, and you can see that the second man had a squeeze to fit his 'quarter' in between the 'at' and the 'to,' showing that the latter were already written. The man who wrote all his words first is undoubtedly the man who planned the affair."

"Excellent!" cried Mr. Acton.

"But very superficial," said Holmes. "We come now, however, to a point which is of importance. You may not be aware that the deduction of a man's age from his writing is one which has been brought to considerable accuracy by experts. In normal cases one can place a man in his true decade with tolerable confidence. I say normal cases, because ill-health and physical weakness reproduce the signs of old age, even when the invalid is a youth. In this case, looking at the bold, strong hand of the one, and the rather broken-backed appearance of the other, which still retains its legibility although the *t*'s have begun to lose their crossing, we can say that the one was a young man and the other was advanced in years without being positively decrepit."

"Excellent!" cried Mr. Acton again.

"There is a further point, however, which is subtler and of greater interest. There is something in common between these hands. They belong to men who are blood-relatives. It may be most obvious to you in the Greek *e*'s, but to me there are many small points which indicate the same thing. I have no doubt at all that a family mannerism can be traced in these two specimens of writing. I am only, of course, giving you the leading results now of my examination of the paper. There were twenty-three other deductions which would be of more interest to experts than to you. They all tend to deepen the impression upon my mind that the Cunninghams, father and son, had written this letter.

"Having got so far, my next step was, of course, to examine into the details of the crime, and to see how far they would help us. I went up to the house with the inspector and saw all that was to be seen. The wound upon the dead man was, as I was able to determine with absolute confidence, fired from a revolver at the distance of something over four yards. There was no powder-blackening on the clothes. Evidently, therefore, Alec Cunningham had lied when he said that the two men were struggling when the shot was fired. Again, both father and son agreed as to the place where the man escaped into the road. At that point, however, as it happens, there is a broadish ditch, moist at the bottom. As there were no indications of boot-marks about this ditch, I was absolutely sure not only that the Cunninghams had again lied but that there had never been any unknown man upon the scene at all.

"And now I have to consider the motive of this singular crime. To get at this, I endeavored first of all to solve the reason of the original burglary at Mr. Acton's. I understood, from something which the colonel told us, that a lawsuit had been going on between you, Mr. Acton, and the Cunninghams. Of course, it instantly occurred to me that they had broken into your library with the intention of getting at some document which might be of importance in the case."

"Precisely so," said Mr. Acton. "There can be no possible doubt as to their intentions. I have the clearest claim upon half of their present estate, and if they could have found a single paper—which, fortunately, was in the strong-box of my solicitors—they would undoubtedly have crippled our case."

"There you are," said Holmes, smiling. "It was a dangerous, reckless attempt in which I seem to trace the influence of young Alec. Having found nothing, they tried to divert suspicion by making it appear to be an ordinary burglary, to which end they carried off whatever they could lay their hands upon. That is all clear enough, but there was much that was still obscure. What I wanted, above all, was to get the missing part of that note. I was certain that Alec had torn it out of the dead man's hand, and almost certain that he must have thrust it into the pocket of his dressing-gown. Where else could he have put it? The only question was whether it was still there. It was worth an effort to find out, and for that object we all went up to the house.

"The Cunninghams joined us, as you doubtless remember, outside the kitchen door. It was, of course, of the very first importance that they should not be reminded of the existence of this paper, otherwise they would naturally destroy it without delay. The inspector was about to tell them the importance which we attached to it when, by the luckiest chance in the world, I tumbled down in a sort of fit and so changed the conversation."

"Good heavens!" cried the colonel, laughing, "do you mean to say all our sympathy was wasted and your fit an imposture?"

"Speaking professionally, it was admirably done," cried I, looking in amazement at this man who was forever confounding me with some new phase of his astuteness.

"It is an art which is often useful," said he. "When I recovered I managed, by a device which had perhaps some little merit of ingenuity, to get old Cunningham to write the word 'twelve,' so that I might compare it with the 'twelve' upon the paper."

"Oh, what an ass I have been!" I exclaimed.

"I could see that you were commiserating me over my weakness," said Holmes, laughing. "I was sorry to cause you the sympathetic pain which I know that you felt. We then went upstairs together, and, having entered the room and seen the dressing-gown hanging up behind the door, I contrived, by upsetting a table, to engage their attention for the moment and slipped back to examine the pockets. I had hardly got the paper, however—which was, as I had expected, in one of them—when the two Cunninghams were on me, and would, I verily believe, have

If you will only come round
to the east gate you will
will very much surprise you and
be of the greatest source to you and also
to Anne Morison. But say nothing to anyone
upon the matter

murdered me then and there but for your prompt and friendly aid. As it is, I feel that young man's grip on my throat now, and the father had twisted my wrist round in the effort to get the paper out of my hand. They saw that I must know all about it, you see, and the sudden change from absolute security to complete despair made them perfectly desperate.

"I had a little talk with old Cunningham afterwards as to the motive of the crime. He was tractable enough, though his son was a perfect demon, ready to blow out his own or anybody else's brains if he could have got to his revolver. When Cunningham saw that the case against him was so strong he lost all heart and made a clean breast of everything. It seems that William had secretly followed his two masters on the night when they made their raid upon Mr. Acton's and, having thus got them into his power, proceeded, under threats of exposure, to levy blackmail upon them. Mr. Alec, however, was a dangerous man to play games of that sort with. It was a stroke of positive genius on his part to see in the burglary scare which was convulsing the countryside an opportunity of plausibly getting rid of the man whom he feared. William was decoyed up and shot, and had they only got the whole of the note and paid a little more attention to detail in their accessories, it is very possible that suspicion might never have been aroused."

"And the note?" I asked.

Sherlock Holmes placed the subjoined paper before us.

"It is very much the sort of thing that I expected," said he. "Of course, we do not yet know what the relations may have been between Alec Cunningham, William Kirwan, and Annie Morrison. The result shows that the trap was skillfully baited. I am sure that you cannot fail to be delighted with the traces of heredity shown in the *p*'s and in the tails of the *g*'s. The absence of the *i*-dots in the old man's writing is also most characteristic. Watson, I think our quiet rest in the country has been a distinct success, and I shall certainly return much invigorated to Baker Street to-morrow."

FOR DISCUSSION: The Reigate Puzzle

1. Part of the fun in reading Sherlock Holmes stories is watching the "great man" extract information from the oddest clues. On a sheet of paper, rule off two columns. In the first, list at least five clues that led to a solution of the mystery. In the second column describe briefly what Holmes was able to deduce from each of these clues.

2. The character of Sherlock Holmes has fascinated readers for well over half a century. Play Sherlock yourself for a moment and see

how many of the following questions you can answer. In each case explain *how* you know your answer is the correct one.

   a. Does Holmes like women?

   b. Does he drink?

   c. Is he modest?

   d. Is he moody?

   e. Does he *enjoy* detecting?

3. In the Sherlock Holmes stories, Watson leads a double life. He assists the detective, of course, but he also assists the author. Describe in separate paragraphs each of these two roles. Include in each paragraph at least one illustration of Watson's work.

INTRODUCTION: Aunt Minnie and the
Accessory After the Fact

One of the first things that a detective learns—and a mystery writer, too—is that in crime the impossible doesn't exist. If something happened, it is possible. If it *seems* impossible, it suggests only that the human mind hasn't been able to find or interpret some of the facts. In such a situation it is the job of the detective to look further, to think logically, to intuit.

In this story the evidence could not be found because it wasn't there. It took a nonprofessional, Aunt Minnie, to see the significance of *that* ... and to march, logically, from there to a solution.

Aunt Minnie and the
Accessory After the Fact
Samuel Hopkins Adams

It was the most open-and-shut case in my police experience. We had everything—corpse, motive, murderer, and a man on the spot at the time. And what was the result? A complete washout.

You remember the West Sixteenth tenement murder last fall, the one the newspapers headlined as the Millionaire Beggar Mystery. I figured on being in those headlines myself. Detective Casey Lane Solves Millionaire Beggar Mystery. And look at me now! I might as well give my badge to Aunt Minnie.

Old Hans Gommer wasn't any millionaire. But he'd made enough out of forty years' street begging to own the tenement. He kept it up decently, too; otherwise Marian and I wouldn't be living there. His room was at the stairhead, second floor, same floor as our apartment. It was a single room. And I mean single; not even a toilet; just a stove, a bed, a stand, a couple of chairs, and a few cooking gadgets. The windows were barred with fixed half-inch iron, five inches apart. The old miser was jittery about being robbed. His door was like a bank vault's.

He hadn't a friend in the world, unless you count a big snarly brindled tomcat that used to crawl the narrow ledge along the wall, squeeze through the bars, and beg for what was left of dinner, and little enough of that, I guess. Old Hans had a relative, though, an ugly little wizened devil of fifty or sixty—you couldn't tell—who used to come in two or three times a week for an unfriendly game of backgammon. His name was Finney, and we found out afterward he was a disbarred lawyer from somewhere out West. When the door was open in summer, you could hear the pair of 'em growling and cursing and swapping charges of crooked play. True, too, I wouldn't wonder.

The door wasn't open this Monday evening. It was cold and rainy. My wife had been busy all day organizing a floor-by-floor bond campaign with a barrier across the foot of the stairs so no tenant could get past without buying. She and Ma Sanderson were on guard from five o'clock on. At half past, old Gommer went out and came back with a flounder tied up in paper, to cook for his dinner, and Marian sold him a twenty-five-cent stamp. That was his limit. An hour later Peter Finney, the nephew, knocked on the door and was let in earlier than he usually came, though if he expected to get a meal out of it, he was a fool.

Maybe they quarreled over that. Maybe over the game. Anyway, Finney stabbed Hans expertly through the spinal cord, and what happened in the next three hours the Police Department is still arguing. All but me.

Don't forget that all this time either my wife or Ma Sanderson, or both, were on the barrier looking right up to old Gommer's door. Even a cockroach couldn't have got in or out without being spotted.

It was half past nine and I was smoking my pipe and jollying with the two females at the foot of the stairs when Finney showed up above us.

"Uncle Hans is dead," he said. He was white but cool enough.

The door hadn't sprung shut. We all ran up and went in. The old boy was dead all right, with a neat hole in the back of his neck, so small you could hardly see it through the fuzz of gray hair. He was in his chair, half slumped over the table. The checkers and dice were scattered over the floor. I put it to Finney.

"Who did it?"

"I don't know."

"Why don't you know? You've been here all the time."

You never saw a fishier eye than the one he gave me. "I was asleep," he said.

I turned to the two women. "Could anyone else have got in here since this man came?"

"No." Both spoke at once.

"Could anyone have got out?"

"Absolutely not," Ma Sanderson answered. But my wife qualified with "Unless those window bars are movable."

I tried them. They were solid.

"I guess that puts it up to you," I told Finney. "Where's the knife?"

"I don't know."

Well, I ought to have called Headquarters, but I figured that, being Johnny-on-the-spot, here was my chance of glory.

"I saw old Gommer having one of these narrow-bladed little fish knives ground by a street grinder one day," Ma Sanderson put in.

"That's it," I said. "We'll find it."

First I frisked Finney. He hadn't so much as a penknife on him. Then the three of us fine-tooth-combed the room. Not a sticker of any sort. That left the window as the only answer. Fifteen feet opposite was a blank wall. Far as it could be thrown, the knife would have to drop into the little back yard. I gave Marian my gun to guard Finney and went down with my flash. No knife. And no footprints in the soft ground, proving that nobody had happened by and picked up the knife.

"It's *got* to be in this room," I said.

So I went through Finney again and the three of us turned the place inside out and made a detailed inventory of everything in it. It was then that my wife said:

"I wish Aunt Minnie was here."

Aunt Minnie was her old schoolmarm at No. 18, now living on the top floor of our tenement. But she was on a visit.

"You can have Aunt Minnie," I said. "I'll take Headquarters." So I phoned.

Then I went after Finney again.

"You killed him."

"I did not. What would I want to kill him for?"

"You're his heir, aren't you?" Marian said.

"I guess so. But I didn't kill him."

"Now, listen," I said. "You got into a stink over your game of backgammon and maybe he made a crack about you cheating and you let him have it. If you didn't, who did?"

"That's for you to find out," he said.

Then the Headquarters push came in and did everything over again with the same result. They took Finney with them when they quit, leaving us with only one new fact: the old man had probably been dead about three hours. So he must have been killed shortly after Finney arrived—which got us a lot nearer nothing.

"I *do* wish Aunt Minnie was here," my wife said.

"What would she do that we haven't?" I growled. I was getting sore. The Headquarters bunch acted like they thought I'd botched the thing somewhere.

"Aunt Minnie'd find something we've overlooked," Marian said. "There was never a trick played in school but what she caught the funny boy that did it."

"Anyway," I said, "we've got the guy, if we haven't got the knife. It's a watertight case for the D.A.'s office."

The district attorney didn't see it in that light. "Find me the knife," he said, "and I'll put him in the chair. But you can't convict a man of murder because nobody else did it."

"That's what Aunt Minnie says," said my wife when I told her the case was at a standstill a week later. "I had a letter from her. She'll be back next week."

When the old dame arrived, she had us up in her room and listened to Marian and Ma Sanderson and me.

"Where's Finney?" she asked.

"Out of jail. He got a lawyer who sprung him."

"Have you got that inventory you made?"

I handed her a copy. She studied it. "Is this everything that was in the room at the time?"

"I'll swear to that," Marian said.

"So will I," said Ma.

"You spoke of the old man bringing in a fish in a parcel."

"That's right."

"Where's the fish?" she asked.

"He ate it, I suppose."

"Did he eat the bones? I don't see 'em here."

Marian and Ma and I looked at the inventory.

"You've got the wrapper down: 'Square of brown paper.' Where's the string?"

"Oh, to hell with the string!" I said. "Are you figuring that he wound up the knife in the string and swallowed it?"

"I never did like comedy cops," Aunt Minnie said. "Not even in the movies. If I were after that knife, I'd look on the roof."

"What roof?"

"This roof and any other roof contiguous."

"Look, Aunt Minnie," I said. "Babe Ruth himself couldn't reach out between those bars and flip a knife five stories up onto a roof."

"You'd better do as Aunt Minnie says," my wife told me.

There's a lot of rubbish on tenement roofs, but I found the knife, two buildings away back of a chimney. Anyway, I found *a* knife and a fish knife at that. Of course there wasn't a chance of fingerprints after it had been out in all that weather. I brought it back to Aunt Minnie.

"Find anything else?"

"I wasn't looking for anything else."

"No fishbones? No string? No brains!" said Aunt Minnie.

So I went back and brought in the lot. "Who put 'em there and why?" I asked.

"In the jargon of your district attorney, the accessory after the fact."

"Oh, yeah? And how did he get 'em?"

"Why, I suppose the murderer passed 'em out through the window."

"Easy, like that! And how did he reach the window? Jump up eighteen feet from the courtyard and hang to the bars? Or scrounge his way across that ledge?"

"Funnier than ever," said Aunt Minnie, "but not too smart. The ledge."

"How could any man navigate a six-inch ledge?" Marian wanted to know.

"He couldn't. A cat could. Many's the time I've watched that ugly tom make it on his way to old Gommer's window."

"Wait a minute!" I said. "Are you telling us that a tomcat would carry away a knife and hide it on a roof?"

"If it was fixed up right, he would."

Then I began to get it, but I didn't like it. "How am I going to put that up to the D.A.?" I asked. "The Department's in wrong enough already on this case without any accessory tomcats."

"I wouldn't," she advised. "I'd leave the D.A. out of it."

"So the murderer not only gets out but collects his legacy, does he? That kind of gripes me, Aunt Minnie."

"Well, I wouldn't be so sure of his collecting," Aunt Minnie said. "You didn't know that I once taught drawing, did you?"

She wouldn't explain that crack until Peter Finney's death. He had received a large envelope in his morning mail and collapsed in the hallway when he opened it. On recovering, he went to the drugstore for medicine, but bought rat poison instead. Beside his bed they found a little heap of ash where he had burned that piece of mail.

Aunt Minnie looked pretty solemn when she got the news. "Perhaps it's just as well," she said, "though I didn't foresee quite that result of my experiment."

"What was in your letter, Aunt Minnie?" my wife asked.

"It wasn't a letter. It was a freehand sketch of a cat crawling on a ledge with a fish bound around with string in his mouth, and a knife handle sticking out beyond the fish."

Which goes to prove, my wife says, that women know more than men about a lot of things, including logic and cats.

Maybe so.

FOR DISCUSSION: Aunt Minnie and the
Accessory After the Fact

1. What was the "impossible situation" that puzzled the police? Why did Aunt Minnie realize almost immediately what must have happened? Which details that they overlooked did she notice?
2. Everyone knows an Aunt Minnie—she's a special kind of person. What clues to her thought processes does the author give *before* she appears in the story?
3. To solve the mystery, does Aunt Minnie use logic, common sense, or intuition—or a blending of all three? Explain.
4. Look closely at Aunt Minnie's dialogue. What are some adjectives that describe her speech pattern? Why has the author given her this particular speech pattern?

As technological advancements develop, the brilliant sleuth, working alone, begins to give way to the police laboratory. Here are all kinds of equipment and experts to use them. Within minutes a fingerprint can lead to an identification; a few drops of blood can eliminate one suspect; lint from a coat pocket can convict another. The modern lab can perform miracles, and it is all done in an orderly, routine, almost prosaic way.

Some of the old excitement and much of the old awe are missing in these fairly new police procedural stories, but wonder is born—a wonder that any criminal still dares to commit a crime. In the long run science and technology can be more persistent pursuers than even the most stubborn "private eye."

D as in Detail

Lawrence Treat

When Detective Inspector Mitch Taylor knocked off for the day, he left Amy's trowel in the Number 4 patrol car. The car was the one he always drove, so he didn't bother anybody about the trowel. He simply left it there under the front seat.

Amy had wanted to buy some marigolds—the dwarf ones she said were just right for the window box in their apartment; but he told her to forget about them—why throw good money away on something he could maybe get for free? Just tell him what they looked like and he'd scrounge them up somewhere. She said, all right, but get some extra ones for the Jub Freemans.

But Mitch's mind didn't exactly run to flowers, and he forgot all about them except when his foot happened to come off the brake and hit against the trowel. Or when he was home, like now. Relaxed. With the kids in bed and Amy sitting at the desk and going over the month's bills.

He watched her, a slim girl with delicate features and bright, teasing eyes, and she could add and subtract as easy as she could rattle off the alphabet. He was thinking what kind of a heel was he, anyhow? He ought to get her those dwarf marigolds even if he had to plant the seeds on his head and make like a flower pot.

The idea sort of bothered him—as if the thing might really happen if he weren't careful; and then the phone rang and Amy picked it up and answered.

She turned to Mitch and said, "It's for you. Official."

"The hell it is," he said, getting up. "What can they want at eleven o'clock?" But he crossed the room briskly and took the phone. "Taylor," he said in his high-pitched tenor.

Sergeant Morty Topps, at headquarters, spoke up. "Central Bureau," he said. "Signal two-nine. They'll pick you up downstairs. They know where to go."

"Right," Mitch said.

Morty grunted and then added in a low voice, as if he were telling a big secret, "Mitch, they think it's him again."

"Huh?" Mitch said. He held onto the phone even after he heard the click at the other end, and then he put the receiver down carefully, as if he were suddenly very tired. "It's him again," he said to Amy. "Only this time, it's a murder."

Amy seemed to wilt, and her voice was almost a wail. "Oh, Mitchell!" she said.

He put his hand on her shoulder for a moment, and he could practically feel the tenderness in her, and maybe in him, too. Then he wheeled, walked over to the closet, and took his gun and holster down from the top shelf where he kept them out of reach of the kids. He strapped on the holster, slipped his jacket over it, and headed for the door.

"Dunno when I'll be back," he said, and he went out.

The patrol car was waiting downstairs, and Mitch slid in. Flaherty was driving but Mitch didn't know the other guy. It was crowded with all three of them in the front seat.

"Where we going?" Mitch asked.

"Irving and Holmes," Flaherty said. "Know anything about it?"

"They said it was him again," Mitch answered.

"Geez!" The two uniformed cops said it at practically the same time. After that none of them felt much like talking.

The first time it happened, it looked like a routine case and the local precinct had handled it. Their report said that around ten o'clock at night a woman had stopped for a traffic light, and a guy with a gun had come over and tried to rob her. She'd screamed and the guy slashed her, and they brought her to the hospital. She was in no condition to be questioned, and the precinct hadn't done much except notify the Homicide Squad. They handled all crimes against the person, so next morning Lieutenant Decker sent Mitch and Balenky over to the hospital to make the investigation.

They found this dame with her face wrapped up in bandages. She'd been carved up and was still in shock, so they only had a few minutes with her. But what they found out was that a kind of giant with a beard two feet long had come over and called her a name. He had a gun in one hand, but his other arm didn't have a hand at all. It had a hook, and he slashed her face with it. Three deep cuts, almost evenly spaced. No attempt to rob—the first precinct report had that part of it all wrong. And no motive. Just the slashing.

That was all. Nothing to go on. Nobody she knew. No leads, no nothing.

Mitch and Balenky had come back the same afternoon and had questioned her some more, but there was nothing much to add. They got a description from her and put it on the teletype, and everybody in the department went looking for this beatnik with a beard. Or maybe he'd shaved it off, so every one-armed man in town got pulled in, but none of them had a hook and none of them could have been at the spot where the assault took place.

A week later it happened again.

Same pattern. A good-looking blonde this time. She stopped for a red light, and this loony came over with his gun and his hook, and he called her a harlot and slashed her face. Same three deep cuts. Again, no reason, no nothing.

Decker talked to her this time, with Mitch present. She had soft blue eyes that were filled with tears, and her voice sounded hurt. Mitch was shook up just hearing it, and he kept wondering what she'd look like when the bandages were finally taken off.

After that the newspapers really piled it on. A maniac was loose, and no woman in the city was safe. They called the guy Captain Hook and wanted to know what was wrong with the police department. The Commissioner advised all women driving alone to watch out when they stopped for red lights. As a result, the traffic detail was going crazy with all the minor accidents. Women went through red lights and they all had the same excuse—they'd seen somebody who might have been this loony. The police didn't give out any tickets—any judge who fined a female for going through a red light would have been howled off the bench.

There were so many tips coming through the police switchboard that they had to set up a special number for the Captain Hook calls. Some of the tips were so phony they could be thrown out without even investigating, but the rest of them had to be checked out. Every damn one of them. But there on the Homicide Squad, it was like slugging against thin air.

With the whole city going hysterical, there was no time to work on anything else. Larceny statistics went up and the crooks had a field day because they knew the police didn't have time to bother with small stuff. The capture of Captain Hook was all that mattered.

The papers proposed a fund to take care of plastic surgery for the two victims. Psychiatrists wrote special articles and went haywire, dreaming up what they thought the guy was like. They said it was all his mother's fault—she'd done something to him when he was a kid and now he was taking it out on the world, or the female part of it, anyhow. Captain Hook, they said, was probably a pillar of the church and a respected member of the community, active in stuff like campaigns for censorship and stiffer penal laws.

Mitch read all the theories, but he didn't learn much. He was right in the middle of it, too, on account he'd made the first investigation. The reports swarmed all over him, but he clammed up the way Lieutenant Decker had ordered him to, and let the Lieutenant handle the questions. Which was no picnic for him, either.

Privately, Mitch didn't have much confidence in the descriptions the two victims had given him. You wear a beard and that's all anybody notices, particularly when they're scared to death. And when you take a cut at them through a car window, you look big even if you're not standing on your toes, which you probably are. So for Mitch's money, those descriptions were like an eight-year-old telling about the big bad man he saw somewhere in the dark.

Anyway, the police were running around in circles and they knew it, and the chances were they'd keep running around for a while, only faster. So Mitch sat there next to the two cops in the squad car and kept his trap shut. And so did they. What was the sense of talking, until they got there and found out what had happened?

It was at the intersection of Irving and Holmes, just as Flaherty had said, and the precinct's cops had already roped off the area. Lieutenant Decker and Balenky were there, and so was Jub Freeman, the lab expert. They were grouped around a cream-colored sedan that had banged into the first tree down on Irving.

Mitch walked over, and in the police spotlight he saw this dame slumped over the wheel. She'd been shot in the head and there were .three jagged wounds on her face, and she looked dead all right. The door of the car was open on her side, and on the floor Mitch could see a small three-pronged cultivator with blood on it—one of those little hand-things for scratching up the soil. Amy used to have one of them for her window box.

Mitch pointed to the cultivator. "So that's Captain Hook, huh?" he said.

Decker, grim and edgy and impatient because he had to hold up everything until the Medical Examiner arrived, answered sharply. "Him, or his kid brother."

Mitch knew what the Lieutenant meant. You get a crime like this, something unusual and different, and every peanut with his brains knocked loose comes along and does the same thing, and it breaks out all over the place, like a rash.

Mitch turned to Jub Freeman. "What happened?"

But it was Decker who answered. "She was shot and marked up when she stopped over there, at the other side of the crossing. Car's got an automatic drive, so it kept crawling until it hit this tree. The guy's arm might have struck the door and had the claw jarred out of his hand after he slashed her. Anyhow, a panel truck was coming down Holmes, so our boy ran."

"He was seen?" Mitch asked hopefully.

"Sure," Decker said. "He's always seen. He has a beard, and he has a claw instead of a hand. Brother! Didn't they tell you?"

Mitch inched away and looked at Jub again, who motioned to him. Out of Decker's hearing Jub spoke in a low voice.

"The truck almost hit her car when the driver slammed down his brakes and swung out. Says he saw the guy run behind that row of houses. They're searching the back yards now, but you know what the chances are."

"Yeah," Mitch said. "But we got that claw thing, and maybe a slug."

Jub nodded. "We'll see," he said. His round face with the puffed-out cheeks gave him a perpetually cheerful look. If he was tense underneath, he didn't show it.

"What I can't figure," Mitch said, "is why a dame would let this guy walk up to the car. Everybody knows about him—that's all they talk about. Why didn't she see him coming at her?"

"Maybe she was thinking about something else," Jub said. "Maybe she was in love."

"Yeah," Mitch said drily. "Love, huh?" Then he heard the sound of a distant siren. That would be the Commissioner or the M.E. In a little while they could get started.

It took about twenty minutes before the M.E. released the body. Lieutenant Decker went over her stuff and found her driver's license. Grace Inskip, 2432 Stowe. She was wearing a wedding ring and she'd been killed only a couple of blocks from home.

The Lieutenant spoke crisply—"Taylor, you go over there and break the news. And find out whatever you can—who she was, where she was going. And get her husband to identify, if he's there."

"Right," Mitch said. He hated this kind of a job, but he couldn't worm out of it. And with the Commissioner there and the Lieutenant acting like a drill sergeant, Mitch was glad to scram.

He was moving away when Jub approached. "Mitch," he said, "get me a soil sample from her place, will you?" Jub took an envelope from his pocket and scribbled the name Inskip on it. "Just a handful, that's all I need."

"Sure," Mitch said. "You think—"

"Too soon to think," Jub said energetically. "I just want stuff to play around with."

It looked as if Jub were reaching, but he was thorough and he'd pulled plenty of miracles in the past. So if he wanted some dirt, Mitch would get it for him.

He scraped up a handful from a well-cultivated flowerbed in front of the house and put it in Jub's envelope. Then Mitch went up the porch steps and rang the bell. There was a light inside, and a gentle, flabby little man wearing a corduroy jacket opened the door. The husband, Mitch supposed.

"Mrs. Grace Inskip lives here?" Mitch asked.

The little man nodded. "Yes, she's my wife. Why? Who are you?"

"Inspector Taylor," Mitch said. "She's had a kind of accident, and—" He stumbled around in his mind for an easy way to break it, gave up, and came straight out with it. "Well, she was killed."

The little guy went white. "Oh, my!" he said. "Oh, my!" He backed off and plunked down on a chair and said, "Oh, my!" a couple more times. Then he asked how it happened and Mitch told him.

"It sounds like that Captain Hook," Inskip gasped.

"Yeah," Mitch said, "but right now I'd like to know where she was going, for instance."

Inskip looked even sicker. "I don't know," he said. "That's what's so awful about it. I don't know! She—"

He gagged and couldn't say it, but Mitch kept prodding him. "You don't know where she went? Or with whom? She told you something, didn't she? Let's have it, Mr. Inskip."

The little man finally choked out an answer. "With one of her boy friends. She had several, but I really didn't mind. I understood her because I—well, I loved her and I'm—I'm—" He couldn't find what he had started to say, so he began again. "I was waiting for her to come home . . ." And then he repeated, "Oh, my!"

"Yeah," Mitch said, feeling sorry for the little guy and wondering where this line of talk was going to lead. "Yeah," he said. "Who were they? The boy friends, I mean."

"I don't know—I didn't want to know. And they really didn't mean anything to her—not one of them. Except—"

"Except who?" Mitch said, and he bore down.

"The one with a sweet tooth. I could tell when she was going to see him because she usually made candy the day before, and took it with her. But she was afraid of him and terribly worried."

"Why?" Mitch asked, getting more interested.

"All I know is what I overheard her saying on the phone one afternoon. The window was open and I was working in the garden, and I guess she didn't know I was there. Whoever it was, she kept telling him he wasn't really bad, he couldn't help himself, and he ought to go see a doctor or else he was liable to do it again."

"Do what?"

"I don't know. But he must have said something to make her real sore, because suddenly her voice sounded angry and she said their relationship was pure and honest and she didn't want him to talk like that."

"When was this conversation?" Mitch asked.

Inskip rocked forward. "Let me think. I came home early that day. It was the day I brought those flowers she liked so much. Dwarf marigolds. I can tell by the bill—it's here somewhere."

"Let's see it," Mitch said.

Inskip got up and rummaged in the pigeonholes of a desk and came up with the bill. "The fourteenth," he said.

"Yeah," Mitch said. That would make it halfway between Captain Hook's two previous assaults. "What else do you know about this guy? The one with the sweet tooth," Mitch asked.

"Nothing. And what difference does it make? She's dead now, and it's all over."

"Sure, but we got to find out how it happened," Mitch said.

Inskip nodded and Mitch questioned him some more. But there wasn't anything else Inskip could tell him, so Mitch took the guy upstairs and got hold of Mrs. Inskip's address book and her phone memos. Then he bundled the little guy into a squad car and sent him down to the morgue, to identify.

It was after one a.m. when Mitch got back to headquarters. Morty Topps was at the big desk that you saw when you came through the double doors before going down the corridor where the offices and Squad Rooms and all the rest of the bureaus and departments and special details were located. He told Mitch that the Lieutenant was up in the lab with Jub, so Mitch went on in and climbed the stairs to the second floor.

All the lights were on in the big examination room with its work benches and the shelves loaded with equipment, all the microscopes and the scales and the jars of casting materials and electric motors and the chromatograph and the U.V. and infra-red stuff, and the test tubes and beakers and jars and hammers and saws and knives and enough stuff to keep you busy for a year just learning what they were and what for. Jub, wearing his tan smock, was busy over a microscope, and Decker was studying the green-handled scratcher and making notes on three different kinds of colored paper.

Jub said, "Hi, Mitch. Got my dirt?"

Mitch took the envelope out of his pocket and handed it to Jub. The Lieutenant said, "Well? Run into anything?"

"Maybe," Mitch said, and told his story.

Jub lost interest in his microscope, and his bright eager eyes were fixed on Mitch. Decker listened intently, and the lines in his face got tougher and deeper.

"Brother!" he exclaimed when Mitch had finished. "It could be. What hit us was why, with all this excitement about Captain Hook, any dame in her right senses would stop there and wait quietly with the car window open, and not see somebody approach. Every woman under ninety would be so jittery she'd wham through the red light with her foot on the gas instead of the brake. But if the Inskip woman recognized the guy, that explains why she waited. If she knew him, we have a lead."

"That's what I figured," Mitch said modestly.

"She was killed a couple of blocks from her home," the Lieutenant said thoughtfully. "Somebody who knew her and knew her probable route could have waited at that intersection. If he called out to her, she'd stop and wouldn't be suspicious. Then he could walk over to the car and kill her."

Mitch nodded, and so did Jub. All three of them—their minds worked the same way. They'd seen the position of the body, noted that there was no sign of a struggle. She must have been shot first and then slashed, so the case was different from the other two. Either Captain Hook knew her and planned the murder, or else this wasn't Captain Hook at all but somebody who'd deliberately used the Hook technique to misdirect the police.

"On the facts we have now," Decker said, "the best guess is either this lover with the sweet tooth, or else her husband. And if it's Inskip—" he picked up the scratcher and stared at it—"then this thing can tell us."

"Prints?" Mitch asked.

Decker shook his head. Jub said, "There was dirt on it. Not much, but enough. If the soil you brought in matches up with it, then—bingo! Where'd you get it?"

"From a flowerbed next to the porch," Mitch said.

"Good," Jub said. "That ought to do it." He spread out a half dozen bits of paper and poured a pinch of dirt from the Inskip envelope onto each of them. "On the other hand," he said—and he didn't finish the sentence.

Decker did. "On the other hand, if the soil doesn't match up, then it looks like Inskip is cleared, and we go after this lover-boy of hers. A do-gooder with a sweet tooth, and his name may be on this list." He opened her address book and glanced through it. "Quite a few names here," he said. "We have some tough work ahead of us."

Mitch knew what that meant. Regular schedules would be suspended, and the Homicide Squad would be on 24-hour duty. Time off to sleep, but they'd be at it every night until they dropped. It had happened before, on a big case, and this was one of the biggest they'd ever had.

Mitch took a long slow breath. He slept at headquarters that night.

In the morning Lieutenant Decker held a conference in the Squad Room and briefed them on what had happened. Most of what Decker summed up was information Mitch already knew, and what he didn't know turned out to be bad news. The soil from the Inskip flowerbed did not match the soil on the handle of the three-pronged scratcher.

Nevertheless, there was a feeling of excitement and tension in the Homicide Squad that morning, and it spread to the entire police force. They were on to something solid at last—negative but solid. Now they were aware that the Inskip murderer might not turn out to be Captain Hook, yet they were pretty sure they'd solve this one. It might not be easy, but they had a start and they all believed that eventually they'd turn up a clue that would break the case. After that, it would snowball.

Down at the Homicide Squad they knew in their bones it would happen exactly like that. Some insignificant detail, maybe overlooked at first, would link up with some other insignificant detail. It had to be that way.

The Homicide Squad spearheaded the investigation, but practically the entire detective force in the city was assigned to help out. Check into Inskip's background, the Inskip marriage, their finances, what the neighbors said about them. Question every person whose name was in Mrs. Inskip's address book. Trace her history, her affairs, where she'd been seen, with whom. Find out everything that people knew about her. Concentrate on where she'd been the night of her death, but don't stop there: find out what she'd done earlier in the day. Check with stores, restaurants, hotels.

Although Inskip's wife had been unfaithful and he stood to inherit a nice chunk of dough from her, the dirt scratcher pretty well cleared him. The police might get around to him again later on, as a last resort, but first things came first: the soil identification was an absolute must—that and finding the lover with the sweet tooth were tops on the list.

Meanwhile, Jub and his assistants went through soil tests, and drew one blank after another. Jub vacuum-cleaned the death car and analyzed every fiber, every bit of dust. But nothing came of it.

Mitch hardly saw Amy these hectic days, but he remembered those dwarf marigolds she wanted, and late one afternoon he drove out to the

Inskip house and rang the bell. A dumpy female with tiny black eyes answered. She looked as if she wanted to go to the movies with Mitch and eat popcorn and hold hands. She said she was Inskip's sister and he wasn't feeling very well, but she wasn't busy right now and would Mitch like to come inside.

"What I came for," Mitch said, "was maybe I could dig up a few of those tiny marigolds. The wife kind of goes for them, and I thought if Mr. Inskip doesn't mind—"

"Oh," she said, as if Mitch's being married had busted up some kind of dream. But she survived all right, and she didn't hold it against him.

"Go ahead," she said, to show her generosity. "Take all you want. They were Mrs. Inskip's, and my brother doesn't particularly like them. They're at the back of the house."

"Thanks," Mitch said.

He got the trowel from his car and dug up a few and packed them in a hunk of newspaper. Then he went back to headquarters and divided them up as Amy had told him to, half for her and half for Jub's wife, and he brought Jub's to the lab.

Jub wasn't there, so Mitch took the bunch and carried it back downstairs and left it in Jub's car. Later on, when Mitch went home to dinner, he brought Amy her half of the marigolds. He'd lost the trowel somewhere on the way, but he was still one up on the case: he'd gotten Amy's flowers out of it.

The next day everybody was still plugging away, but you could kind of feel the letdown. They'd gone off half cocked, they'd been too sure of themselves, and the papers were riding the police again.

One by one the names in Mrs. Inskip's address book got crossed off, and the Homicide Squad was slipping back into the nightmare of having nothing to grab hold of. And the Captain Hook switchboard was getting twice the calls it used to—from all the cranks who knew a do-gooder with a sweet tooth as well as those who knew a psycho with a beard.

On the fifth day Mitch was running down a tip about a Boy Scout leader who liked fudge and bought it wholesale, and Mitch felt like a dope when he asked his questions. He was driving Number 4, his regular car, and he'd just spoken to the manager of a candy factory and had drawn another blank, along with some wisecracks about whether the police were tracking down a killer or just wanted to learn the caramel business.

When Mitch came out to start his car, his radio phone buzzed and he picked it up.

"Taylor, Car Four," he said.

"Report to Lieutenant Decker at once," the sergeant said. "Please acknowledge."

Mitch did, then hung up and started back. He drove at his usual pace, wondering what the hell the Lieutenant wanted now. And why pick on him, for Pete's sake. He was feeling low, like the rest of the squad, and asking himself how long they could keep looking for somebody who maybe didn't even exist. After all, how did they know there was such a guy, except that Inskip had heard his wife say something on the phone, and he'd told how she made candy for someone. And maybe Inskip was all mixed up.

Nobody was excited about anything when Mitch got back to headquarters, and the girl in the outer office said Decker was up in the lab, to go see him there. So Mitch trudged up the flight of stairs and walked in. Jub whirled and looked happy, and Decker jumped off a stool like he'd been goosed.

"Taylor," he said, "Where'd you get that trowel?"

"Trowel?" Mitch said, stalling and trying to get his bearings.

"The one you left here for me. The other day," Jub said, "while I was out."

"That?" Mitch said, glad that he hadn't lost the thing after all. "It's Amy's. I been looking for it. Why?"

"Because the soil on it matches the soil on the scratcher," Decker said, and he was all steamed up. "Where did you use it?"

Mitch blinked. "I dug up some marigolds at the Inskips," he said. "They were in a special flowerbed in the back."

"Brother!" Decker yelled. "If the Inskips brought in special soil for that flowerbed, then it would be different from all the other samples around the house. That's why we went wrong, but now we've got him!"

So, as Mitch told Amy that night, without her and those dwarf marigolds she wanted, maybe the case of Captain Hook would never have been cracked. But on account of them, they had Inskip cold. Once they went to work on him and got a warrant and tore the place apart, they found the false beard and the gun. And it was the same gun that had killed Grace Inskip.

After that the guy confessed. His wife's two-timing was more than he could take, but divorce was no good because she had all the dough and in a divorce she'd hang onto it. Then he hit on this idea of slashing a couple of dames and setting up a pattern so that, when he killed his wife, it would look like another Captain Hook murder, unmotivated and completely unconnected with the Inskip marital troubles.

Amy listened in a kind of shock. "How horrible!" she said, when Mitch had finished. "And those marigolds—I don't want them, I don't even want to see them. Throw them out."

"Look," Mitch said. "What's there to get so excited about?"

"I can't look at them," Amy exclaimed. "It's awful—you just don't understand."

Mitch frowned at her and tried to figure it out. She wanted flowers, didn't she? So if she had something against marigolds, he'd get her some other kind. That florist up on Emerson, for instance, could give him some good advice. If Mitch went up there and asked him, and then maybe mentioned a violation or two, the guy would be glad to give him some stuff for free. No real problem there.

The only thing was, Mitch had to get another trowel, on account Amy's was up in the lab and Jub was hanging onto it. And somehow, it just didn't seem right—Mitch having to get Amy another trowel. And he'd have to buy it too—there was no way he could think of to get one for free.

FOR DISCUSSION: **D as in Detail**

1. Successful police detection is the result, as the title suggests, of attention to details. List five examples of attention to detail that helped to lead to a solution.
2. In this particular story coincidence plays a part several times. This is usually considered "unfair," but coincidences do exist in life. List all the coincidences you can remember; then analyze them. Are they farfetched, or are they natural? Might they really occur?
3. Treat begins and ends with references to a trowel and some marigolds. Why does he emphasize these unexciting objects?
4. The last paragraph sums up Mitch's personality and at the same time provides contrast with the technological core of the story. What does it tell the reader about Mitch and about his attitude toward his work?
5. Modern detection frequently uses the team approach. Who are the members of the team? What kind of work is each team member responsible for?

INTRODUCTION: The Red Silk Scarf

Unlike the detectives in the preceding stories of this unit, Arsène Lupin is a scoundrel. He steals joyfully (usually from the rich), ridicules with abandon (especially the pompous), and delights in both his mental and physical agility. He's a sort of twentieth-century Robin Hood who espouses not amorality, but a morality of his own.

Like the traditional detectives, though, Lupin knows full well the value of physical clues, of "fingerprints and footprints." With an ingenuity that is truly awe-inspiring, he interprets clues left by another criminal while casually sprinkling a few new ones to distract and delude the police. He juggles simultaneously circumstantial evidence, a knowledge of human nature, and a desire to avenge the real victims of crime and oppression. But Lupin's most endearing—and enduring—trait is his marvelous zest for life, including his own.

The Red Silk Scarf
Maurice Leblanc

That morning, leaving his home at the usual time to go to the law court, Chief Inspector Ganimard noted the rather curious activity of a man walking ahead of him along Rue Pergolèse.

Shabbily dressed and wearing a straw hat despite the November weather, every fifty or sixty feet, the man bent over either to pick up his cane, or tie his shoelaces, or for some other reason. And each time, he drew a tiny bit of orange peel from his pocket and furtively left it on the very edge of the sidewalk.

Simply an idiosyncrasy, no doubt, a childish amusement to which no one else would have paid any attention; but Ganimard was one of those perspicacious observers who overlook nothing and who are not satisfied until they know the secret reason for things. And so he began to follow the man.

Now at the very moment that the man turned right into Avenue de la Grande-Armée, Ganimard caught him exchanging signs with an urchin of some twelve years who was walking in front of the houses on the left-hand side.

Twenty yards farther on, the man bent down and lifted the bottom of his trouser leg. A piece of orange peel marked his passage. At the same instant, the little boy stopped in front of a house, and, using a piece of chalk, drew a white cross within a circle on the wall.

The two of them continued their promenade. A moment later, they stopped again. The man picked up a pin and dropped another piece of orange peel, and instantly the little boy drew another white cross and a white circle around it on the wall.

"This looks like it might lead to something," thought the inspector with a pleased grunt. "What in the world could those two be up to?"

"Those two" went down Avenue Friedland and along Rue du Faubourg Saint Honoré without anything unusual occurring.

At rather regular intervals, the double operation recommenced—mechanically, as it were. However, it was obvious that the man with the orange peels never performed his part before choosing the house to be marked, while the boy did not mark the house until he had observed his companion's signal.

There must have been some previous agreement, and the astonishing maneuver was of considerable interest in the eyes of Chief Inspector Ganimard.

At Place Beauvau, the man hesitated. Then, apparently making up his mind, he lifted and dropped the bottom of his trouser leg twice. Thereupon, the boy sat down on the edge of the sidewalk in front of the soldier mounting guard at the Ministry of the Interior, and drew two small crosses in two small circles on the cobblestones.

At the Champs Elysées, they performed the very same ceremony. But on the pavement where the sentinel walked up and down before the house of the President of the Republic, there were three signs instead of two.

"What does this mean?" mumbled Ganimard, pale with agitation. He couldn't help but think of his eternal enemy Lupin, just as he thought of him every time any mysterious event occurred. . . .

"What does this mean?"

He very nearly collared the two to interrogate them. But Ganimard was too crafty to commit such a blunder. Besides, the man with the orange peels had lit a cigarette, and the little boy, holding a cigarette stub, had come over to him, apparently to ask him for a light.

The two of them exchanged a few words. The boy quickly handed his companion an object which, as far as the inspector could tell, had the form of a revolver in a holster. The man and the boy huddled over this object, and, facing the wall, the man reached into his pocket six times and seemed to be loading the gun.

When he was done, they retraced their steps and turned into Rue de Surène; the inspector trailed behind as closely as possible, even at the risk of being noticed by them. He watched them pass through the portico of an old house, all of whose shutters, with the exception of those on the third and top floor, were closed.

Off he went after them. From the carriage gateway he could see into a huge courtyard: at the back, there was a house painter's sign, and at the left, a stairway.

He mounted the steps; reaching the first floor, he began to hurry, hearing from way up high a noise like the sound of blows or knocking.

On the top landing, he came to an open door. He stepped through, cocked his ear for a moment, made out the sounds of a struggle, dashed into the room from which the din seemed to be coming, and stopped short at the threshold, out of breath and extremely surprised to see the man with the orange peels and the boy, both of whom were banging chairs against the floor.

Just at that moment, a third person entered from the next room: a young man of twenty-eight or thirty, with short sideburns, eyeglasses, and an astrakhan smoking jacket. He looked foreign, Russian probably.

"*Bonjour*, Ganimard," he said.

And to his companions:

"Thank you so much, my friends, and my compliments on your success. Here is the little reward I promised you."

He gave them a hundred-franc note, motioned for them to leave, and then closed both doors.

"My apologies, old friend," he said to Ganimard. "I simply had to talk to you . . . it's most urgent."

He offered him his hand, and since the inspector stood there flabbergasted, his face ravaged with anger, the young man exclaimed:

"You don't seem to understand. Yet it's quite simple . . . I *had* to see you. And so . . ."

And, as if replying to an objection:

"No, no, old friend, you're quite wrong. If I had written or rung you up, you wouldn't have come . . . or else you would have arrived with a whole regiment of your cohorts. And I wanted to see you alone, so I thought I could simply send out those two people to meet you. I told them to leave a trail of orange peels as well as crosses in circles so that you might find your way here. What is it? You looked bewildered. Is something the matter? Don't you recognize me . . . Arsène Lupin? Rack your brain. Doesn't that name evoke anything for you?"

"Devil!" snapped Ganimard through clenched teeth.

Looking somewhat heartbroken, Lupin replied affectionately, "You're angry? Yes, I can see it in your eyes. . . . Because of the Dugrival affair, I suppose. I should have waited for you to come and arrest me? I'm afraid, however, that the thought never entered my mind! But I swear to you that next time—"

"Swindler!" muttered Ganimard.

"And I thought you'd be so pleased. Why, I said to myself, 'Good old Ganimard, it's been such a long time since we've seen one another. He'll probably fling his arms around me.'"

Ganimard, who still hadn't budged, seemed to be shaking off his stupor. He glanced around him, looked at Lupin, and obviously wondered whether he might not really fling his arms around him, but with more violent intent. Pulling himself together, he grabbed a chair and sat down, apparently having made up his mind to listen to his adversary.

"Go ahead, talk," he said, "but no nonsense. I'm in a hurry."

"Fine," said Lupin, "let's talk. I couldn't imagine a more tranquil place. This is an old mansion, and it belongs to the Duke de Rochelaure. Since he never uses it, he rented this whole floor out to me and he allows me to share the grounds with a house-painting enterprise. I have several homes of this sort, all of them highly practical. Here, although I may look like a Russian lord, my name is Monsieur Jean Dubreuil, a former minister. . . . As you can see, I chose a slightly overcrowded profession so as not to attract attention—"

"What makes you think I'm at all interested?" Ganimard broke in.

"You're so right, here I am chattering away, and you're pressed for time. My apologies, but it won't take long. Five minutes . . . I'll begin. A cigar? No? Fine. I won't smoke either."

He sat down, drummed his fingers on the table as he reflected, and began:

"On October 17, 1599, on a lovely day that was both hot and joyous— are you following?—well, on October 17, 1599. . . . But really, must I go back to the reign of Henry the Fourth and review the chronicle of the Pont Neuf? No, you're probably not up on your French history, and I don't want to run the risk of confusing you. It's enough for you to know that last night, toward one o'clock, a bargeman passing beneath the leftmost arch of that selfsame Pont Neuf, near the Left Bank, heard something drop onto the prow of his *péniche,* something that had been thrown from the bridge and was obviously destined for a watery grave. The bargeman's dog started barking and dashed after it, and when the master came to the front of his barge, he saw the dog shaking a piece of newspaper in which several curious objects were wrapped. The bargeman picked up these objects which hadn't fallen into the water and, returning to his cabin, he examined them. What he saw struck him as most interesting, and since he knows a friend of mine, he asked that I be informed. This very morning, someone woke me up to tell me the whole story and give me the objects. And here they are."

He pointed to them, spread out on a table. First of all, there were the torn pieces of a newspaper. Next, there was a large crystal inkwell, with a long piece of string tied to the lid. Next, a tiny fragment of glass, then a sort of flexible cardboard reduced to pulp. And finally, a piece of scarlet silk with a tassel of the same color.

"Exhibit A, old friend," said Lupin. "We'd have an easier time solving the problem if the dog hadn't been so stupid as to lose the other objects. But I think we'll manage, with a bit of reflection and intelligence. And after all, those are your best qualities, aren't they? What do you think?"

Ganimard didn't turn a hair. He was willing to submit to Lupin's chatter, but his dignity did not permit him to reply, either verbally or by nodding or shaking his head.

"I see that we're in complete agreement," continued Lupin, apparently unaware of the inspector's silence. "Let me sum up in a succinct sentence the whole case in terms of what this evidence reveals. *Last night, between nine and midnight, an unmarried woman of rather eccentric ways was stabbed several times and then choked to death by a gentleman who was well-dressed, wore a monocle, frequented racetrack society, and with whom the aforesaid lady had just eaten three meringues and an éclair in a café.*"

Lupin lit a cigarette, and seizing Ganimard's sleeve, said:

"Well, sort of takes the wind out of your sails, Inspector, doesn't it? You thought that in the domain of detective work, such tours de force were forbidden to the layman. That was a mistake, monsieur. Lupin juggles deductions like a detective in a flashy novel. What proof do I have? Proof that's blinding and infantile."

And, going through the objects, he said, "First of all: *last night after nine* (this scrap of newspaper bears yesterday's date and says 'evening paper'; furthermore, as you can see, there's a bit of a yellow strip attached to it, one of those yellow strips in which the gazettes are mailed to subscribers, and they only arrive with the nine P.M. mail). And so, after nine o'clock, *a well-dressed gentleman* (please note that the small fragment of glass has the round rim of a monocle, and that the monocle is essentially an aristocratic accessory), *a well-dressed gentleman entered a bakery* (here is the very thin cardboard in the form of a box, and you can still make out a bit of meringue cream and a trace of the éclair, which were crowded together in the usual way). Carrying his package, the man in the monocle met the young woman whose scarlet silk scarf is a sufficient indication of her *eccentric ways*. Next, for reasons that are still unknown, *he stabbed her with a knife several times, and then strangled her with the silk scarf*. (If you reach for your magnifying glass, Inspector, and examine the silk, you'll notice spots of a darker red, the marks of a knife that was wiped, and here you see the traces of a bloodstained hand clutching the silk.) The gentleman, upon committing his crime and so as not to leave any traces behind, took from his pocket: first, the newspaper he subscribes to, and which (take a look at the scrap) is a racing gazette, whose title you can easily find out; second, a piece of cord which turns out to be a whipcord (and these two details prove that our man is interested in horseracing and is directly involved with horses himself). Next, he picked up the pieces of his monocle, the string of which had ripped during the fight. He used his scissors (note the cutting marks) to cut off the stained part of the scarf, leaving the remaining part in the clenched hands of the victim. Then he crumpled up the baker's cardboard box into a ball. He also added certain incriminating objects, which are probably at the bottom of the Seine now—for example, the knife. He rolled up everything into the newspaper, used some string to attach the crystal inkwell in order to weight the parcel down, then off he went. A moment later, the package dropped onto the barge. *Voilà.* Ouf! The whole thing makes me quite uncomfortable. What do you think of it?"

He stared at Ganimard to see what effect his words had had on him. But Ganimard maintained a stubborn silence.

Lupin burst out laughing.

"Staggering, isn't it? But you're on your guard. Why is that devil Lupin letting me in on this, instead of keeping it for himself, going after the murderer, and robbing him of anything he stole? It's a logical question. But—there's always a but—I don't have the time. A burglary in London, another in Lausanne, then I have to substitute a child in Marseilles, and rescue a girl stalked by death. In short, everything is descending on me at the same time. So I thought to myself: 'Why not let good old Ganimard in on it? Now that it's half solved, he ought to be able to finish it off. And what a great favor I'm doing him! He'll distinguish himself no end.'

"No sooner said than done. At eight o'clock this morning I sent the man with the orange peels out to meet you. You swallowed the bait, and at nine o'clock you arrived here, wriggling like a fish on a hook."

Lupin had gotten up. He leaned toward the inspector and said, looking him straight in the eye:

"And that's that. The matter is settled. You'll probably know who the victim is soon enough . . . some ballet dancer or café singer. On the other hand, there's a good chance that the murderer lives near the Pont Neuf, probably on the Left Bank. Well, here's the evidence. Be my guest. And do a good job. I'll just keep this piece of scarf. If you need to piece the scarf together, bring me the other end, the part that the law will find on the victim's neck. Hand it over to me a month from today, the twenty-eighth of December at ten A.M. You can be sure of finding me here. And don't be afraid: the whole matter is quite serious, old friend, my word of honor. I'm not playing a practical joke on you.

Forge ahead! Incidentally, a detail of some importance: when you arrest the man with the monocle, be careful—he's left-handed. So long, old chum, and best of luck."

Lupin twirled about, strode to the door, opened it, and vanished. Ganimard did not wait to make up his mind. He leaped over to the door —only to discover that due to some device or other, the knob did not turn. It took Ganimard ten minutes to unscrew the lock, and ten more to unscrew the lock in the front room. He rushed down the stairs without the slightest hope of catching up with Arsène Lupin.

It never even occurred to him that he could. Lupin evoked a strange and complex feeling in him, a mixture of fear and bitterness, involuntary admiration and a dim sense that despite all his efforts, all the persistence of his pursuit, he would never get the better of such an adversary. His pursuit was a blend of duty and ego, but he was haunted by the constant fear of being duped by this formidable mystifier and made a fool of before a public that was always ready to laugh at his misfortunes.

And the affair of the red scarf seemed rather dubious to him. An interesting enough hypothesis, but so improbable! And Lupin's explanation, so logical on the surface, would hardly survive a thorough examination.

"No," said Ganimard, "the whole thing's a joke . . . a mass of guesswork without any basis. I won't bother with it."

By the time he reached his office at 36 Quai des Orfèvres, he had absolutely made up his mind to declare the incident null and void.

He went upstairs to the Sûreté, the criminal investigation department.

"Have you seen the chief?" one of his colleagues asked.

"No."

"He was asking for you a little while ago."

"Really?"

"Yes, go join him."

"Where?"

"On Rue de Berne. A murder was committed there last night."

"Who was the victim?"

"I don't know for sure . . . some café singer, I think."

"Good Lord!"

Twenty minutes later, he came out of the *métro* and walked toward Rue de Berne.

The victim, known in the theater world by her stage name, Jenny Saphir, had occupied a modest apartment on the third floor of the building. Led by a policeman, Chief Inspector Ganimard crossed two rooms and entered the bedroom to find the investigating magistrates, the head of the Sûreté, and a medical expert.

Ganimard began trembling the moment he looked. On the couch lay the corpse of a young woman, her hands still gripping a piece of red silk. Her shoulder, revealed by the V-shaped neckline, bore two wounds clotted with blood. Her face was convulsed, almost black, and the expression was one of insane terror.

The coroner, finishing his examination, said, "My initial conclusions are quite certain. The victim was stabbed twice with a dagger and then strangled. A clear case of death by asphyxia."

"Good Lord!" thought Ganimard once more, recalling Lupin's words, his depiction of the crime.

"But her neck shows no signs of ecchymosis," the investigating magistrate objected.

"The strangling," said the doctor, "could have been done with this silk scarf, which the victim was wearing, and a piece of which is clutched in her hands in what must have been an attempt to defend herself."

"But why is this piece all that's left?" asked the magistrate. "What happened to the other part?"

"The other piece may have been bloodstained, and perhaps the killer took it with him. You can still make out the quick slashing marks of scissors."

"Good Lord!" repeated Ganimard through his teeth for the third time. "That devil Lupin saw everything without even being here!"

"And what about the motive?" asked the judge. "All the locks have been broken, the closets and wardrobes have been turned inside out. Do you have any information, Monsieur Dudouis?"

The head of the Sûreté replied:

"I can at least advance a hypothesis, based on the cleaning woman's statements. The victim was not very talented as a singer, but she *was* known for her good looks. Two years ago she took a trip to Russia and returned with a magnificent sapphire which was said to have been given to her by someone at the Czar's court. From then on, people called her Jenny Saphir; she was very proud of the gift, although for reasons of prudence she never had it on her. Isn't it possible that the murderer wanted to steal the sapphire?"

"But the cleaning woman knew where it was hidden, didn't she?"

"No, nobody knew. And judging by the chaos in this room, the murderer didn't know either."

"We ought to interrogate the cleaning woman," said the investigating magistrate.

Dudouis took Chief Inspector Ganimard aside and said, "You look rather odd, Ganimard. Is something amiss? Do you suspect something?"

"Nothing at all, chief."

"Too bad. The Sûreté could really use a coup. Several crimes of this sort have been committed, and we haven't been able to find the culprit. This time, we've got to get him, and right away!"

"That won't be easy, chief."

"We've got to, I tell you. Listen to me, Ganimard. According to the chambermaid, Jenny Saphir led a very regular life: for the past month, when she came home from the theater, around ten-thirty in the evening, she always had company, a man who stayed until midnight. 'He's high society,' Jenny Saphir would say, 'he wants to marry me.' This gentleman took every precaution not to be seen: he always drew up his coat collar and pulled his hat brim down over his face when he passed the concierge. And Jenny Saphir always sent her chambermaid away before he arrived."

"Did he leave any clues, any traces at all?"

"None. We're obviously up against a very sly customer. He planned his crime and carried it out with every possible precaution. If we get him, it will be a feather in our cap. I'm counting on you, Ganimard."

"You're counting on me, are you?" replied the chief inspector. "Well, we'll see . . . I'm not saying no . . . only . . ."

He seemed very nervous, and his agitation struck Monsieur Dudouis.

"Only," continued Ganimard, "only I swear . . . do you hear me? I swear . . ."

"You swear what?"

"Nothing. We'll see. We'll see."

It was only after he left that Ganimard finished his sentence. And he finished it out loud, stamping his foot as he exclaimed furiously:

"Only, I swear before God that I'll catch the murderer my own way, and without using any of the information that Lupin gave me."

Cursing Lupin, enraged at getting involved in the case, and determined to solve it, he wandered about aimlessly. His brain was teeming, he tried to straighten out his thoughts and discover among the few available facts some tiny detail which had eluded both Lupin and the others, and which might lead him to success.

He had a quick lunch at a café and then continued walking—only to halt suddenly, puzzled and stupefied. He had come to the portico on Rue de Surène, the very house to which Lupin had lured him a few hours earlier. A force more powerful than his own will had brought him back. The solution to the problem was there. All the elements of the truth were there. Do what he might, Lupin's assertions were so exact, his calculations so precise, that Ganimard, cut to the quick by such prodigious theorizing, could only take up the work where his enemy had left off.

No longer resisting, he mounted the three flights. The apartment was open. No one had touched the evidence. He pocketed it.

From that moment on, he thought and acted almost mechanically, prompted by the Master whom he had no choice but to obey.

If the murderer did live near Pont Neuf, Ganimard had to find the bakery where the cakes had been bought; it must lie on a street connecting the bridge with Rue de Berne. His investigations did not take long. Near the Saint Lazare Station, a baker showed him small cardboard boxes, identical in form and material to the one Ganimard had. Furthermore, one of the shopgirls recalled that the night before she had waited on a man whose face was covered by his fur collar, although she had noticed that he was wearing a monocle.

"Our first clue has been checked out," thought Ganimard. "Our man wears a monocle."

Next, he pieced together the shreds of the racing gazette and showed them to a newspaper dealer who instantly recognized *Le Turf Illustré*. Thereupon, he went to the *Turf* office and asked to see the list of subscribers, noting all those who lived near the Pont Neuf, and especially those on the Left Bank, *because Lupin had said so.*

Then he returned to the Sûreté, recruited a half-dozen men, and sent them out with the necessary instructions.

At seven P.M., the last of these men came back and told him the good news. A certain Monsieur Prévailles, who subscribed to *Le Turf Illustré*, had a second-floor apartment on the Quai des Augustins. The previous evening, he had left his home, dressed in a fur-lined coat; the concierge had handed him his mail, including *Le Turf Illustré;* he had gone out, and then returned around midnight.

Monsieur Prévailles wore a monocle. He was a racetrack habitué and even owned several horses, which he rode or put out for hire.

The investigation had been so rapid, the results so much in keeping with Lupin's predictions, that Ganimard remained speechless upon hearing the detective's report. Once again, he gauged the tremendous resources at Lupin's disposal. Never in all his life had he come across such clairvoyance, such sharpness of mind, such alert thinking.

He went to see Monsieur Dudouis.

"Everything's set. Get me a warrant."

"What?"

"I said everything's all set for the arrest."

"You know who killed Jenny Saphir?"

"Yes."

"But how did you do it? Tell me."

Ganimard felt some qualms, reddened slightly, but answered:

"A fluke, chief. The murderer threw a mass of incriminating evidence into the Seine. Part of the package was recovered and given to me."

"By whom?"

"A bargeman who didn't want to reveal his name—he was afraid they'd get him. But I obtained all the necessary evidence. The rest was easy."

And Ganimard told how he had gone about it.

"And you call that a fluke!" exclaimed Dudouis. "And you say it was easy. Why, that's one of your best jobs. Carry it out on your own, Ganimard, and be careful."

Ganimard was in a hurry to complete the case. He went straight to Quai des Augustins with his men, whom he told to surround the place. He questioned the concierge, and she declared that her tenant always ate out, but usually came home after dinner.

And in point of fact, shortly before nine o'clock, the concierge, leaning out her window, signaled to Ganimard, who immediately emitted a low whistle. A gentleman in a high hat and a pelisse was coming down the sidewalk along the Seine. He crossed the street in the direction of the house.

Ganimard accosted him.

"Are you Monsieur Prévailles?"

"Yes, who are you?"

"I have the duty—"

There was no time for him to finish. At the sight of the men who were emerging from the darkness, Prévailles had quickly backed up against the wall; still facing his adversaries, he kept his back toward the door of a ground-floor shop whose shutters were closed.

"Keep away," he shouted. "I don't know who you are."

His right hand clutched a heavy cane, while his left hand, slipping behind him, tried to open the door.

Ganimard realized that the man might slip inside and then escape by some secret exit.

"Come along, no funny business," he said, drawing nearer. "You're caught. Now surrender peacefully."

But the very instant he grabbed Prévailles' cane, Ganimard recalled Lupin's warning: the man was left-handed, and he was obviously reaching for his revolver.

Ganimard ducked quickly, for he had seen Prévailles' abrupt motion. Two shots shattered the silence. No one was hurt.

A few seconds later, Prévailles was struck in the jaw by a gun butt and dropped to the ground. At nine o'clock, they consigned him to a cell at police headquarters.

Ganimard now enjoyed a great reputation. The quick capture, carried out by such simple means, which the police immediately divulged, brought him sudden fame. Prévailles was charged with all sorts of unsolved crimes, and the newspapers extolled Ganimard's prowess.

The case moved ahead swiftly. First, it was established that Prévailles, whose real name was Thomas Derocq, had already had a skirmish or two with the law. His home was searched and although no new evidence was found, the police discovered a ball of cord similar to the cord used to tie up the package; in addition, they came upon daggers capable of producing wounds like those on the victim.

But a week later, everything changed. Prévailles had refused to answer any questions, and now, with his lawyer's help he came up with an airtight alibi: on the evening of the crime, he had been at the Folies-Bergère.

And in point of fact, after going through his tuxedo, they found a ticket stub and a program, both bearing that evening's date.

The investigating magistrate suggested that the alibi had been prepared beforehand.

"Prove it," said Prévailles.

Confrontations! The salesgirl in the bakery *seemed to recall* the gentleman with the monocle. The concierge in Rue de Berne *seemed to recall* the gentleman who visited Jenny Saphir. But no one could testify to more than that.

The investigation could turn up nothing more precise, no solid ground on which to base a serious accusation.

The magistrate sent for Ganimard and told him of their troubles.

"It's impossible for me to labor the point any further; I need sound evidence."

"But you know you're right, Magistrate! Prévailles would never have offered resistance when we arrested him if he weren't guilty."

"He claims he thought he was being attacked. He even claims he never saw Jenny Saphir, and we haven't found anyone who can testify against him. And besides, if the sapphire was stolen, we haven't been able to find it at his place."

"Nor anywhere else," objected Ganimard.

"Perhaps, but that's not incriminating evidence. Do you know what we need, Monsieur Ganimard, and right away? The other half of the red scarf."

"The other half?"

"Yes. It's obvious that the murderer carried it off with him, because his bloodstained fingerprints were on it."

Ganimard did not answer. Several days earlier, he had come to realize that the whole affair was leading in that direction. There was no other evidence possible. With the silk scarf, and with that alone, Prévailles' guilt was certain. And Ganimard had to insure the man's guilt. For having brought about his arrest and acquired renown for doing so, he was extolled as the redoubtable adversary of the underworld, and if Prévailles were released, Ganimard would become the laughingstock of Paris.

Unfortunately, the unique and indispensable proof was in the pocket of Arsène Lupin. What could Ganimard do?

He searched and searched, he exhausted himself with more investigations, reopened the inquiry, spent sleepless nights sifting through the mystery of Rue de Berne, reconstructed Prévailles' existence, mobilized ten men to discover the whereabouts of the vanished sapphire. All of it useless!

On December 27, the investigating magistrate summoned him to the court.

"Well, Ganimard, anything new?"

"No, sir."

"In that case, I'll have to give up."

"Wait just one more day."

"Why? We need the other half of the scarf: have you got it?"

"I'll have it tomorrow."

"Tomorrow?"

"Yes, but give me the part that's in your possession."

"What will you give me in return?"

"The entire scarf."

"Very well."

Ganimard entered the magistrate's private study. He came back out with the tattered piece of scarf.

"*Crenom de bon sang,* I'll go after the evidence," he grumbled, "and I'll get it. If only Lupin has the courage to appear at our rendezvous."

Actually, he didn't have the slightest doubt that Lupin would have the audacity, and that was what particularly annoyed him. Why was Lupin so set on the appointment? What was he aiming at?

Gnawed by anxiety, furious, filled with hate, he resolved to take all the necessary precautions, not only to keep from falling into a trap, but also, since the opportunity presented itself, to trap his old enemy. And the next day, the twenty-eighth of December, the date set by Lupin, Ganimard went to his appointment. The whole night before, he had studied the old mansion on Rue de Surène. Making sure that there was no exit other than the large front gate, he told his men that he was going out on a dangerous expedition and arrived with them on the field of battle.

He stationed them in a café. The instructions were simple: if he appeared at one of the windows on the third floor or if he didn't return within an hour, the detectives were to surround the house and arrest anyone trying to leave.

Ganimard made sure that his revolver was working and that he could pull it out easily. Then he went upstairs.

He was rather surprised to see that everything was the way it had been left; the doors were open and the locks broken. After establishing that the windows of the main room really did face the street, he checked the other three rooms that made up the apartment. No one was there.

"Lupin lost his nerve," he murmured, not without a certain satisfaction.

"Don't be a fool," said a voice behind him.

Turning around he saw an old worker in the long smock of a house painter.

"Don't rack your brains," said the man. "It's I, Lupin. I've been working all day at the house painter's establishment. As we've just stopped for lunch, I thought I'd come up."

He stared at Ganimard with a joyful smile and exclaimed: "Ah, Ganimard, I'm indebted to you for the pleasure of this moment. As fond of you as I am, I wouldn't have missed it for the world. What do you think, you artist you? Did I do a good job of solving the mystery of the scarf? I won't claim there were no holes in my logic and no links missing in the chain . . . but what a masterpiece of intelligence! What a reconstruction, Ganimard! What superb intuition, what an exquisite hypothesis of everything that happened and *was* to happen—from the discovery of the crime until your arrival here in search of evidence! What truly brilliant guesswork! Have you got the scarf?"

"Half of it. Have you got the rest?"

"Here it is. Let's compare."

They spread the two pieces of silk out on the table. The scissors cuts fitted exactly. Moreover the color was identical.

"But I suppose," said Lupin, "that you didn't just come for that. What interests you are the bloodstains. Let's go into the other room; the light's not strong enough here."

They passed into the adjoining room, which faced the court and was actually much lighter. Lupin held up his part of the scarf against the windowpane.

"Look," he said, making room for Ganimard.

The inspector trembled with joy. There were distinct traces of five fingers and the palm of a hand. The proof was unchallengeable. The murderer's bloodstained hand, the same hand that had stabbed Jenny Saphir, had clutched the scarf and twisted it around her neck.

"And it's obviously a left hand," said Lupin. "Which is why I warned you; it was no miracle, you see. I don't mind your considering my mind superior, but I don't care to have you treat me like a magician."

Ganimard quickly pocketed the scrap of silk. Lupin expressed his approval.

"That's right, old boy, it's yours. I'm so happy to see you happy! And you see, there was no trap laid for you . . . it was merely a favor . . . a friendly service for an old friend. And also, I must admit, a modicum of curiosity. . . . Yes, I wanted to examine the other piece of silk. The one the police found. Don't be afraid, I'll give it back. . . . One second."

Nonchalantly he played with the tassel at the other end of the scarf, while Ganimard listened to him in spite of himself.

"They're so ingenious, these examples of women's handiwork! Did you notice a detail during your investigation? Jenny Saphir was quite skillful and made all her own hats and clothing. This scarf was obviously her own handiwork. And I realized it immediately. Curious dog that I am. I found that the poor girl had put a tiny St. Christopher's medal as a sort of good-luck charm into the tassel. A poignant touch, don't you think? A tiny St. Christopher's medal."

The inspector's eyes were riveted on Lupin, who went on:

"And so I thought to myself: how interesting it would be to explore the other half of the scarf, the part the police would find twisted around the victim's neck! For the other half, *which I finally have in my hand*, has the same kind of tassel at its end. I wanted to see if it had the same hidingplace and I wanted to inspect its contents. Just look at this, how cleverly it's worked! And so uncomplicated! All you have to do is take a skein of red silk and braid it around a knob so that a little space is left in the middle of the tassel, a rather narrow space, to be sure, but large enough for a tiny medal or anything else . . . a jewel, for example . . . a sapphire."

That very instant, he undid the strands of silk and from the center of the tassel plucked an admirable blue stone, perfectly pure and superbly cut.

"Well, what do you say to that, my friend?"

He looked up. Ganimard was livid, his eyes were haggard; he stood there gaping, fascinated by the sparkling jewel. Now he understood everything.

"You swindler!" he murmured, falling back on the insult he had used at their first encounter.

The two men were facing one another.

"Hand it over," said Ganimard.

Lupin gave him the piece of silk.

"The sapphire, too," commanded Ganimard.

"Are you crazy?"

"Give it to me, or else . . ."

"Or else what, you fool?" exclaimed Lupin. "Why do you think I passed the case on to you?"

"Give that back to me!"

"Surely you must be joking? For a month now I've been making you run around like the simpleton that you are. 'Here, Ganimard, fetch this, carry that, like a good little dog.' That's all you've been for the past four weeks . . . 'Good little puppy-wuppy! Stand on your hind legs . . . here's a little bone for you. . . .' "

Barely containing the anger boiling up in him, Ganimard thought of only one thing: to call his men. And since the room he was in faced the back, he slowly edged toward the door. He would jump to the window in the other room and smash one of the panes.

"You and the others at the Sûreté really are a bit thick," continued Lupin. "During all this time that you've had the scrap of silk, it never occurred to a single one of you to feel it, not a single one of you ever wondered why the poor girl hung on to her scarf so desperately. Not a single one! You simply bumble on, without ever reflecting or thinking ahead!"

The inspector had reached his goal. Taking advantage of a moment when Lupin had moved away, Ganimard dashed around and grabbed the doorknob—only to emit an oath: the knob wouldn't budge.

Lupin positively roared with laughter.

"Not even that! You didn't even think of that! You try to ambush me, and it never occurs to you that I might realize it beforehand. And you let yourself be taken into this room without even wondering whether I'm not leading you here on purpose, and without even recalling that the locks have special mechanisms! In all frankness, tell me, what do you say to all this!"

"What I say to all this?" Ganimard spat out, beside himself.

He pulled out his gun and aimed it at Lupin point-blank.

"Get your hands up!" he cried.

Lupin stood in front of him and shrugged.

"One more blunder."

"Get your hands up, I tell you."

"One more blunder. Your gadget won't work."

"What?"

"Your cleaning woman, old Catherine . . . she's in my pay. She wet the powder this morning while you were drinking your coffee."

Ganimard was furious. He pocketed the revolver and leaped upon Lupin.

"What now?" said Lupin, stopping him short with a kick in the leg.

They were almost touching. Their eyes dared one another, like those of two adversaries about to come to blows.

But there was no battle. The recollection of past fights made the struggle futile. And Ganimard, remembering all his past defeats, his vain attacks, the lightning reactions of Lupin, refused to move. He felt there was nothing he could do. Lupin had forces at his disposal that made individual effort pointless. What could he do? Nothing.

"You're so right," said Lupin in a friendly voice. "Better stay where you are. Besides, old friend, just think what this affair has brought you: glory, the assurance of being promoted soon, and thanks to this, the prospect of a happy old age. You don't really want to add the sapphire *and* poor Lupin's head to all that! Would that be fair? In addition, you seem to have forgotten that poor old Lupin saved your life. Oh, but he did! Who warned you right here in this very room that Prévailles was left-handed? And is this what you call gratitude? How ungenerous of you, Ganimard. Really, I'm quite distressed."

As he spoke, Lupin repeated Ganimard's maneuver and inched his way over to the door.

Ganimard realized that his enemy was about to escape. Throwing prudence to the wind, he tried to stop him. But Lupin smashed his head into Ganimard's stomach, and the inspector sprawled backward against the opposite wall.

With three swift movements, Lupin set off a spring, turned the knob, opened the door, and slipped off in a burst of guffaws.

Twenty minutes later, when Ganimard finally managed to rejoin his men, he was told, "One of the painters came out of the house just as the others were coming back from lunch; he gave me a letter. 'Give this to your chief,' he said. 'What do you mean?' I asked him. But he was already far away. I guess he meant you."

"Let me see."

Ganimard tore open the letter. It had been penciled in haste and read:

> *Just a few lines to put you on your guard against excessive credulity, old friend. When a person or persons unknown tell(s) you that the cartridges in your revolver are damp, no matter how great your trust in the aforesaid party may be, and even if his name is Arsène Lupin, don't be taken in. Shoot first, and if the party does a pirouette into eternity, you will have proof: (1) that the cartridges are perfectly dry and (2) that old Catherine is the most honest cleaning woman in the world.*
>
> *Trusting that I will someday have the honor of making her acquaintance, I remain, your faithful friend.*
>
> ARSÈNE LUPIN

FOR DISCUSSION: The Red Silk Scarf

1. Arsène Lupin is an amazing man—half criminal, half detective. In addition, he possesses the agility of an acrobat and the mental shrewdness of an Einstein. In this story, what is the single, specific goal toward which Lupin concentrates all his effort and talents? How does he employ both his criminal and detection abilities to attain this goal?

2. Lupin's reconstruction of the crime from a handful of objects is a fine display of the marshaling of circumstantial evidence. List the six objects and the conclusions Lupin developed from each.

3. A complex relationship links Lupin and Chief Inspector Ganimard. The two men are enemies, yet they respect each other. In the text find several specific incidents that illustrate Lupin's primary attitude toward the Chief Inspector, and several specific incidents that illustrate Ganimard's primary attitude toward Lupin.

4. Arsène Lupin is, above all, a show-off. He glories in his own brilliance. Skim the story again, and see if you can find three occasions when Lupin makes comments that are basically irrelevant but that do indulge his vanity.

5. Most readers find that they sympathize strongly with Lupin even though he is a criminal. How does Leblanc deliberately arouse this sympathy? Can you suggest a reason why many people occasionally like to side with a criminal of this type rather than with the established forces of law and order?

Cerebrating Sleuths

CHAPTER FOUR

Two different trends appeared in this century that have altered the course of history. The first is the apotheosis of the intellectual, and the second is the popularization of Freudian and other schools of psychology.

¶ *The Apotheosis of the Intellectual.* The attitude of the masses toward the intellectual has exhibited a pendulumlike quality since 1900. Sometimes the intellectual has been excessively admired, and sometimes he has been derided. Either way he has been talked and argued about. Always he has been in the spotlight. Notice how epithets like "high brow" and "egghead" have become parts of our daily language.

¶ *The Popularization of Psychology.* The second trend started in the nineteenth century with Sigmund Freud, who explored the human mind and described his discoveries. Psychology was essentially limited to the doctor's office, and it had little effect on the average person. But soon the new vocabulary—"subconscious," "ego," "free association," "repression," and "guilt"—caught the public's fancy. Before long, psychology was beginning to have tremendous impact on society. For example, in an attempt to depict intimate realities of the human mind and extremely personal feelings, new artistic techniques were developed. Artists were using splashes of color and geometric shapes, musicians were playing with dissonance, and writers—heady with all the fresh possibilities—

were probing into the subconscious, exposing psychological flaws, and manipulating egos and libidos.

In the cauldron of mystery writing, a curious thing happened. The two trends merged, and a new creature was born: the cerebrating sleuth. He had a respectable ancestry—Sherlock Holmes (Arthur Conan Doyle) and C. Auguste Dupin (Edgar Allan Poe) had already left their mark on an earlier, more inhibited age. But the new sleuth was different—more human, less detached, more given to idiosyncrasies, above all, more aware of neuroses and psychoses, of whys and wherefores. These cerebrating sleuths keep coming into existence with a dizzying rapidity.

Our age, more than most, is the age of the antihero. There are few real heroes in our fiction or in our lives, yet we need heroes to admire and to emulate. The intellectual detective who is knowledgeable about popular psychology satisfies these needs. We feel awe as we watch him at work, and we identify with him, finding in ourselves unsuspected talents for perception and analysis.

With his advent, the mystery story has grown in variety and in depth. Earlier, it was limited to crime- and puzzle-solving; now it is concerned also with human behavior and its causes. The smart detective still searches for a weapon, but he seeks also, in the criminal's childhood, the origin of ruthlessness. He is aware that dreams reflect fears and desires and is relentless in drawing from these dreams the least significant clue. He knows that the habit of many years does not change in one night; and he knows that each profession, each trade, is marked by small but distinctive characteristics. These characteristics reflect the interests or values of those involved. And he uses this knowledge to convict the guilty and to clear the innocent.

This powerful injection of psychological inquiry has brought the mystery novel and the short story closer than ever before to traditional literature. No longer is it enough for the writer to have a thug gun down a victim, lead the police on a wild chase, and die dramatically in a melodramatic confrontation. Today's readers, weaned on magazine articles by sociologists and psychiatrists, demand more fully drawn characters, more astute descriptions of motive, more sophisticated understanding and analysis of actions and speech. The new writers and their new detectives provide exactly this, in works that often exhibit fine craftsmanship as well as the expected suspense.

Some of these new detectives work purely by *intuition*—but an intuition that is a blend of sophisticated knowledge and skillful inference. Some work by employing a knowledge of history and the insights it gives about human nature. Some use the new psychology openly and directly, reflecting current interests. Still others use actual tests to identify the criminal or to trap him. All think fast and accurately, their aim more sure and more deadly than the lead spray from a machine gun. And, of course, in the world of fiction, all eventually "get their man."

They're a fascinating lot, these cerebrating sleuths, providing individuality and color and verve in a world gone bland. In this unit you will meet four of them, each working in his own inscrutable way.

INTRODUCTION: The Nine Mile Walk

An *inference* is a conclusion or a deduction based on evidence. The evidence may be substantial (physical clues) or insubstantial (ideas or facts). An example of the first: the saucer that was filled with cream is now empty. Your cat is purring happily and a smidgin of cream remains on its whiskers. You *infer* that the cat lapped up the cream. An example of the second: your friend says, "It is raining." You *infer* that the sun is not shining (probably), that it is not snowing or sleeting, that your friend is outside or has access to a window. You may further *infer* that it began raining fairly recently since otherwise he would have said, "It is *still* raining." Since he did not modify his statement at all, you can also *infer* that the rain is heavier than a mist but not so heavy as a downpour, and that it is not accompanied by high winds or thunder and lightning.

All these inferences *can* be drawn from the three words, "It is raining." The fact that they *can* be drawn does not necessarily mean they are true, but a number of inferences, responsibly arrived at, can lead to the truth. "The Nine Mile Walk" is a tour de force, a remarkable display of skill, by a master of inference.

The Nine Mile Walk

Harry Kemelman

I had made an ass of myself in a speech I had given at the Good Government Association dinner, and Nicky Welt had cornered me at breakfast at the Blue Moon, where we both ate occasionally, for the pleasure of rubbing it in. I had made the mistake of departing from my prepared speech to criticize a statement my predecessor in the office of County Attorney had made to the press. I had drawn a number of inferences from his statement and had thus left myself open to a rebuttal which he had promptly made and which had the effect of making me appear intellectually dishonest. I was new to this political game, having but a few months before left the Law School faculty to become the Reform Party candidate for County Attorney. I said as much in extenuation, but Nicholas Welt, who could never drop his pedagogical manner (he was Snowdon Professor of English Language and Literature), replied in much

154

the same tone that he would dismiss a request from a sophomore for an extension on a term paper, "That's no excuse."

Although he is only two or three years older than I, in his late forties, he always treats me like a schoolmaster hectoring a stupid pupil. And I, perhaps because he looks so much older with his white hair and lined, gnomelike face, suffer it.

"They were perfectly logical inferences," I pleaded.

"My dear boy," he purred, "although human intercourse is well-nigh impossible without inference, most inferences are usually wrong. The percentage of error is particularly high in the legal profession where the intention is not to discover what the speaker wishes to convey, but rather what he wishes to conceal."

I picked up my check and eased out from behind the table.

"I suppose you are referring to cross-examination of witnesses in court. Well, there's always an opposing counsel who will object if the inference is illogical."

"Who said anything about logic?" he retorted. "An inference can be logical and still not be true."

He followed me down the aisle to the cashier's booth. I paid my check and waited impatiently while he searched in an old-fashioned change purse, fishing out coins one by one and placing them on the counter beside his check, only to discover that the total was insufficient. He slid them back into his purse and with a tiny sigh extracted a bill from another compartment of the purse and handed it to the cashier.

"Give me any sentence of ten or twelve words," he said, "and I'll build you a logical chain of inferences that you never dreamed of when you framed the sentence."

Other customers were coming in, and since the space in front of the cashier's booth was small, I decided to wait outside until Nicky completed his transaction with the cashier. I remember being mildly amused at the idea that he probably thought I was still at his elbow and was going right ahead with his discourse.

When he joined me on the sidewalk I said, "A nine mile walk is no joke, especially in the rain."

"No, I shouldn't think it would be," he agreed absently. Then he stopped in his stride and looked at me sharply. "What the devil are you talking about?"

"It's a sentence and it has eleven words," I insisted. And I repeated the sentence, ticking off the words on my fingers.

"What about it?"

"You said that given a sentence of ten or twelve words—"

"Oh, yes." He looked at me suspiciously. "Where did you get it?"

"It just popped into my head. Come on now, build your inferences."

"You're serious about this?" he asked, his little blue eyes glittering with amusement. "You really want me to?"

It was just like him to issue a challenge and then to appear amused when I accepted it. And it made me angry.

"Put up or shut up," I said.

"All right," he said mildly. "No need to be huffy. I'll play. Hm-m, let me see, how did the sentence go? 'A nine mile walk is no joke, especially in the rain.' Not much to go on there."

"It's more than ten words," I rejoined.

"Very well." His voice became crisp as he mentally squared off to the problem. "First inference: the speaker is aggrieved."

"I'll grant that," I said, "although it hardly seems to be an inference. It's really implicit in the statement."

He nodded impatiently. "Next inference: the rain was unforeseen, otherwise he would have said, 'A nine mile walk in the rain is no joke,' instead of using the 'especially' phrase as an afterthought."

"I'll allow that," I said, "although it's pretty obvious."

"First inferences should be obvious," said Nicky tartly.

I let it go at that. He seemed to be floundering and I didn't want to rub it in.

"Next inference: the speaker is not an athlete or an outdoors man."

"You'll have to explain that one," I said.

"It's the 'especially' phrase again," he said. "The speaker does not say that a nine mile walk in the rain is no joke, but merely the walk—just the distance, mind you—is no joke. Now, nine miles is not such a terribly long distance. You walk more than half that in eighteen holes of golf—and golf is an old man's game," he added slyly. "I play golf."

"Well, that would be all right under ordinary circumstances," I said, "but there are other possibilities. The speaker might be a soldier in the jungle, in which case nine miles would be a pretty good hike, rain or no rain."

"Yes," and Nicky was sarcastic, "and the speaker might be one-legged. For that matter, the speaker might be a graduate student writing a Ph.D. thesis on humor and starting by listing all the things that are not funny. See here, I'll have to make a couple of assumptions before I continue."

"How do you mean?" I asked, suspiciously.

"Remember, I'm taking this sentence *in vacuo*, as it were. I don't know who said it or what the occasion was. Normally a sentence belongs in the framework of a situation."

"I see. What assumptions do you want to make?"

"For one thing, I want to assume that the intention was not frivolous, that the speaker is referring to a walk that was actually taken, and that the purpose of the walk was not to win a bet or something of that sort."

"That seems reasonable enough," I said.

"And I also want to assume that the locale of the walk is here."

"You mean here in Fairfield?"

"Not necessarily. I mean in this general section of the country."

"Fair enough."

"Then, if you grant those assumptions, you'll have to accept my last inference that the speaker is no athlete or outdoors man."

"Well, all right, go on."

"Then my next inference is that the walk was taken very late at night or very early in the morning—say, between midnight and five or six in the morning."

"How do you figure that one?" I asked.

"Consider the distance, nine miles. We're in a fairly well-populated section. Take any road and you'll find a community of some sort in less than nine miles. Hadley is five miles away, Hadley Falls is seven and a half, Goreton is eleven, but East Goreton is only eight and you strike East Goreton before you come to Goreton. There is local train service along the Goreton road and bus service along the others. All the highways are pretty well traveled. Would anyone have to walk nine miles in a rain unless it were late at night when no buses or trains were running and when the few automobiles that were out would hesitate to pick up a stranger on the highway?"

"He might not have wanted to be seen," I suggested.

Nicky smiled pityingly. "You think he would be less noticeable trudging along the highway than he would be riding in a public conveyance where everyone is usually absorbed in his newspaper?"

"Well, I won't press the point," I said brusquely.

"Then try this one: he was walking toward a town rather than away from one."

I nodded. "It is more likely, I suppose. If he were in a town, he could probably arrange for some sort of transportation. Is that the basis for your inference?"

"Partly that," said Nicky, "but there is also an inference to be drawn from the distance. Remember, it's a *nine* mile walk and nine is out of the exact numbers."

"I'm afraid I don't understand."

That exasperated schoolteacher-look appeared on Nicky's face again. "Suppose you say, 'I took a ten mile walk' or 'a hundred mile drive'; I would assume that you actually walked anywhere from eight to a dozen miles, or that you rode between ninety and a hundred and ten miles. In other words, *ten* and *hundred* are round numbers. You might have walked *exactly* ten miles or just as likely you might have walked *approximately* ten miles. But when you speak of walking *nine* miles, I have a right to assume that you have named an exact figure. Now, we are far more likely to know the distance of the city from a given point than we are to know the distance of a given point from the city. That is, ask anyone in the city how far out Farmer Brown lives, and if he knows him, he will say, 'Three or four miles.' But ask Farmer Brown how far he lives from the city and he will tell you. 'Three and six-tenths miles—measured it on my speedometer many a time.'"

"It's weak, Nicky," I said.

"But in conjunction with your own suggestion that he could have arranged transportation if he had been in a city—"

"Yes, that would do it," I said. "I'll pass it. Any more?"

"I've just begun to hit my stride," he boasted. "My next inference is that he was going to a definite destination and that he had to be there at a particular time. It was not a case of going off to get help because his car broke down or his wife was going to have a baby or somebody was trying to break into his house."

"Oh, come now," I said, "the car breaking down is really the most likely situation. He could have known the exact distance from having checked the mileage just as he was leaving the town."

Nicky shook his head. "Rather than walk nine miles in the rain, he would have curled up on the back seat and gone to sleep, or at least stayed by his car and tried to flag another motorist. Remember, it's nine miles. What would be the least it would take him to hike it?"

"Four hours," I offered.

He nodded. "Certainly no less, considering the rain. We've agreed that it happened very late at night or very early in the morning. Suppose he had his breakdown at one o'clock in the morning. It would be five o'clock before he would arrive. That's daybreak. You begin to see a lot of cars on the road. The buses start just a little later. In fact, the first buses hit Fairfield around five-thirty. Besides, if he were going for help, he would not have to go all the way to town—only as far as the nearest telephone. No, he had a definite appointment, and it was in a town, and it was for some time before five-thirty."

"Then why couldn't he have got there earlier and waited?" I asked. "He could have taken the last bus, arrived around one o'clock, and waited until his appointment. He walks nine miles in the rain instead, and you said he was no athlete."

We had arrived at the Municipal Building where my office is. Normally, any arguments begun at the Blue Moon ended at the entrance to the Municipal Building. But I was interested in Nicky's demonstration and I suggested that he come up for a few minutes.

When we were seated I said, "How about it, Nicky, why couldn't he have arrived early and waited?"

"He could have," Nicky retorted. "But since he did not, we must assume that he was either detained until after the last bus left, or that he had to wait where he was for a signal of some sort, perhaps a telephone call."

"Then according to you, he had an appointment some time between midnight and five-thirty—"

"We can draw it much finer than that. Remember, it takes him four hours to walk the distance. The last bus stops at twelve-thirty A.M. If he doesn't take that, but starts at the same time, he won't arrive at his destination until four-thirty. On the other hand, if he takes the first bus in the morning, he will arrive around five-thirty. That would mean that his appointment was for some time between four-thirty and five-thirty."

"You mean that if his appointment was earlier than four-thirty, he would have taken the last night bus, and if it was later than five-thirty, he would have taken the first morning bus?"

"Precisely. And another thing: if he was waiting for a signal or a phone call, it must have come not much later than one o'clock."

"Yes, I see that," I said. "If his appointment is around five o'clock and it takes him four hours to walk the distance, he'd have to start around one."

He nodded, silent and thoughtful. For some queer reason I could not explain, I did not feel like interrupting his thoughts. On the wall was a large map of the county and I walked over to it and began to study it.

"You're right, Nicky," I remarked over my shoulder, "there's no place as far as nine miles away from Fairfield that doesn't hit another town first. Fairfield is right in the middle of a bunch of smaller towns."

He joined me at the map. "It doesn't have to be Fairfield, you know," he said quietly. "It was probably one of the outlying towns he had to reach. Try Hadley."

"Why Hadley? What would anyone want in Hadley at five o'clock in the morning?"

"The Washington Flyer stops there to take on water about that time," he said quietly.

"That's right, too," I said. "I've heard that train many a night when I couldn't sleep. I'd hear it pulling in and then a minute or two later I'd hear the clock on the Methodist Church banging out five." I went back to my desk for a timetable. "The Flyer leaves Washington at twelve forty-seven A.M. and gets into Boston at eight A.M."

Nicky was still at the map measuring distances with a pencil.

"Exactly nine miles from Hadley is the Old Sumter Inn," he announced.

"Old Sumter Inn," I echoed. "But that upsets the whole theory. You can arrange for transportation there as easily as you can in a town."

He shook his head. "The cars are kept in an enclosure and you have to get an attendant to check you through the gate. The attendant would remember anyone taking out his car at a strange hour. It's a pretty conservative place. He could have waited in his room until he got a call from Washington about someone on the Flyer—maybe the number of the car and the berth. Then he could just slip out of the hotel and walk to Hadley."

I stared at him, hypnotized.

"It wouldn't be difficult to slip aboard while the train was taking on water, and then if he knew the car number and the berth—"

"Nicky," I said portentously, "as the Reform District Attorney who campaigned on an economy program, I am going to waste the taxpayer's money and call Boston long distance. It's ridiculous, it's insane—but I'm going to do it!"

His little blue eyes glittered and he moistened his lips with the tip of his tongue.

"Go ahead," he said hoarsely.

I replaced the telephone in its cradle.

"Nicky," I said, "this is probably the most remarkable coincidence in the history of criminal investigation: *a man was found murdered in his berth on last night's twelve-forty-seven from Washington!* He'd been dead about three hours, which would make it exactly right for Hadley."

"I thought it was something like that," said Nicky. "But you're wrong about its being a coincidence. It can't be. Where did you get that sentence?"

"It was just a sentence. It simply popped into my head."

"It couldn't have! It's not the sort of sentence that pops into one's head. If you had taught composition as long as I have, you'd know that when you ask someone for a sentence of ten words or so, you get an ordinary statement such as 'I like milk'—with the other words made up by a modifying clause like, 'because it is good for my health.' The sentence you offered related to a *particular situation.*"

"But I tell you I talked to no one this morning. And I was alone with you at the Blue Moon."

"You weren't with me all the time I paid my check," he said sharply. "Did you meet anyone while you were waiting on the sidewalk for me to come out of the Blue Moon?"

I shook my head. "I was outside for less than a minute before you joined me. You see, a couple of men came in while you were digging out your change and one of them bumped me, so I thought I'd wait—"

"Did you ever see them before?"

"Who?"

"The two men who came in," he said, the note of exasperation creeping into his voice again.

"Why, no—they weren't anyone I knew."

"Were they talking?"

"I guess so. Yes, they were. Quite absorbed in their conversation, as a matter of fact—otherwise, they would have noticed me and I would not have been bumped."

"Not many strangers come into the Blue Moon," he remarked.

"Do you think it was they?" I asked eagerly. "I think I'd know them again if I saw them."

Nicky's eyes narrowed. "It's possible. There had to be two—one to trail the victim in Washington and ascertain his berth number, the other to wait here and do the job. The Washington man would be likely to come down here afterwards. If there was theft as well as murder, it would be to divide the spoils. If it was just murder, he would probably have to come down to pay off his confederate."

I reached for the telephone.

"We've been gone less than half an hour," Nicky went on. "They were just coming in and service is slow at the Blue Moon. The one who walked all the way to Hadley must certainly be hungry and the other probably drove all night from Washington."

"Call me immediately if you make an arrest," I said into the phone and hung up.

Neither of us spoke a word while we waited. We paced the floor, avoiding each other almost as though we had done something we were ashamed of.

The telephone rang at last. I picked it up and listened. Then I said, "O.K." and turned to Nicky.

"One of them tried to escape through the kitchen but Winn had someone stationed at the back and they got him."

"That would seem to prove it," said Nicky with a frosty little smile.

I nodded agreement.

He glanced at his watch. "Gracious," he exclaimed, "I wanted to make an early start on my work this morning, and here I've already wasted all this time talking with you."

I let him get to the door. "Oh, Nicky," I called, "what was it you set out to prove?"

"That a chain of inferences could be logical and still not be true," he said.

"Oh."

"What are you laughing at?" he asked snappishly. And then he laughed too.

FOR DISCUSSION: The Nine Mile Walk

1. Explain briefly the irony in Nicky's statement that "an inference can be logical and still not be true."
2. List in outline form the inferences Nicky made throughout the story. Is each one logical? At what point does the logical become the true?
3. The use of inference is, to some extent, dependent on a knowledge of basic psychology, an understanding of human nature. How is this shown in the narrator's choice of an eleven-word sentence? It may also be dependent on common sense. How is *this* shown in Nicky's assertion that the two criminals could probably still be found in the restaurant?
4. From the text of the story, try to decide *through inferences* the career Kemelman followed before he became a professional writer.
5. Write a sentence about ten words in length. Have a friend do the same thing. After exchanging sentences, see how many inferences each of you can draw from the other's sentence.

INTRODUCTION: The President's Half Disme

Less concrete than the clues of Sherlock Holmes, less intangible than the inferences of Nicky Welt, is the intellectual or mental clue. It is the favorite of the thinking sleuth—of Ellery Queen, for instance.

Ellery Queen is the brainchild of two men, Frederic Dannay and Manfred Lee. Over the years Ellery, in dozens of novels and short stories, has taken on a life and reality of his own, much as Sherlock Holmes did in an earlier age. Ellery is slight but strong, with a penchant for wit-shaking puzzlers. Nothing fascinates him so much as an apparently unsolvable problem.

In this story Ellery stumbles upon a challenge which he cannot resist. The mystery lies in the far past—which makes it tougher—and it revolves around the venerable figure of George Washington. To solve it, Ellery needs patience and wit, a knowledge of mathematics and history, and an understanding of how Washington's precise mind operated.

The President's Half Disme

Ellery Queen

Those few curious men who have chosen to turn off the humdrum highway to hunt for their pleasure along the back trails expect—indeed, they look confidently forward to—many strange encounters; and it is the dull stalk which does not turn up at least a hippogriff. But it remained for Ellery Queen to experience the ultimate excitement. On one of his prowls he collided with a President of the United States.

This would have been joy enough if it had occurred as you might imagine: by chance, on a dark night, in some back street of Washington, D.C., with Secret Service men closing in on the delighted Mr. Queen to question his motives by way of his pockets while a large black bullet-proof limousine rushed up to spirit the President away. But mere imagination fails in this instance. What is required is the power of fancy, for the truth is fantastic. Ellery's encounter with the President of the United States took place, not on a dark night, but in the unromantic light of several days (although the night played its role, too). Nor was it by chance: the meeting was arranged by a farmer's daughter. And it was not in Washington, D.C., for this President presided over the affairs of the nation from a different city altogether. Not that the meeting took place in that city, either; it did not take place in a city at all, but on a farm some miles south of Philadelphia. Oddest of all, there was no limousine to spirit the Chief Executive away, for while the President was a man of great wealth, he was still too poor to possess an automobile and, what is more, not all the resources of his Government—indeed, not all the riches of the world—could have provided one for him.

There are even more curious facets to this jewel of paradox. This was an encounter in the purest sense, and yet, physically, it did not occur at all. The President in question was dead. And while there are those who would not blink at a rubbing of shoulders or a clasping of hands even though one of the parties was in his grave, and to such persons the thought might occur that the meeting took place on a psychic plane— alas, Ellery Queen is not of their company. He does not believe in ghosts, consequently he never encounters them. So he did not collide with the President's shade, either.

And yet their meeting was as palpable as, say, the meeting between two chess masters, one in London and the other in New York, who never leave their respective armchairs and still play a game to a decision. It is even more wonderful than that, for while the chess players merely annihilate space, Ellery and the father of his country annihilated time—a century and a half of it.

In fine, this is the story of how Ellery Queen matched wits with George Washington.

Those who are finicky about their fashions complain that the arms of coincidence are too long; but in this case the Designer might say that He cut to measure. Or, to put it another way, an event often brews its own mood. Whatever the cause, the fact is The Adventure of the President's Half Disme, which was to concern itself with the events surrounding President Washington's fifty-ninth birthday, actually first engrossed Ellery on February the nineteenth and culminated three days later.

Ellery was in his study that morning of the nineteenth of February, wrestling with several reluctant victims of violence, none of them quite flesh and blood, since his novel was still in the planning stage. So he was annoyed when Nikki came in with a card.

"James Ezekiel Patch," growled the great man; he was never in his best humor during the planning stage. "I don't know any James Ezekiel Patch, Nikki. Toss the fellow out and get back to transcribing those notes on Possible Motives—"

"Why, Ellery," said Nikki. "This isn't like you at all."

"What isn't like me?"

"To renege on an appointment."

"Appointment? Does this Patch character claim—?"

"He doesn't merely claim it. He proves it."

"Someone's balmy," snarled Mr. Queen; and he strode into the living room to contend with James Ezekiel Patch. This, he perceived as soon as James Ezekiel Patch rose from the Queen fireside chair, was likely to be a heroic project. Mr. Patch, notwithstanding his mild, even studious, eyes, seemed to rise indefinitely; he was a large, a very large, man.

"Now what's all this, what's all this?" demanded Ellery fiercely; for after all Nikki was there.

"That's what I'd like to know," said the large man amiably. "What did you want with me, Mr. Queen?"

"What did I want with you! What did you want with me?"

"I find this very strange, Mr. Queen."

"Now see here, Mr. Patch, I happen to be extremely busy this morning—"

"So am I." Mr. Patch's large thick neck was reddening and his tone was no longer amiable. Ellery took a cautious step backward as his visitor lumbered forward to thrust a slip of yellow paper under his nose. "Did you send me this wire, or didn't you?"

Ellery considered it tactically expedient to take the telegram, although for strategic reasons he did so with a bellicose scowl.

IMPERATIVE YOU CALL AT MY HOME TOMORROW FEBRUARY NINETEEN PROMPTLY TEN A.M. SIGNED ELLERY QUEEN

"Well sir?" thundered Mr. Patch. "Do you have something on Washington for me, or don't you?"

"Washington?" said Ellery absently, studying the telegram.

"*George* Washington, Mr. Queen! I'm Patch the antiquarian. I *collect* Washington, I'm an *authority* on Washington. I have a large fortune and I spend it all on Washington! I'd never have wasted my time this morning if your name hadn't been signed to this wire! This is my busiest week of the year. I have engagements to speak on Washington—"

"Desist, Mr. Patch," said Ellery. "This is either a practical joke, or—"

"The Baroness Tchek," announced Nikki clearly. "With another telegram." And then she added: "And Professor John Cecil Shaw, ditto."

The three telegrams were identical.

"Of course I didn't send them," said Ellery thoughtfully, regarding his three visitors. Baroness Tchek was a short powerful woman, resembling a dumpling with gray hair; an angry dumpling. Professor Shaw was lank and long-jawed, wearing a sack suit which hung in some places and failed in its purpose by inches at the extremities. Along with Mr. Patch, they constituted as deliciously queer a trio as had ever congregated in the Queen apartment. Their host suddenly determined not to let go of them. "On the other hand, someone obviously did, using my name . . ."

"Then there's nothing more to be said," snapped the Baroness, snapping her bag for emphasis.

"I should think there's a great deal more to be said," began Professor Shaw in a troubled way. "Wasting people's time this way—"

"It's not going to waste any more of *my* time," growled the large Mr. Patch. "Washington's Birthday only three days off—!"

"Exactly," smiled Ellery. "Won't you sit down? There's more in this than meets the eye. . . . Baroness Tchek, if I'm not mistaken, you're the one who brought that fabulous collection of rare coins into the United States just before Hitler invaded Czechoslovakia? You're in the rare-coin business in New York now?"

"Unfortunately," said the Baroness coldly, "one must eat."

"And you, sir? I seem to know you."

"Rare books," said the Professor in the same troubled way.

"Of course. John Cecil Shaw, the rare-book collector. We've met at Mim's and other places. I abandon my first theory. There's a pattern here, distinctly unhumorous. An antiquarian, a coin dealer, and a collector of rare books—Nikki? Whom have you out there this time?"

"If this one collects anything," muttered Nikki into her employer's ear, "I'll bet it has two legs and hair on its chest. A darned pretty girl—"

"Named Martha Clarke," said a cool voice; and Ellery turned to find himself regarding one of the most satisfying sights in the world.

"Ah. I take it, Miss Clarke, you also received one of these wires signed with my name?"

"Oh, no," said the pretty girl. "I'm the one who sent them."

There was something about the comely Miss Clarke which inspired, if not confidence, at least an openness of mind. Perhaps it was the self-possessed manner in which she sat all of them, including Ellery, down in Ellery's living room while she waited on the hearth-rug, like a conductor on the podium, for them to settle in their chairs. And it was the measure of Miss Clarke's assurance that none of them was indignant, only curious.

"I'll make it snappy," said Martha Clarke briskly. "I did what I did the way I did it because, first, I had to make sure I could see Mr. Patch, Baroness Tchek, and Professor Shaw today. Second, because I may need a detective before I'm through. . . . Third," she added, almost absently, "because I'm pretty desperate.

"My name is Martha Clarke. My father Tobias is a farmer. Our farm lies just south of Philadelphia, it was built by a Clarke in 1761, and it's been in our family ever since. I won't go gooey on you. We're broke and there's a mortgage. Unless Papa and I can raise six thousand dollars in the next couple of weeks we lose the old homestead."

Professor Shaw looked vague. But the Baroness said: "Deplorable, Miss Clarke. Now if I'm to run my auction this afternoon—"

And James Ezekiel Patch grumbled: "If it's money you want, young woman—"

"Certainly it's money I want. But I have something to sell."

"Ah!" said the Baroness.

"Oh?" said the Professor.

"Hm," said the antiquarian.

Mr. Queen said nothing, and Miss Porter zealously chewed the end of her pencil.

"The other day while I was cleaning out the attic, I found an old book."

"Well, now," said Professor Shaw indulgently. "An old book, eh?"

"It's called *The Diary of Simeon Clarke*. Simeon Clarke was Papa's great-great-great-something or other. His *Diary* was privately printed in 1792 in Philadelphia, Professor, by a second cousin of his, Jonathan, who was in the printing business there."

"Jonathan Clarke. *The Diary of Simeon Clarke*," mumbled the cadaverous book collector. "I don't believe I know either, Miss Clarke. Have you . . . ?"

Martha Clarke carefully unclasped a large Manila envelope and drew forth a single yellowed sheet of badly printed paper. "The title page was loose, so I brought it along."

Professor Shaw silently examined Miss Clarke's exhibit, and Ellery got up to squint at it. "Of course," said the Professor after a long scrutiny, in which he held the sheet up to the light, peered apparently at individual characters, and performed other mysterious rites, "mere age doesn't connote rarity, nor does rarity of itself constitute value. And while this page looks genuine for the purported period and is rare enough to be unknown to me, still . . ."

"Suppose I told you," said Miss Martha Clarke, "that the chief purpose of the *Diary*—which I have at home—is to tell the story of how George Washington visited Simeon Clarke's farm in the winter of 1791—"

"Clarke's farm? 1791?" exclaimed James Ezekiel Patch. "Preposterous. There's no record of—"

"And of what George Washington buried there," the farmer's daughter concluded.

By executive order, the Queen telephone was taken off its hook, the door was bolted, the shades were drawn, and the long interrogation began. By the middle of the afternoon, the unknown chapter in the life of the Father of His Country was fairly sketched.

Early on an icy gray February morning in 1791, Farmer Clarke had looked up from the fence he was mending to observe a splendid cortège galloping down on him from the direction of the City of Philadelphia.

Outriders thundered in the van, followed by a considerable company of gentlemen on horseback and several great coaches-and-six driven by liveried Negroes. To Simeon Clarke's astonishment, the entire equipage stopped before his farmhouse. He began to run. He could hear the creak of springs and the snorting of sleek and sweating horses. Gentlemen and lackeys were leaping to the frozen ground, and, by the time Simeon had reached the farmhouse, all were elbowing about the first coach, a magnificent affair bearing a coat of arms. Craning, the farmer saw within the coach a very large, great-nosed gentleman clad in a black velvet suit and a black cloak faced with gold; there was a cocked hat on his wigged head and a great sword in a white leather scabbard at his side. This personage was on one knee, leaning with an expression of considerable anxiety over a chubby lady of middle age, swathed in furs, who was half-sitting, half-lying on the upholstered seat, her eyes closed and her cheeks waxen under the rouge. Another gentleman, soberly attired, was stooping over the lady, his fingers on one pale wrist.

"I fear," he was saying with great gravity to the kneeling man, "that it would be imprudent to proceed another yard in this weather, Your Excellency. Lady Washington requires physicking and a warm bed immediately."

Lady Washington! Then the large, richly dressed gentleman was the President! Simeon Clarke pushed excitedly through the throng.

"Your Mightiness! Sir!" he cried. "I am Simeon Clarke. This is my farm. We have warm beds, Sarah and I!"

The President considered Simeon briefly. "I thank you, Farmer Clarke. No, no, Dr. Craik. I shall assist Lady Washington myself."

And George Washington carried Martha Washington into the little Pennsylvania farmhouse of Simeon and Sarah Clarke. An aide informed the Clarkes that President Washington had been on his way to Virginia to celebrate his fifty-ninth birthday in the privacy of Mount Vernon.

Instead, he passed his birthday on the Clarke farm, for the physician insisted that the President's lady could not be moved, even back to the nearby Capital, without risking complications. On His Excellency's order, the entire incident was kept secret. "It would give needless alarm to the people," he said. But he did not leave Martha's bedside for three days and three nights.

Presumably during those seventy-two hours, while his lady recovered from her indisposition, the President devoted some thought to his hosts, for on the fourth morning he sent black Christopher, his body servant, to summon the Clarkes. They found George Washington by the kitchen fire, shaven and powdered and in immaculate dress, his stern features composed.

"I am told, Farmer Clarke, that you and your good wife refuse reimbursement for the livestock you have slaughtered in the accommodation of our large company."

"You're my President, Sir," said Simeon. "I wouldn't take money."

"We—we wouldn't take money, Your Worship," stammered Sarah.

"Nevertheless, Lady Washington and I would acknowledge your hospitality in some kind. If you give me leave, I shall plant with my own hands a grove of oak saplings behind your house. And beneath one of the saplings I propose to bury two of my personal possessions." Washington's eyes twinkled ever so slightly. "It is my birthday—I feel a venturesome spirit. Come, Farmer Clarke and Mistress Clarke, would you like that?"

"What—what were they?" choked James Ezekiel Patch, the Washington collector. He was pale.

Martha Clarke replied: "The sword at Washington's side, in its white leather scabbard, and a silver coin the President carried in a secret pocket."

"Silver *coin?*" breathed Baroness Tchek, the rare-coin dealer. "What kind of coin, Miss Clarke?"

"The *Diary* calls it 'a half disme,' with an *s*," replied Martha Clarke, frowning. "I guess that's the way they spelled dime in those days. The book's full of queer spellings."

"A United States of America half disme?" asked the Baroness in a very odd way.

"That's what it says, Baroness."

"And this was in 1791?"

"Yes."

The Baroness snorted, beginning to rise. "I thought your story was too impossibly romantic, young woman. The United States Mint didn't begin to strike off half dismes until 1792!"

"Half dismes or any other U.S. coinage, I believe," said Ellery. "How come, Miss Clarke?"

"It was an experimental coin," said Miss Clarke coolly. "The *Diary* isn't clear as to whether it was the Mint which struck it off, or some private agency—maybe Washington himself didn't tell Simeon—but the President did say to Simeon that the half disme in his pocket had been coined from silver he himself had furnished and had been presented to him as a keepsake."

"There's a half disme with a story like that behind it in the possession of The American Numismatic Society," muttered the Baroness, "but it's definitely called one of the earliest coins struck off by the Mint. It's possible, I suppose, that in 1791, the preceding year, some specimen coins may have been struck off—"

"Possible my foot," said Miss Clarke. "It's so. The *Diary* says so. I imagine President Washington was pretty interested in the coins to be issued by the new country he was head of."

"Miss Clarke, I—I want that half disme. I mean—I'd like to buy it from you," said the Baroness.

"And I," said Mr. Patch carefully, "would like to ah . . . purchase Washington's sword."

"The *Diary*," moaned Professor Shaw. "I'll buy *The Diary of Simeon Clarke* from you, Miss Clarke!"

"I'll be happy to sell it to you, Professor Shaw—as I said, I found it in the attic and I have it locked up in a highboy in the parlor at home. But as for the other two things . . ." Martha Clarke paused, and Ellery looked delighted. He thought he knew what was coming. "I'll sell you the sword, Mr. Patch, and you the half disme, Baroness Tchek, provided"— and now Miss Clarke turned her clear eyes on Ellery—"provided you, Mr. Queen, will be kind enough to find them."

And there was the farmhouse in the frosty Pennsylvania morning, set in the barren winter acres, and looking as bleak as only a little Revolutionary house with a mortgage on its head can look in the month of February.

"There's an apple orchard over there," said Nikki as they got out of Ellery's car. "But where's the grove of oaks? I don't see any!" And then she added, sweetly: "Do you, Ellery?"

Ellery's lips tightened. They tightened further when his solo on the front-door knocker brought no response.

"Let's go around," he said briefly; and Nikki preceded him with cheerful step.

Behind the house there was a barn; and beyond the barn there was comfort, at least for Ellery. For beyond the barn there were twelve ugly holes in the earth, and beside each hole lay either a freshly felled oak tree and its stump, or an ancient stump by itself, freshly uprooted. On one of the stumps sat an old man in earth-stained blue jeans, smoking a corncob pugnaciously.

"Tobias Clarke?" asked Ellery.

"Yump."

"I'm Ellery Queen. This is Miss Porter. Your daughter visited me in New York yesterday—"

"Know all about it."

"May I ask where Martha is?"

"Station. Meetin' them there other folks." Tobias Clarke spat and looked away—at the holes. "Don't know what ye're all comin' down here for. Wasn't nothin' under them oaks. Dug 'em all up t'other day. Trees that were standin' and the stumps of the ones that'd fallen years back. Look at them holes. Hired hand and me dug down most to China. Washin'ton's Grove, always been called. Now look at it. Firewood—for someone else, I guess." There was iron bitterness in his tone. "We're losin' this farm, Mister, unless..." And Tobias Clarke stopped. "Well maybe we won't," he said. "There's always that there book Martha found."

"Professor Shaw, the rare-book collector, offered your daughter two thousand dollars for it if he's satisfied with it, Mr. Clarke," said Nikki.

"So she told me last night when she got back from New York," said Tobias Clarke. "Two thousand—and we need six." He grinned, and he spat again.

"Well," said Nikki sadly to Ellery, "that's that." She hoped Ellery would immediately get into the car and drive back to New York—immediately.

But Ellery showed no disposition to be sensible. "Perhaps, Mr. Clarke, some trees died in the course of time and just disappeared, stumps, roots, and all. Martha—Martha!—said the *Diary* doesn't mention the exact number Washington planted here."

"Look at them holes. Twelve of 'em ain't there? In a triangle. Man plants trees in a triangle, he plants trees in a triangle. Ye don't see no place between holes big enough for another tree, do you? Anyways, there was the same distance between all the trees. No, sir, Mister, twelve was all there was ever; and I looked under all twelve."

"What's the extra tree doing in the center of the triangle? You haven't uprooted that one, Mr. Clarke."

Tobias Clarke spat once more. "Don't know much about trees, do ye? That's a cherry saplin' I set in myself six years ago. Ain't got nothin' to do with George Washington."

Nikki tittered.

"If you'd sift the earth in those holes—"

"I sifted it. Look, Mister, either somebody dug that stuff up a hundred years ago or the whole yarn's a Saturday night whopper. Which it most likely is. There's Martha now with them other folks." And Tobias Clarke added, spitting for the fourth time: "Don't let me be keepin' ye."

"It reveals Washington rather er...out of character," said James Ezekiel Patch that evening. They were sitting about the fire in the parlor, as heavy with gloom as with Miss Clarke's dinner; and that, at least in Miss Porter's view, was heavy indeed. Baroness Tchek wore the expression of one who is trapped in a cave; there was no further train until morning, and she had not yet resigned herself to a night in a farmhouse bed. The better part of the day had been spent poring over *The Diary of Simeon Clarke*, searching for a clue to the buried Washingtonia. But there was no clue; the pertinent passage referred merely to "a Triangle of Oake Trees behinde the red Barn which His Excellency the

President did plant with his own Hands, as he had promis'd me, and then did burie his Sworde and the Half Disme for his Pleasure in a Case of copper beneathe one of the Oakes, the which, he said (the Case), had been fashion'd by Mr. Revere of Boston who is experimenting with this Mettle in his Furnasses."

"How out of character, Mr. Patch?" asked Ellery. He had been staring into the fire for a long time, scarcely listening.

"Washington wasn't given to romanticism," said the large man dryly. "No folderol about him. I don't know of anything in his life which prepares us for such a yarn as this. I'm beginning to think—"

"But Professor Shaw himself says the *Diary* is no forgery!" cried Martha Clarke.

"Oh, the book's authentic enough." Professor Shaw seemed unhappy. "But it may simply be a literary hoax, Miss Clarke. The woods are full of them. I'm afraid that unless the story is confirmed by the discovery of that copper case with its contents . . ."

"Oh, dear," said Nikki impulsively; and for a moment she was sorry for Martha Clarke, she really was.

But Ellery said: "I believe it. Pennsylvania farmers in 1791 weren't given to literary hoaxes, Professor Shaw. As for Washington, Mr. Patch —no man can be so rigidly consistent. And with his wife just recovering from an illness—on his own birthday . . ." And Ellery fell silent again.

Almost immediately he leaped from his chair. "Mr. Clarke!"

Tobias stirred from his dark corner. "What?"

"Did you ever hear your father, or grandfather—anyone in your family —talk of *another barn behind the house?*"

Martha stared at him. Then she cried: "Papa, that's it! It was a different barn, in a different place, and the original Washington's Grove was cut down, or died—"

"Nope," said Tobias Clarke. "Never was but this one barn. Still got some of its original timbers. Ye can see the date burned into the cross-tree—1761."

Nikki was up early. A steady *hack-hack-hack* borne on the frosty air woke her. She peered out of her back window, the coverlet up to her nose, to see Mr. Ellery Queen against the dawn, like a pioneer, wielding an ax powerfully.

Nikki dressed quickly, shivering, flung her mink-dyed muskrat over her shoulders, and ran downstairs, out of the house, and around it past the barn.

"Ellery! What do you think you're doing? It's practically the middle of the night!"

"Chopping," said Ellery, chopping.

"There's *mountains* of firewood stacked against the barn," said Nikki. "Really, Ellery, I think this is carrying a flirtation too far." Ellery did not reply. "And anyway, there's something—something gruesome and indecent about chopping up trees George Washington planted. It's vandalism."

"Just a thought," panted Ellery, pausing for a moment. "A hundred and fifty-odd years is a long time, Nikki. Lots of queer things could happen, even to a tree, in that time. For instance—"

"The copper case," breathed Nikki, visibly. "The roots grew *around* it. It's *in* one of these stumps!"

"Now you're functioning," said Ellery, and he raised the ax again.

He was still at it two hours later, when Martha Clarke announced breakfast.

At 11:30 A.M. Nikki returned from driving the Professor, the Baroness, and James Ezekiel Patch to the railroad station. She found Mr. Queen seated before the fire in the kitchen in his undershirt, while Martha Clarke caressed his naked right arm.

"Oh!" said Nikki faintly. "I *beg* your pardon."

"Where you going, Nikki?" said Ellery irritably. "Come in. Martha's rubbing liniment into my biceps."

"He's not very accustomed to chopping wood, is he?" asked Martha Clarke in a cheerful voice.

"Reduced those foul 'oakes' to splinters," groaned Ellery. "Martha, ouch!"

"I should think you'd be satisfied *now*," said Nikki coldly. "I suggest we imitate Patch, Shaw, and the Baroness, Ellery—there's a 3:05. We can't impose on Miss Clarke's hospitality forever."

To Nikki's horror, Martha Clarke chose this moment to burst into tears.

"Martha!"

Nikki felt like leaping upon her and shaking the cool look back into her perfidious eyes.

"Here—here, now, Martha." That's right, thought Nikki contemptuously. Embrace her in front of me! "It's those three rats. Running out that way! Don't worry—I'll find that sword and half disme for you yet."

"You'll never find them," sobbed Martha, wetting Ellery's undershirt. "Because they're not here. They *never* were here. When you s-stop to think of it . . . *burying* that coin, his sword . . . if the story were true, he'd have given them to Simeon and Sarah . . ."

"Not necessarily, not necessarily," said Ellery with a hateful haste. "The old boy had a sense of history, Martha. They all did in those days. They knew they were men of destiny and that the eyes of posterity were upon them. Burying 'em is *just* what Washington would have done!"

"Do you really th-think so?"

Oh ... *pfui.*

"But even if he did bury them," Martha sniffled, "it doesn't stand to reason Simeon and Sarah would have let them *stay* buried. They'd have dug that copper box up like rabbits the minute G-George turned his back."

"Two simple countryfolk?" cried Ellery. "Salt of the earth? The new American earth? Disregard the wishes of His Mightiness, George Washington, First President of the United States? Are you out of your mind? And anyway, what would Simeon do with a dress-sword?"

Beat it into a plowshare, thought Nikki spitefully—*that's* what he'd do.

"And that half disme. How much could it have been worth in 1791? Martha, they're here under your farm somewhere. You wait and see—"

"I wish I could b-believe it ... Ellery."

"Shucks, child. Now stop crying—"

From the door Miss Porter said stiffly: "You might put your shirt back on, Superman, before you catch pneumonia."

Mr. Queen prowled about the Clarke acres for the remainder of that day, his nose at a low altitude. He spent some time in the barn. He devoted at least twenty minutes to each of the twelve holes in the earth. He reinspected the oaken wreckage of his axwork, like a paleontologist examining an ancient petrifaction for the impression of a dinosaur foot. He measured off the distance between the holes; and, for a moment, a faint tremor of emotion shook him. George Washington had been a surveyor in his youth; here was evidence that his passion for exactitude had not wearied with the years. As far as Ellery could make out, the twelve oaks had been set into the earth at exactly equal distances, in an equilateral triangle.

It was at this point that Ellery had seated himself upon the seat of a cultivator behind the barn, wondering at his suddenly accelerated circulation. Little memories were knocking at the door. And as he opened to admit them, it was as if he were admitting a personality. It was, of course, at this time that the sense of personal conflict first obtruded. He had merely to shut his eyes in order to materialize a tall, large-featured man carefully pacing off the distances between twelve points—pacing them off in a sort of objective challenge to the unborn future. George Washington . . .

The man Washington had from the beginning possessed an affinity for numbers. It had remained with him all his life. To count things, not so much for the sake of the things, perhaps, as for the counting, had been of the utmost importance to him. As a boy in Mr. Williams's school in Westmoreland, he excelled in arithmetic. Long division, subtraction, weights and measures—to calculate cords of wood and pecks of peas, pints and gallons and avoirdupois—young George delighted in these as other boys delighted in horseplay. As a man, he merely directed his passion into the channel of his possessions. Through his possessions he apparently satisfied his curious need for enumeration. He was not content simply to keep accounts of the acreage he owned, its yield, his slaves, his pounds and pence. Ellery recalled the extraordinary case of Washington and the seed. He once calculated the number of seeds in a pound troy weight of red clover. Not appeased by the statistics on red clover, Washington then went to work on a pound of timothy seed. His conclusions were: 71,000 and 298,000. His appetite unsatisfied, he thereupon fell upon the problem of New River grass. Here he tackled a calculation worthy of his prowess: his mathematical labors produced the great, pacifying figure of 844,800.

This man was so obsessed with numbers, Ellery thought, staring at the ruins of Washington's Grove, that he counted the windows in each house of his Mount Vernon estate and the number of "Paynes" in each window of each house, and then triumphantly recorded the exact number of each in his own handwriting.

It was like a hunger, requiring periodic appeasement. In 1747, as a boy of fifteen, George Washington drew "A Plan of Major Law: Washington's Turnip Field as Survey'd by me." In 1786, at the age of fifty-four, General Washington, the most famous man in the world, occupied himself with determining the exact elevation of his piazza above the Potomac's high-water mark. No doubt he experienced a warmer satisfaction thereafter for knowing that when he sat upon his piazza looking down upon the river he was exactly 124 feet 10½ inches above it.

And in 1791, as President of the United States, Ellery mused, he was striding about right here, setting saplings into the ground, twelve of them in an equilateral triangle, and beneath one of them he buried a copper case containing his sword and the half disme coined from his own silver. Beneath one of them . . . But it was not beneath one of them. Or had it been? And had long ago been dug up by a Clarke? But the story had apparently died with Simeon and Sarah. On the other hand . . .

Ellery found himself irrationally reluctant to conclude the obvious.

George Washington's lifelong absorption with figures kept intruding. Twelve trees, equidistant, in an equilateral triangle.

"What is it?" he kept asking himself, almost angrily. "Why isn't it satisfying me?"

And then, in the gathering dusk, a very odd explanation insinuated itself. *Because it wouldn't have satisfied him!*

That's silly, Ellery said to himself abruptly. It has all the ear-marks of a satisfying experience. There is no more satisfying figure in all geometry than an equilateral triangle. It is closed, symmetrical, definite, a whole and balanced and finished thing.

But it wouldn't have satisfied George Washington... for all its symmetry and perfection.

Then perhaps there is a symmetry and perfection beyond the cold beauty of figures?

At this point, Ellery began to question his own postulates ... lost in the dark and to his time ...

They found him at ten-thirty, crouched on the cultivator seat, numb and staring.

He permitted himself to be led into the house, he suffered Nikki to subject him to the indignity of having his shoes and socks stripped off and his frozen feet rubbed to life, he ate Martha Clarke's dinner—all with a detachment and indifference which alarmed the girls and even made old Tobias look uneasy.

"If it's going to have this effect on him," began Martha, and then she said: "Ellery, give it up. Forget it." But she had to shake him before he heard her.

He shook his head. "They're there."

"*Where?*" cried the girls simultaneously.

"In Washington's Grove."

"Ye found 'em?" croaked Tobias Clarke, half-rising.

"No."

The Clarkes and Nikki exchanged glances.

"Then how can you be so certain they're buried there, Ellery?" asked Nikki gently.

Ellery looked bewildered. "Darned if I know *how* I know," he said, and he even laughed a little. "Maybe George Washington told me." Then he stopped laughing and went into the firelit parlor and—pointedly —slid the doors shut.

At ten minutes past midnight Martha Clarke gave up the contest.

"Isn't he *ever* going to come out of there?" she said, yawning.

"You never can tell what Ellery will do," replied Nikki.

"Well, I can't keep my eyes open another minute."

"Funny," said Nikki. "I'm not the least bit sleepy."

"You city girls."

"You country girls."

They laughed. Then they stopped laughing, and for a moment there was no sound in the kitchen but the patient sentry-walk of the grandfather clock and the snores of Tobias assaulting the ceiling from above.

"Well," said Martha. Then she said: "I just *can't*. Are you staying up, Nikki?"

"For a little while. You go to bed, Martha."

"Yes. Well. Good night."

"Good night, Martha."

At the door Martha turned suddenly: "Did he say *George Washington told him?*"

"Yes."

Martha went rather quickly up the stairs.

Nikki waited fifteen minutes. Then she tiptoed to the foot of the stairs and listened. She heard Tobias snuffling and snorting as he turned over in his bed, and an uneasy moan from the direction of Martha's bedroom, as if she were dreaming an unwholesome dream. Nikki set her jaw grimly and went to the parlor doors and slid them open.

Ellery was on his knees before the fire. His elbows were resting on the floor. His face was propped in his hands. In this attitude his posterior was considerably higher than his head.

"Ellery!"

"Huh?"

"Ellery, what on earth—?"

"Nikki. I thought you'd gone to bed long ago." In the firelight his face was haggard.

"But what have you been *doing*? You look exhausted!"

"I am. I've been wrestling with a man who could bend a horseshoe with his naked hands. A very strong man. In more ways than one."

"What are you talking about? Who?"

"George Washington. Go to bed, Nikki."

"George . . . Washington?"

"Go to bed."

". . . *Wrestling* with him?"

"Trying to break through his defenses. Get into his mind. It's not an easy mind to get into. He's been dead such a long time—that makes the difference. The dead are stubborn, Nikki. Aren't you going to bed?"

Nikki backed out shivering.

The house *was* icy.

It was even icier when an inhuman bellow accompanied by a thunder that shook the Revolutionary walls of her bedroom brought Nikki out of bed with a yelping leap.

But it was only Ellery.

He was somewhere up the hall, in the first glacial light of dawn, hammering on Martha Clarke's door.

"Martha. *Martha!* Wake up, damn you, and tell me where I can find a book in this damned house! A biography of Washington—a history of the United States—an almanac . . . *anything!*"

The parlor fire had long since given up the ghost. Nikki and Martha in wrappers, and Tobias Clarke in an ancient bathrobe over his marbled long underwear, stood around shivering and bewildered as a disheveled, daemonic Ellery leafed eagerly through a 1921 edition of *The Farmer's Fact Book and Complete Compendium*.

"Here it is!" The words shot out of his mouth like bullets, leaving puffs of smoke.

"What is it, Ellery?"

"What on earth are you looking for?"

"He's loony, I tell ye!"

Ellery turned with a look of ineffable peace, closing the book.

"That's it," he said. "That's it."

"What's it?"

"Vermont. The State of Vermont."

"Vermont . . . ?"

"*Vermont?*"

"Vermont. What in the crawlin' creeper's Vermont got to do with—?"

"Vermont," said Ellery with a tired smile, "did not enter the Union until March fourth, 1791. So that proves it, don't you see?"

"Proves *what?*" shrieked Nikki.

"Where George Washington buried his sword and half disme."

"Because," said Ellery in the rapidly lightening dawn behind the barn, "Vermont was the fourteenth State to do so. The *fourteenth.* Tobias, would you get me an ax, please?"

"An ax," mumbled Tobias. He shuffled away, shaking his head.

"Come on, Ellery, I'm d-dying of c-cold!" chattered Nikki, dancing up and down before the cultivator.

"Ellery," said Martha Clarke piteously, "I don't understand any of this."

"It's very simple, Martha—oh, thank you, Tobias—as simple," said Ellery, "as simple arithmetic. Numbers, my dears—numbers tell this remarkable story. Numbers and their influence on our first President who was, above all things, a number-man. That was my key. I merely had to discover the lock to fit it into. Vermont was the lock. And the door's open."

Nikki seated herself on the cultivator. You had to give Ellery his head in a situation like this; you couldn't drive him for beans. Well, she thought grudgingly, seeing how pale and how tired-looking he was after a night's wrestling with George Washington, he's earned it.

"The number was wrong," said Ellery solemnly, leaning on Tobias's ax. "Twelve trees. Washington apparently planted twelve trees—Simeon Clarke's *Diary* never did mention the number twelve, but the evidence seemed unquestionable—there were twelve oaks in an equilateral triangle, each one an equal distance from its neighbor.

"And yet . . . I felt that *twelve* oaks couldn't be, perfect as the triangle was. Not if they were planted by George Washington. Not on February the twenty-second, New Style, in the year of our Lord 1791.

"Because on February the twenty-second, 1791—in fact, until March the fourth, when Vermont entered the Union to swell its original number by one—there was *another* number in the United States so important, so revered, so much a part of the common speech and the common living—and dying—that it was more than a number; it was a solemn and sacred thing; almost not a number at all. It overshadowed other numbers like the still-unborn Paul Bunyan. It was memorialized on the new American flag in the number of its stars and the number of its stripes. It was a number of which George Washington was the standard-bearer!—the head and only recently the strong right arm of the new Republic which had been born out of the blood and muscle of its integers. It was a number which was in the hearts and minds and mouths of all Americans.

"No. If George Washington, who was not merely the living symbol of all this but carried with him that extraordinary compulsion toward numbers which characterized his whole temperament besides, had wished to plant a number of oak trees to commemorate a birthday visit in the year 1791 . . . he would have, he could have, selected only one number out of all the mathematical trillions at his command—*the number thirteen.*"

The sun was looking over the edge of Pennsylvania at Washington's Grove.

"George Washington planted thirteen trees here that day, and under one of them he buried Paul Revere's copper case. Twelve of the trees he arranged in an equilateral triangle, and we know that the historic treasure was not under any of the twelve. Therefore he must have buried the case under the thirteenth—a thirteenth oak sapling which grew to oakhood and, some time during the past century and a half, withered and died and vanished, vanished so utterly that it left no trace, not even its roots.

"Where would Washington have planted that thirteenth oak? Because beneath the spot where it once stood—there lies the copper case containing his sword and the first coin to be struck off in the new United States."

And Ellery glanced tenderly at the cherry sapling which Tobias Clarke had set into the earth in the middle of Washington's Grove six years before.

"Washington the surveyor, the geometer, the man whose mind cried out for integral symmetries? Obviously, in only one place: *In the center of the triangle.* Any other place would be unthinkable."

And Ellery hefted Tobias's ax and strode toward the six-year-old tree. He raised the ax.

But suddenly he lowered it, and turned, and said in a rather startled way: "See here! Isn't today ... ?"

"Washington's Birthday," said Nikki.

Ellery grinned and began to chop down the cherry tree.

FOR DISCUSSION: The President's Half Disme

1. Ellery Queen uses clues, inferences, and pure logic just as many of his predecessors did, but—being very much a child of the twentieth century—he is keenly aware of the power of psychology. He knows that one way to find out *what* a man did is to find out *how* he thought. In what sense are Washington's thought processes of major importance in this story?

2. Writing a mystery story based on an historical character can be perilous. Readers indignantly report any historical inaccuracies they detect. What specific historical information about the past did the author use in this story? What part of the story is truly historical and what part is fictitious? What advantage is there in using a real person from history in an otherwise fictitious short story?

3. At one point in this story Nikki asks Ellery how he can be so sure that Washington really did bury something on the farm. Ellery replies, "Maybe George Washington told me." He wasn't mad, as one character seemed to think. What, then, did he mean?

4. A key line in solving the mystery is the half-question—"Then perhaps there is a symmetry and perfection beyond the cold beauty of figures?" What exactly does this mean? What does it tell us about Washington? About this country's view of itself in 1791?

5. Like Sherlock Holmes, Ellery Queen has a distinctive and memorable personality. After reading this story, you should be able to answer the following questions:
   a. What would be the most effective approach if you wanted to win Ellery's interest in a case?
   b. What positions and conditions best help Ellery to *think?*
   c. Is he persistent?
   d. Is he kind?
   e. Does he have a sense of humor?
   Substantiate each answer by referring to specific incidents in the story.

INTRODUCTION: The Dream

Outstanding among the cerebrating sleuths is little Hercule Poirot, the 5-foot-4-inch Belgian who exercises his "little grey cells" in pursuit of justice and truth. Poirot's egg-shaped head, his sharp green eyes, and his cherished mustache make him a memorable figure in the hall of fame of fictitious detectives.

His "creator," Agatha Christie, wrote over eighty novels. An intriguing sample is "The Dream," a work that could hardly have been written before Freud's intensive studies on the significance of dreams. In this story Poirot's sensitivity to the psychological flaw in his fellow humans enables him to perceive the truth even though it is blanketed by deception.

The Dream
Agatha Christie

Hercule Poirot gave the house a steady appraising glance. His eyes wandered a moment to its surroundings, the shops, the big factory building on the right, the blocks of cheap mansion flats opposite.

Then once more his eyes returned to Northway House, relic of an earlier age—an age of space and leisure, when green fields had surrounded its well-bred arrogance. Now it was an anachronism, submerged and forgotten in the hectic sea of modern London, and not one man in fifty could have told you where it stood.

Furthermore, very few people could have told you to whom it belonged, though its owner's name would have been recognized as one of the world's richest men. But money can quench publicity as well as flaunt it. Benedict Farley, that eccentric millionaire, chose not to advertise his choice of residence. He himself was rarely seen, seldom making a public appearance. From time to time he appeared at board meetings, his lean figure, beaked nose, and rasping voice easily dominating the assembled directors. Apart from that, he was just a well-known figure of legend. There were his strange meannesses, his incredible generosities, as well as more personal details—his famous patchwork dressing-gown, now reputed to be twenty-eight years old, his invariable diet of cabbage soup and caviar, his hatred of cats. All these things the public knew.

Hercule Poirot knew them also. It was all he did know of the man he was about to visit. The letter which was in his coat pocket told him little more.

181

After surveying this melancholy landmark of a past age for a minute or two in silence, he walked up the steps to the front door and pressed the bell, glancing as he did so at the neat wrist-watch which had at last replaced an earlier favorite—the large turnip-faced watch of earlier days. Yes, it was exactly nine-thirty. As ever, Hercule Poirot was exact to the minute.

The door opened after just the right interval. A perfect specimen of the genus butler stood outlined against the lighted hall.

"Mr. Benedict Farley?" asked Hercule Poirot.

The impersonal glance surveyed him from head to foot, inoffensively but effectively.

"*En gros et en détail,*" thought Hercule Poirot to himself with appreciation.

"You have an appointment, sir?" asked the suave voice.

"Yes."

"Your name, sir?"

"M. Hercule Poirot."

The butler bowed and drew back. Hercule Poirot entered the house. The butler closed the door behind him.

But there was yet one more formality before the deft hands took hat and stick from the visitor.

"You will excuse me, sir. I was to ask for a letter."

With deliberation Poirot took from his pocket the folded letter and handed it to the butler. The latter gave it a mere glance, then returned it with a bow. Hercule Poirot returned it to his pocket. Its contents were simple.

Northway House, W. 8

M. HERCULE POIROT.

DEAR SIR,

    Mr. Benedict Farley would like to have the benefit of your advice. If convenient to yourself he would be glad if you would call upon him at the above address at 9:30 tomorrow (Thursday) evening.

Yours truly,

HUGO CORNWORTHY.

(Secretary).

P.S.—Please bring this letter with you.

Deftly the butler relieved Poirot of hat, stick, and overcoat. He said: "Will you please come up to Mr. Cornworthy's room?"

He led the way up the broad staircase. Poirot followed him, looking with appreciation at such *objets d'art* as were of an opulent and florid nature! His taste in art was always somewhat bourgeois.

On the first floor the butler knocked on a door.

Hercule Poirot's eyebrows rose very slightly. It was the first jarring note. For the best butlers do not knock at doors—and yet indubitably this was a first-class butler!

It was, so to speak, the first intimation of contact with the eccentricity of a millionaire.

A voice from within called out something. The butler threw open the door. He announced (and again Poirot sensed the deliberate departure from orthodoxy):

"The gentleman you are expecting, sir."

Poirot passed into the room. It was a fair-sized room, very plainly furnished in a workmanlike fashion. Filing cabinets, books of reference, a couple of easy chairs, and a large and imposing desk covered with neatly docketed papers. The corners of the room were dim, for the only light came from a big green-shaded reading-lamp which stood on a small table by the arm of one of the easy chairs. It was placed so as to cast its full light on anyone approaching from the door. Hercule Poirot blinked a little, realizing that the lamp bulb was at least 150 watts. In the arm-chair sat a thin figure in a patchwork dressing-gown—Benedict Farley. His head was stuck forward in a characteristic attitude, his beaked nose projecting like that of a bird. A crest of white hair like that of a cockatoo rose above his forehead. His eyes glittered behind thick lenses as he peered suspiciously at his visitor.

"Hey," he said at last—and his voice was shrill and harsh, with a rasping note in it. "So you're Hercule Poirot, hey?"

"At your service," said Poirot politely and bowed, one hand on the back of the chair.

"Sit down—sit down," said the old man testily.

Hercule Poirot sat down—in the full glare of the lamp. From behind it the old man seemed to be studying him attentively.

"How do I know you're Hercule Poirot—hey?" he demanded fretfully. "Tell me that—hey?"

Once more Poirot drew the letter from his pocket and handed it to Farley.

"Yes," admitted the millionaire grudgingly. "That's it. That's what I got Cornworthy to write." He folded it up and tossed it back. "So you're the fellow, are you?"

With a little wave of his hand Poirot said:

"I assure you there is no deception!"

Benedict Farley chuckled suddenly.

"That's what the conjurer says before he takes the goldfish out of the hat! Saying that is part of the trick, you know."

Poirot did not reply. Farley said suddenly:

"Think I'm a suspicious old man, hey? So I am. Don't trust anybody!

That's my motto. Can't trust anybody when you're rich. No, no, it doesn't do."

"You wished," Poirot hinted gently, "to consult me?"

The old man nodded.

"That's right. Always buy the best. That's my motto. Go to the expert and don't count the cost. You'll notice, M. Poirot, I haven't asked you your fee. I'm not going to! Send me in the bill later—I shan't cut up rough over it. Damned fools at the dairy thought they could charge me two and nine for eggs when two and seven's the market price—lot of swindlers! I won't be swindled. But the man at the top's different. He's worth the money. I'm at the top myself—I know."

Hercule Poirot made no reply. He listened attentively, his head poised a little on one side.

Behind his impassive exterior he was conscious of a feeling of disappointment. He could not exactly put his finger on it. So far Benedict Farley had run true to type—that is, he had conformed to the popular idea of himself; and yet—Poirot was disappointed.

"The man," he said disgustedly to himself, "is a mountebank—nothing but a mountebank!"

He had known other millionaires, eccentric men too, but in nearly every case he had been conscious of a certain force, an inner energy that had commanded his respect. If they had worn a patchwork dressing-gown, it would have been because they liked wearing such a dressing-gown. But the dressing-gown of Benedict Farley, or so it seemed to Poirot, was essentially a stage property. And the man himself was essentially stagey. Every word he spoke was uttered, so Poirot felt assured, sheerly for effect.

He repeated again unemotionally, "You wished to consult me, Mr. Farley?"

Abruptly the millionaire's manner changed.

He leaned forward. His voice dropped to a croak.

"Yes. Yes . . . I want to hear what you've got to say—what you think. . . . Go to the top! That's my way! The best doctor—the best detective —it's between the two of them."

"As yet, Monsieur, I do not understand."

"Naturally," snapped Farley. "I haven't begun to tell you."

He leaned forward once more and shot out an abrupt question.

"What do you know, M. Poirot, about dreams?"

The little man's eyebrows rose. Whatever he had expected, it was not this.

"For that, Monsieur Farley, I should recommend Napoleon's *Book of Dreams*—or the latest practicing psychologist from Harley Street."

Benedict Farley said soberly, "I've tried both. . . ."

There was a pause, then the millionaire spoke, at first almost in a whisper, then with a voice growing higher and higher.

"It's the same dream—night after night. And I'm afraid, I tell you— I'm afraid. . . . It's always the same. I'm sitting in my room next door to this. Sitting at my desk, writing. There's a clock there and I glance at it and see the time—exactly twenty-eight minutes past three. Always the same time, you understand.

"And when I see the time, M. Poirot, I know I've got to do it. I don't want to do it—I loathe doing it—but I've got to. . . ."

His voice had risen shrilly.

Unperturbed, Poirot said, "And what is it that you have to do?"

"At twenty-eight minutes past three," Benedict Farley said hoarsely, "I open the second drawer down on the right of my desk, take out the revolver that I keep there, load it, and walk over to the window. And then —and then—"

"Yes?"

Benedict Farley said in a whisper:

"Then I shoot myself. . . ."

There was silence.

Then Poirot said, "That is your dream?"

"Yes."

"The same every night?"

"Yes."

"What happens after you shoot yourself?"

"I wake up."

Poirot nodded his head slowly and thoughtfully. "As a matter of interest, do you keep a revolver in that particular drawer?"

"Yes."

"Why?"

"I have always done so. It is as well to be prepared."

"Prepared for what?"

Farley said irritably, "A man in my position has to be on his guard. All rich men have enemies."

Poirot did not pursue the subject. He remained silent for a moment or two, then he said:

"Why exactly did you send for me?"

"I will tell you. First of all I consulted a doctor—three doctors to be exact."

"Yes?"

"The first told me it was all a question of diet. He was an elderly man. The second was a young man of the modern school. He assured me that it all hinged on a certain event that took place in infancy at that particular time of day—three twenty-eight. I am so determined, he says, not to remember that event, that I symbolize it by destroying myself. That is his explanation."

"And the third doctor?" asked Poirot.

Benedict Farley's voice rose in shrill anger.

"He's a young man, too. He has a preposterous theory! He asserts that I, myself, am tired of life, that my life is so unbearable to me that I deliberately want to end it! But since to acknowledge that fact would be to acknowledge that essentially I am a failure, I refuse in my waking moments to face the truth. But when I am asleep, all inhibitions are removed, and I proceed to do that *which I really wish to do*. I put an end to myself."

"His view is that you really wish, unknown to yourself, to commit suicide?" said Poirot.

Benedict Farley cried shrilly:

"And that's impossible—impossible! I'm perfectly happy! I've got everything I want—everything money can buy! It's fantastic—unbelievable even to suggest a thing like that!"

Poirot looked at him with interest. Perhaps something in the shaking hands, the trembling shrillness of the voice, warned him that the denial was *too* vehement, that its very insistence was in itself suspect. He contented himself with saying:

"And where do I come in, Monsieur?"

Benedict Farley calmed down suddenly. He tapped with an emphatic finger on the table beside him.

"There's another possibility. And if it's right, you're the man to know about it! You're famous, you've had hundreds of cases—fantastic, improbable cases! You'd know if anyone does."

"Know what?"

Farley's voice dropped to a whisper.

"Supposing someone wants to kill me. . . . Could they do it this way? Could they make me dream that dream night after night?"

"Hypnotism, you mean?"

"Yes."

Hercule Poirot considered the question.

"It would be possible, I suppose," he said at last. "It is more a question for a doctor."

"You don't know of such a case in your experience?"

"Not precisely on those lines, no."

"You see what I'm driving at? I'm made to dream the same dream, night after night, night after night—and then—one day the suggestion is too much for me—*and I act upon it*. I do what I've dreamed of so often —kill myself!"

Slowly Hercule Poirot shook his head.

"You don't think that is possible?" asked Farley.

"*Possible?*" Poirot shook his head. "That is not a word I care to meddle with."

"But you think it improbable?"

"Most improbable."

Benedict Farley murmured, "The doctor said so too. . . ." Then his voice rising shrilly again, he cried out, "But why do I have this dream? Why? Why?"

Hercule Poirot shook his head. Benedict Farley said abruptly, "You're sure you've never come across anything like this in your experience?"

"Never."

"That's what I wanted to know."

Delicately, Poirot cleared his throat.

"You permit," he said, "a question?"

"What is it? What is it? Say what you like."

"Who is it you suspect of wanting to kill you?"

Farley snapped out, "Nobody. Nobody at all."

"But the idea presented itself to your mind?" Poirot persisted.

"I wanted to know—if it was a possibility."

"Speaking from my own experience, I should say no. Have you ever been hypnotized, by the way?"

"Of course not. D'you think I'd lend myself to such tomfoolery?"

"Then I think one can say that your theory is definitely improbable."

"But the dream, you fool, the dream."

"The dream is certainly remarkable," said Poirot thoughtfully. He paused and then went on. "I should like to see the scene of this drama—the table, the clock, and the revolver."

"Of course, I'll take you next door."

Wrapping the folds of his dressing-gown round him, the old man half-rose from his chair. Then suddenly, as though a thought had struck him, he resumed his seat.

"No," he said. "There's nothing to see there. I've told you all there is to tell."

"But I should like to see for myself—"

"There's no need," Farley snapped. "You've given me your opinion. That's the end."

Poirot shrugged his shoulders. "As you please." He rose to his feet. "I am sorry, Mr. Farley, that I have not been able to be of assistance to you."

Benedict Farley was staring straight ahead of him.

"Don't want a lot of hanky-pankying around," he growled out. "I've told you the facts—you can't make anything of them. That closes the matter. You can send me in a bill for a consultation fee."

"I shall not fail to do so," said the detective dryly. He walked towards the door.

"Stop a minute." The millionaire called him back. "That letter—I want it."

"The letter from your secretary?"

"Yes."

Poirot's eyebrows rose. He put his hand into his pocket, drew out a folded sheet, and handed it to the old man. The latter scrutinized it, then put it down on the table beside him with a nod.

Once more Hercule Poirot walked to the door. He was puzzled. His busy mind was going over and over the story he had been told. Yet in the midst of his mental preoccupation, a nagging sense of something wrong obtruded itself. And that something had to do with himself—not with Benedict Farley.

With his hand on the doorknob, his mind cleared. He, Hercule Poirot, had been guilty of an error! He turned back into the room once more.

"A thousand pardons! In the interest of your problem I have committed a folly! That letter I handed to you—by mischance I put my hand into my right-hand pocket instead of the left—"

"What's all this? What's all this?"

"The letter that I handed you just now—an apology from my laundress concerning the treatment of my collars." Poirot was smiling, apologetic. He dipped into his left-hand pocket. "This is *your* letter."

Benedict Farley snatched at it—grunted: "Why the devil can't you mind what you're doing?"

Poirot retrieved his laundress's communication, apologized gracefully once more, and left the room.

He paused for a moment outside on the landing. It was a spacious one. Directly facing him was a big old oak settle with a refectory table in front of it. On the table were magazines. There were also two armchairs and a table with flowers. It reminded him a little of a dentist's waiting-room.

The butler was in the hall below waiting to let him out.

"Can I get you a taxi, sir?"

"No, I thank you. The night is fine. I will walk."

Hercule Poirot paused a moment on the pavement waiting for a lull in the traffic before crossing the busy street.

A frown creased his forehead.

"No," he said to himself. "I do not understand at all. Nothing makes sense. Regrettable to have to admit it, but I, Hercule Poirot, am completely baffled."

That was what might be termed the first act of the drama. The second act followed a week later. It opened with a telephone call from one John Stillingfleet, M.D.

He said with a remarkable lack of medical decorum:

"That you, Poirot, old horse? Stillingfleet here."

"Yes, my friend. What is it?"

"I'm speaking from Northway House—Benedict Farley's."

"Ah, yes?" Poirot's voice quickened with interest. "What of—Mr. Farley?"

"Farley's dead. Shot himself this afternoon."

There was a pause, then Poirot said:

"Yes. . . ."

"I notice you're not overcome with surprise. Know something about it, old horse?"

"Why should you think that?"

"Well, it isn't brilliant deduction or telepathy or anything like that. We found a note from Farley to you making an appointment about a week ago."

"I see."

"We've got a tame police inspector here—got to be careful, you know, when one of these millionaire blokes bumps himself off. Wondered whether you could throw any light on the case. If so, perhaps you'd come round?"

"I will come immediately."

"Good for you, old boy. Some dirty work at the cross-roads—eh?"

Poirot merely repeated that he would set forth immediately.

"Don't want to spill the beans over the telephone? Quite right. So long."

A quarter of an hour later Poirot was sitting in the library, a low long room at the back of Northway House on the ground floor. There were five other persons in the room. Inspector Barnett, Dr. Stillingfleet, Mrs. Farley, the widow of the millionaire, Joanna Farley, his only daughter, and Hugo Cornworthy, his private secretary.

Of these, Inspector Barnett was a discreet soldierly-looking man. Dr. Stillingfleet, whose professional manner was entirely different from his telephonic style, was a tall, long-faced young man of thirty. Mrs. Farley was obviously very much younger than her husband. She was a handsome dark-haired woman. Her mouth was hard and her black eyes gave absolutely no clue to her emotions. She appeared perfectly self-possessed. Joanna Farley had fair hair and a freckled face. The prominence of her nose and chin was clearly inherited from her father. Her eyes were intelligent and shrewd. Hugo Cornworthy was a somewhat colorless young man, very correctly dressed. He seemed intelligent and efficient.

After greetings and introductions, Poirot narrated simply and clearly the circumstances of his visit and the story told him by Benedict Farley. He could not complain of any lack of interest.

"Most extraordinary story I've ever heard!" said the inspector. "A dream, eh? Did you know anything about this, Mrs. Farley?"

She bowed her head.

"My husband mentioned it to me. It upset him very much. I—I told him it was indigestion—his diet, you know, was very peculiar—and suggested his calling in Dr. Stillingfleet."

That young man shook his head.

"He didn't consult me. From M. Poirot's story, I gather he went to Harley Street."

"I would like your advice on that point, doctor," said Poirot. "Mr. Farley told me that he consulted three specialists. What do you think of the theories they advanced?"

Stillingfleet frowned.

"It's difficult to say. You've got to take into account that what he passed on to you wasn't exactly what had been said to him. It was a layman's interpretation."

"You mean he had got the phraseology wrong?"

"Not exactly. I mean they would put a thing to him in professional terms, he'd get the meaning a little distorted, and then recast it in his own language."

"So that what he told me was not really what the doctors said."

"That's what it amounts to. He's just got it all a little wrong, if you know what I mean."

Poirot nodded thoughtfully. "Is it known whom he consulted?" he asked.

Mrs. Farley shook her head, and Joanna Farley remarked:

"None of us had any idea he had consulted anyone."

"Did he speak to *you* about his dream?" asked Poirot.

The girl shook her head.

"And you, Mr. Cornworthy?"

"No, he said nothing at all. I took down a letter to you at his dictation, but I had no idea why he wished to consult you. I thought it might possibly have something to do with some business irregularity."

Poirot asked: "And now as to the actual facts of Mr. Farley's death?"

Inspector Barnett looked interrogatively at Mrs. Farley and at Dr. Stillingfleet, and then took upon himself the rôle of spokesman.

"Mr. Farley was in the habit of working in his own room on the first floor every afternoon. I understand that there was a big amalgamation of businesses in prospect—"

He looked at Hugo Cornworthy who said, "Consolidated Coachlines."

"In connection with that," continued Inspector Barnett, "Mr. Farley had agreed to give an interview to two members of the Press. He very seldom did anything of the kind—only about once in five years, I understand. Accordingly two reporters, one from the Associated Newsgroups, and one from Amalgamated Press-sheets, arrived at a quarter past three by appointment. They waited on the first floor outside Mr. Farley's door —which was the customary place for people to wait who had an appointment with Mr. Farley. At twenty past three a messenger arrived from the office of Consolidated Coachlines with some urgent papers. He was shown into Mr. Farley's room where he handed over the documents. Mr. Farley accompanied him to the door of the room, and from there spoke to the two members of the Press. He said:

" 'I am sorry, gentlemen, to have to keep you waiting, but I have some urgent business to attend to. I will be as quick as I can.'

"The two gentlemen, Mr. Adams and Mr. Stoddart, assured Mr. Farley that they would await his convenience. He went back into his room, shut the door—and was never seen alive again!"

"Continue," said Poirot.

"At a little after four o'clock," went on the inspector, "Mr. Cornworthy here came out of his room which is next door to Mr. Farley's, and was surprised to see the two reporters still waiting. He wanted Mr. Farley's signature to some letters and thought he had also better remind him that these two gentlemen were waiting. He accordingly went into Mr. Farley's room. To his surprise he could not at first see Mr. Farley and thought the room was empty. Then he caught sight of a boot sticking out behind the desk (which is placed in front of the window). He went quickly across and discovered Mr. Farley lying there dead, with a revolver beside him.

"Mr. Cornworthy hurried out of the room and directed the butler to ring up Dr. Stillingfleet. By the latter's advice, Mr. Cornworthy also informed the police."

"Was the shot heard?" asked Poirot.

"No. The traffic is very noisy here, the landing window was open. What with lorries and motor horns it would be most unlikely if it had been noticed."

Poirot nodded thoughtfully. "What time is it supposed he died?" he asked.

Stillingfleet said:

"I examined the body as soon as I got here—that is, at thirty-two minutes past four. Mr. Farley had been dead at least an hour."

Poirot's face was very grave.

"So then, it seems possible that his death could have occurred at the time he mentioned to me—that is, at twenty-eight minutes past three."

"Exactly," said Stillingfleet.

"Any finger-marks on the revolver?"

"Yes, his own."

"And the revolver itself?"

The inspector took up the tale.

"Was one which he kept in the second right-hand drawer of his desk, just as he told you. Mrs. Farley has identified it positively. Moreover, you understand, there is only one entrance to the room, the door giving on to the landing. The two reporters were sitting exactly opposite that door and they swear that no one entered the room from the time Mr. Farley spoke to them, until Mr. Cornworthy entered it at a little after four o'clock."

"So that there is every reason to suppose that Mr. Farley committed suicide?"

Inspector Barnett smiled a little.

"There would have been no doubt at all but for one point."

"And that?"

"The letter written to you."

Poirot smiled too.

"I see! Where Hercule Poirot is concerned—immediately the suspicion of murder arises!"

"Precisely," said the inspector dryly. "However, after your clearing up of the situation—"

Poirot interrupted him. "One little minute." He turned to Mrs. Farley. "Had your husband ever been hypnotized?"

"Never."

"Had he studied the question of hypnotism? Was he interested in the subject?"

She shook her head. "I don't think so."

Suddenly her self-control seemed to break down. "That horrible dream! It's uncanny! That he should have dreamed that—night after night—and then—and then—it's as though he were—*hounded* to death!"

Poirot remembered Benedict Farley saying—"*I proceed to do that which I really wish to do. I put an end to myself.*"

He said, "Had it ever occurred to you that your husband might be tempted to do away with himself?"

"No—at least—sometimes he was very queer. . . ."

Joanna Farley's voice broke in clear and scornful. "Father would never have killed himself. He was far too careful of himself."

Dr. Stillingfleet said, "It isn't the people who threaten to commit suicide who usually do it, you know, Miss Farley. That's why suicides sometimes seem unaccountable."

Poirot rose to his feet. "Is it permitted," he asked, "that I see the room where the tragedy occurred?"

"Certainly. Dr. Stillingfleet—"

The doctor accompanied Poirot upstairs.

Benedict Farley's room was a much larger one than the secretary's next door. It was luxuriously furnished with deep leather-covered armchairs, a thick pile carpet, and a superb outsize writing-desk.

Poirot passed behind the latter to where a dark stain on the carpet showed just before the window. He remembered the millionaire saying, *"At twenty-eight minutes past three I open the second drawer down on the right of my desk, take out the revolver that I keep there, load it, and walk over to the window. And then—and then I shoot myself."*

He nodded slowly. Then he said:

"The window was open like this?"

"Yes. But nobody could have got in that way."

Poirot put his head out. There was no sill or parapet and no pipes near. Not even a cat could have gained access that way. Opposite rose the blank wall of the factory, a dead wall with no windows in it.

Stillingfleet said, "Funny room for a rich man to choose as his own sanctum with that outlook. It's like looking out on to a prison wall."

"Yes," said Poirot. He drew his head in and stared at the expanse of solid brick. "I think," he said, "that that wall is important."

Stillingfleet looked at him curiously. "You mean—psychologically?"

Poirot had moved to the desk. Idly, or so it seemed, he picked up a pair of what are usually called lazytongs. He pressed the handles; the tongs shot out to their full length. Delicately, Poirot picked up a burnt match stump with them from beside a chair some feet away and conveyed it carefully to the waste-paper basket.

"When you've finished playing with those things . . ." said Stillingfleet irritably.

Hercule Poirot murmured, "An ingenious invention," and replaced the tongs neatly on the writing-table. Then he asked:

"Where were Mrs. Farley and Miss Farley at the time of the—death?"

"Mrs. Farley was resting in her room on the floor above this. Miss Farley was painting in her studio at the top of the house."

Hercule Poirot drummed idly with his fingers on the table for a minute or two. Then he said:

"I should like to see Miss Farley. Do you think you could ask her to come here for a minute or two?"

"If you like."

Stillingfleet glanced at him curiously, then left the room. In another minute or two the door opened and Joanna Farley came in.

"You do not mind, mademoiselle, if I ask you a few questions?"

She returned his glance coolly. "Please ask anything you choose."

"Did you know that your father kept a revolver in his desk?"

"No."

"Where were you and your mother—that is to say your stepmother—that is right?"

"Yes, Louise is my father's second wife. She is only eight years older than I am. You were about to say—?"

"Where were you and she on Thursday of last week? That is to say, on Thursday night."

She reflected for a minute or two.

"Thursday? Let me see. Oh, yes, we had gone to the theater. To see *Little Dog Laughed.*"

"Your father did not suggest accompanying you?"

"He never went out to theaters."

"What did he usually do in the evenings?"

"He sat in here and read."

"He was not a very sociable man?"

The girl looked at him directly. "My father," she said, "had a singularly unpleasant personality. No one who lived in close association with him could possibly be fond of him."

"That, mademoiselle, is a very candid statement."

"I am saving you time, M. Poirot. I realize quite well what you are getting at. My stepmother married my father for his money. I live here because I have no money to live elsewhere. There is a man I wish to marry—a poor man; my father saw to it that he lost his job. He wanted me, you see, to marry well—an easy matter since I was to be his heiress!"

"Your father's fortune passes to you?"

"Yes. That is, he left Louise, my stepmother, a quarter of a million free of tax, and there are other legacies, but the residue goes to me." She smiled suddenly. "So you see, M. Poirot, I had every reason to desire my father's death!"

"I see, mademoiselle, that you have inherited your father's intelligence."

She said thoughtfully, "Father was clever.... One felt that with him—that he had force—driving power—but it had all turned sour—bitter—there was no humanity left...."

Hercule Poirot said softly, "*Grand Dieu,* but what an imbecile I am...."

Joanna Farley turned towards the door. "Is there anything more?"

"Two little questions. These tongs here," he picked up the lazytongs, "were they always on the table?"

"Yes. Father used them for picking up things. He didn't like stooping."

"One other question. Was your father's eyesight good?"

She stared at him.

"Oh, no—he couldn't see at all—I mean he couldn't see without his glasses. His sight had always been bad from a boy."

"But with his glasses?"

"Oh, he could see all right then, of course."

"He could read newspapers and fine print?"

"Oh, yes."

"That is all, mademoiselle."

She went out of the room.

Poirot murmured, "I was stupid. It was there, all the time, under my nose. And because it was so near I could not see it."

He leaned out of the window once more. Down below, in the narrow way between the house and the factory, he saw a small dark object.

Hercule Poirot nodded, satisfied, and went downstairs again.

The others were still in the library. Poirot addressed himself to the secretary:

"I want you, Mr. Cornworthy, to recount to me in detail the exact circumstances of Mr. Farley's summons to me. When, for instance, did Mr. Farley dictate that letter?"

"On Wednesday afternoon—at five-thirty, as far as I can remember."

"Were there any special directions about posting it?"

"He told me to post it myself."

"And you did so?"

"Yes."

"Did he give any special instructions to the butler about admitting me?"

"Yes. He told me to tell Holmes (Holmes is the butler) that a gentleman would be calling at 9:30. He was to ask the gentleman's name. He was also to ask to see the letter."

"Rather peculiar precautions to take, don't you think?"

Cornworthy shrugged his shoulders.

"Mr. Farley," he said carefully, "was rather a peculiar man."

"Any other instructions?"

"Yes. He told me to take the evening off."

"Did you do so?"

"Yes, immediately after dinner I went to the cinema."

"When did you return?"

"I let myself in about a quarter past eleven."

"Did you see Mr. Farley again that evening?"

"No."

"And he did not mention the matter the next morning?"

"No."

Poirot paused a moment, then resumed, "When I arrived I was not shown into Mr. Farley's own room."

"No. He told me that I was to tell Holmes to show you into my room."

"Why was that? Do you know?"

Cornworthy shook his head. "I never questioned any of Mr. Farley's orders," he said dryly. "He would have resented it if I had."

"Did he usually receive visitors in his own room?"

"Usually, but not always. Sometimes he saw them in my room."

"Was there any reason for that?"

Hugo Cornworthy considered.

"No—I hardly think so—I've never really thought about it."

Turning to Mrs. Farley, Poirot asked:

"You permit that I ring for your butler?"

"Certainly, M. Poirot."

Very correct, very urbane, Holmes answered the bell.

"You rang, madam?"

Mrs. Farley indicated Poirot with a gesture. Holmes turned politely. "Yes, sir?"

"What were your instructions, Holmes, on the Thursday night when I came here?"

Holmes cleared his throat, then said:

"After dinner Mr. Cornworthy told me that Mr. Farley expected a Mr. Hercule Poirot at 9:30. I was to ascertain the gentleman's name, and I was to verify the information by glancing at a letter. Then I was to show him up to Mr. Cornworthy's room."

"Were you also told to knock on the door?"

An expression of distaste crossed the butler's countenance.

"That was one of Mr. Farley's orders. I was always to knock when introducing visitors—business visitors, that is," he added.

"Ah, that puzzled me! Were you given any other instructions concerning me?"

"No, sir. When Mr. Cornworthy had told me what I have just repeated to you he went out."

"What time was that?"

"Ten minutes to nine, sir."

"Did you see Mr. Farley after that?"

"Yes, sir, I took him up a glass of hot water as usual at nine o'clock."

"Was he then in his own room or in Mr. Cornworthy's?"

"He was in his own room, sir."

"You noticed nothing unusual about that room?"

"Unusual? No, sir."

"Where were Mrs. Farley and Miss Farley?"

"They had gone to the theater, sir."

"Thank you, Holmes, that will do."

Holmes bowed and left the room. Poirot turned to the millionaire's widow.

"One more question, Mrs. Farley. Had your husband good sight?"

"No. Not without his glasses."

"He was very short-sighted?"

"Oh, yes, he was quite helpless without his spectacles."

"He had several pairs of glasses?"

"Yes."

"Ah," said Poirot. He leaned back. "I think that that concludes the case. . . ."

There was silence in the room. They were all looking at the little man who sat there complacently stroking his mustache. On the inspector's face was perplexity, Dr. Stillingfleet was frowning, Cornworthy merely stared uncomprehendingly, Mrs. Farley gazed in blank astonishment, Joanna Farley looked eager.

Mrs. Farley broke the silence.

"I don't understand, M. Poirot." Her voice was fretful. "The dream—"

"Yes," said Poirot. "That dream was very important."

Mrs. Farley shivered. She said:

"I've never believed in anything supernatural before—but now—to dream it night after night beforehand—"

"It's extraordinary," said Stillingfleet. "Extraordinary! If we hadn't got your word for it, Poirot, and if you hadn't had it straight from the horse's mouth—" he coughed in embarrassment, and readopting his professional manner, "I beg your pardon, Mrs. Farley. If Mr. Farley himself had not told that story—"

"Exactly," said Poirot. His eyes, which had been half-closed, opened suddenly. They were very green. *"If Benedict Farley hadn't told me—"*

He paused a minute, looking round at a circle of blank faces.

"There are certain things, you comprehend, that happened that evening which I was quite at a loss to explain. First, why make such a point of my bringing that letter with me?"

"Identification," suggested Cornworthy.

"No, no, my dear young man. Really that idea is too ridiculous. There must be some more valid reason. For not only did Mr. Farley require to see that letter produced, but he definitely demanded that I should leave it behind me. And moreover even then he did not destroy it! It was found among his papers this afternoon. *Why did he keep it?"*

Joanna Farley's voice broke in. "He wanted, in case anything happened to him, that the facts of his strange dream should be made known."

Poirot nodded approvingly.

"You are astute, mademoiselle. That must be—that can only be—the point of the keeping of the letter. When Mr. Farley was dead, the story of that strange dream was to be told! That dream was very important. That dream, mademoiselle, was *vital!*

"I will come now," he went on, "to the second point. After hearing his story I ask Mr. Farley to show me the desk and the revolver. He seems about to get up to do so, then suddenly refuses. Why did he refuse?"

This time no one advanced an answer.

"I will put that question differently. *What was there in that next room that Mr. Farley did not want me to see?*"

There was still silence.

"Yes," said Poirot, "it is difficult, that. And yet there was some reason —some *urgent* reason why Mr. Farley received me in his secretary's room and refused point blank to take me into his own room. *There was something in that room he could not afford to have me see.*

"And now I come to the third inexplicable thing that happened on that evening. Mr. Farley, just as I was leaving, requested me to hand him the letter I had received. By inadvertence I handed him a communication from my laundress. He glanced at it and laid it down beside him. Just before I left the room I discovered my error—and rectified it! After that I left the house and—I admit it—I was completely at sea! The whole affair and especially that last incident seemed to me quite inexplicable."

He looked round from one to the other.

"You do not see?"

Stillingfleet said, "I don't really see how your laundress comes into it, Poirot."

"My laundress," said Poirot, "was very important. That miserable woman who ruins my collars, was, for the first time in her life, useful to somebody. Surely you see—it is so obvious. Mr. Farley glanced at that communication—*one glance* would have told him that it was the wrong letter—and yet he knew nothing. Why? *Because he could not see it properly!*"

Inspector Barnett said sharply, "Didn't he have his glasses on?"

Hercule Poirot smiled. "Yes," he said. "He had his glasses on. That is what makes it so very interesting."

He leaned forward.

"Mr. Farley's dream was very important. He dreamed, you see, that he committed suicide. And a little later on, he did commit suicide. That is to say he was alone in a room and was found there with a revolver by him, and no one entered or left the room at the time that he was shot. What does that mean? It means, does it not, that it *must* be suicide!"

"Yes," said Stillingfleet.

Hercule Poirot shook his head.

"On the contrary," he said. "It was murder. An unusual and a very cleverly planned murder."

Again he leaned forward, tapping the table, his eyes green and shining. "Why did Mr. Farley not allow me to go into his own room that evening? What was there in there that I must not be allowed to see? I think, my friends, that there was—Benedict Farley himself!"

He smiled at the blank faces.

"Yes, yes, it is not nonsense what I say. Why could the Mr. Farley to whom I had been talking not realize the difference between two totally dissimilar letters? Because, *mes amis*, he was a man of *normal sight* wearing a pair of very powerful glasses. Those glasses would render a man of normal eyesight practically blind. Isn't that so, doctor?"

Stillingfleet murmured, "That's so—of course."

"Why did I feel that in talking to Mr. Farley I was talking to a *mountebank*, to an actor playing a part? Because he *was* playing a part! Consider the setting. The dim room, the green shaded light turned blindingly away from the figure in the chair. What did I see—the famous patchwork dressing-gown, the beaked nose (faked with that useful substance, nose putty) the white crest of hair, the powerful lenses concealing the eyes. What evidence is there that Mr. Farley ever had a dream? Only the story I was told and the evidence of *Mrs. Farley*. What evidence is there that Benedict Farley kept a revolver in his desk? Again only the story told me and the word of Mrs. Farley. Two people carried this fraud through—Mrs. Farley and Hugo Cornworthy. Cornworthy wrote the letter to me, gave instructions to the butler, went out ostensibly to the cinema, but let himself in again immediately with a key, went to his room, made himself up, and played the part of Benedict Farley.

"And so we come to this afternoon. The opportunity for which Mr. Cornworthy has been waiting arrives. There are two witnesses on the landing to swear that no one goes in or out of Benedict Farley's room. Cornworthy waits until a particularly heavy batch of traffic is about to pass. Then he leans out of his window, and with the lazytongs which he has purloined from the desk next door he holds an object against the window of that room. Benedict Farley comes to the window. Cornworthy snatches back the tongs and as Farley leans out, and the lorries are passing outside, Cornworthy shoots him with the revolver that he has ready. There is a blank wall opposite, remember. There can be no witness of the crime. Cornworthy waits for over half an hour, then gathers up some papers, conceals the lazytongs and the revolver between them and goes out on to the landing and into the next room. He replaces the tongs on the desk, lays down the revolver after pressing the dead man's fingers on it, and hurries out with the news of Mr. Farley's 'suicide.'

"He arranges that the letter to me shall be found and that I shall arrive with my story—the story I heard *from Mr. Farley's own lips*—of his extraordinary 'dream'—the strange compulsion he felt to kill himself! A few credulous people will discuss the hypnotism theory—but the main result will be to confirm without a doubt that the actual hand that held the revolver was Benedict Farley's own."

Hercule Poirot's eyes went to the widow's face—the dismay—the ashy pallor—the blind fear.

"And in due course," he finished gently, "the happy ending would have been achieved. A quarter of a million and two hearts that beat as one. . . .'"

John Stillingfleet, M.D., and Hercule Poirot walked along the side of Northway House. On their right was the towering wall of the factory. Above them, on their left, were the windows of Benedict Farley's and Hugo Cornworthy's rooms. Hercule Poirot stopped and picked up a small object—a black stuffed cat.

"*Voilà*" he said. "That is what Cornworthy held in the lazytongs against Farley's window. You remember, he hated cats? Naturally he rushed to the window."

"Why on earth didn't Cornworthy come out and pick it up after he'd dropped it?"

"How could he? To do so would have been definitely suspicious. After all, if this object were found what would anyone think—that some child had wandered round here and dropped it."

"Yes," said Stillingfleet with a sigh. "That's probably what the ordinary person *would* have thought. But not good old Hercule! D'you know, old horse, up to the very last minute I thought you were leading up to some subtle theory of highfalutin psychological 'suggested' murder? I bet those two thought so too! Nasty bit of goods, the Farley. Goodness, how she cracked! Cornworthy might have got away with it if she hadn't had hysterics and tried to spoil your beauty by going for you with her nails. I only got her off you just in time."

He paused a minute and then said:

"I rather like the girl. Grit, you know, and brains. I suppose I'd be thought to be a fortune hunter if I had a shot at her . . . ?"

"You are too late, my friend. There is already someone *sur le tapis*. Her father's death has opened the way to happiness."

"Take it all round, *she* had a pretty good motive for bumping off the unpleasant parent."

"Motive and opportunity are not enough," said Poirot. "There must also be the criminal temperament!"

"I wonder if you'll ever commit a crime, Poirot?" said Stillingfleet. "I bet you could get away with it all right. As a matter of fact, it would be *too* easy for you—I mean the thing would be off as definitely too un-sporting."

"That," said Poirot, "is a typically English idea."

FOR DISCUSSION: The Dream

1. Hercule Poirot (like his creator, Agatha Christie) has a fine eye and ear for "jarring notes"—those small details that aren't quite right. List three "jarring notes" that make Poirot uneasy during his first visit to Benedict Farley's home.

2. Poirot at one point indicates that during his visit, three inexplicable things happened: (a) Farley wanted the letter he had sent to Poirot; (b) Farley refused to let Poirot go into the next room; (c) when Poirot returned the letter, Farley looked at it and accepted it even though it was the wrong letter. How does Hercule Poirot finally explain each of these "inexplicable" things?

3. How exactly does Poirot use his knowledge of psychology (of human behavior) to arrive at a solution? Consider especially his "reading" of Farley.

4. Christie spends little energy in depicting the "foreignness" of Poirot. She achieves it with a word here, a phrase there. Find four or five of these words and phrases. What effect do they have on the reader's "reading" of Poirot?

5. Near the end of the story Poirot says—"Motive and opportunity are not enough. There must also be the criminal temperament!" Do you agree or disagree? Support your answer.

INTRODUCTION: The Professor's Manuscript

The "trade sleuth" is a fairly recent arrival in the field of fictional crime. During the last few years Emma Lathen has created the banker-sleuth, Dick Francis has created the jockey-sleuth, and Harry Kemelman has created the rabbi-sleuth. In each case the "detective" is primarily a banker or a jockey or a rabbi; he slips into detecting through circumstances, and the cases in which he becomes involved deal with his primary milieu. In fact, he usually solves his cases precisely *because* of his expertise in his own field.

In most of her novels and short stories, Dorothy Sayers wrote about the exploits of Lord Peter Wimsey, who spent most of his time tracking down criminals. In this story, however, written in 1939, Sayers abandoned Wimsey and created a true trade-sleuth—Montague Egg, salesman par excellence, and detective only incidentally. It is a paradigm of the trade-sleuth story in that much of Egg's insight is the result of his occupation. Of course it is also true that few salesmen have Egg's peculiar erudition.

The Professor's Manuscript

Dorothy L. Sayers

"See here, Monty," said Mr. Hopgood (traveling representative for Messrs. Brotherhood, Ltd.) to Mr. Egg (traveling representative for Messrs. Plummett & Rose); "while you're here, why don't you have a go at old Professor Pindar? I should say he was just about in your line."

Mr. Egg brought his mind back—a little unwillingly—from the headlines in his morning paper ("SCREEN STAR'S MARRIAGE ROMANCE PLANE DASH"—"CONTINENT COMB-OUT FOR MISSING FINANCIER"—"BUDGET INCOME-TAX REMISSION POSSIBILITY"), and inquired who Professor Pindar might be when he was at home.

"He's a funny old bird that's come and settled down at Wellingtonia House," replied Mr. Hopgood. "You know, where the Fennells used to live. Bought the place last January and moved in about a month ago. Writes books, or something. I went along yesterday to see if there was anything doing in our way. Heard he was a retired sort of old party. Thought he might be good for a case of Sparkling Pompayne or something else in the soft drinks line. Quite rude to me, he was. Called it 'gut-rot,' and spilled a piece of poetry about 'windy waters.' Shouldn't have expected such strong expressions from a brainy-looking old gent like him. Apologized for taking up his time, of course, and said to myself, 'Here's where young Monty gets in with his matured spirits and fine old fruity.' Thought I'd give you the tip, that's all—but suit yourself, of course."

Mr. Egg thanked Mr. Hopgood, and agreed that Professor Pindar sounded like a useful prospect.

"One gets to see him all right, then?" he asked.

"Yes—only you have to state your business," said Mr. Hopgood. "Housekeeper's a bit of a dragon. No good trying on the old tale of being sent round by his dear friend Mr. So-and-so, because, for one thing, he's got no friends round here and, for another, they know that one."

"In that case—" began Mr. Egg; but Mr. Hopgood did not appear to notice that he had said anything odd, and he felt it was hardly worth while to start an argument, especially as the morning was getting on, and he had not yet read about the film-star's marriage dash or the country-house arson suspicions. He turned his attention to these, discovered that the romance was the lady's fifth marriage and that the fire was thought to be yet another ramification of the insurance ramp, went on to ascertain that the person detained the day before in Constantinople was not, after all, the absconding head of Mammoth Industries, Ltd., and that the hope of sixpence off the income-tax was little more than the *Daily Trumpet* correspondent's dream of wish-fulfillment, and then embarked upon a juicy leader-page article headed ""CAN COMMERCIAL TRAVELERS BE CHRISTIANS?—by One of Them," which interested him, not so much because he had any doubts about commercial morality as because he fancied he knew who the author was.

Before very long, however, his own commercial conscience (which was sensitive) reminded him that he was wasting his employer's time, and he went out to inquire into a complaint received from the landlord of the Ring of Bells that the last case of Plummett & Rose's Superior Old Tawny (full body, fine masculine flavor) was not up to sample, owing to alleged faulty corking.

Having disposed of this little unpleasantness, and traced the trouble to the fact that the landlord had thoughtlessly run the main pipe of a new heating installation behind the racks housing the Superior Old Tawny, Mr. Egg asked to be directed to Wellingtonia House.

"It's about five miles out of the town," said the landlord. "Take the road to Great Windings, turn off to the left by the tower they call Grabb's Folly and then it's down the lane on the right past the old water-mill. Biggish place with a high brick wall, right down in the hollow. Damp, in my opinion. Shouldn't care to live there myself. All right if you like peace and quiet, but I prefer to see a bit of life myself. So does the missis. But this old chap ain't married, so I suppose it's all right for him. Lives there alone with a housekeeper and a handy-man and about fifty million tons of books. I was sorry to hear he'd taken the house. What we want there is a family with a bit of money, to bring some trade into the town."

"Not a rich man, then?" asked Mr. Egg, mentally substituting a cheaper line for the Cockburn 1896 (a grand ancient wine thirty-five years in bottle) with which he had hoped to tempt the Professor.

"He may have," replied the landlord; "must have, I suppose, since he's bought the place freehold. But what's the odds if he don't spend it? Never goes anywhere. No entertaining. Bit of a crank, by what they tell me."

"Butcher's meat?" inquired Mr. Egg.

"Oh, yes," said the landlord, "and only the best cuts. But what's one old gentleman's steak and chop when you come to think of it? That don't make a lot of difference in the week's turn-over."

However, the thought of the steak and chops comforted Mr. Egg as he drove by Grabb's Folly and the old watermill and turned down the little, winding lane between high hedgerows starred with dog-violets and the lesser celandine. Grilled meat and wine went together almost as certainly as nut-cutlets and home-made lemonade.

The door of Wellingtonia House was opened by a middle-aged woman in an apron, at sight of whom Mr. Egg instantly dismissed the manner he used for domestic servants and substituted the one reserved for persons "out of the top drawer," as he phrased it. A pre-War gentlewoman in a post-War job, he decided. He produced his card and stated his business frankly.

"Well," said the housekeeper. She looked Mr. Egg searchingly up and down. "Professor Pindar is a very busy man, but he may like to see you. He is very particular about his wines—especially vintage port."

"Vintage port, madam," replied Mr. Egg, "is a speciality with us."

"*Real* vintage port?" asked the housekeeper, smiling.

Mr. Egg was hurt, though he tried not to show it. He mentioned a few of Messrs. Plummett & Rose's choicer shipments, and produced a list.

"Come in," said the housekeeper. "I'll take the list to Professor Pindar. He may like to see you himself, though I can't promise. He is very hard at work upon his book, and he can't possibly spare very much time."

"Certainly not, madam," said Mr. Egg, stepping in and wiping his boots carefully. They were perfectly clean, but the ritual was part of his regular routine, as laid down by *The Salesman's Handbook*. ("Be clean and courteous; raise your hat, And wipe your boots upon the mat: Such proofs of gentlemanly feeling Are to the ladies most appealing.") "In my opinion," he added, as he followed his conductress through a handsome hall and down a long and thickly carpeted passage, "more sales are lost through being too persistent than through not being persistent enough. There's a little verse, madam, that I try to bear in mind: 'Don't stay too long; the customer has other things to do than sitting in the parlor and listening to you; And if, through your loquacity, she lets the dinner burn, She will not soon forget it, and it does you a bad turn.' I will just show the professor my list, and if he is not interested, I will promise to go away at once."

The housekeeper laughed. "You are more reasonable than most of them," she said, and showed him into a large and lofty room, lined from floor to ceiling with bookshelves. "Wait here a minute, and I will see what Professor Pindar says."

She was gone for some time, and Mr. Egg, being left to contemplate, with awe and some astonishment, the array of learning all about him, became restless, and even a little reckless. He walked about the library, trying to ascertain from the titles of the books what Professor Pindar was professor of. His interests, however, appeared to be catholic, for the books dealt with many subjects. One of them, a stout, calf-bound octavo in a long row of calf-bound octavos, attracted Mr. Egg's attention. It was an eighteenth-century treatise on brewing and distilling, and he extended a cautious finger to hook it from the shelf. It was, however, too tightly wedged between a bound collection of pamphlets and a play by Ben Jonson to come out easily, and he abandoned the attempt. Curiosity made him next tiptoe over to the formidable great desk strewn with manuscripts. This gave more information. In the center, near the typewriter, lay a pile of neatly typed sheets, embellished with footnotes and a good many passages of what looked to Mr. Egg like Greek, though it might, of course, have been Russian or Arabic, or any other language with a queer alphabet. The half-finished page upon the blotter broke off abruptly with the words: "This was the opinion of St. Augustine, though Clement of Alexandria expressly declares—" Here the sentence ended, as though the writer had paused to consult his authority. The open folio on the table was, however, neither St. Augustine nor Clement of Alexandria, but Origen. Close beside it stood a metal strong-box with a combination-lock, which Mr. Egg judged to contain some rare manuscript or other.

The sound of a hand upon the door-handle caused him to start guiltily away from the table, and when the door opened he had whisked round with his back to the desk and was staring abstractedly at a shelf crammed with immense tomes, ranging from Aristotle's works to a Jacobean *Life of Queen Elizabeth*.

Professor Pindar was a very bent and tottery old gentleman, and the hairiest person Mr. Egg had ever set eyes upon. His beard began at his cheekbones and draped his chest as far as the penultimate waistcoat-button. Over a pair of very sharp grey eyes, heavy grey eyebrows hung like a penthouse. He wore a black skull-cap, from beneath which more grey hair flowed so as to conceal his collar. He wore a rather shabby black velvet jacket, grey trousers, which had forgotten the last time they had ever seen a trousers-press, and a pair of carpet slippers, over which grey woolen socks wreathed themselves in folds. His face (what could be seen of it) was thin, and he spoke with a curious whistle and click due to an extremely ill-fitting set of dentures.

"Hso you are the young man from the wine-merchant's, hish, click," said the Professor. "Hsit down. Click." He waved his hand to a chair some little distance away, and himself shuffled to the desk and seated himself. "You brought me a list—where have I—ah! yesh! click! here it is, hish. Let me hsee." He fumbled about himself and produced a pair of steel spectacles. "Hish! yesh! Very interesting. What made you think of calling on me, click, hey? Hish."

Mr. Egg said that he had been advised to call by Messrs. Brotherhood's representative.

"I thought, sir," he said, ingenuously, "that if you disapproved so much of soft drinks, you might appreciate something more, shall we say, full-bodied."

"You did, did you?" said the Professor. "Very shrewd of you. Click! Hsmart of you, hish. Got some good hish stuff here." He waved the list. "Don't believe in highclassh wine-merchants touting for customers shthough. Infra dig. Hey?"

Mr. Egg explained that the pressure of competition had driven Messrs. Plummett & Rose to this undoubtedly rather modern expedient. "But of course, sir," he added, "we exercise our discretion. I should not dream of showing a gentleman like yourself the list we issue to licensed houses."

"Humph!" said Professor Pindar. "Well—" He entered upon a discussion of the wine-list, showing himself remarkably knowledgeable for an aged scholar whose interests were centered upon the Fathers of the Church. He was, he said, thinking of laying down a small cellar, though he should have to get some new racks installed, since the former owners had allowed that part of the establishment to fall into decay.

Mr. Egg ventured on a mild witticism about "rack and ruin," and booked a useful little order for some Warre, Dow & Cockburn ports, together with a few dozen selected burgundies, to be delivered in a month's time, when the cellar accommodation should be ready for them.

"You are thinking of settling permanently in this part of the country, sir?" he ventured, as he rose (mindful of instructions) to take his leave.

"Yes. Why not, hey?" snapped the Professor.

"Very glad to hear it, sir," said Monty. "Always very glad to hear of a good customer, you know."

"Yes, of coursh," replied Professor Pindar. "Naturally. I exshpect to be here till I have finished my book, at any rate. May take years, click! *Hishtory of the Early Chrishtian Chursh*, hish, click." Here his teeth seemed to take so alarming a leap from his jaws that Mr. Egg made an instinctive dive forward to catch them, and wondered why the Professor should have hit on a subject and title so impossible of pronunciation.

"But that means nothing to *you*, I take it, hey?" concluded the Professor, opening the door.

"Nothing, I'm sorry to say, sir," said Mr. Egg, who knew where to draw the line between the pretence of interest and the confession of ignorance. "Like the Swan of Avon, if I may put it that way, I have small Latin and less Greek, and that's the only resemblance between me and him, I'm afraid."

The Professor laughed, perilously, and followed up this exercise with a terrific click.

"Mrs. Tabbitt!" he called, "show this gentleman out."

The housekeeper reappeared and took charge of Mr. Egg, who departed, full of polite thanks for esteemed favors.

"Well," thought Montague Egg, "that's a puzzler, that is. All the same, it's no business of mine, and I don't want to make a mistake. I wonder who I could ask. Wait a minute. Mr. Griffiths—he's the man. He'd know in a moment."

It so happened that he was due to return to town that day. He attended to his business and then, as soon as he was free, went round to call upon a very good customer and friend of his, who was the senior partner in the extremely respectable publishing firm of Griffiths & Seabright. Mr. Griffiths listened to his story with considerable interest.

"Pindar?" said he. "Never heard of him. Early Fathers of the Church, eh? Well, Dr. Abcock is the man for that. We'll ring him up. Hullo! is that Dr. Abcock? Sorry to bother you, but have you ever heard of a Professor Pindar who writes your kind of stuff? You haven't?... I don't know. Wait a moment."

He took down various stout volumes and consulted them.

"He doesn't seem to hold any English or Scotch professorship," he observed, presently. "Of course, it might be foreign or American—did he speak with any sort of accent, Egg?—No?—Well, that proves nothing, of course. Anybody can get a professorship from those odd American universities. Well, never mind, Doctor, don't bother. Yes, a book. I rather wanted to get the thing vetted. I'll let you know again later."

He turned to Monty.

"Nothing very definite there," he said, "but I'll tell you what I'll do. I'll call on this man—or perhaps it will be better to write. I'll say I've heard about the work and would like to make an offer for it. That might produce something. You're a bit of a terror, aren't you, Egg? Have a spot of one of your own wares before you go."

It was some time before Mr. Egg heard again from Mr. Griffiths. Then a letter was forwarded to him in York, whither his travels had taken him.

"Dear Egg,

"I wrote to your Professor, and with a good bit of trouble extracted an answer and a typescript. Now, there's no doubt at all about the MS. It's first-class, of its kind. Rather unorthodox, in some ways, but stuffed as full of scholarship as an egg (sorry) is of meat. But his letter was what I should call evasive. He doesn't say where he got his professorship. Possibly he bestowed the title on himself, *honoris causa*. But the book is so darned good that I'm going to make a stiff push to get it for G. & S. I'm writing to ask the mysterious Professor for an appointment and will send you a line if I get it."

The next communication reached Mr. Egg in Lincoln.

"Dear Egg,

"Curiouser and curiouser. Professor Pindar absolutely refuses to see me or to discuss his book with me, though he is ready to consider an offer. Abcock is getting excited about it, and has written to ask for further information on several controversial points in the MS. We cannot understand how a man of such remarkable learning and ability should have remained all this time unknown to the experts in his particular subject. I think our best chance is to get hold of old Dr. Wilverton. He knows all about everything and everybody, only he is so very eccentric that it is rather difficult to get anything out of him. But you can be sure of one thing—the man who wrote that book is a bona fide scholar, so your doubts must have been ill-founded. But I'm immensely grateful to you for putting me on to Professor Pindar, whoever he is. The work will make a big noise in the little world of learning."

Mr. Egg had returned to London before he heard from Mr. Griffiths again. Then he was rung up and requested, in rather excited tones, to come round and meet the great and eccentric Dr. Lovell Wilverton at

Mr. Griffiths' house. When he got there, he found the publisher and Dr. Abcock seated by the fire, while a strange little man in a check suit and steel spectacles ramped irritably up and down the room.

"It's no use," spluttered Dr. Wilverton, "it's no use to tell me. I know. I say I *know*. The views expressed—the style—the—everything points the same way. Besides, I tell you, I've seen that passage on Clement of Alexandria before. Poor Donne! He was a most brilliant scholar—*the* most brilliant scholar who ever passed through my hands. I went to see him once, at that horrible little hut on the Essex Marshes that he retired to after the—collapse, you know—and he showed me the stuff then. Mistaken? Of course I'm not mistaken. I'm never mistaken. Couldn't be. I've often wondered since where that manuscript went to. If only I'd been in England at the time I should have secured it. Sold with the rest of his things, for junk, I suppose, to pay the rent."

"Just a moment, Wilverton," said Dr. Abcock, soothingly. "You're going too fast for us. You say this *History of the Early Christian Church* was written by a young man called Roger Donne, a pupil of yours, who unfortunately took to drink and went to live in very great poverty in a hut on the Essex Marshes. Now it turns up, in typescript, which you say Donne wouldn't have used, masquerading as the work of an old person calling himself Professor Pindar, of Wellingtonia House, in Somerset. Are you suggesting that Pindar stole the manuscript or bought it from Donne? Or that he is Donne in disguise?"

"Of course he isn't Donne," said Dr. Wilverton, angrily. "I told you, didn't I? Donne's dead. He died last year when I was in Syria. I suppose this old imposter bought the manuscript at the sale."

Mr. Egg smote his thigh with his palm.

"Why, of course, sir," he said. "The deed-box I saw on the table. That would have the original manuscript in it, and this old professor-man just copied it out on his own typewriter."

"But what for?" asked Mr. Griffiths. "It's a remarkable book, but it's not a thing one would get a lot of money out of."

"No," agreed Monty, "but it would be an awfully good proof that the professor really was what he pretended to be. Suppose the police made investigations—there was the professor, and there was the book, and any expert they showed it to (unless they had the luck to hit on Dr. Wilverton, of course) would recognize it for the work of a really learned gentleman."

"Police?" said Dr. Abcock, sharply. "Why the police? Who do you suppose this Pindar really is?"

Mr. Egg extracted a newspaper cutting from his pocket.

"Him, sir," he said. "Greenholt, the missing financier, who absconded with all the remaining assets of Mammoth Industries, Ltd., just a week before Professor Pindar came and settled at Wellingtonia House. Here's his description: sixty years old, grey eyes, false teeth. Why, a bunch of hair and a bad set of dentures, a velvet coat and skullcap, and there you are. There's your Professor Pindar. I did think the hair was just a bit overdone. And that Mrs. Tabbitt was a lady, all right, and here's a photo of Mrs. Greenholt. Take away the make-up and scrag her hair back in a bun, and they're as like as two peas."

"Great heavens!" exclaimed Mr. Griffiths. "And they've been combing Europe for the fellow. Egg, I shouldn't wonder if you're right. Give me the 'phone. We'll get on to Scotland Yard. Hullo! Give me Whitehall 1212."

"You seem to be something of a detective, Mr. Egg," said Dr. Lovell Wilverton, later in the evening, when word had come through of the arrest of Robert Greenholt at Wellingtonia House. "Do you mind telling me what first put this idea into your head?"

"Well, sir," replied Mr. Egg, modestly, "I'm not a brainy man, but in my line one learns to size a party up pretty quickly. The first thing that seemed odd was that this Professor wouldn't see my friend, Hopgood, of Brotherhood, Ltd., till he knew where he came from, and then, when he did see him, told him he couldn't stick soft drinks. Now, you know, sir, as a rule, a busy gentleman won't see a commercial at all if he's not interested in the goods. It's one of our big difficulties. It looked as though the Professor wanted to be seen, in his character as a professor, by anybody and everybody, provided that it wasn't anybody who knew too much about books and so on. Then there was the butcher. He supplied steaks and chops to the household, which looked like a gentleman with good teeth; but when I got there, I found a hairy old boy whose dental plate was so wonky he could hardly have chewed scrambled eggs with it. But the thing that really bothered me was the books in that library. I'm no reader, unless it's a crook yarn or something of that kind, but I visit a good many learned gentlemen, and I've now and again cast my eye on their shelves, always liking to improve myself. Now, there were three things in that library that weren't like the library of any gentleman that uses his books. First, the books were all mixed up, with different subjects alongside one another, instead of all the same subject together. Then, the books were too neat, all big books in one place and all small ones in another. And then they were too snug in the shelves. No gentleman that likes books or needs to consult them quickly keeps them as tight as that—they won't come out when you want them and besides, it breaks the bindings. That's true, I know, because I asked a friend of mine in the second-hand book business. So you see," said Mr. Egg, persuasively, "Greek or no Greek, I couldn't believe that gentleman ever read any of his books. I expect he just bought up somebody's library—or you can have 'em delivered by the yard; it's often done by rich gentlemen who get their libraries done by furnishing firms."

"Bless my soul," said Dr. Lovell Wilverton, "is Saul also among the prophets? You seem to be an observant man, Mr. Egg."

"I try to be," replied Mr. Egg. "Never miss a chance of learning for that word spells '£' plus 'earning.'—You'll find that in *The Salesman's Handbook*. Very neat, sir, don't you think?"

FOR DISCUSSION: The Professor's Manuscript

1. When Professor Pindar first appears in this story, he is portrayed vividly and dramatically. What two or three features of the Professor are most memorable? Why might an author use exaggeration in describing a character?

2. Montague Egg, though strictly an amateur detective, has a keen eye for detail and a sharp understanding of people. List five facts about the Professor and the Professor's household that Egg considered suspicious. Next to each, describe briefly the deduction Egg was able to draw.

3. Sayers is known for the odd, whimsical humor that pervades her works. Often (but not always) it is intellectual. Sometimes it appears in the name of a person or place, sometimes in word-play, sometimes in metaphor or hyperbole. From the text, choose half a dozen examples of Sayers's humor. Does humor add or detract from the effectiveness of a mystery story? Explain.

4. This story is extremely British, in tone and in content. Suppose someone changed the setting to New York City and transformed the characters into Americans. Would the story still make sense? Which elements of the story would then have to be changed? Why would each change be necessary?

Things
Are Seldom as
They Seem

CHAPTER FIVE

A *paradox* is an expression that *seems* (but is *not*) self-contradictory or absurd. One often hears someone say, "I am never lonely when I am alone." We know immediately what is meant; the apparent contradiction actually leads to truth. What seems to be true is not; what seems to be false is true.

But the term *paradox* is not limited to a statement. An idea, an argument, a belief, or an incident can be paradoxical too. When Kipling wished to suggest that Englishmen were made ignorant by their insularity, he wrote: "What can they know of England who only England know?"—to which G. K. Chesterton retorted: "The globe-trotter lives in a smaller world than the peasant."

In the world of paradox, Chesterton is king. He used the paradox to startle and to amuse, but above all to probe past superficiality to truth. When he decided to write mystery stories, he created Father Brown, a detective who is a living paradox: a fumbling adept, a brilliant fool. The puzzles themselves are often paradoxical, and the way to solution lies through paradox. They are, in short, studies of apparent contradiction. Therein lie their fascination and mystery.

Being human, we crave consistency. When one thug with cauliflower ears guns down a second thug with a battered nose and this happens on a fog-swaddled waterfront, well, then, things are as they should be. A battle between two gangsters doesn't worry us much, but it doesn't amaze us much, either. The characters and locale are consistent with the action.

Now change the characters and the locale. Instead of the waterfront, substitute a suburban lawn or a pleasant, well-kept park. For the thug, substitute a nice, middle-aged lady with white gloves. When she quietly stabs her nephew and gives as her sole reason "I felt like doing it," then crime becomes frightening, because it becomes inexplicable—because "things are not as they seem." Consistency has been violated, and in the apparent contradiction lies a truth we fear to recognize.

This paradox bothers us. Crime among gangsters shares our physical world but not our *real* world. It is not of us, nor we of it. But crime that does not seem criminal, or legal activity that does seem criminal, enters our world by the back door. It is suddenly in our own living room; it is our neighbor or our brother; it is even, perhaps, ourselves.

Such crime can come about through rumor, through fear, or through a moral lapse.

Rumor, skillfully constructed, carefully placed, and well timed, can create a facade so sturdy it takes a howitzer to penetrate it. It can make good look evil, and evil look good.

Fear is just as potent. Fear for oneself, for one's loved ones, for one's home or job—these can possess and obsess until someone who has always been law-abiding resorts to poison or bullets or blades.

The *moral lapse* is even more destructive. It can happen to anyone at any time. It is a blind spot that distorts both vision and judgment, a sickness that afflicts the law-abiding and the religious. When "good" people turn to crime, it is doubly terrifying because "they" and "we" are interchangeable; in the pursuit of morality there is always the danger of becoming too caught up in a cause to be able to see straight. Those who fight intolerance sometimes become intolerant of the intolerant.

In this section four writers illustrate that "things are seldom as they seem." They cut across time—from Nathaniel Hawthorne in the early nineteenth century, to the master himself, Chesterton, in the early twentieth, to Allingham and Jackson in our own time. They cut across national boundaries, from the United States to Great Britain. They share only one belief: that the curtain of deceit, whether deliberate or involuntary, is both a precursor and a reflector of the small touch of evil that taints each human soul.

INTRODUCTION: Mr. Higginbotham's Catastrophe

One of the finest short story writers of all time is Nathaniel Hawthorne, a man who knew, better than most, that "things are seldom as they seem." One of his own ancestors had been a judge at the Salem witchcraft trials, and Nathaniel knew all too well how inbreeding and climate could lead to family quirks and polite idiosyncrasies. Strange things happened in his New England of the nineteenth century. Paradoxically, the long, hard, sterile winters were a fertile ground for rumor-growing.

Even so, how do you explain three murders on three successive nights, all with the same victim? Or a dead man signing a paper, or passing through a toll booth? Or a dead man who is afraid of dying? There is no witchcraft, no magic in this story—just Hawthorne's creative realization that human beings are strange; that their actions cannot be taken literally; that they are, above all, human.

Mr. Higginbotham's Catastrophe
Nathaniel Hawthorne

A young fellow, a tobacco pedlar by trade, was on his way from Morristown, where he had dealt largely with the Deacon of the Shaker settlement, to the village of Parker's Falls, on Salmon River. He had a neat little cart, painted green, with a box of cigars depicted on each side panel, and an Indian chief, holding a pipe and a golden tobacco stalk, on the rear. The pedlar drove a smart little mare, and was a young man of excellent character, keen at a bargain, but none the worse liked by the Yankees; who, as I have heard them say, would rather be shaved with a sharp razor than a dull one. Especially was he beloved by the pretty girls along the Connecticut, whose favor he used to court by presents of the best smoking tobacco in his stock; knowing well that the country lasses of New England are generally great performers on pipes. Moreover, as will be seen in the course of my story, the pedlar was inquisitive, and something of a tattler, always itching to hear the news and anxious to tell it again.

After an early breakfast at Morristown, the tobacco pedlar, whose name was Dominicus Pike, had traveled seven miles through a solitary piece of woods, without speaking a word to anybody but himself and his little gray mare. It being nearly seven o'clock, he was as eager to hold a morning gossip as a city shopkeeper to read the morning paper. An opportunity seemed at hand when, after lighting a cigar with a sun-glass, he looked up, and perceived a man coming over the brow of the hill, at the foot of which the pedlar had stopped his green cart. Dominicus watched him as he descended, and noticed that he carried a bundle over his shoulder on the end of a stick, and traveled with a weary, yet determined pace. He did not look as if he had started in the freshness of the morning, but had footed it all night, and meant to do the same all day.

"Good morning, mister," said Dominicus, when within speaking distance. "You go a pretty good jog. What's the latest news at Parker's Falls?"

The man pulled the broad brim of a gray hat over his eyes, and answered, rather suddenly, that he did not come from Parker's Falls, which, as being the limit of his own day's journey, the pedlar had naturally mentioned in his inquiry.

"Well then," rejoined Dominicus Pike, "let's have the latest news where you did come from. I'm not particular about Parker's Falls. Any place will answer."

Being thus importuned, the traveler—who was as ill looking a fellow as one would desire to meet in a solitary piece of woods—appeared to hesitate a little, as if he was either searching his memory for news, or weighing the expediency of telling it. At last, mounting on the step of the cart, he whispered in the ear of Dominicus, though he might have shouted aloud and no other mortal would have heard him.

"I do remember one little trifle of news," said he. "Old Mr. Higginbotham, of Kimballton, was murdered in his orchard, at eight o'clock last night, by an Irishman and a black man. They strung him up to the branch of a St. Michael's pear-tree, where nobody would find him till the morning."

As soon as this horrible intelligence was communicated, the stranger betook himself to his journey again, with more speed than ever, not even turning his head when Dominicus invited him to smoke a Spanish cigar and relate all the particulars. The pedlar whistled to his mare and went up the hill, pondering on the doleful fate of Mr. Higginbotham whom he had known in the way of trade, having sold him many a bunch of long nines, and a great deal of pigtail, lady's twist, and fig tobacco. He was rather astonished at the rapidity with which the news had spread. Kimballton was nearly sixty miles distant in a straight line; the murder had been perpetrated only at eight o'clock the preceding night; yet Dominicus had heard of it at seven in the morning, when, in all probability, poor Mr. Higginbotham's own family had but just discovered his corpse, hanging on the St. Michael's pear-tree. The stranger on foot must have worn seven-league boots to travel at such a rate.

"Ill news flies fast, they say," thought Dominicus Pike; "but this beats railroads. The fellow ought to be hired to go express with the President's Message."

The difficulty was solved by supposing that the narrator had made a mistake of one day in the date of the occurrence; so that our friend did not hesitate to introduce the story at every tavern and country store along the road, expending a whole bunch of Spanish wrappers among at least twenty horrified audiences. He found himself invariably the first bearer of the intelligence, and was so pestered with questions that he could not avoid filling up the outline, till it became quite a respectable narrative. He met with one piece of corroborative evidence. Mr. Higginbotham was a trader; and a former clerk of his, to whom Dominicus related the facts, testified that the old gentleman was accustomed to return home through the orchard about nightfall, with the money and valuable papers of the store in his pocket. The clerk manifested but little grief at Mr. Higginbotham's catastrophe, hinting, what the pedlar had discovered in his own dealings with him, that he was a crusty old fellow, as close as a vice. His property would descend to a pretty niece who was now keeping school in Kimballton.

What with telling the news for the public good, and driving bargains for his own, Dominicus was so much delayed on the road that he chose to put up at a tavern, about five miles short of Parker's Falls. After supper, lighting one of his prime cigars, he seated himself in the bar-room, and went through the story of the murder, which had grown so fast that it took him half an hour to tell. There were as many as twenty people in the room, nineteen of whom received it all for gospel. But the twentieth was an elderly farmer, who had arrived on horseback a short time before, and was now seated in a corner smoking his pipe. When the story was concluded, he rose up very deliberately, brought his chair right in front of Dominicus, and stared him full in the face, puffing out the vilest tobacco smoke the pedlar had ever smelt.

"Will you make affidavit," demanded he, in the tone of a country justice taking an examination, "that old Squire Higginbotham of Kimballton was murdered in his orchard the night before last, and found hanging on his great pear-tree yesterday morning?"

"I tell the story as I heard it, mister," answered Dominicus, dropping his half-burnt cigar; "I don't say that I saw the thing done. So I can't take my oath that he was murdered exactly in that way."

"But I can take mine," said the farmer, "that if Squire Higginbotham was murdered night before last, I drank a glass of bitters with his ghost this morning. Being a neighbor of mine, he called me into his store, as I was riding by, and treated me, and then asked me to do a little business for him on the road. He didn't seem to know any more about his own murder than I did."

"Why, then, it can't be a fact!" exclaimed Dominicus Pike.

"I guess he'd have mentioned, if it was," said the old farmer; and he removed his chair back to the corner, leaving Dominicus quite down in the mouth.

Here was a sad resurrection of old Mr. Higginbotham! The pedlar had no heart to mingle in the conversation any more, but comforted himself with a glass of gin and water, and went to bed where, all night long, he dreamed of hanging on the St. Michael's pear-tree. To avoid the old farmer (whom he so detested that his suspension would have pleased him better than Mr. Higginbotham's), Dominicus rose in the gray of the morning, put the little mare into the green cart, and trotted swiftly away towards Parker's Falls. The fresh breeze, the dewy road, and the pleasant summer dawn, revived his spirits, and might have encouraged him to repeat the old story had there been anybody awake to hear it. But he met neither ox team, light wagon, chaise, horseman, nor foot traveler, till, just as he crossed Salmon River, a man came trudging down to the bridge with a bundle over his shoulder, on the end of a stick.

"Good morning, mister," said the pedlar, reining in his mare. "If you come from Kimballton or that neighborhood, may be you can tell me the real fact about this affair of old Mr. Higginbotham. Was the old fellow actually murdered two or three nights ago, by an Irishman and a black man?"

Dominicus had spoken in too great a hurry to observe, at first, that the stranger himself had a deep tinge of negro blood. On hearing this sudden question, the Ethiopian appeared to change his skin, its yellow hue becoming a ghastly white, while, shaking and stammering, he thus replied:—

"No! no! There was no colored man! It was an Irishman that hanged him last night, at eight o'clock. I came away at seven! His folks can't have looked for him in the orchard yet."

Scarcely had the yellow man spoken, when he interrupted himself, and though he seemed weary enough before, continued his journey at a pace which would have kept the pedlar's mare on a smart trot. Dominicus stared after him in great perplexity. If the murder had not been committed till Tuesday night, who was the prophet that had foretold it, in all its circumstances, on Tuesday morning? If Mr. Higginbotham's corpse were not yet discovered by his own family, how came the mulatto, at above thirty miles' distance, to know that he was hanging in the orchard, especially as he had left Kimballton before the unfortunate man was hanged at all? These ambiguous circumstances, with the stranger's surprise and terror, made Dominicus think of raising a hue and cry after him, as an accomplice in the murder; since a murder, it seemed, had really been perpetrated.

"But let the poor devil go," thought the pedlar. "I don't want his black blood on my head; and hanging the black man wouldn't unhang Mr. Higginbotham. Unhang the old gentleman! It's a sin, I know; but I should hate to have him come to life a second time and give me the lie!"

With these meditations, Dominicus Pike drove into the street of Parker's Falls, which, as everybody knows, is as thriving a village as three cotton factories and a slitting mill can make it. The machinery was not in motion, and but a few of the shop doors unbarred, when he alighted in the stable yard of the tavern, and made it his first business to order the mare four quarts of oats. His second duty, of course, was to impart Mr. Higginbotham's catastrophe to the hostler. He deemed it advisable, however, not to be too positive as to the date of the direful fact, and also to be uncertain whether it were perpetrated by an Irishman and a mulatto, or by the son of Erin alone. Neither did he profess to relate it on his own authority, or that of any one person; but mentioned it as a report generally diffused.

The story ran through the town like fire among girdled trees, and became so much the universal talk that nobody could tell whence it had originated. Mr. Higginbotham was as well known at Parker's Falls as any citizen of the place, being part owner of the slitting mill, and a considerable stockholder in the cotton factories. The inhabitants felt their own prosperity interested in his fate. Such was the excitement, that the Parker's Falls Gazette anticipated its regular day of publication, and came out with half a form of blank paper and a column of double pica emphasized with capitals, and headed HORRID MURDER OF MR. HIGGINBOTHAM! Among other dreadful details, the printed account described the mark of the cord round the dead man's neck, and stated the number of thousand dollars of which he had been robbed; there was much pathos also about the affliction of his niece, who had gone from one fainting fit to another, ever since her uncle was found hanging on the St. Michael's pear-tree with his pockets inside out. The village poet likewise commemorated the young lady's grief in seventeen stanzas of a ballad. The selectmen held a meeting, and, in consideration of Mr. Higginbotham's claims on the town, determined to issue handbills, offering a reward of five hundred dollars for the apprehension of his murderers, and the recovery of the stolen property.

Meanwhile the whole population of Parker's Falls, consisting of shop-keepers, mistresses of boarding-houses, factory girls, millmen, and school-boys, rushed into the street and kept up such a terrible loquacity as more than compensated for the silence of the cotton machines, which refrained from their usual din out of respect to the deceased. Had Mr. Higginbotham cared about posthumous renown, his untimely ghost would have exulted in this tumult. Our friend Dominicus, in his vanity of heart, forgot his intended precautions, and mounting on the town pump, announced himself as the bearer of the authentic intelligence which had caused so wonderful a sensation. He immediately became the great man of the moment, and had just begun a new edition of the narrative, with a voice like a field preacher, when the mail stage drove into the village street. It had traveled all night, and must have shifted horses at Kimballton, at three in the morning.

"Now we shall hear all the particulars," shouted the crowd.

The coach rumbled up to the piazza of the tavern, followed by a thousand people; for if any man had been minding his own business till then, he now left it at sixes and sevens, to hear the news. The pedlar, foremost in the race, discovered two passengers, both of whom had been startled from a comfortable nap to find themselves in the center of a mob. Every man assailing them with separate questions, all propounded at once, the couple were struck speechless, though one was a lawyer and the other a young lady.

"Mr. Higginbotham! Mr. Higginbotham! Tell us the particulars about old Mr. Higginbotham!" bawled the mob. "What is the coroner's verdict? Are the murderers apprehended? Is Mr. Higginbotham's niece come out of her fainting fits? Mr. Higginbotham! Mr. Higginbotham!!"

The coachman said not a word, except to swear awfully at the hostler for not bringing him a fresh team of horses. The lawyer inside had generally his wits about him even when asleep; the first thing he did, after learning the cause of the excitement, was to produce a large, red pocketbook. Meantime Dominicus Pike, being an extremely polite young man, and also suspecting that a female tongue would tell the story as glibly as a lawyer's, had handed the lady out of the coach. She was a fine, smart girl, now wide awake and bright as a button, and had such a sweet pretty mouth, that Dominicus would almost as lief have heard a love tale from it as a tale of murder.

"Gentlemen and ladies," said the lawyer to the shopkeepers, the millmen, and the factory girls, "I can assure you that some unaccountable mistake, or, more probably, a willful falsehood, maliciously contrived to injure Mr. Higginbotham's credit, has excited this singular uproar. We passed through Kimballton at three o'clock this morning, and most certainly should have been informed of the murder had any been perpetrated. But I have proof nearly as strong as Mr. Higginbotham's own oral testimony, in the negative. Here is a note relating to a suit of his in the Connecticut courts, which was delivered me from that gentleman himself. I find it dated at ten o'clock last evening."

So saying, the lawyer exhibited the date and signature of the note, which irrefragably proved, either that this perverse Mr. Higginbotham was alive when he wrote it, or—as some deemed the more probable case, of two doubtful ones—that he was so absorbed in worldly business as to continue to transact it even after his death. But unexpected evidence was forthcoming. The young lady, after listening to the pedlar's explanation, merely seized a moment to smooth her gown and put her curls in order, and then appeared at the tavern door, making a modest signal to be heard.

"Good people," said she, "I am Mr. Higginbotham's niece."

A wondering murmur passed through the crowd on beholding her so rosy and bright; that same unhappy niece, whom they had supposed, on the authority of the Parker's Falls Gazette, to be lying at death's door in a fainting fit. But some shrewd fellows had doubted, all along, whether a young lady would be quite so desperate at the hanging of a rich old uncle.

"You see," continued Miss Higginbotham, with a smile, "that this strange story is quite unfounded as to myself; and I believe I may affirm it to be equally so in regard to my dear uncle Higginbotham. He has the kindness to give me a home in his house, though I contribute to my own support by teaching a school. I left Kimballton this morning to spend the vacation of commencement week with a friend, about five miles from Parker's Falls. My generous uncle, when he heard me on the stairs, called me to his bedside, and gave me two dollars and fifty cents to pay my stage fare, and another dollar for my extra expenses. He then laid his pocket-book under his pillow, shook hands with me, and advised me to take some biscuit in my bag, instead of breakfasting on the road. I feel confident, therefore, that I left my beloved relative alive, and trust that I shall find him so on my return."

The young lady curtsied at the close of her speech, which was so sensible and well worded, and delivered with such grace and propriety, that everybody thought her fit to be preceptress of the best academy in the State. But a stranger would have supposed that Mr. Higginbotham was an object of abhorrence at Parker's Falls, and that a thanksgiving had been proclaimed for his murder; so excessive was the wrath of the inhabitants on learning their mistake. The millmen resolved to bestow public honors on Dominicus Pike, only hesitating whether to tar and feather him, ride him on a rail, or refresh him with an ablution at the town pump, on the top of which he had declared himself the bearer of the news. The selectmen, by advice of the lawyer, spoke of prosecuting him for a misdemeanor, in circulating unfounded reports, to the great disturbance of the peace of the Commonwealth. Nothing saved Dominicus, either from mob law or a court of justice, but an eloquent appeal made by the young lady in his behalf. Addressing a few words of heartfelt gratitude to his benefactress, he mounted the green cart and rode out of town, under a discharge of artillery from the schoolboys, who found plenty of ammunition in the neighboring clay-pits and mud holes. As he turned his head to exchange a farewell glance with Mr. Higginbotham's niece, a ball, of the consistence of hasty pudding, hit him slap in the mouth, giving him a most grim aspect. His whole person was so bespattered with the like filthy missiles, that he had almost a mind to ride back, and supplicate for the threatened ablution at the town pump; for, though not meant in kindness, it would now have been a deed of charity.

However, the sun shone bright on poor Dominicus, and the mud, an emblem of all stains of undeserved opprobrium, was easily brushed off when dry. Being a funny rogue, his heart soon cheered up; nor could he refrain from a hearty laugh at the uproar which his story had excited. The handbills of the selectmen would cause the commitment of all the vagabonds in the State; the paragraph in the Parker's Falls Gazette would be reprinted from Maine to Florida, and perhaps form an item in the London newspapers; and many a miser would tremble for his money bags and life, on learning the catastrophe of Mr. Higginbotham. The pedlar meditated with much fervor on the charms of the young schoolmistress, and swore that Daniel Webster never spoke nor looked so like an angel as Miss Higginbotham, while defending him from the wrathful populace at Parker's Falls.

Dominicus was now on the Kimballton turnpike, having all along determined to visit that place, though business had drawn him out of the most direct road from Morristown. As he approached the scene of the supposed murder, he continued to revolve the circumstances in his mind, and was astonished at the aspect which the whole case assumed. Had nothing occurred to corroborate the story of the first traveler, it might now have been considered as a hoax; but the yellow man was evidently acquainted either with the report or the fact; and there was a mystery in his dismayed and guilty look on being abruptly questioned. When, to this singular combination of incidents, it was added that the rumor tallied exactly with Mr. Higginbotham's character and habits of life; and that he had an orchard, and a St. Michael's pear-tree, near which he always passed at nightfall; the circumstantial evidence appeared so strong that Dominicus doubted whether the autograph produced by the lawyer, or even the niece's direct testimony, ought to be equivalent. Making cautious inquiries along the road, the pedlar further learned that Mr. Higginbotham had in his service an Irishman of doubtful character, whom he had hired without a recommendation, on the score of economy.

"May I be hanged myself," exclaimed Dominicus Pike aloud, on reaching the top of a lonely hill, "if I'll believe old Higginbotham is unhanged till I see him with my own eyes, and hear it from his own mouth! And as he's a real shaver, I'll have the minister or some other responsible man for an indorser."

It was growing dusk when he reached the toll-house on Kimballton

222

turnpike, about a quarter of a mile from the village of this name. His little mare was fast bringing him up with a man on horseback, who trotted through the gate a few rods in advance of him, nodded to the toll-gatherer, and kept on towards the village. Dominicus was acquainted with the tollman, and, while making change, the usual remarks on the weather passed between them.

"I suppose," said the pedlar, throwing back his whiplash, to bring it down like a feather on the mare's flank, "you have not seen anything of old Mr. Higginbotham within a day or two?"

"Yes," answered the toll-gatherer. "He passed the gate just before you drove up, and yonder he rides now, if you can see him through the dusk. He's been to Woodfield this afternoon, attending a sheriff's sale there. The old man generally shakes hands and has a little chat with me; but to-night, he nodded,—as if to say, 'Charge my toll,' and jogged on; for wherever he goes, he must always be at home by eight o'clock."

"So they tell me," said Dominicus.

"I never saw a man look so yellow and thin as the squire does," continued the toll-gatherer. "Says I to myself, to-night, he's more like a ghost or an old mummy than good flesh and blood."

The pedlar strained his eyes through the twilight, and could just discern the horseman now far ahead on the village road. He seemed to recognize the rear of Mr. Higginbotham; but through the evening shadows, and amid the dust from the horse's feet, the figure appeared dim and unsubstantial; as if the shape of the mysterious old man were faintly moulded of darkness and gray light. Dominicus shivered.

"Mr. Higginbotham has come back from the other world, by way of the Kimballton turnpike," thought he.

He shook the reins and rode forward, keeping about the same distance in the rear of the gray old shadow, till the latter was concealed by a bend of the road. On reaching this point, the pedlar no longer saw the man on horseback, but found himself at the head of the village street, not far from a number of stores and two taverns, clustered round the meeting-house steeple. On his left were a stone wall and a gate, the boundary of a wood-lot, beyond which lay an orchard, farther still, a mowing field, and last of all, a house. These were the premises of Mr. Higginbotham, whose dwelling stood beside the old highway, but had been left in the background by the Kimballton turnpike. Dominicus knew the place; and the little mare stopped short by instinct; for he was not conscious of tightening the reins.

"For the soul of me, I cannot get by this gate!" said he, trembling. "I never shall be my own man again, till I see whether Mr. Higginbotham is hanging on the St. Michael's pear-tree!"

He leaped from the cart, gave the rein a turn round the gate post, and ran along the green path of the wood-lot as if Old Nick were chasing behind. Just then the village clock tolled eight, and as each deep stroke fell, Dominicus gave a fresh bound and flew faster than before, till, dim in the solitary center of the orchard, he saw the fated pear-tree. One great branch stretched from the old contorted trunk across the path, and threw the darkest shadow on that one spot. But something seemed to struggle beneath the branch!

The pedlar had never pretended to more courage than befits a man of peaceable occupation, nor could he account for his valor on this awful emergency. Certain it is, however, that he rushed forward, prostrated a sturdy Irishman with the butt end of his whip, and found—not indeed hanging on the St. Michael's pear-tree, but trembling beneath it, with a halter round his neck—the old, identical Mr. Higginbotham!

"Mr. Higginbotham," said Dominicus tremulously, "you're an honest man, and I'll take your word for it. Have you been hanged or not?"

If the riddle be not already guessed, a few words will explain the simple machinery by which this "coming event" was made to "cast its shadow before." Three men had plotted the robbery and murder of Mr. Higginbotham; two of them, successively, lost courage and fled, each delaying the crime one night by their disappearance; the third was in the act of perpetration, when a champion, blindly obeying the call of fate, like the heroes of old romance, appeared in the person of Dominicus Pike.

It only remains to say, that Mr. Higginbotham took the pedlar into high favor, sanctioned his addresses to the pretty schoolmistress, and settled his whole property on their children, allowing themselves the interest. In due time, the old gentleman capped the climax of his favors, by dying a Christian death, in bed, since which melancholy event Dominicus Pike has removed from Kimballton, and established a large tobacco manufactory in my native village.

FOR DISCUSSION: Mr. Higginbotham's Catastrophe

1. Hawthorne takes great care to develop the personality and character of Dominicus Pike. What kind of man is Dominicus? Is he credulous or shrewd? Is his acceptance of the first story sound? Of the second?
2. Hawthorne had tremendous insight into human nature. How do the people—the crowds—behave when they hear that Higginbotham is dead? When they hear he is alive? What do their mass reactions tell us about human nature?
3. The phrase "hanging on the St. Michael's pear-tree" is repeated a

number of times. What effect does this repetition have on the rumor of Higginbotham's death? What effect does it have on the general tone of the story?

4. A few readers have felt that Hawthorne's ending of this story is a "cop-out." Although the ending as he wrote it is absolutely possible and even logical, it does strain one's belief. If the ending were rewritten, perhaps with ESP accounting for the first and second "murders," would you find it more or less believable? Go one step further and rewrite the ending. Work on it individually, and see how many different endings you can create.

INTRODUCTION: The Absence of Mr. Glass

If you see a pickpocket slip a watch into her reticule, then move calmly to the door, you have seen a pickpocket at work, haven't you? Or have you?

Things are seldom as they seem . . .

Here, G. K. Chesterton, creator of that marvelous, fumblingly astute detective, Father Brown, creates a second detective, Dr. Orion Hood, who step by step can match Sherlock Holmes in observation and deduction. The great Hood observes and deduces while Father Brown giggles, and young Todhunter chokes, and love-stricken Maggie wonders whether she should swoon or smite.

In this story Chesterton, as always, outdoes everyone else. Not only are things seldom as they seem, but they *seem* different to every character in the story. That may make this one of the most realistic, and one of the most profound, stories of the twentieth century.

The Absence of Mr. Glass
G. K. Chesterton

Dr. Orion Hood paced the length of his string of apartments, bounded —as the boys' geographies say—on the east by the North Sea and on the west by the serried ranks of his sociological and criminologist library. He was clad in an artist's velvet, but with none of an artist's negligence; his hair was heavily shot with grey, but growing thick and healthy; his face was lean, but sanguine and expectant. Everything about him and his room indicated something at once rigid and restless, like that great Northern Sea by which (on pure principles of hygiene) he had built his home.

Fate, being in a funny mood, pushed the door open and introduced into those long, strict, sea-flanked apartments one who was perhaps the most startling opposite of them and their master. In answer to a curt but civil summons, the door opened inwards and there shambled into the room a shapeless little figure, which seemed to find its own hat and umbrella as unmanageable as a mass of luggage. The umbrella was a black and prosaic bundle long past repair, the hat was a broad-curved black hat, clerical but not common in England, the man was the very embodiment of all that is homely and helpless.

The doctor regarded the newcomer with a restrained astonishment, not unlike that he would have shown if some huge but obviously harmless sea-beast had crawled into his room. The newcomer regarded the doctor with that beaming but breathless geniality which characterizes a corpulent charwoman who has just managed to stuff herself into an omnibus. It is a rich confusion of social self-congratulation and bodily disarray. His hat tumbled to the carpet, his heavy umbrella slipped between his knees with a thud; he reached after the one and ducked after the other, but with an unimpaired smile on his round face spoke simultaneously as follows:

"My name is Brown. Pray excuse me. I come about that business of the MacNabs. I have heard you often help people out of such troubles. Pray excuse me if I am wrong."

By this time he had sprawlingly recovered the hat, and made an odd little bobbing bow over it, as if setting everything quite right.

"I hardly understand you," replied the scientist, with a cold intensity of manner. "I fear you have mistaken the chambers. I am Dr. Hood, and my work is almost entirely literary and educational. It is true that I have sometimes been consulted by the police in cases of peculiar difficulty and importance, but—"

"Oh, this is of the greatest importance," broke in the little man called Brown. "Why, her mother won't let them get engaged." And he leaned back in his chair in radiant rationality.

The brows of Dr. Hood were drawn down darkly, but the eyes under them were bright with something that might be anger or might be amusement. "And still," he said, "I do not quite understand."

"You see, they want to get married," said the man with the clerical hat. "Maggie MacNab and young Todhunter want to get *married*. Now, what can be more important than that?"

The great Orion Hood's scientific triumphs had deprived him of many things—some said of his health, others of his God; but they had not wholly despoiled him of his sense of the absurd. At the last plea of the ingenuous priest a chuckle broke out of him from inside, and he threw himself into an armchair in an ironical attitude of the consulting physician.

"Mr. Brown," he said gravely, "it is quite fourteen and a half years since I was personally asked to test a personal problem: then it was the case of an attempt to poison the French President at a Lord Mayor's Banquet. It is now, I understand, a question of whether some friend of yours called Maggie is a suitable fiancée for some friend of hers called Todhunter. Well, Mr. Brown, I am a sportsman. I will take it on. I will give the MacNab family my best advice, as good as I gave the French Republic and the King of England—no, better: fourteen years better. I have nothing else to do this afternoon. Tell me your story."

The little clergyman called Brown thanked him with unquestionable warmth, but still with a queer kind of simplicity. It was rather as if he were thanking a stranger in a smoking-room for some trouble in passing the matches, than as if he were (as he was) practically thanking the Curator of Kew Gardens for coming with him into a field, to find a four-leaved clover. With scarcely a semicolon after his hearty thanks, the little man began his recital:

"I told you my name was Brown; well, that's the fact, and I'm the priest of the little Catholic Church I dare say you've seen beyond those straggly streets, where the town ends towards the north. In the last and straggliest of those streets which runs along the sea like a sea-wall there is a very honest but rather sharp-tempered member of my flock, a widow called MacNab. She has one daughter, and she lets lodgings; and between her and the daughter, and between her and the lodgers—well, I dare say there is a great deal to be said on both sides. At present she has only one lodger, the young man called Todhunter; but he has given more trouble than all the rest, for he wants to marry the young woman of the house."

"And the young woman of the house," asked Dr. Hood, with huge and silent amusement, "what does she want?"

"Why, she wants to marry him," cried Father Brown, sitting up eagerly. "That is just the awful complication."

"It is indeed a hideous enigma," said Dr. Hood.

"This young James Todhunter," continued the cleric, "is a very decent man so far as I know; but then nobody knows very much. He is a bright, brownish little fellow, agile like a monkey, clean-shaven like an actor, and obliging like a born courier. He seems to have quite a pocketful of money, but nobody knows what his trade is. Mrs. MacNab, therefore (being of a pessimistic turn), is quite sure it is something dreadful, and probably connected with dynamite. The dynamite must be of a shy and noiseless sort, for the poor fellow only shuts himself up for several hours of the day and studies something behind a locked door. He declares his privacy is temporary and justified, and promises to explain before the wedding. That is all that anyone knows for certain, but Mrs. MacNab will tell you a great deal more than even she is certain of. You know how the tales grow like grass on such a patch of ignorance as that. There are tales of two voices heard talking in the room; though, when the door is opened, Todhunter is always found alone. There are tales of a mysterious tall man in a silk hat, who once came out of the sea-mists and apparently out of the sea, stepping softly across the sandy fields and through the small back garden at twilight, till he was heard talking to the lodger at his open back window. The colloquy seemed to end in a quarrel: Todhunter dashed down his window with violence, and the man in the high hat melted into the sea-fog again. This story is told by the family with the fiercest mystification, but I really think Mrs. MacNab prefers her own original tale: that the Other Man (or whatever it is) crawls out every night from the big box in the corner, which is kept locked all day. You see, therefore, how this sealed door of Todhunter's is treated as the gate of all the fancies and monstrosities of the *Thousand and One Nights*. And yet there is the little fellow in his respectable black jacket, as punctual and innocent as a parlor clock. He pays his rent to the tick; he is practically a teetotaler; he is tirelessly kind with the younger children, and can keep them amused for a day on end; and, last and most urgent of all, he has made himself equally popular with the eldest daughter, who is ready to go to church with him tomorrow."

A man warmly concerned with any large theories has always a relish for applying them to any triviality. The great specialist, having condescended to the priest's simplicity, condescended expansively. He settled himself with comfort in his armchair and began to talk in the tone of a somewhat absent-minded lecturer:

"Even in a minute instance, it is best to look first to the main tendencies of Nature. A particular flower may not be dead in early winter, but the flowers are dying; a particular pebble may never be wetted with the tide, but the tide is coming in. To the scientific eye all human history is a series of collective movements, destructions or migrations, like the massacre of flies in winter or the return of birds in spring. Now the root fact in all history is Race. Race produces religion; Race produces legal and ethical wars. There is no stronger case than that of the wild, unworldly and perishing stock which we commonly call the Celts, of whom your friends the MacNabs are specimens. Small, swarthy, and of this dreamy and drifting blood, they accept easily the superstitious explanation of any incidents, just as they still accept (you will excuse me for saying) that superstitious explanation of all incidents which you and your Church represent. It is not remarkable that such people, with the sea moaning behind them and the Church (excuse me again) droning in front of them, should put fantastic features into what are probably plain events. You, with your small parochial responsibilities, see only this particular Mrs. MacNab, terrified with this particular tale of two voices and a tall man out of the sea. But the man with the scientific imagination sees, as it were, the whole clan of MacNabs scattered over the whole world, in its ultimate average as uniform as a tribe of birds. He sees thousands of Mrs. MacNabs, in thousands of houses, dropping their little drop of morbidity in the tea-cups of their friends; he sees—"

Before the scientist could conclude his sentence, another and more impatient summons sounded from without; someone with swishing skirts was marshaled hurriedly down the corridor, and the door opened on a young girl, decently dressed but disordered and red-hot with haste. She had sea-blown blonde hair, and would have been entirely beautiful if her cheekbones had not been, in the Scotch manner, a little high in relief as well as in color. Her apology was almost as abrupt as a command.

"I'm sorry to interrupt you, sir," she said; "but I had to follow Father Brown at once; it's nothing less than life or death."

Father Brown began to get to his feet in some disorder. "Why, what has happened, Maggie?" he said.

"James has been murdered, for all I can make out," answered the girl, still breathing hard from her rush. "That man Glass has been with him again; I heard them talking through the door quite plain. Two separate voices; for James speaks low, with a burr, and the other voice was high and quavery."

"That man Glass?" repeated the priest in some perplexity.

"I know his name is Glass," answered the girl, in great impatience. "I heard it through the door. They were quarreling—about money, I think —for I heard James say again and again, 'That's right, Mr. Glass,' or 'No, Mr. Glass,' and then, 'Two and three, Mr. Glass.' But we're talking too much; you must come at once, and there may be time yet."

"But time for what?" asked Dr. Hood, who had been studying the young lady with marked interest. "What is there about Mr. Glass and his money troubles that should impel such urgency?"

"I tried to break down the door and couldn't," answered the girl shortly. "Then I ran round to the back yard, and managed to climb on to the windowsill that looks into the room. It was all dim, and seemed to be empty, but I swear I saw James lying huddled up in a corner, as if he were drugged or strangled."

"This is very serious," said Father Brown, gathering his errant hat and umbrella and standing up; "in point of fact, I was just putting your case before this gentleman, and his view—"

"Has been largely altered," said the scientist gravely. "I do not think this young lady is so Celtic as I had supposed. As I have nothing else to do, I will put on my hat and stroll down the town with you."

In a few minutes all three were approaching the dreary tail of the MacNabs' street; the girl with the stern and breathless stride of the mountaineer, the criminologist with a lounging grace (which was not without a certain leopard-like swiftness), and the priest at an energetic trot entirely devoid of distinction. The aspect of this edge of the town was not entirely without justification for the doctor's hints about desolate moods and environments. The scattered houses stood farther and farther apart in a broken string along the seashore, the afternoon was closing with a premature and partly lurid twilight; the sea was of an inky purple and murmuring ominously. In the scrappy back garden of the MacNabs which ran down towards the sand, two black, barren-looking trees stood up like demon hands held up in astonishment, and as Mrs. MacNab ran down the street to meet them with lean hands similarly spread, and her fierce face in shadow, she was a little like a demon herself. The doctor and the priest made scant reply to her shrill reiterations of her daughter's story, with more disturbing details of her own, to the divided vows of vengeance against Mr. Glass for murdering, and against Mr. Todhunter for being murdered, or against the latter for having dared to want to marry her daughter, and for not having lived to do it. They passed through the narrow passages in the front of the house until they came to the lodger's door at the back, and there Dr. Hood, with the trick of an old detective, put his shoulder sharply to the panel and burst in the door.

It opened on a scene of silent catastrophe. No one seeing it, even for a flash, could doubt that the room had been the theater of some thrilling collision between two, or perhaps more, persons. Playing-cards lay littered across the table or fluttered about the floor as if a game had been interrupted. Two wine glasses stood ready for wine on a side-table, but a third lay smashed in a star of crystal upon the carpet. A few feet from it lay what looked like a long knife or short sword, straight, but with an ornamental and pictured handle; its dull blade just caught a grey glint from the dreary window behind, which showed the black trees against the leaden level of the sea. Towards the opposite corner of the room was rolled a gentleman's silk top hat, as if it had just been knocked off his head; so much so, indeed, that one almost looked to see it still rolling. And in the corner behind it, thrown like a sack of potatoes, but corded like a railway trunk, lay Mr. James Todhunter, with a scarf across his mouth, and six or seven ropes knotted round his elbows and ankles. His brown eyes were alive and shifted alertly.

Dr. Orion Hood paused for one instant on the door mat and drank in the whole scene of voiceless violence. Then he stepped swiftly across the carpet, picked up the tall silk hat, and gravely put it upon the head of the yet pinioned Todhunter. It was so much too large for him that it almost slipped down on to his shoulders.

"Mr. Glass's hat," said the doctor, returning with it and peering into the inside with a pocket lens. "How to explain the absence of Mr. Glass and the presence of Mr. Glass's hat? For Mr. Glass is not a careless man with his clothes. This hat is of a stylish shape and systematically brushed and burnished, though not very new. An old dandy, I should think."

"But, good heavens!" called out Miss MacNab, "aren't you going to untie the man first?"

"I say 'old' with intention, though not with certainty," continued the expositor; "my reason for it might seem a little farfetched. The hair of human beings falls out in very varying degrees, but almost always falls out slightly, and with the lens I should see the tiny hairs in a hat recently worn. It has none, which leads me to guess that Mr. Glass is bald. Now when this is taken with the high-pitched and querulous voice which Miss MacNab described so vividly (patience, my dear lady, patience), when we take the hairless head together with the tone common in senile anger, I should think we may deduce some advance in years. Nevertheless, he was probably vigorous, and he was almost certainly tall. I might rely in some degree on the story of his previous appearance at the window, as a tall man in a silk hat, but I think I have more exact indication. This wine glass has been smashed all over the place, but one of its splinters lies on the high bracket beside the mantelpiece. No such fragment could have fallen there if the vessel had been smashed in the hand of a comparatively short man like Mr. Todhunter."

"By the way," said Father Brown, "might it not be as well to untie Mr. Todhunter?"

"Our lesson from the drinking vessels does not end here," proceeded the specialist. "I may say at once that it is possible that the man Glass was bald or nervous through dissipation rather than age. Mr. Todhunter, as has been remarked, is a quiet, thrifty gentleman, essentially an abstainer. These cards and wine cups are no part of his normal habit; they have been produced for a particular companion. But, as it happens, we may go farther. Mr. Todhunter may or may not possess this wine-service, but there is no appearance of his possessing any wine. What, then, were these vessels to contain? I would at once suggest some brandy or whiskey, perhaps of a luxurious sort, from a flask in the pocket of Mr. Glass. We have thus something like a picture of the man, or at least of the type: tall, elderly, fashionable, but somewhat frayed, certainly fond of play and strong waters, and perhaps rather too fond of them. Mr. Glass is a gentleman not unknown on the fringes of society."

"Look here," cried the young woman, "if you don't let me pass to untie him I'll run outside and scream for the police."

"I should not advise *you*, Miss MacNab," said Dr. Hood gravely, "to be in any hurry to fetch the police. Father Brown, I seriously ask you to compose your flock, for their sakes, not for mine. Well, we have seen something of the figure and quality of Mr. Glass; what are the chief facts known of Mr. Todhunter? They are substantially three: that he is economical, that he is more or less wealthy, and that he has a secret. Now surely it is obvious that these are the three chief marks of the kind of man who is blackmailed. And surely it is equally obvious that the faded finery, the profligate habits, and the shrill irritation of Mr. Glass are the unmistakable marks of the kind of man who blackmails him. We have the two typical figures of a tragedy of hush money: on the one hand, the respectable man with a mystery, on the other, the west-end vulture with a scent for a mystery. These two men have met here today and have quarreled, using blows and a bare weapon."

"Are you going to take those ropes off?" asked the girl stubbornly.

Dr. Hood replaced the silk hat carefully on the side-table, and went across to the captive. He studied him intently, even moving him a little and half-turning him round by the shoulders, but he only answered:

"No, I think these ropes will do very well till your friends the police bring the handcuffs."

Father Brown, who had been looking dully at the carpet, lifted his round face and said, "What do you mean?"

The man of science had picked up the peculiar dagger-sword from the carpet and was examining it intently as he answered.

"Because you find Mr. Todhunter tied up," he said, "you all jump to the conclusion that Mr. Glass had tied him up; and then, I suppose, escaped. There are four objections to this. First, why should a gentleman so dressy as our friend Glass leave his hat behind him, if he left of his own free will? Second," he continued, moving towards the window, "this is the only exit, and it is locked on the inside. Third, this blade here has a tiny touch of blood at the point, but there is no wound on Mr. Todhunter. Mr. Glass took that wound away with him, dead or alive. Add to all this primary probability. It is much more likely that the blackmailed person would try to kill his incubus, rather than that the blackmailer would try to kill the goose that lays his golden eggs. There, I think, we have a pretty complete story."

"But the ropes?" inquired the priest, whose eyes had remained open with a rather vacant admiration.

"Ah, the ropes," said the expert with a singular intonation. "Miss MacNab very much wanted to know why I did not set Mr. Todhunter free from his ropes. Well, I will tell her. I did not do it because Mr. Todhunter can set himself free from them at any minute he chooses."

"What?" cried the audience in quite different notes of astonishment.

"I have looked at all the knots on Mr. Todhunter," reiterated Hood quietly. "I happen to know something about knots; they are quite a branch of criminal science. Every one of those knots he has made himself and could loosen himself; not one of them would have been made by an enemy really trying to pinion him. The whole of this affair of the ropes is a clever fake, to make us think him the victim of the struggle instead of the wretched Glass, whose corpse may be hidden in the garden or stuffed up the chimney."

The face of the little Catholic priest, which was commonly complacent and even comic, had suddenly become knotted with a curious frown. It was not the blank curiosity of his first innocence. It was rather that creative curiosity which comes when a man has the beginnings of an idea.

"Say it again, please," he said in a simple, bothered manner; "do you mean that Todhunter can tie himself up all alone and untie himself all alone?"

"That is what I mean," said the doctor.

"Jerusalem!" ejaculated Brown suddenly, "I wonder if it could possibly be that!"

He scuttled across the room rather like a rabbit, and peered with quite a new impulsiveness into the partially covered face of the captive. Then he turned his own rather fatuous face to the company. "Yes, that's it!" he cried in a certain excitement. "Can't you see it in the man's face? Why, look at his eyes!"

Both the Professor and the girl followed the direction of his glance. And though the broad black scarf completely masked the lower half of Todhunter's visage, they did grow conscious of something struggling and intense about the upper part of it.

"His eyes do look queer," cried the young woman, strongly moved. "You brutes; I believe it's hurting him!"

"Not that, I think," said Dr. Hood, "the eyes have certainly a singular expression. But I should interpret those transverse wrinkles as expressing rather such slight psychological abnormality—"

"Oh, bosh!" cried Father Brown, "can't you see he's laughing?"

"Laughing!" repeated the doctor, with a start, "but what on earth can he be laughing at?"

"Well," replied the Reverend Brown apologetically, "not to put too fine a point on it, I think he is laughing at you. And indeed, I'm a little inclined to laugh at myself, now I know about it."

"Now you know about what?" asked Hood, in some exasperation.

"Now I know," replied the priest, "the profession of Mr. Todhunter."

He shuffled about the room looking at one object after another, with what seemed to be a vacant stare, and then invariably bursting into an equally vacant laugh, a highly irritating process for those who had to watch it. He laughed very much over the hat, still more uproariously over the broken glass, but the blood on the sword point sent him into mortal convulsions of amusement. Then he turned to the fuming specialist.

"Dr. Hood," he cried enthusiastically, "you are a great poet! You have called an uncreated being out of the void. How much more god-like that is than if you had only ferreted out the mere facts! Indeed, the mere facts are rather commonplace and comic by comparison."

"I have no notion what you are talking about," said Dr. Hood rather haughtily; "my facts are all inevitable, though necessarily incomplete. A place may be permitted to intuition, perhaps (or poetry if you prefer the term), but only because the corresponding details cannot as yet be ascertained. In the absence of Mr. Glass—"

"That's it, that's it," said the little priest, nodding quite eagerly, "that's the first idea to get fixed; the absence of Mr. Glass. He is so extremely absent. I suppose," he added reflectively, "that there was never anybody so absent as Mr. Glass."

"Do you mean he is absent from the town?" demanded the doctor.

"I mean he is absent from everywhere," answered Father Brown; "he is absent from the Nature of Things, so to speak."

"Do you seriously mean," said the specialist with a smile, "that there is no such person?"

The priest made a sign of assent. "It does seem a pity," he said.

Orion Hood broke into a contemptuous laugh. "Well," he said, "before we go on to the hundred and one other evidences, let us take the first proof we found; the first fact we fell over when we fell into this room. If there is no Mr. Glass, whose hat is this?"

"It is Mr. Todhunter's," replied Brown.

"But it doesn't fit him," cried Hood impatiently. "He couldn't possibly wear it!"

Father Brown shook his head with ineffable mildness. "I never said he could wear it," he answered. "I said it was his hat. Or, if you insist on a shade of difference, a hat that is his."

"And where is the shade of difference?" asked the criminologist with a slight sneer.

"My good sir," cried the mild little man, with his first movement akin to impatience, "if you will walk down the street to the nearest hatter's shop, you will see that there is, in common speech, a difference between a man's hat and the hats that are his."

"But a hatter," protested Hood, "can get money out of his stock of new hats. What could Todhunter get out of this one old hat?"

"Rabbits," replied Father Brown promptly.

"*What?*" cried Dr. Hood.

"Rabbits, ribbons, sweetmeats, goldfish, rolls of colored paper," said the reverend gentleman with rapidity. "Don't you see it all when you found out the faked ropes? It's just the same with the sword. Mr. Todhunter hasn't got a scratch on him, as you say; but he's got a scratch in him, if you follow me."

"Do you mean inside Mr. Todhunter's clothes?" inquired Mrs. MacNab sternly.

"I do not mean inside Mr. Todhunter's clothes," said Father Brown. "I mean inside Mr. Todhunter."

"Well, what in the name of Bedlam *do* you mean?"

"Mr. Todhunter," explained Father Brown placidly, "is learning to be a professional conjurer, as well as juggler, ventriloquist, and expert in the rope trick. The conjuring explains the hat. It is without traces of hair, not because it is worn by the prematurely bald Mr. Glass, but because it has never been worn by anybody. The juggling explains the three glasses, which Todhunter was teaching himself to throw up and catch in rotation. But, being only at the stage of practice, he smashed one glass against the ceiling. And the juggling also explains the sword, which it was Mr. Todhunter's professional pride and duty to swallow. But, again, being at the stage of practice, he very slightly grazed the inside of his throat with the weapon. Hence he has a wound inside him, which I am sure (from the expression of his face) is not a serious one. He was also practicing the trick of a release from ropes, and he was just about to free himself when we all burst in the room. The cards, of course, are for card tricks, and they are scattered on the floor because he had just been practicing one of those dodges of sending them flying through the air. He merely kept his trade secret, because he had to keep his tricks secret, like any other conjurer. But the mere fact of an idler in a top hat having once looked in at his back window, and been driven away by him with great indignation, was enough to set us all on a wrong track of romance, and make us imagine his whole life overshadowed by the silk-hatted specter of Mr. Glass."

"But what about the two voices?" asked Maggie, staring.

"Have you never heard a ventriloquist?" asked Father Brown. "Don't you know they speak first in their natural voice, and then answer themselves in just that shrill, squeaky, unnatural voice that you heard?"

There was a long silence, and Dr. Hood regarded the little man who had spoken with a dark and attentive smile. "You are certainly a very ingenious person," he said; "it could not have been done better in a book. But there is just one part of Mr. Glass you have not succeeded in explaining away, and that is his name. Miss MacNab distinctly heard him so addressed by Mr. Todhunter."

The Rev. Mr. Brown broke into a rather childish giggle. "Well, that," he said, "that's the silliest part of the whole silly story. When our juggling friend here threw up the three glasses in turn, he counted them aloud as he caught them, and also commented aloud when he failed to catch them. What he really said was 'One, two, and three—missed a glass; one, two—missed a glass.' And so on."

There was a second of stillness in the room, and then everyone with one accord burst out laughing. As they did so the figure in the corner complacently uncoiled all the ropes and let them fall with a flourish. Then, advancing into the middle of the room with a bow, he produced from his pocket a big bill printed in blue and red, which announced that

ZALADIN, the World's Greatest Conjurer, Contortionist, Ventriloquist and Human Kangaroo, would be ready with an entirely new series of Tricks at the Empire Pavilion, Scarborough, on Monday next at eight o'clock precisely.

FOR DISCUSSION: The Absence of Mr. Glass

1. Do a quick comparison/contrast of Dr. Hood and Father Brown as *people*. What is the major difference between them?
2. Now try a comparison/contrast of Dr. Hood and Father Brown as *detectives*. Again, what is the major difference between them?
3. Why is the title of this unit, "Things Are Seldom as They Seem," especially appropriate for Todhunter?
4. People see what they wish to see, not what is. The result is that four people can look at the same room and come up with four different interpretations of what happened there. In this story how is each person's character or personality related to his or her interpretation of Todhunter's dilemma?
5. Although almost every writer is fascinated by words, this is more true of G. K. Chesterton than of most. He holds them up to the light, manipulates them, views them from different angles. Can you find several places in the text where this kind of word-play occurs?

INTRODUCTION: The Dove and the Hawk

Hawks are large, predatory birds. They nest in tall trees, on rock ledges, in hollow logs, and on cliffs. They are swift, deliberate, and accurate in spotting their prey and in plunging down for the kill. They attack fish, rodents, reptiles, lizards, and small mammals. Among the best-known are the Red-tailed Hawk, the Cooper's Hawk, the Bald Eagle, and the Osprey.

Doves are slim, fairly gentle birds. Their call is melancholy—"coo-ah, coo, coo." They eat seeds and berries and fruit. They are natural victims—the prey rather than the predator. Among the best-known are the White-winged Dove, the Inca Dove, and the Mourning Dove.

Hawks and doves are distinctly different species. No one who knows anything about birds could ever mistake a hawk for a dove. Or vice versa. Nature is careful about these things.

However, when one considers the human hawk and the human dove, one finds the distinction blurred.

The Dove and the Hawk
Anthony Gilbert

Penelope came into my life when I was 21. She was my father's child by his second wife, more like a niece than a half sister, and for years she called me Aunt Helen.

I'll never forget the night I first set eyes on her mother.

As a rule I spent my holidays in London with my Aunt Olive—I was an only child—while my father went to his beloved mountains; but that year I developed a sudden sharp attack of influenza and had to stay at home. On the fifth evening, when my temperature was rapidly subsiding, I heard a sudden commotion in the hall and crept out of bed to find out what was going on. To my amazement I saw my father in the hall and with him a girl of about my own age, whom I'd certainly never seen before. My father looked up and saw me. He was a handsome, unpredictable, undemonstrative man.

"What on earth are you doing here, Helen? Why aren't you in London?"

I murmured something apologetic about influenza, but before I could finish, the girl came running up the stairs.

"You're Helen," she said. "Oh, isn't it lovely for me that you should be here? There's so much to learn and you'll know all the answers. You must think of me as a sister, never as a stepmother. Ugh!" She pulled her lovely mouth into a grimace.

I was gawky with amazement. She was never to my thinking quite so beautiful as her daughter, Penelope, was to be, but at that time she was the loveliest creature I had ever seen. Like a living beam of sunlight—and for some incredible reason she had wanted to marry a man 30 years her senior. It took me a long time to realize that she was in love with him, and she stayed in love with him all her life. She was a small woman, neatly formed as a bird, dark and glowing—like a beam of a living sun.

"You'd better go back to bed, Helen," my father said. "Jenny, my dear, be careful. Influenza can be very infectious."

"He's right—you must go back," Jenny told me. "I'll come and talk to you."

I don't know where she learned her skills, but within five minutes our glowering Mrs. Mopp had turned into a ministering angel and was bringing me cold drinks and a fresh hot-water bottle.

"What a homecoming!" I said shakily. "But no one told me . . ."

"I know. It was awful of us. I knew we ought to cable you, and you could have flown out or something, but I thought—suppose she feels she can't share him—I wouldn't blame you a bit. Darling Peregrine!"

I realized dazedly she was talking about my unapproachable father.

"But it'll be all right, you'll see. I shan't take your place, just pop into an empty room in his life. Tell me about your mother. It must have been dreadful for you when she died."

Jenny was right, as always. During the year I lived on at home I was never once asked to have a tray in my room when company came; she took over the reins of office by degrees and so unobtrusively that I hardly realized they were slipping out of my hands.

At the year's end my father said, "It's time you thought of your own future, Helen, my dear." He'd become kinder since his second marriage; Jenny softened everything she touched. "You've great potentialities. It occurred to me you might like to take a secretarial course. There are excellent openings, and, I believe, a great shortage of competent young women. If you manage an employer as well as you managed this house you should go far."

His idea was that I should occupy Aunt Olive's spare room in London, but Jenny put a stop to that.

"Darling, do have a heart," I heard her say. "Helen's young, she wants some fun, not just a collection of Aunt Olive's grisly old bores. And you know you've never really done anything for her."

"I brought you into the family," he said simply. "She's had a year with you under the same roof."

He explained he'd make me an allowance until I was trained. I'd come into some money from my mother when I was 25, and after that I should be able to make my own way.

Aunt Olive found me a bed-sitting room in a rather dingy but respectable street and had me enrolled in London's most famous secretarial college. I loved it from the start. Sitting in an office, keeping books, arranging appointments—it was like housekeeping all over again but with a much wider scope. At that stage I didn't envisage the Helen Bryce Employment and Secretarial Agency—headquarters in London and two provincial branches, all doing very nicely, thank you—but I knew in my bones I was bound to succeed. I wrote to tell my father, but he'd lost interest in me by now, because Jenny was going to have a baby. This time, he was convinced, it would be a boy.

But it wasn't. It was another girl whom they christened Penelope. I saw her when she was two weeks old. I suppose she wasn't really beautiful then—they can't be at that age—but from the moment I set eyes on her, Jenny occupied a second place in my heart. It was a different form of "love at first sight."

It says a lot for Penelope that before she was two she had reconciled her father to her disappointing sex. She captivated everyone wherever she went. Strangely, I never connected her closely with my father—as well, I thought, expect a toad to hatch out a butterfly. She was just the zenith of the miracles that Jenny had worked on our dull, uncheerful house.

The child took to me from the first. By this time I accepted the fact that I was unlikely to marry. I was doing well at my job, and my prospects were bright. When Penelope was five Jenny said one day, "If anything should happen to me, Helen, you'd look after Penelope, wouldn't you? Even in the grave I wouldn't worry if I knew she was with you."

Second sight? I don't know. Anyway, nothing did happen for several years. Except in my career. As soon as I came into my inheritance I bought a partnership with a Miss Carless, who ran a secretarial bureau. We were doing well and would do better.

Three years later Miss Carless had a stroke and I bought her out. When she died a year later, I turned the concern into the Helen Bryce Agency. They say a recommendation from me goes a long way to help a girl to get a particular job.

When Penelope was 14 the blow fell. Both her parents were killed in a plane crash over the Alps. Under my father's will she became a ward of court. There was a good deal of money involved and practically everything was left to her. My Aunt Olive had died two years previously, so I was her only living relative.

Mr. Prendergast, the lawyer, hemmed and ha-ed a bit when I said

Penelope's home would henceforth be with me. She had just started boarding school, but she'd need a place for the holidays. I was my own boss by now, could fix my holidays as I chose, so Penelope wouldn't be neglected; but I should see to it, too, that she didn't lack companionship of her own age. What settled the question was the child herself.

"I shall go to Aunt Helen," she said. "It's what Mother wanted."

I had recently bought a house in the suburbs. I furnished the top floor as a sort of flat, remembering how much I'd longed for privacy at Penelope's age. She had her own bathroom and sitting room, where she could entertain her friends, and there was a sofa if she wanted to invite them to stay over. But she had the run of the whole house.

She was up in that flat less than I anticipated. I had dreamed of her joining me when she started work—she could be a junior executive in no time, and no nonsense about nepotism, but Penelope wouldn't hear of it.

"I wouldn't be any good at it. If I was anyone else you'd give me the sack in a week. Besides, I've sort of promised Marjorie to join her—she's starting a shop for kookie clothes. She thinks I could model and perhaps design."

"But you don't know anything about clothes," I protested.

"Darling, everyone knows about clothes."

I wasn't in love with the idea. The Cochranes were a young couple embarking on a rather hazardous enterprise with inadequate capital. Penelope was 18, and when she was 21 she'd be a very rich young woman. I was resolved not to be coaxed into putting any money into the concern.

"All right," said Penelope, obviously disappointed, "but actually it would be a very good investment."

"If they're solvent at the end of a year I'll reconsider," I promised.

"If they're solvent at the end of a year they won't need it."

She didn't stay with me long after she started the job. She didn't make any excuses about difficulty of transportation, or anything like that; she just said she wanted to share a flat with a girl she knew. I hid my disappointment—after all, I hadn't wanted to live with my aunt when I was her age, and aunts are aunts the world over. The funny thing was, that was how I thought of her—as my niece rather than my half sister, though about this time she stopped calling me Aunt Helen. But all her friends—the few I met, that is—all assumed I was her aunt and neither of us bothered to correct them.

Penelope moved out the following week. Secretly I thought her new flat deplorable and the morals of her friend pretty dubious, but I had the wit to say nothing. After a time she moved casually into another flat in Regent's Park, where I went once or twice by invitation. But though she still came to see me, nothing would induce her to bring her companions.

"Darling, you're so efficient they'd be terrified. They'd think you square."

She'd been at work for about a year when Tim Driscoll loomed on her horizon.

Loomed? He leaped, he bounded, he was as sudden as Jenny must have seemed to my father. I met him of all places at Penelope's bedside. She had been involved in a car accident, of which she made pretty light. "Darling Helen,"—it was Jenny over again—"your generation does fuss so. Just be grateful for our wonderful Health Service—it won't cost us a penny."

When I arrived with a basket of fruit and some flowers, I found her looking like Pallas Athene, arising out of a sea of flowers, cards, books, bottles of perfume, and chocolates—there was hardly any room for her in the bed. But my eyes were all for Tim. He was a dark vital man, oozing with that unscrupulous charm that sweeps young girls off their feet, and a good many older women, too. I knew he was no good to Penelope the instant I set eyes on him; but I knew, too, I was going to have the hardest job of my life persuading Penelope of this. He was 30, at least, and I wouldn't be surprised to know there were already one or two broken marriages behind him.

Penelope held out her hand. "Helen darling, this is Tim. We're in love." She might have been introducing the Archangel Gabriel.

"How are you, Aunt Helen?" Which was absurd, for there were only a few years between us. "Don't tell me you don't like Irishmen, but how about the Englishman's sense of fair play? When I was a boy there was a man who lived on the corner, kept a few pigs, and in bad weather you could hardly tell the pigs from the muck they wallowed in. He put up a notice. 'Don't judge the pigs by the sty, but wait till you get the flavor of the bacon.' You get the message—Aunt Helen?"

Penelope watched him with adoration in her eyes. She seemed to throw her love over him in handfuls, so that he glittered in consequence.

"I knew how it would be." Tim Driscoll turned to her with an air of comic dismay. "Your aunt doesn't think I'm good enough for you. Well, that's one thing we can agree on right away. But where on earth are you going to find the man who is?"

I thought he would realize that I wanted a little time alone with Penelope, but he made no move. He carried on a conversation practically nonstop.

"What a girl! She's so popular, her visitors come in droves. I have to act as a sort of social secretary and space them out."

He looked at me impudently, as if to suggest I ought to have made an appointment, but I wasn't having any of that.

"There are a few things I want to talk to you about, Penelope," I announced, and even he couldn't pretend not to notice that.

242

"I can take a hint," he said. "Now don't let Aunt Helen put you against me, sweetie." But he had no fears of that. The child was completely under his spell.

"Where did you meet him?" I asked Penelope, when we were alone.

"At the races."

"I didn't know you were a gambler."

"Aren't we all? Helen, you *must* like him. He's nervous about you— that's why he tried to sound so confident. He's terrified you'll try and break it up."

"Why should he suppose I'd want to do that?"

"Well—you might think he was too old, for one thing."

"He is. He'll never see thirty again."

"He's thirty-four. My mother was twenty when she got married, and my father was fifty. You're not going to try to tell me that wasn't a success. Why, everything I know about love I learned from her—until I met Tim, of course. I knew it was right the first minute we met—it was like the sun coming out."

"I didn't know your sun had ever gone in."

"Well, not the ordinary sun. But this was different. This was—well, like a radiance, the light that never was on sea or land. If you're not going to like him it'll be the first barrier there's ever been between us. Because I could never give him up—never."

"How long have you known him?"

"What difference does that make?"

"I suppose you're not thinking of getting married right away? You're barely twenty."

"Why waste time? Oh, you're thinking about me being a minor, but I'm sure the courts wouldn't object, even if it got that far. Not if you said you approved. And you must. You've always put my happiness ahead of everything, even your beloved business. I used to wonder if I could ever love anyone as much as that. Now, of course . . ."

Her smile finished the sentence. She meant that now, of course, she had outstripped me, that I could never hope to catch up.

He was there the next time I went, though I'd written in advance this time. I wondered what kind of job he had that he could turn up on an afternoon. Penelope was as sweet as ever, but I realized she had started to move away from me, and wouldn't be coming back.

It was somehow like being on an island just offshore—I could see what was going on, I could wave, and she could wave back, but there was that implacable sea between us.

Some young things came piling in when I'd been there about fifteen minutes—one worked in a coffee bar, one was on the stage, none of her friends seemed to have steady jobs or regular hours—and the gulf between us perceptibly widened.

Things Are Seldom as They Seem   243

Mind you, they were charming, they glowed in a way I don't remember youth glowing when I was a girl, as if they lived in a blaze of perpetual sunlight. They accepted Tim as casually as if he'd been a poodle or a Persian cat, someone belonging exclusively to Penelope, but on show just the same. I came away feeling about 80, and cold, as though I'd been sitting in a howling draft.

The following time Tim brought me back in his car. It was a handsome affair, a red Alvis with a hood twice the size of the chassis. He drove well, I'll say that for him, but in a manner I can only describe as anti-social. Like most women drivers, I have a great sense of what I owe to my fellow drivers, but Tim was absolutely ruthless.

When we reached my door I asked him in—conversation had been impossible en route—and gave him a whiskey and soda. I wasn't going to waste my good sherry on him.

"I want you to tell me something, Mr. Driscoll," I said.

"Tim. After all, I call you Aunt Helen."

"Very premature of you," I snapped.

"It's no good, you know—you're not going to break us up," he warned me. "If you insist on a tug of war, I promise you there isn't a bookmaker between here and John o' Groats who'd give you evens."

"You do realize Penelope's a minor?"

"Of course. But I don't think even you would invoke the law. At best you could only get the wedding postponed, and at worst—well, it wouldn't do you any good."

"Strangely enough," I told him, "it's not my good I'm thinking of."

"People have such filthy minds, don't they. And an old maid—forgive me, Aunt Helen, but we have got the gloves off, haven't we?—who tries to stop a girl from getting married—well, jealousy has an ugly name."

"Jealousy!" I exclaimed. I couldn't stop myself. "What! Of you?"

I got him under the skin there, though he kept his temper. "Of her happiness," he said.

"I wish I could be persuaded it lies in your hands. But I wanted to ask you something, didn't I? I'm her only living relative. Are you in a position to support a wife?"

"Pen and I'll get by," he said.

"That's what I'm wondering. You see, she can't touch her money till she's twenty-one."

"You think that's the only reason I'm marrying her, isn't that so? Well, for your information I have a business of my own."

It turned out that the business consisted of a riding school in some placed unnamed—Surrey, he finally said airily, when I pressed him. It hadn't been going long, but it would grow. Eventually—when he could lay hands on Penelope's money, I suppose—he intended to branch out, to breed his own horses. Blood stock, he said, and with the export market being what it was, there should be a packet in it.

"Oh, no doubt," I agreed. "But it costs a packet to get started. Stud fees are pretty heavy, and you can't breed from inferior animals."

He gestured toward the decanter. "May I?" But he didn't wait for an answer.

"If there's one thing I do know about it's horses," he went on. "I don't say we shall be millionaires from the start, but—well, its like having a kid. At first you have to carry him about, but one day he may turn into the prizefighter of his time."

"I hope," I said dryly, "your business is a little older than that."

"And, of course," he said, "Pen will keep on with her job to begin with. It's what she wants. Well, it would be ridiculous to throw her chances away."

"Penelope will want children," I assured him bluntly.

"Naturally. In due course. Look, Aunt Helen, why can't we be friends? We both love Pen. I'm going to marry her—make up your mind to that. If you think she's making such a bad bargain I'd have expected you to stick closer than ever."

"Oh, you could charm a hippopotamus out of its pool on a hot day," I acknowledged. "Unfortunately for you, I'm not a hippopotamus."

"That could be an advantage to me." His manner was as smooth as cream. "I've always heard hippos can do a lot of damage."

All the same, I had enough sense to know that I had been wasting my breath.

As soon as she left the hospital, Penelope spent every spare minute looking at apartments.

"I thought Tim's riding stables or whatever they are were out of London," I said.

"They are, of course, but he can commute. I have to be on the spot." She seemed to do about a fourteen-hour day. "What do you mean by whatever they are? Don't you believe they exist?"

Well, if they did I was pretty sure they weren't registered in his name. He might be a riding-master, but by temperament and profession he was a gambler, and that's no foundation for married life with a girl like Penelope. Now and again he might hit the jackpot and they'd unroll the red carpet, but the rest of the time Penelope would, as they say, "carry the can." I knew she'd be far too proud to let me help her, once she became Mrs. Driscoll.

I was pretty busy myself that summer. I was opening my second provincial office, and there'd been some tiresome setbacks. I was away from London a lot, but at last everything was ironed out. It was a Saturday when I started back to London.

I don't believe in predestination, a set pattern arranged by some invisible and inscrutable Deity, absolving us from personal responsibility. People have to answer for their own actions. But I do agree that chance plays a big part. If Jenny hadn't gone to Switzerland that summer, her first visit—if Penelope hadn't gone to the races—if I hadn't stopped at St. Aubyns Racecourses that afternoon on sheer impulse, all our lives would be different.

I hadn't intended to stop—I didn't even realize there was a racecourse there—but going past I saw there was a big meeting that afternoon. I had time on my hands, so I parked my car and bought a ticket. That was the first and last time in my life I felt any sympathy with Tim Driscoll.

I've always wanted perfection—in my office, in my work. You don't get it, of course, but you do aim for it, and it seemed to me that these splendid horses had achieved it. The noble carriage, the rolling eye, the velvet coats, the sheer majesty of them—oh, I could see how they'd appeal to a gambler like Tim Driscoll. Or did he only see them, as I was convinced he saw Penelope, as a source of personal profit?

Since I didn't expect to come a second time I decided to complete the experiment by making a few bets. I chose four horses haphazardly, and backed them to place. Three of the four came home. I wasn't triumphant, I was horrified. If a month's pay could be gleaned in an afternoon under such thrilling circumstances, how could I expect a go-getter like Tim to turn his hand to honest work?

I decided not to stay for the last race, but get away before the roads were jammed with traffic. I went into the refreshment tent for a cup of tea that I was disgusted to find was being served in paper cups. The tent was packed—I didn't see how I'd ever manage to get my cup to my mouth. And, in fact, I never did. I was trying to maneuver a little space when I heard a voice behind me that turned me rigid.

I didn't have to turn to see who it was. I'd have known that voice if it had spoken beside my grave.

"But, darling," it coaxed, "I promise you it won't make any difference to us, none whatsoever."

I heard a woman's laugh. "What do you mean, no difference? You'll be a married man, won't you?"

I couldn't see the speaker, but it didn't matter. I'd heard that particular voice before, and other voices exactly like it. They came into my office—the greedy ones, the What's-in-it-for-Walter ones, to whom scruple isn't even a word in the dictionary.

"So what?" Tim demanded. "I've got business all over the country, haven't I? I'm not tied to an office desk. And Pen's no camp follower. Anyway, she's got her own job."

The blatancy of it, the crudeness and cruelty of it, made me sick. But

246

Penelope's innocence was no match for a woman like this—the dove and the hawk, I thought, and the hawk knows no pity.

"But if she finds out—"

"Why should she? Even your husband hasn't a suspicion—after four years."

"Lucky for you. If he had he'd clap a divorce on me before you could wink. Would you marry me, if he did?"

"Flo, don't be absurd."

There was a warning note of impatience in Tim's voice. I could read the situation easily enough. He was one of those men who command women's love but never give it back—because he has no love to give. Pitiful? Perhaps. But it would take a more Christian woman than I am to spare compassion for such a rogue.

"If you got divorced," Tim went on brutally, "you couldn't even get alimony, and Teddy's such a vengeful type he'd probably claim fantastic damages. No, we're far better off as we are. Oh, darling, don't be like that. It's worked for four years—it'll be all right, you'll see."

"I suppose she's over the moon for you?" cried the jealous voice.

"Well, darling . . ."

I couldn't have moved if my life had depended on it. I found I was crushing the horrible paper cup till the tea spurted over the front of my dress. I've never been a violent type, but I understood in that moment how a person armed with a flickknife or even a stone will employ direct action, on impulse, with reason driven out of the mind.

"If I thought you cared for *her*," began Flo slowly, and Tim laughed.

"Darling, she's a kid, a cute kid, but I've always preferred my women grown up. You'd love her, Flo—a sweet little innocent."

That was a bit thick, even for him. "Don't be a bloody fool," said the woman roughly. "I hate her before I've even seen her. If you're sensible you'll keep her out of my way. All right, Tim. If that's the situation, come round tonight. Teddy's away on some conference—I suppose you're not spending your *nights* with Little Miss Muffet yet?"

"I can't see you tonight, angel. I'm booked for dinner. As a matter of fact, we have to be damn careful for the next few weeks. That grisly horror of an aunt—well, she's a half sister really—would smash us if she had half an opportunity, and I can't afford to pass up a chance like this, not even for you, baby."

"Tomorrow night then?"

"I'll ring you," he said. "You can count on me, darling."

His voice dripped butter all over the place. I was afraid he might see me, but he didn't even turn his head.

"You'd better not forget," said Flo. "You're betting on lives now, Tim, not just horseflesh."

If I'd been capable of even a shred of pity I'd have been sorry for her.

She might be worthless, but this was love all right, the agonizing love that isn't sure of the object of its affections. In a way you could say she loved him even more than Penelope did—because she saw his rottenness, and she didn't care.

"Don't fret," Tim told her. "I have to keep sweetie pie happy for all our sakes. Even being seen here together is risky. You know what people are like—they have tongues for more than licking ice cream. And if it came to dear old Auntie's ears, she'd somehow lay hands on a poison dart and send it to me in an envelope with Happy Birthday written on it, and she's so bloody clever she'd have fourteen alibis at the inquest to prove it couldn't be her."

He was right about that, too. I caught sight of him as he moved away, saying, "Can't miss the last race. I've got something on Falconer. Let's hope he changes the luck or I'll be in Queer Street before I reach the altar."

Off he went, as graceful as one of the horses he loved. I really believe he loved horses, as it wasn't in him to love a woman.

When he was gone I ground my paper cup underfoot and went along to the cloakroom to bathe my burning face and make some repairs. I had the room to myself. People had either gone off already or were packing the rails for the start of the last race.

I looked like a glowing ember of a woman—it was as if in five minutes I'd aged 25 years. Somehow, I knew, I had to find some way to save Penelope from a future of humiliation and despair.

There were a number of gaps in the car park ranks when I arrived. I showed the attendant my ticket and went in. I was looking for a red Alvis, and it wasn't hard to find. It was typical of Tim that he hadn't even bothered to lock the car.

I opened the door and put my bag on the seat. Then I lifted the hood. If anyone had seen me I'd have been an owner checking some trifling fault, but on occasions like these you're never truly *seen*. I only had a few minutes before the last race would be over, and I had to be away before Tim appeared.

Fortunately, I've always been independent. I'm a good mechanic, I can paper a wall, mend an electric socket, change a tire in record time. What I had to do now didn't take long, and by the time I had driven my own car out of the park I had insured that Penelope's marriage to Tim Driscoll would never take place.

The odd thing was I felt perfectly calm. As I saw it, my first duty was to Jenny's child. I'd tried everything else; this, it seemed to me—only I didn't phrase it in such a hifalutin fashion—was the love that is faithful unto death—in this case, Tim's death. But if it had involved mine it wouldn't have made any difference.

248

The cars were moving out fairly regularly now, and I was just one of a crowd. I had no fear of detection—everyone knew I never went near a racecourse; besides, I'd placed my bets on the tote, so there were no records, and I destroyed my car park ticket a quarter of a mile away from the course.

It's a funny thing, but I never really thought about Flo. When you play chess, which is one of my relaxations, you know you may have to sacrifice a pawn to guard your Queen. Flo was just one of the pawns.

I slept quite peacefully that night. Next morning was Sunday, and I came down a little later than usual to collect my papers. There was nothing in the two literary ones, but the *Echo* had the full story. There was even a photograph of the scene of the disaster. Wherever I look these days, I see that story in letters of flame.

FATAL CRASH NEAR ST. AUBYNS

Mr. Tim Driscoll, a well-known racing enthusiast, was killed instantaneously when his Alvis car went out of control as he was returning from the races yesterday evening. With Mr. Driscoll was his fiancee, Miss Penelope Bryce, who was also killed.

You've heard the phrase—time stood still. Time stopped for me that morning—I can't even be certain how long ago.

How was I to guess that it was Penelope and not Flo whom he had brought with him? The meeting with Flo in the tea tent might have been just chance—or, more likely, Flo's jealousy had driven her there, perhaps to catch a glimpse of her rival.

I was brought up to believe in the immortal spirit of man. Eternity's a terrifying thought—time without end, a road that goes on and on and presumably leads you somewhere in the end.

It won't be like that for me. My share of eternity is approximately 18 hours—between teatime on a Saturday afternoon and ten o'clock the next morning. The wheel turns and I turn with it; the clock moves from four to ten, from four to ten, and back again, always back again. And on that wheel I'll go round and round and round—forever and ever.

FOR DISCUSSION: The Dove and the Hawk

1. At one point Helen says of Penelope and Flo: "But Penelope's innocence was no match for a woman like this—the dove and the hawk, I thought, and the hawk knows no pity." This seems to explain the

title, but "things are seldom as they seem." Explain Gilbert's intent by labeling each of the following characters as *dove* or *hawk*.

Helen Bryce
Penelope Bryce
Tim Driscoll
Flo

2. Keeping in mind the information given in the introduction about doves and hawks, ask yourself whether each of these four characters *remained* a dove or a hawk throughout the story. Did anyone change from one species to another? Explain. (At least one did. The answer to this question should suggest a second meaning for the title of this story.)

3. Is anyone of us *all* hawk or *all* dove? Or are we all a combination of the two? How does this further our knowledge of *our* species, the human race?

4. Once again irony plays an important part in the development of a story. What are some of the small ironic touches throughout the story? How is the final scene especially ironic?

INTRODUCTION: The Possibility of Evil

If you have read Shirley Jackson's story "The Lottery," you know that the one thing you can expect in a Jackson story is the unexpected. In that story the author explored the nature of evil. In this story the author cuts still deeper into the same human problem. What is evil? How can it be recognized? What is its immediate cause? Its long-range cause?

This story takes place on a lovely day in a lovely town filled with lovely people. Yet the most *unlovely* things happen. Overt evil is tolerable, but evil lurking unsuspected beneath serene goodness is abominable.

The Possibility of Evil
Shirley Jackson

Miss Adela Strangeworth came daintily along Main Street on her way to the grocery. The sun was shining, the air was fresh and clear after the night's heavy rain, and everything in Miss Strangeworth's little town looked washed and bright. Miss Strangeworth took deep breaths and thought that there was nothing in the world like a fragrant summer day.

She knew everyone in town, of course; she was fond of telling strangers —tourists who sometimes passed through the town and stopped to admire Miss Strangeworth's roses—that she had never spent more than a day outside this town in all her long life. She was seventy-one, Miss Strangeworth told the tourists, with a pretty little dimple showing by her lip, and she sometimes found herself thinking that the town belonged to her. "My grandfather built the first house on Pleasant Street," she would say, opening her blue eyes wide with the wonder of it. "This house, right here. My family has lived here for better than a hundred years. My grandmother planted these roses, and my mother tended them, just as I do. I've watched my town grow; I can remember when Mr. Lewis, Senior, opened the grocery store, and the year the river flooded out the shanties on the low road, and the excitement when some young folks wanted to move the park over to the space in front of where the new post office is today. They wanted to put up a statue of Ethan Allen"—Miss Strangeworth would frown a little and sound stern—"but it should have been a statue of my grandfather. There wouldn't have been a town here at all if it hadn't been for my grandfather and the lumber mill."

Miss Strangeworth never gave away any of her roses, although the tourists often asked her. The roses belonged on Pleasant Street, and it bothered Miss Strangeworth to think of people wanting to carry them away, to take them into strange towns and down strange streets. When the new minister came, and the ladies were gathering flowers to decorate the church, Miss Strangeworth sent over a great basket of gladioli; when she picked the roses at all, she set them in bowls and vases around the inside of the house her grandfather had built.

Walking down Main Street on a summer morning, Miss Strangeworth had to stop every minute or so to say good morning to someone or to ask after someone's health. When she came into the grocery, half a dozen people turned away from the shelves and the counters to wave at her or call out good morning.

"And good morning to you, too, Mr. Lewis," Miss Strangeworth said at last. The Lewis family had been in the town almost as long as the Strangeworths; but the day young Lewis left high school and went to work in the grocery, Miss Strangeworth had stopped calling him Tommy and started calling him Mr. Lewis, and he had stopped calling her Addie and started calling her Miss Strangeworth. They had been in high school together, and had gone to picnics together, and to high-school dances and basketball games; but now Mr. Lewis was behind the counter in the grocery, and Miss Strangeworth was living alone in the Strangeworth house on Pleasant Street.

"Good morning," Mr. Lewis said, and added politely, "Lovely day."

"It is a very nice day," Miss Strangeworth said, as though she had only just decided that it would do after all. "I would like a chop, please, Mr. Lewis, a small, lean veal chop. Are those strawberries from Arthur Parker's garden? They're early this year."

"He brought them in this morning," Mr. Lewis said.

"I shall have a box," Miss Strangeworth said. Mr. Lewis looked worried, she thought, and for a minute she hesitated, but then she decided that he surely could not be worried over the strawberries. He looked very tired indeed. He was usually so chipper, Miss Strangeworth thought, and almost commented, but it was far too personal a subject to be introduced to Mr. Lewis, the grocer, so she only said, "And a can of cat food and, I think, a tomato."

Silently, Mr. Lewis assembled her order on the counter, and waited. Miss Strangeworth looked at him curiously and then said, "It's Tuesday, Mr. Lewis. You forgot to remind me."

"Did I? Sorry."

"Imagine your forgetting that I always buy my tea on Tuesday," Miss Strangeworth said gently. "A quarter pound of tea, please, Mr. Lewis."

"Is that all, Miss Strangeworth?"

"Yes, thank you, Mr. Lewis. Such a lovely day, isn't it?"

"Lovely," Mr. Lewis said.

Miss Strangeworth moved slightly to make room for Mrs. Harper at the

252

counter. "Morning, Adela," Mrs. Harper said, and Miss Strangeworth said, "Good morning, Martha."

"Lovely day," Mrs. Harper said, and Miss Strangeworth said, "Yes, lovely," and Mr. Lewis, under Mrs. Harper's glance, nodded.

"Ran out of sugar for my cake frosting," Mrs. Harper explained. Her hand shook slightly as she opened her pocketbook. Miss Strangeworth wondered, glancing at her quietly, if she had been taking proper care of herself. Martha Harper was not as young as she used to be, Miss Strangeworth thought. She probably could use a good strong tonic.

"Martha," she said, "you don't look well."

"I'm perfectly all right," Mrs. Harper said shortly. She handed her money to Mr. Lewis, took her change and her sugar, and went out without speaking again. Looking after her, Miss Strangeworth shook her head slightly. Martha definitely did *not* look well.

Carrying her little bag of groceries, Miss Strangeworth came out of the store into the bright sunlight and stopped to smile down on the Crane baby. Don and Helen Crane were really the two most infatuated young parents she had ever known, she thought indulgently, looking at the delicately embroidered baby cap and the lace-edged carriage cover.

"That little girl is going to grow up expecting luxury all her life," she said to Helen Crane.

Helen laughed. "That's the way we want her to feel," she said. "Like a princess."

"A princess can see a lot of trouble sometimes," Miss Strangeworth said dryly. "How old is Her Highness now?"

"Six months next Tuesday," Helen Crane said, looking down with rapt wonder at her child. "I've been worrying, though, about her. Don't you think she ought to move around more? Try to sit up, for instance?"

"For plain and fancy worrying," Miss Strangeworth said, amused, "give me a new mother every time."

"She just seems—slow," Helen Crane said.

"Nonsense. All babies are different. Some of them develop much more quickly than others."

"That's what my mother says." Helen Crane laughed, looking a little bit ashamed.

"I suppose you've got young Don all upset about the fact that his daughter is already six months old and hasn't yet begun to learn to dance?"

"I haven't mentioned it to him. I suppose she's just so precious that I worry about her all the time."

"Well, apologize to her right now," Miss Strangeworth said. "*She* is probably worrying about why you keep jumping around all the time." Smiling to herself and shaking her old head, she went on down the sunny street, stopping once to ask little Billy Moore why he wasn't out riding in

Things Are Seldom as They Seem   253

his daddy's shiny new car, and talking for a few minutes outside the library with Miss Chandler, the librarian, about the new novels to be ordered and paid for by the annual library appropriation. Miss Chandler seemed absent-minded and very much as though she were thinking about something else. Miss Strangeworth noticed that Miss Chandler had not taken much trouble with her hair that morning, and sighed. Miss Strangeworth hated sloppiness.

Many people seemed disturbed recently, Miss Strangeworth thought. Only yesterday the Stewarts' fifteen-year-old Linda had run crying down her own front walk and all the way to school, not caring who saw her. People around town thought she might have had a fight with the Harris boy, but they showed up together at the soda shop after school as usual, both of them looking grim and bleak. Trouble at home, people concluded, and sighed over the problems of trying to raise kids right these days.

From halfway down the block Miss Strangeworth could catch the heavy scent of her roses, and she moved a little more quickly. The perfume of roses meant home, and home meant the Strangeworth House on Pleasant Street. Miss Strangeworth stopped at her own front gate, as she always did, and looked with deep pleasure at her house, with the red and pink and white roses massed along the narrow lawn, and the rambler going up along the porch; and the neat, the unbelievably trim lines of the house itself, with its slimness and its washed white look. Every window sparkled, every curtain hung stiff and straight, and even the stones of the front walk were swept and clear. People around town wondered how old Miss Strangeworth managed to keep the house looking the way it did, and there was a legend about a tourist once mistaking it for the local museum and going all through the place without finding out about his mistake. But the town was proud of Miss Strangeworth and her roses and her house. They had all grown together.

Miss Strangeworth went up her front steps, unlocked her front door with her key, and went into the kitchen to put away her groceries. She debated about having a cup of tea and then decided that it was too close to midday dinnertime; she would not have the appetite for her little chop if she had tea now. Instead she went into the light, lovely sitting room, which still glowed from the hands of her mother and her grandmother, who had covered the chairs with bright chintz and hung the curtains. All the furniture was spare and shining, and the round hooked rugs on the floor had been the work of Miss Strangeworth's grandmother and her mother. Miss Strangeworth had put a bowl of her red roses on the low table before the window, and the room was full of their scent.

Miss Strangeworth went to the narrow desk in the corner and unlocked it with her key. She never knew when she might feel like writing letters, so she kept her notepaper inside and the desk locked. Miss Strangeworth's usual stationery was heavy and cream-colored, with STRANGE-WORTH HOUSE engraved across the top, but, when she felt like writing her other letters, Miss Strangeworth used a pad of various-colored paper bought from the local newspaper shop. It was almost a town joke, that colored paper, layered in pink and green and blue and yellow; everyone in town bought it and used it for odd, informal notes and shopping lists. It was usual to remark, upon receiving a note written on a blue page, that so-and-so would be needing a new pad soon—here she was, down to the blue already. Everyone used the matching envelopes for tucking away recipes, or keeping odd little things in, or even to hold cookies in the school lunchboxes. Mr. Lewis sometimes gave them to the children for carrying home penny candy.

Although Miss Strangeworth's desk held a trimmed quill pen which had belonged to her grandfather, and a gold-frosted fountain pen which had belonged to her father, Miss Strangeworth always used a dull stub of pencil when she wrote her letters, and she printed them in a childish block print. After thinking for a minute, although she had been phrasing the letter in the back of her mind all the way home, she wrote on a pink sheet: DIDN'T YOU EVER SEE AN IDIOT CHILD BEFORE? SOME PEOPLE JUST SHOULDN'T HAVE CHILDREN SHOULD THEY?

She was pleased with the letter. She was fond of doing things exactly right. When she made a mistake, as she sometimes did, or when the letters were not spaced nicely on the page, she had to take the discarded page to the kitchen stove and burn it at once. Miss Strangeworth never delayed when things had to be done.

After thinking for a minute, she decided that she would like to write another letter, perhaps to go to Mrs. Harper, to follow up the ones she had already mailed. She selected a green sheet this time and wrote quickly: HAVE YOU FOUND OUT YET WHAT THEY WERE ALL LAUGHING ABOUT AFTER YOU LEFT THE BRIDGE CLUB ON THURSDAY? OR IS THE WIFE REALLY ALWAYS THE LAST ONE TO KNOW?

Miss Strangeworth never concerned herself with facts; her letters all dealt with the more negotiable stuff of suspicion. Mr. Lewis would never have imagined for a minute that his grandson might be lifting petty cash from the store register if he had not had one of Miss Strangeworth's letters. Miss Chandler, the librarian, and Linda Stewart's parents would have gone unsuspectingly ahead with their lives, never aware of possible evil lurking nearby, if Miss Strangeworth had not sent letters opening their eyes. Miss Strangeworth would have been genuinely shocked if there *had* been anything between Linda Stewart and the Harris boy, but, as long as evil existed unchecked in the world, it was Miss Strangeworth's duty to keep her town alert to it. It was far more sensible for Miss Chandler to wonder what Mr. Shelley's first wife had really died of than to take a chance on not knowing. There were so many wicked people in the world and only one Strangeworth left in the town. Besides, Miss Strangeworth liked writing her letters.

She addressed an envelope to Don Crane after a moment's thought, wondering curiously if he would show the letter to his wife, and using a pink envelope to match the pink paper. Then she addressed a second envelope, green, to Mrs. Harper. Then an idea came to her and she selected a blue sheet and wrote: YOU NEVER KNOW ABOUT DOCTORS. REMEMBER THEY'RE ONLY HUMAN AND NEED MONEY LIKE THE REST OF US. SUPPOSE THE KNIFE SLIPPED ACCIDENTALLY. WOULD DR. BURNS GET HIS FEE AND A LITTLE EXTRA FROM THAT NEPHEW OF YOURS?

She addressed the blue envelope to old Mrs. Foster, who was having an operation next month. She had thought of writing one more letter, to the head of the school board, asking how a chemistry teacher like Billy Moore's father could afford a new convertible, but, all at once, she was tired of writing letters. The three she had done would do for one day. She could write more tomorrow; it was not as though they all had to be done at once.

She had been writing her letters—sometimes two or three every day for a week, sometimes no more than one in a month—for the past year. She never got any answers, of course, because she never signed her name. If she had been asked, she would have said that her name, Adela Strangeworth, a name honored in the town for so many years, did not belong on such trash. The town where she lived had to be kept clean and sweet, but people everywhere were lustful and evil and degraded, and needed to be watched; the world was so large, and there was only one Strangeworth left in it. Miss Strangeworth sighed, locked her desk, and put the letters into her big black leather pocketbook, to be mailed when she took her evening walk.

She broiled her little chop nicely, and had a sliced tomato and a good cup of tea ready when she sat down to her midday dinner at the table in her dining room, which could be opened to seat twenty-two, with a second table, if necessary, in the hall. Sitting in the warm sunlight that came through the tall windows of the dining room, seeing her roses massed outside, handling the heavy, old silverware and the fine, translucent china, Miss Strangeworth was pleased; she would not have cared to be doing anything else. People must live graciously, after all, she thought, and sipped her tea. Afterward, when her plate and cup and saucer were washed and dried and put back onto the shelves where they belonged, and her silverware was back in the mahogany silver chest, Miss Strangeworth went up the graceful staircase and into her bedroom, which was the front room overlooking the roses, and had been her mother's and her grandmother's. Their Crown Derby dresser set and furs had been kept here, their fans and silver-backed brushes and their own bowls of roses; Miss Strangeworth kept a bowl of white roses on the bed table.

She drew the shades, took the rose satin spread from the bed, slipped out of her dress and her shoes, and lay down tiredly. She knew that no doorbell or phone would ring; no one in town would dare to disturb Miss Strangeworth during her afternoon nap. She slept, deep in the rich smell of roses.

After her nap she worked in her garden for a little while, sparing herself because of the heat; then she came in to her supper. She ate asparagus from her own garden, with sweet-butter sauce and a soft-boiled egg, and, while she had her supper, she listened to a late-evening news broadcast and then to a program of classical music on her small radio. After her dishes were done and her kitchen set in order, she took up her hat—Miss Strangeworth's hats were proverbial in the town; people believed that she had inherited them from her mother and her grandmother—and, locking the front door of her house behind her, set off on her evening walk, pocketbook under her arm. She nodded to Linda Stewart's father, who was washing his car in the pleasantly cool evening. She thought that he looked troubled.

There was only one place in town where she could mail her letters, and that was the new post office, shiny with red brick and silver letters. Although Miss Strangeworth had never given the matter any particular thought, she had always made a point of mailing her letters very secretly; it would, of course, not have been wise to let anyone see her mail them. Consequently, she timed her walk so she could reach the post office just as darkness was starting to dim the outlines of the trees and the shapes of people's faces, although no one could ever mistake Miss Strangeworth, with her dainty walk and her rustling skirts.

There was always a group of young people around the post office, the very youngest roller-skating upon its driveway, which went all the way around the building and was the only smooth road in town; and the slightly older ones already knowing how to gather in small groups and chatter and laugh and make great, excited plans for going across the street to the soda shop in a minute or two. Miss Strangeworth had never had any self-consciousness before the children. She did not feel that any of them were staring at her unduly or longing to laugh at her; it would have been most reprehensible for their parents to permit their children to mock Miss Strangeworth of Pleasant Street. Most of the children stood back respectfully as Miss Strangeworth passed, silenced briefly in her presence, and some of the older children greeted her, saying soberly, "Hello, Miss Strangeworth."

Miss Strangeworth smiled at them and quickly went on. It had been a long time since she had known the name of every child in town. The mail slot was in the door of the post office. The children stood away as Miss Strangeworth approached it, seemingly surprised that anyone should want to use the post office after it had been officially closed up for the night and turned over to the children. Miss Strangeworth stood by the door, opening her black pocketbook to take out the letters, and heard a voice which she knew at once to be Linda Stewart's. Poor little Linda was crying again, and Miss Strangeworth listened carefully. This was, after all, her town, and these were her people; if one of them was in trouble she ought to know about it.

"I can't tell you, Dave," Linda was saying—so she *was* talking to the Harris boy, as Miss Strangeworth had supposed—"I just *can't*. It's just *nasty*."

"But why won't your father let me come around any more? What on earth did I do?"

"I can't tell you. I just wouldn't tell you for *anything*. You've got to have a dirty, dirty mind for things like that."

"But something's happened. You've been crying and crying, and your father is all upset. Why can't *I* know about it, too? Aren't I like one of the family?"

"Not any more, Dave, not any more. You're not to come near our house again; my father said so. He said he'd horsewhip you. That's all I can tell you: You're not to come near our house any more."

"But I didn't *do* anything."

"Just the same, my father said . . ."

Miss Strangeworth sighed and turned away. There was so much evil in people. Even in a charming little town like this one, there was still so much evil in people.

She slipped her letters into the slot, and two of them fell inside. The third caught on the edge and fell outside, onto the ground at Miss Strangeworth's feet. She did not notice it because she was wondering whether a letter to the Harris boy's father might not be of some service in wiping out this potential badness. Wearily Miss Strangeworth turned to go home to her quiet bed in her lovely house, and never heard the Harris boy calling to her to say that she had dropped something.

"Old lady Strangeworth's getting deaf," he said, looking after her and holding in his hand the letter he had picked up.

"Well, who cares?" Linda said. "Who cares any more, anyway?"

"It's for Don Crane," the Harris boy said, "this letter. She dropped a letter addressed to Don Crane. Might as well take it on over. We pass his house anyway." He laughed. "Maybe it's got a check or something in it and he'd be just as glad to get it tonight instead of tomorrow."

"Catch old lady Strangeworth sending anybody a check," Linda said. "Throw it in the post office. Why do anyone a favor?" She sniffled. "Doesn't seem to me anybody around here cares about us," she said. "Why should we care about them?"

"I'll take it over anyway," the Harris boy said. "Maybe it's good news for them. Maybe they need something happy tonight, too. Like us."

258

Sadly, holding hands, they wandered off down the dark street, the Harris boy carrying Miss Strangeworth's pink envelope in his hand.

Miss Strangeworth awakened the next morning with a feeling of intense happiness and, for a minute wondered why, and then remembered that this morning three people would open her letters. Harsh, perhaps, at first, but wickedness was never easily banished, and a clean heart was a scoured heart. She washed her soft old face and brushed her teeth, still sound in spite of her seventy-one years, and dressed herself carefully in her sweet, soft clothes and buttoned shoes. Then, coming downstairs and reflecting that perhaps a little waffle would be agreeable for breakfast in the sunny dining room, she found the mail on the hall floor and bent to pick it up. A bill, the morning paper, a letter in a green envelope that looked oddly familiar. Miss Strangeworth stood perfectly still for a minute, looking down at the green envelope with the penciled printing, and thought: It looks like one of my letters. Was one of my letters sent back? No, because no one would know where to send it. How did this get here?

Miss Strangeworth was a Strangeworth of Pleasant Street. Her hand did not shake as she opened the envelope and unfolded the sheet of green paper inside. She began to cry silently for the wickedness of the world when she read the words: LOOK OUT AT WHAT USED TO BE YOUR ROSES.

FOR DISCUSSION: The Possibility of Evil

1. During the first several pages of this story, everything seems quiet and friendly, yet slowly one grows aware of a restlessness, a general discomfort. How does Shirley Jackson make the reader aware of this restlessness and of the type of restlessness it is?
2. "The town where she lived had to be kept clean and sweet, but people everywhere were lustful and evil and degraded, and needed to be watched. . . ." What do these words suggest about Adela Strangeworth's character?
3. In this story roses and a sense of order form two separate strands that come together, separate, and come together again. What effect do you think the author was trying to achieve? Would the story be as powerful if you eliminated either strand?
4. This story ends with the sentence: "LOOK OUT AT WHAT USED TO BE YOUR ROSES." These words tell the reader a great deal about the person who wrote them. How do they add a new dimension of meaning to the title, "The Possibility of Evil"?
5. Is evil contagious? Discuss.

Murder-
Up-To-Date

CHAPTER SIX

There's an eerie inverse relationship between man's technological development and his regression to barbarity. As he improves intellectually, he degenerates morally. As he learns the laws of the universe, he learns also how to violate those laws. As he masters the machine for his comfort, he makes machines masters to the discomfort of others.

This twentieth century has placed mechanical marvels in all too human hands. Consider just five:

> Telephone
> Radio
> Television
> Automobile
> Airplane

All five have contributed to the health and happiness of human beings, yet all five have also contributed to crime.

The *telephone* had barely come into existence when it was being used to plot crimes, to terrorize women, and, most recently, to spy (thanks to the "bug").

The *radio* has been used, in life and in fiction, as a murder weapon.

Innocuous in itself, it becomes a potential murderer if it is perched precariously on the rim of a bathtub filled with water.

Television has turned thousands of apparently good citizens into "fences." The person who would be horrified at the idea of buying a hot car hardly thinks twice when he is offered a 25-inch color set for $150. Television has also served as a learning machine: to learn how crooks operate; how escapes are planned and executed; how to set up an alibi.

The *automobile,* which has become America's extra pair of legs, takes children to school and men and women to work; but it also enables the criminal to make a fast getaway, and on dark nights offers him an ore-rich mine for criminal activity.

The *airplane,* beyond the reach of the private citizen, seems safe for legitimate purposes. Yet it too has been misused. The small plane makes criminals mobile as they never were before. The large number of passengers entering and leaving the countries of the world provides smuggling possibilities beyond the old rum-runner's dream. And in the last few years the giant jet is the perfect "sitting duck" for the warped, embittered brain of a skyjacker. Where else do you have so many hostages in so vulnerable a position?

The above five mechanical marvels have all been used by large numbers of criminals; they have also been used by hundreds of mystery writers seeking a new twist or an unexpected solution. In fact, these five are no longer novelties: they have become staples both in life and in fiction.

What about NOW? What new gimmicks, what new developments are available?

Space Travel
Transplants
Computers
Robots
Freezing (after death)
Genetic Manipulation and Selection

To lengthen this list, simply scan the daily newspaper. New "things," new ideas are—like the population—increasing geometrically, not mathematically.

It is interesting to trace the path of one of these new developments. It begins frequently with a couple of scientists who have an idea and talk about it before it has been thoroughly researched. Then it is picked up by a group of alert science fiction writers who embroider and enlarge on it. Next it goes back to the laboratory where it is perfected. Now all kinds of people, including criminals, play with it, discovering unsuspected talents in the new toy. Finally the mystery writer picks it up and uses it to the delight of thousands of readers or viewers. After this, it becomes old hat—stale—banal—trite.

The pattern is not unchangeable. Some inventions appeared in science fiction *before* they appeared in any orthodox scientific laboratory. And some mystery writers discovered destructive uses for certain things before the criminals did. When the latter happens, the police and the public may be horrified, but the writer is still more appalled as he finds himself the creator not of fiction but of life. In her 81st year, the veteran mystery writer Agatha Christie was upset when she learned that an earlier novel of hers (*The Pale Horse*, 1961) may have been used as a blueprint by a young man in Hertfordshire who was murdering his fellow factory workers by putting thallium in their tea and coffee. At about the same time a science fiction writer considered giving up writing when he learned that one of his stories had suggested an ingenious procedure to an otherwise unimaginative skyjacker.

Fortunately this kind of thing happens rarely, and most mystery writers go cheerfully on, using their well-honed imaginations on the changing world. For the reader, the result is pure delight. Who does not shiver deliciously when he realizes that slow-changing laws can allow a murderer to act with impunity? Who, after reading Gerald Kersh, will not study newspaper stories of transplants with new interest and awakened curiosity? Who has not wondered if it would be possible to program a computer to solve, or even to commit, a crime?

The mystery writer of 2,000 years ago as well as the mystery writer of today has three obligations to his readers: to entertain, to sharpen observation, and to stimulate deduction. Today's writers, as they write about Murder-Up-To-Date, are fulfilling these obligations. They are helping us to see our world, to know it, to understand it. And they sugar-coat their instruction with suspense and vicarious fear. An appealing package, as the next three stories vividly prove.

In this age, change has become a constant. Inventions and explorations open doors faster than we can grab the knobs. Willy-nilly, more by accident than by plan, we manage to sidle through these doors as we ascend and descend alien corridors. So intent are we on discovering the next door that we neglect the walls of these corridors: the ramifications, the 1,001 problems that follow in the wake of each new thrust.

Miriam deFord in this short story deals with one of these ramifications. It describes a situation that is already almost commonplace, yet the legal niceties ruling the situation are still undetermined. She raises an interesting question—what happens when man's reach exceeds his law? Under what rules does he then operate? Or is he then, truly, a law unto himself? It is a question which our airborne age must soon answer.

A Case for the UN
Miriam Allen deFord

The one-class DC-4 plane, bound east from Montreal to Paris, was carrying less than its capacity of 40 passengers. It was the off-season, and Canadian Transatlantic was not the biggest or most favored airline. But it was comfortably full, and Mavis Brook, the stewardess, looked the passengers over with an approving eye. There were no babies and no farewell-party drunks; it would be an easy trip.

"Any freaks aboard this time?" teased Bob Kemper, the pilot, when she went up front to take the first cups of coffee to Kemper, Ed Rodman the copilot, and Louis Pellereaux the flight engineer. Mavis had round hazel eyes, curly hair, a cuddly figure, and was easy to tease—she had no sense of humor.

"No, thank goodness," she answered seriously. "Just one man who seems a little—well, odd. He was the first one on, grabbed a rear seat, and has sat ever since with his face behind a newspaper that he isn't reading. He didn't want a cocktail, and he hardly touched his dinner."

Kemper winked at Rodman. "*Must* be something wrong," he announced solemnly, still teasing, "with anyone who wants privacy, huh, Ed?"

"Sure thing. Anyone who doesn't get chummy with everybody else—watch out, Mavis, he might be an escaping criminal!"

"Oh, do you think so?" Mavis turned pale.

"For heaven's sake, girl, we're only kidding. Go on back and forget it."

When she returned to the cabin her eyes darted again to the man in the back seat. He was still buried in his newspaper. He looked harmless —a bald, middle-aged little man with dark glasses . . . but you never could tell.

Mavis glanced at the other passengers as she took away the dinner dishes and answered queries. All of them were unremarkable, except—

She peered curiously at a man and a woman sitting up front, on opposite sides of the aisle. They had come in separately and had never spoken to each other; but every once in a while the woman would turn and look at the man, or the man at the woman, and if ever two people were crazy about each other it was those two—who nevertheless acted like strangers.

When she had a minute, Mavis consulted the passenger list. The little man in the rear was Bartholomew Evans, of New York. She must be mistaken about the seemingly enamored couple: he was Italian, Giuseppe Falconari, from Rome; she was Renée Blanc, from Lyons. And, Mavis noted, the nearest thing to a V.I.P. aboard was Sir Eric Milbanke, Q.C., whatever that meant. She stole a look at him—a tall, white-haired man immersed in a legal-looking tome from which he was making notes in red ink.

Mavis sighed; as a celebrity he was a complete washout, not worth approaching for an autograph. Mavis was an ardent autograph collector —but she preferred movie stars.

Everything was serene when the plane left Gander and started for Shannon. The passengers settled down to sleep. Sir Eric had been the last to turn out his reading light. Mavis settled down too, in a rear seat across the aisle from the little man, who now seemed to be asleep. The only sound was a duet of snores from two passengers. Mavis took off her shoes and fell into a catnap which even the softest signal would interrupt.

At three o'clock in the morning they were over the mid-Atlantic.

It was then that the little man in the rear, Bartholomew Evans, got quietly to his feet. No one paid any attention to him; others had arisen from time to time and gone back to the lavatory.

Evans stepped forward silently until he stood in the aisle between Renée Blanc and Giuseppe Falconari, who were now sound asleep, their heads buried in pillows.

Very calmly and deliberately, Evans drew a pistol from his pocket, and shot each of them through the head.

Immediately there was pandemonium. Startled passengers awoke, jumped up, cried out. Mavis ran to the cockpit, forgetting her shoes, and almost collided with Kemper as he opened the door and hurried to the scene.

The murderer made no attempt to move. He stood there with the smoking pistol still in his hand. Not a sound came from either of his victims; there was not even much blood. Both had been killed instantly.

The pilot took command at once.

"Please resume your seats," Kemper ordered, hoping his voice was steady. He had heard plenty of stories of sensational events on other planes, but this was his first and, he hoped, his last experience of this kind. "See to this lady," he added to Mavis; an elderly woman sitting nearby was in hysterics. Mavis, her legs trembling, ministered to the woman and got her quieted down. There was little noise otherwise; most of the passengers were too shocked to speak.

A heavy-set man stood up and started toward the murderer. Kemper stopped him with a gesture. The responsibility—and the danger—were his.

"Give me the gun," he demanded of Evans.

The coolest person on board was the murderer.

"Certainly, Captain," Evans replied politely, placing the gun in Kemper's outstretched hand. "And you needn't tie me up. I'm not going to pull any doors open and jump out, or do anything foolish."

Unexpectedly somebody laughed. Someone else reached blindly for a paper bag and was sick in it.

"Ladies and gentlemen, please keep your seats," the pilot said, his voice steady now. "I know how distressing this must be for you, but there is nothing we can do until we arrive at Shannon. Mavis, I think everybody could use a drink. But first get some blankets to cover these—these two people. And if you, madam, and you, sir, who were sitting next to them would find places elsewhere—"

The suggestion was unnecessary; the victims' neighbors were already hunched in seats farther away.

"Now"—Kemper turned to the still unmoving Evans—"I shall have you placed under guard until I can turn you over to the Eire authorities when we land. Our copilot will have wired ahead, and the police will have been notified. They'll be waiting for you. Now, if two of you gentlemen will volunteer to keep an eye on him—"

The burly man and another stepped forward.

Bartholomew Evans smiled.

"You know, Captain," he said conversationally, "I happen to be a lawyer, and I know a few things that you don't. For instance, though an aircraft in flight has the legal status of a ship at sea, its pilot does not have the power of arrest and detention that a ship's captain has. You have no right whatever to hold or guard me.

"And the authorities you say will be waiting to apprehend me can do nothing whatever. Eire has no jurisdiction over me. I waited deliberately to do my—deed until we were over the mid-Atlantic. My whole action depended on the fact that no nation in the world has jurisdiction in this matter. I've made very sure of the law. There is *nowhere* I can be held, *nowhere* I can be tried. There is no such thing as a code of international criminal air law, nor is there any Air Police Force."

"Interpol," Kemper muttered uncertainly.

"Interpol," replied the murderer smoothly, "has no police force of its own; it is merely a clearing house for international criminal information. And if you try to invoke the World Court, that has nothing to do with civilian crime. It deals only with cases submitted to it by member countries of the United Nations."

"Is there anything I can do?" Sir Eric murmured. "I'm a lawyer." He gave his name.

Kemper looked helplessly at Sir Eric. The barrister shook his head.

"I'm afraid he's right on all points, so far," Sir Eric said.

"Moreover," Evans continued, "my crucial point is impregnable. While every country has jurisdiction over any aircraft passing over its territory, no country on earth has jurisdiction over a plane that is more than three miles off the coast of any nation.

"Besides which, I might add that this ship is owned by a Canadian company, I myself am a citizen of the United States, and the persons whom I brought to justice belonged to two other nations—she was a French citizen who, though she resided in New York for a long time, never became naturalized, and he was an Italian citizen. Why, even the witnesses, if there were any—"

"I was awake," said Sir Eric curtly. "I saw you rise from your seat and come down the aisle, and before I realized what was happening, I saw you commit a double murder. If you think you are going to go scot-free because of some legal technicality—"

"Oh, come now. I heard you say you're a lawyer yourself, so you know better than anyone how invulnerable my position is. What I was going to say was that even witnesses would probably be of still other nationalities, and I was right. You, sir, are obviously British; and if there are any others—"

A short plump passenger who had not yet uttered a word stood up diffidently.

"Kyashi Nakamura, export business, Tokyo," he said with a jerky little bow. "I too was not asleep. I too saw this happen. It is my eternal regret that I could not in time—"

"Still another nationality," Evans interrupted him evenly. "This is better than I could possibly have anticipated. Are you going to assemble witnesses against me from the ends of the earth? And just where would you assemble them?

"Captain, ask this gentleman of my own profession if I am not in fact entirely right—not right 'so far,' as he said, but right all the way. Who has jurisdiction here? Who has the right to arrest me? Where could I be tried? Where could I be—punished, I believe, is the word—if I were convicted? How can I possibly be held at all?"

"Canada—" Kemper suggested feebly.

"Afraid not, old man," said Sir Eric. "The crime was not committed in or over Canada, and a plane is not like an embassy or a consulate, a part of its country of origin."

Suddenly the burly man who had volunteered to guard Evans erupted. He grabbed the imperturbable murderer, only half his size, and thrust out an angry fist. Kemper intercepted the blow before it landed.

"No, please," he begged. "We've had enough violence already. Let's keep our heads and act like adults."

"And let this filthy murderer get away with it? I'll be damned if I'll stand by and see a vicious criminal—"

"I resent those terms, sir," said Bartholomew Evans sharply. "I am an agent of justice. Those two deserved to die." For the first time he showed a sign of emotion. His face reddened and his voice roughened. "That woman—she was traveling under the name she had when I first met her; but she was my wife. And the man with her, pretending not to be, was her lover. Look up her baggage in the hold. You'll find a bag stuffed with everything that was in my safe at home—money, negotiable securities, jewels—everything valuable she could lay her hands on.

"I've had a private detective watching her for months. And I picked one who would understand—I represented him five years ago when he was divorced from a wife just as rotten as mine was. He told me then, 'I wish I'd bumped her off.' Well, he didn't; he even let her get the divorce, and he's been kept poor by alimony ever since. So I knew he'd put his heart into working for me. I paid him plenty, but he did a fine job. He kept right on her track every minute.

"When he told me she and that blackguard were planning to run off, I rushed home from my office, but I was too late. I found her already gone and the safe empty. I'd been planning to divorce her as soon as I had the evidence against her—the only grounds possible in New York—but she knew she'd never have got a cent of alimony out of me, so she beat me to it. She wasn't going to face poverty for her grand passion—not Renée. And he—that scoundrel called himself an artist. He had nothing but what she gave him, and that was stolen from me.... Well, what would you have done? Let them get away with it?"

"Following them, under the circumstances, is understandable," said the

British barrister stiffly. "Even following them on the same plane so as not to lose track of them—though how you kept them from knowing you were here in the same cabin—"

"Oh, that. I had luck all the way. They drove to Montreal—in the car I'd given her"—once again his voice choked with rage—"and I flew up with the private detective and got there before they did. It was easy to follow them after that. She'd had her French passport renewed—that's what first alerted my man. I suppose her boy friend had his Italian one, and I travel often and always keep mine up-to-date. They took a room in a hotel, sold my car, and bought their tickets. My detective booked a seat for me on the same plane—"

"In your own name?"

"Why not? I knew I was perfectly safe. The only tricky thing was getting aboard before they did and keeping them from seeing me. I'd shaved off my mustache and bought these dark glasses, but of course if they had spotted me they'd have run for it. So I arrived early and asked the stewardess for a back seat—said I had paper work to do and would be grateful if I could be the first one permitted aboard—"

"Oh!" cried Mavis, her face scarlet.

"Then all I had to do was keep hidden behind a newspaper and hope they'd not sit near me. Fortunately, they didn't. They were too busy making eyes at each other to look at anyone else. The detective had told me they were traveling separately and pretending not to know each other —I was amused to see they didn't even take seats next to each other."

"But when we got off at Gander? What then?" the pilot asked. Evans' nonchalance was infectious; the murder inquiry was degenerating into a discussion.

"I simply didn't get off. The stewardess said I could stay if I wanted to. After that, it wasn't long before everybody settled down to sleep— at least, I thought everybody had; not that it really mattered. I waited till I was sure we were far enough out over the ocean, and I knew that even if any of the passengers were awake and watching me—as two of you were—I'd be far too quick for them to realize what was happening and to stop me."

"Go back to your seat," Kemper ordered brusquely, casting off the spell. "And you two gentlemen, keep an eye on him."

"I won't give you any trouble," Evans said quietly. The passengers drew back as he went by. The murderer smiled.

"If you'll come into the cockpit with me, Sir Eric," said the pilot, "I'd like to have a few words with you."

"You're not going to find any way out, I assure you," Evans called after them blandly. "I'll walk off this plane at Shannon as free as a bird."

Milbanke and Kemper both shuddered as they passed the two motionless forms, now shrouded in blankets. Behind them the passengers broke into whispers, as if the dead could hear. Their horrified, fascinated glances veered from the two victims to the killer. He sat silent, his eyes fixed, his face a mask. The two men assigned to guard him stood in the aisle, blocking him off from the rest of the cabin. Evans ignored them.

Rodman and Pellereaux looked up as the pilot and the barrister entered. Kemper took over the controls.

"I guess you've heard most of it," he said. "This is Sir Eric Milbanke, an English lawyer." They nodded. "I'm hoping he'll be able to suggest some way out of this mess. Have you heard from Shannon yet, Ed?"

"Police will meet the plane. But from what I've gathered, they aren't going to be able to hold him."

"Hey, how about this?" Louis Pellereaux burst out. "If anybody can kill a person on a plane over the ocean and get away with it, why don't we just open a door and push Evans through it?"

"Don't be funny, Louis," said Kemper. "*He* may be a murderer, but I'm not. Any ideas, Sir Eric?"

The barrister wrinkled his forehead as he braced his long lean body against the door.

"None that would be useful, I'm afraid." He paused, then his eyes lit up. "Unless—yes, that's a bare possibility.... No, I think it may be more than that."

The others waited, hardly breathing.

"This private detective he hired—hmm, let me think . . ."

When Sir Eric Milbanke went back to his seat, the pilot knew what to do.

Just before they reached Shannon, Kemper returned to the cabin and walked up to Bartholomew Evans. The man turned a sardonic gaze on him.

"Couldn't figure out anything, could you?" Evans said. "I noticed that the great Q.C. came back looking pretty downhearted. You might as well wire those Irish cops to go back home. If they lay a hand on me, I'll sue them for false arrest."

Kemper turned his back. "Ladies and gentlemen," he said, "I know you want to get away from this plane just as fast as you can; it hasn't been a pleasant trip, and I'm sorry. If Mr. Nakamura will let me know where he can be reached, I'll be obliged; I've already got that information from Sir Eric Milbanke. And if you two gentlemen—Mr. Goss, is it, and Mr. Hagedorn?—will wait and keep this man in charge until the other passengers have debarked, the rest of you can leave promptly. I'm grateful to all of you for your help. There'll be reporters at the airport, of course, and you can do as you like about talking to them. But I must ask all of you not to leave until the police have entered and taken away the bodies of this unfortunate couple."

There was a murmur of assent.

"As for you—" he turned to Evans.

"I'm warning you, Captain. The Irish police can't touch me, and if you turn me over to them I'll make you and your company sorry you did. I can't fight my way out physically against these two big bullies, but—"

"That will be all, I think," said Kemper wearily. The sign went on to stop smoking and fasten seat belts.

The headlines in the Dublin *News* read:

YANK HELD FOR MURDER ON PLANE

LAWYER SHOOTS WIFE, PARAMOUR

EXTRADITION ASKED

"It was just an idea I had," Sir Eric Milbanke said modestly to the reporters. "I wondered exactly what he'd told that private detective. It seemed reasonable to assume that the detective understood very well that his employer intended to commit murder. The police will probably find that even the pistol was his—Evans had no permit to carry one.

"The pilot sent a radiogram to his company in Canada; they telephoned the New York police, and the Homicide Department there quickly identified the private detective—we told them that Evans had been the detective's attorney five years ago in a divorce suit. The detective is under arrest now, and Evans will be put under lock and key in Dublin to await the extradition papers.

"Evans was too clever for his own good—that's the long and short of it. The murder itself was committed in one of the few places on earth where there is no jurisdiction whatever over crime, but—and here's the legal point that Evans, a lawyer, overlooked—the *original conspiracy* was perpetrated in the States. And they'll make that charge stick against both of them—conspiracy.

"I'd like to add that if it hadn't been for the cool thinking and courage of the pilot, a vicious murderer might well have escaped unscathed. The entire crew of the plane showed admirable calmness, and the passengers were exemplary in their conduct."

There was a little tug at his coat sleeve.

"Yes, young lady?" asked Sir Eric.

"If you don't mind," said Mavis, her hazel eyes wide and a pretty blush on her face, "would you kindly give me your autograph?"

FOR DISCUSSION: A Case for the UN

1. Notice how Miriam deFord carefully paints the background for this murder. It is a small plane, with rather ordinary passengers. Mavis Brooke, the stewardess, even thinks "it would be an easy trip." Why is this exactly the right background for this particular crime?

2. Evans commits the murders in a matter-of-fact fashion; he even explains his position in a matter-of-fact tone. How does this heighten the special horror that accompanies this crime? Are there any crimes today that seem especially terrifying precisely because they also seem unpunishable? Why does an unpunishable crime seem to cause almost unbearable fear in most people? Does this suggest the real reason for punishment?

3. This story was written in 1964. Some student who knows a lawyer may be interested in researching any change in laws that would prevent this type of situation from occurring today. Since 1964, skyjacking has become practically a daily happening. What national and international legal problems have been caused by skyjackers? Have they been resolved? How? Does modern psychology help or hinder us in handling these new and often complex problems?

INTRODUCTION: Murderer's Eye

Transplants have become so commonplace that most of them no longer make the front page. There are kidney transplants, and eye transplants, and heart transplants.

We know all about the dangers that may accompany transplants—the physical dangers, that is. We know, for example, that a body may reject the alien organ, causing death. That is an understandable danger.

But there may be dangers that we do not yet understand—dangers that we do not even know about. Suppose one cell keeps duplicating until it gains control of the host body. Or suppose a cell grafted on to a hand retains a manual skill, a bit of special dexterity. Or suppose a cell of the eye is somehow capable of memory. Would you see with your eyes, or with the original owner's? Would your brain receive a vision from you— or from him? If from him, would *your* brain still be independent, or would it be somehow influenced by the small trespasser?

These are only a few of the questions that may plague society in the coming decades . . . and the answers may transform both the operating room and the criminal code.

Murderer's Eye
Gerald Kersh

The generosity of the criminal generally consists in the giving away of something that never was, or no longer is, his own property. A case in point is that of the robber and murderer Rurik Duncan, whose last empty gesture was thick and sticky with sentiment. Duncan gave away his eyes to be delivered after his death. It was regarded as a vital act of charity —in effect, a ticket to salvation—that this singularly heartless fellow gave permission for his eyes to be grafted onto some person or persons un- known. Similar cases have been printed in the newspapers. As it is with most philanthropists who give their all, so it was with this man Duncan. Having no further need for what he donated, he made a virtue of relin- quishing it—stealing from his own grave; conning to the bitter end.

I knew a billionaire whose ears were stopped during his lifetime against any plea for charity, but who, when his claws relaxed in death, gave what he had to orphans. I knew a Snow Maiden of an actress whose body was bequeathed to science. All that they were proud of, the billionaire and the beauty, they let go because they had to. Rurik will rank with them, no doubt, on the everlasting plane. And why not? Rurik prized his eyes, of a strange, flecked, yellowish color. He could expand or contract the irises at will, and seemed to look in a different direction while he watched your every movement.

Born on an eroded farm between the rocks and the desert, Rurik was what in my day was called a "nuisance," but is now termed a "juvenile delinquent." Physical force used to be applied to such, whereafter they generally lived to die in their beds; now they bring in psychologists, and only in extreme cases is a Rurik stopped in his career with a tingling jolt and—first and last restraint—the pressure of certain heavy leather straps. He killed chickens, maimed sheep, corrupted and led a mob of fourteen-year-old muggers; graduated to the rackets, in which he was employed to his pleasure and profit in nineteen states of the Union; got hot, gathered about him two coadjutors and went plundering from bank to bank, one of the most formidable operators since Dillinger. Something was missing from him that makes society possible—call it a heart, call it a soul, call it what you like, but say that he wanted to be alone. And so he was, right to his convulsive end, with a high-backed chair all to himself, and a secret which he thought he would carry on his own, locked within himself, to a narrow place where nobody could touch him.

This secret was the whereabouts of certain buried treasure. I mean the location of $2,600,000 which he had stolen and hidden nobody knew where.

It was Rurik and his two companions who stole the armored truck in Butte, Montana. At any moment now the pulp writers will rehash the Rurik snatch as a perfect crime. The details are available in the files of all the newspapers in the world. Here it is sufficient to say simply that one second there was an armored truck loaded with an immense payroll together with nearly all the money that had been in the vault of a great bank. Next second there were three or four bewildered guards, loosely holding pistols they did not know what to point at; three streets full of traffic had stopped for the lights, and a great fortune was on its way to nowhere. Only one shot was fired, and that by a bank guard named Larkin, who, when the three bandits appeared, let fly with a short-barreled .38. As it later transpired, the robbers carried unloaded automatics—it seems that Rurik was very particular about this. So, in about as long as it takes a man to say, "Was that a backfire?" one of the greatest robberies of our time was perpetrated. "Timing, timing, timing," said the Sunday-supplement criminologists; until one became sick and tired of the word.

Reconstructing the affair, the Federal authorities arrived at the conclusion that Rurik and his men, halting somewhere on the outskirts of Butte, hid the money in some place tantalizingly close to town, known only to themselves. Each took $8000 for current expenses. About fifteen miles farther, the truck was abandoned at a point near where they had secreted a getaway car. Rurik drove them away; then they separated, arranging to meet when it was expedient to do so. But Little Dominic, trying to buy a used car in Helena, was recognized and died fighting it out with state troopers, and MacGinnis lost his way northwards among the rocks and died there, in his pigheaded way, rather than give himself up.

Only Rurik was taken alive, having fainted through loss of blood in a filling station; Larkin, the bank guard, had hit him in the hip and so precipitated his capture. When he was convicted of bank robbery, the FBI furnished the additional information that, under another name, Rurik was wanted in the state of New York for murder. So he was shipped East and there, after fair trial, sentenced to death by electrocution. And while Rurik was playing pinochle in the death house, there came to him a certain Father Jellusik, who said that Doctor Holliday, the eye surgeon, wanted Rurik's eyes.

The condemned man, laughing heartily, said, "Listen, the D.A. offers me my life if I sing where the dough is stashed! No disrespect, father, but d'you think I never heard how you can see things in a dead man's eye?"

Father Jellusik said, "My son, that's an old wives' tale. A dead man's eye is no more revealing than an unloaded camera."

Rurik began, "Once, I looked into— Well, anyway, I never saw nothing. What do they want my eyes for?"

"An eye," said Father Jellusik, "is nothing but a certain arrangement of body tissues. Put it like this: you are you, Rurik. If one of your fingers were chopped off, would you still be Rurik?"

"Who else?"

"Without your arms and legs, who would you be?"

"Rurik."

"Now say you had an expensive miniature camera and were making your will, wouldn't you give it away?"

"To the cops, no."

"But to an innocent child?"

"I guess I might."

"And the eye, you know, is nothing but a camera."

In the end, Rurik signed a document bequeathing his eyes to Doctor Holliday for the benefit of this remarkable surgeon's child patients.

"You can't take 'em with you," Rurik is alleged to have said, thereby letting loose a tidal wave of emotion. The sob sisters took him to their bosoms and put into his mouth all kinds of scrapbook philosophy, such as: "If more folks thought more about more folks, the world—" His last words, which were: "Hold it, I changed my mind," were reported as: "I feel kind of at peace now." The general public completely ignored the little matter of two and a half million dollars which Rurik had, to all practical intents and purposes, taken with him. Little Dominic and MacGinnis being dead, no one had a clue to its whereabouts; it was buried treasure.

To Doctor Holliday, the grafting of corneal tissue from the eye of a man recently dead to the eye of a living child was a routine affair which he regarded much as a tailor regards the stitching of a collar. He was at once savagely possessive, devilishly proud and bitterly contemptuous of the craft to which he was married. Years before, when he first became famous and the reporters came to interview him, his face set in a look of intense distaste and, talking in an overemphasized reedy voice, Doctor Holliday said, "Human eyes? A fly's are far more remarkable. Your eye is nothing but a makeshift arrangement for receiving light rays upon a sensitive surface—a camera, and damned inefficient at that. Well?"

A reporter said, "But you've restored sight, Doctor Holliday. A camera can't see without an eye behind it."

Doctor Holliday snapped, "Neither can an eye see, as anybody but an absolute fool must know."

"Well, you can't see without your eyes," another reporter said.

"You can't see with them," said Doctor Holliday. "Even if I had the time to explain the difference between looking and seeing, you have not the power to understand me; and even if you had, how would you convey what you understood to the louts who buy your journal? Let it be sufficient for me to say, therefore, that vision comes from behind the eye."

One of the reporters who wrote up things like viruses and astronomy for the Sunday supplement said, "Optic nerve—" at which Doctor Holliday swooped at him like a sparrow hawk.

"Optic nerve! A wiring job, so to speak, eh? Splice it, like a rope, eh? Oh, I love these popular scientists, I love them! My dear sir, you know nothing about the tiniest and most insignificant nerve in your body, and neither do I. But you will suck on your scientific jargon, like a baby. Can you name me thirty parts, say, of the mere eye—just name them— that you talk with such facility of optic nerves?"

The reporter, abashed, said, "I'm sorry, Doctor Holliday. I was only going to ask if it might be possible—I don't mean in our time, but some-time—really to graft a whole eye and, as you put it, splice an optic nerve?"

In his disagreeable way, mocking the hesitancy of the reporter's voice, Doctor Holliday said, "One thing is impossible, and that is to predict what may or may not be surgically possible or impossible in our time. But I can tell you this, sir: it is about as possible to graft a whole eye as it might be to graft a whole head. As every schoolboy must know, nervous tissue does not regenerate itself in the vertebrate—except in the case of the salamander, in which the regenerative process remains a mystery."

A lady reporter asked, "Aren't salamanders those lizards that are supposed to live in fire, or something?"

Doctor Holliday started to snap, but, meeting the wide gaze of this young woman, liked her irises and, gently for him, explained, "The salamander resembles a lizard, but it is an amphibian with a long tail. An amphibian lives both in and out of water. Have you never seen a salamander? I'll show you one"—and he led the way to an air-conditioned room that smelled somewhat of dead vegetation, through which ran a miniature river bordered with mud. In this mud languid little animals stirred.

A man from the South said, "Heck, they're mud eels!"

At him Doctor Holliday curled a lip, saying, "Same thing."

The Sunday-supplement man said, "Doctor Holliday, may I ask whether you are studying the metabolic processes of the salamander with a view to their application—"

"No, you may not!"

Next day there were photographs of a salamander in the papers, and headlines like this:

HEAD GRAFT NEXT?
MYSTERY OF SALAMANDER

After that, Doctor Holliday would not speak to anybody connected with the press, and was dragged into the limelight again only when he grafted the right eye of Rurik into the head of a four-year-old boy named Dicky Aldous, son of Richard Aldous, a wealthy paint manufacturer of Greenwich, Connecticut.

It was not one operation, but eight, over a period of about six weeks, during which time the child's eye was kept half in and half out of a certain fluid which Doctor Holliday has refused to discuss. The Sunday-supplement writer, the "sensationalist," has hinted that this stuff is derived from the salamander. It is not for me to express an opinion; only I will insist that Jules Verne was a sensationalist, and now we are discussing man-powered rockets to the moon; H. G. Wells was a sensationalist, but there really are such things as heavier-than-air-aircraft, automatic sights, and atomic bombs. I, for one, refuse to discount the Sunday-supplement man's conjecture that from the humble salamander Doctor Holliday extracted a regenerative principle for human nervous tissue. And why not? Alexander Fleming found penicillin in the mold on lemon rind. Believe me, if it were not for such cranks, medicine would still be witch-doctoring, and brain surgery a hole in the head to let the devils out.

Anyway, when the bandages were lifted, Dicky Aldous, born blind, could see out of his new right eye. The lady reporter made quite a piece out of his first recognition of the color blue. The Sunday-supplement man wrote an article suggesting that the delicate tissues of the human eye, especially of the optic nerve, might be seriously altered by the tremendous shock of electrocution; he noted that Doctor Holliday was frequently found in consultation with the English brain specialist, Mr. Donne, and Doctor Felsen, the neurologist. Doctor Holliday himself, after a few outbursts against the press, became silent.

Paragraph by paragraph, the case of Dicky Aldous dropped out of the papers. Other matters came up to occupy our attention—Russia, the hydrogen bomb, Israel, the World Series—and the fly trap of the public mind closed upon and digested what once it had gapingly received as The Dicky Aldous Miracle. But this is far from being the whole of the story; and since, now, it can do no harm and might do some good, I feel that I have the right to offer the public a brief account of subsequent events.

Richard Aldous was a third-generation millionaire; genteel, sensitive, a collector of engravings. His wife, whom he had met in Lucca, was an Italian princess—finely engraved herself, and almost fanatically fastidious. Tourists used to wonder how it was possible for a high-bred aristocrat to live in a *palazzo* surrounded with filth. The explanation is in the Three Wise Monkeys: "See no evil, speak no evil, hear no evil"—and there you are, divorced from humanity. In extreme cases, stop your nose, having previously sprinkled yourself with strong perfume.

As you can imagine, therefore, little Dicky Aldous in his fifth year was in complete ignorance of the ugliness that exists in the world. The servants in the Aldous household had been examined, as it were, through a magnifying glass—generally imported from Europe, expense being no object. Dicky's nurse was a sweet-natured English gentlewoman. From her he could have heard nothing but old-fashioned nursery songs—sung off-key, perhaps, but kindly and innocuous—and no story more dangerous than the one about the pig that wouldn't jump over the stile. The housekeeper was from Lucca; she had followed her mistress six years previously, with her husband, the butler. Neither of them could speak more than two or three phrases in English. Mrs. Aldous' maid, Beatrice, also was an Italian girl; a wonderful needlewoman and hairdresser, she seldom spoke at all—she preferred to sing, which the little boy liked, being blind. Here were no evil communications to corrupt the good manners of poor Dicky Aldous.

Yet one day, about a month after the sensational success of Doctor

Holliday's operation had been fully established, the English nurse came down from the nursery to make the required announcement that Master Dicky was asleep, and there was something in her manner which made the father ask, "Anything wrong, Miss Williams?" Rachel Williams, the English nanny, didn't like to say, but at last she burst out—that somebody must have been teaching little Dicky to use bad language. She could not imagine who might be responsible. Closely pressed, she spelled out a word or two—she could not defile her tongue by uttering them whole—and Aldous began to laugh.

All the same, when the nurse was at supper, Mr. Aldous went to the nursery where his son lay sleeping. On the way into the room he met his wife hurrying out, evidently on the verge of tears.

She said, "Oh, Richard, our boy is possessed by a devil! He just said, in his sleep, 'For crying out loud, cease, you rousy sandwich!' Where did he ever hear a word like 'cease'?"

Her husband sent her to bed, saying, "Why, darling, little Dicky has had to suffer the impact of too many new sensations, too suddenly. The shock must be something like the shock of being born. Rest, sweetheart." Then he went into the nursery and sat by the child's crib.

After a little while, stirring uneasily in his sleep, speaking in the accents of the gutters of the West, Dicky Aldous said quite clearly, "Ah, shup! Aina kina guya rat!"—distinguishable to his father as: "Ah, shut up! I ain't the kind of guy to rat!" Then, tossing feverishly from side to side, his face curiously distorted so that he spoke almost without moving his lips, Dicky Aldous said, in baby talk with which I will not trouble your eyes or distract your attention by writing it phonetically, "Listen, and get it right, this time, you son—" He added a string of expletives which, coming from him, were indescribably shocking. Perhaps "horrifying" is the better word, because you can understand shock, being aware of its cause, but horror makes no sense. That is why it is horrible—there lies the quintessence of nightmare, in the truth divorced from reason.

Presently, in a tense whisper, while the entire face of the child seemed to age and alter, Dicky said, "Dom, you take the big forty-five. . . . Mac, take the cut-down, snub-nose blue-barrel thirty-eight. . . . What for? Because I'm telling you. A big gun looks five times bigger on a runt like Little Dominic. Get me? And a blue belly-gun looks twice as dangerous in the mitt of a big lug like Mac. Me, I take the Luger, because one look at a Luger, you know it's made for business. But empty—I want 'em empty. . . . You got an argument, Dom? O.K., so have I. In Montana, brother, they hang you up. . . . O.K., O.K., call it unscientific, but you'll do as I say because, believe me, this job'll be pulled using those things just for show. My weapon is time. Cease, Dominic. . . . Gimme a feel of that forty-five. Empty. Good, let it stay like that. . . . O.K., then, I want this straight; I want this right from the start. We'll go over this again."

Then Dicky Aldous stopped talking. His face reassumed its proper contours, and he slept peacefully.

Mr. Aldous met Miss Williams on the stairs. "It's worrying me to death," she said. "I cannot for the life of me imagine where Dicky darling picked up the word 'cease.'"

Mr. Aldous said, "I think, just for a few nights, Miss Williams, I'll sleep in his room." He lay down on the nurse's bed, and stayed awake, listening. He made careful notes of what poor Dicky said in his sleep—and many of the things the child said were concerned with visual memory, which the boy could not have had, since he was born blind.

"... They's a whole knot o' cottonmouths on the island past Miller's Bend. What'll you give me if I show you? What, you never seen a cottonmouth? It's a snake, see, a great big poison snake, and it's got a mouth like it's full of cotton, and poison teeth longer'n your finger. C'mon, give me what you got and I'll show you the cottonmouths," Dicky said, his voice growing uglier.... "What d'you mean, you ain't got nothing? Ever learn the Indian twist, so you can break a growed man's elbow? All right, boy, I'll show you for free.... Oh, that hurts, does it? Too bad. A bit more pressure and it'll hurt you for keeps—like that.... You still ain't got nothing to see the cottonmouths all tangled in a knot? ... Oh, you'll get it, will you? You'd better. And you owe me an extra dime for learning you the Indian twist.... No, sir, just for wasting my time I ain't going to show you them cottonmouths today—not till you bring me twenty cents, you punk, you. And then, maybe, I'll show you that nest o' diamondback rattlesnakes at Geranium Creek. But if you don't deliver, Malachi Westbrook—mind me, now—I'll show you the Seminole jaw grip. That takes a man's head clear off. And I'll show it to you good, Malachi. Yes, sir, me and Teddy Pinchbeck will sure show you good! Mind me, now; meet me and Teddy Pinchbeck at the old Washington Boathouse eight o'clock tomorrow morning, and bring Charley Greengrass with you. He better have twenty cents with him, too, or else."

Mr. Aldous wrote all this down. At about three o'clock in the morning, Dicky said, "O.K., kids. You paid up. You're O.K. O.K., I'll just borrow Three-Finger Mike's little old boat, and Teddy Pinchbeck and me'll take you and Charley Greengrass to look at them cottonmouths. Only see here, you kids, me and Teddy Pinchbeck got to pole you way past Burnt Swamp and all the way to Miller's Bend.... That'll cost 'em, won't it, Teddy? ... You ain't got it? Get it. And stop crying. It makes me nervous, don't it, Teddy? And when I'm nervous I'm liable to show you the Indian hip grip, so you'll never walk again as long as you live. You mind me, now!"

At about nine o'clock in the morning, Mr. Aldous made an appointment with a psychologist, one Doctor Asher, who, finding himself caught on the horns of this dilemma—carte blanche and an insoluble problem—double-talked himself into one of those psychiatric serials that are longer than human patience. But what was Doctor Asher to say? Little Dicky Aldous had no vision to remember with; there was nothing in his head upon which juvenile imagination might conceivably fall back.

It was by sheer accident that Mr. Aldous met a lieutenant of detectives named Neetsfoot, to whom he confided the matter, hoping against hope, simply because Neetsfoot had worked on the Rurik Duncan case.

The detective said, "That's very strange, Mr. Aldous. Let's have it all over again."

"I have it written down verbatim, lieutenant."

"I'd be grateful if you'd let me make a copy, Mr. Aldous. And look—I have children of my own. My boy has had polio, in fact, and I've kind of got the habit of talking to kids without upsetting them. Would you have any objection—this is unofficial—would you have any objection to my talking to your son a little bit?"

"What in the world for?" asked Mr. Aldous.

Lieutenant Neetsfoot said, "Mr. Aldous, if you haven't got a clue to something—well, that's that. In that case, if you see what I mean, it doesn't even come within range of being understood. At a certain point you stop trying to understand it. Now sometimes something that makes absolutely no sense at all, flapping about in the dark, throws a switch. And there you've got a mystery."

"I don't get what you're driving at, lieutenant."

"Neither do I, Mr. Aldous. But I'll give you the leading points, if you like. A, I know all there is to know about Rurik Duncan—saw him electrocuted, in fact. And a miserable show he made of it.. B, I don't like to dig these matters up, but your son, four years old and born blind, had one of Rurik's eyes grafted into his head by Doctor Holliday. And now, C, the child is going word for word and point by point into details of things that happened about sixteen years before he was born and two thousand miles away!"

"Oh, no, surely not!" cried Mr. Aldous.

"Oh, yes, surely so," said the lieutenant. "And geographically accurate, at that. What's more remarkable, your son has got the names right of people that he never heard of and who died before he was born. What d'you make of that? Teddy Pinchbeck was shot in a fight outside a church it must be ten, eleven years ago. A bad boy, that one. And where did I get my information? From Malachi Westbrook—he's a real-estate man now. There was an old Washington Boathouse, and Malachi Westbrook's the man that tore it down to make space for Westbrook Landing. Charley Greengrass runs his father's store. There was a Three-Finger Mike, but he just disappeared. There really is a Cottonmouth Island just past a Miller's Bend, and in the mating season it's one writhing mass. And Rurik Duncan did break Malachi Westbrook's arm before your son was born. Well?"

"This I do not understand," said Richard Aldous.

"Me neither. Mind if I sit with the boy a bit?"

"No, lieutenant, no. . . . But how on earth could he know about cotton-mouths? He never saw one. He never saw anything, poor child. To be frank with you, neither my wife nor I have ever seen a cottonmouth snake. I simply don't get it."

"Then you don't mind?"

"Go ahead by all means, lieutenant," said Mr. Aldous.

Neetsfoot went ahead—in other words, he sacrificed two weeks of his vacation in a dead silence, listening by Dicky's bed while the child slept. Mrs. Aldous was in the grip of a nervous breakdown, so that her husband was present only half the time. But he bears witness—and so, at a later date, does an official stenographer—to what Dicky Aldous said, in what was eventually termed his "delirium."

First, the child struggled left and right. It appeared to the detective that he was somehow trying to writhe away from something; that he was in the clutch of a nightmare. His temperature went up to 103 degrees, and then he said, "Look. This is the setup, you kids. The Pan keeps the engine running. . . . Get that right from the start, Pan. . . . Little Joe sticks a toothpick under the bell push. I put the heat on. O.K.? O.K.!"

Lieutenant Neetsfoot knew what to make of this. The man who was called The Pan on account of his rigid face was driver for several gang-sters; Little Joe Ricardo was a sort of assistant gunman who was trying to make the grade with the big mobs. The heat, as Neetsfoot construed it, was put on a union leader named M'Turk, for whose murder Rurik Duncan was tried, but acquitted for lack of evidence.

M'Turk was shot down in his own doorway; the street was aroused less by the noise of the shot than by the constant ringing of M'Turk's door-bell, under which somebody had stuck a toothpick.

But all this had happened at least eight years before Dicky Aldous was born.

"And this I don't quite get," said Lieutenant Neetsfoot.

"There is something distinctly peculiar here," Mr. Aldous said. "But I won't have the child bothered."

"I'm not bothering the child, Mr. Aldous; the child's bothering me.

Heaven's my judge, I haven't opened my mouth. Not even to smoke! The kid does all the talking, and Gregory takes it down on the machine. You can believe me when I tell you there's something funny here. Your little boy has gone into details about the M'Turk shooting, and this I can't understand. Tell me, Mr. Aldous, do you remember the details of M'Turk?"

"No, I can't say I do, lieutenant."

"Then how does the kid?"

"I must have told your people a thousand times: my son couldn't possibly have heard anything about the people or the events you keep harping on."

"I know he couldn't, Mr. Aldous. This is off the record and on my own time. That's understood, isn't it?"

"It is a most extraordinary situation, lieutenant."

"You can say that again."

Mr. Aldous said, with a kind of detached enthusiasm that somehow disgusted the detective, "You know what? The eye of this man Rurik Duncan having been grafted, complete with optic nerve, it's almost as if the child's actually seeing through Rurik Duncan's optic nerve!"

"Almost as if," said the lieutenant.

"But how?"

"Ask the doctor, don't ask me."

And Doctor Holliday was, indeed, the fourth witness to the last, and most important, utterances of the boy into whose orbit he had grafted the right eye of Rurik Duncan. It happened, as previously, between two and three o'clock in the morning.

Dicky said, "Now listen. You, Dom, listen. . . . And you listen, Mac. . . . You heard it before? Then hear it again. This is the way I want it, and this is the way it's going to be. . . . Dom, you always were trigger-happy. First, no loads in the rods. I want these guns ice-cold. One thing I won't do, and that's hang. And in Montana they hang you on a rope. Never forget that. . . . Second, follow my timing and you can't go wrong. We beat the lights. Remember, it's two million and a half in small bills. Better men than you have died for less. My Uncle Gabe died through getting bitten in the leg by a hog. This way's more fun. . . . Third, the short haul in the armored truck and the swift stash in the rocks, you know where. Got it? . . . Fourth, the quick scatter. Now somebody could get hurt. So let's get this right. O.K.? I'll go over it again."

At this point, Mr. Aldous, carried away by sheer excitement, cried, "Yes, but exactly where is the money? Where did we put it?"

Dicky sneered in his sleep, "And exactly where d'you get that 'did'? It ain't put there yet. . . . And who's 'we'? Little Dom and Mac I told already. There ain't no more 'we.' Go burn me, mister, and sniff for it. 'We,' for cryin' out loud! Well, I guess you got to be dumb or you wouldn't be a cop. O.K. You want to know where the dough is? I'll tell you. It's in Montana. Got that wrote down? Montana. It's going to be loaded in a great big armored truck in Butte. And taken where?" The child laughed in a singularly ugly way. "It'll be my pleasure to tell you, mister: somewhere in Montana. All you got to do when I stash this dough is scratch. O.K., Mr. Dickins?"

"Wasn't Dickins the name of the district attorney who offered Rurik Duncan his life if he would divulge the whereabouts of the stolen money?" whispered Mr. Aldous.

Lieutenant Neetsfoot replied, not without bitterness, "Yes, it was. For Pete's sake, shut up! I think you've already talked us out of that two and a half million. And here I've sat like a stone for fifteen days, and right at the end you must bust in and open your yap."

Deeply hurt, Mr. Aldous said, "My son has always responded to my voice."

The lieutenant looked at him with disdain, and then said, in a carefully controlled voice, "Yes, Mr. Aldous. Your son has always responded to your voice, Mr. Aldous. But damn it, that wasn't your son who was talking—that was Rurik Duncan! That was Rurik Duncan running over orders with Little Dominic and MacGinnis before the truck was snatched and the money stashed away! I told you to keep quiet like me; I begged you to keep your mouth shut like I did. But no, your son has always responded to your voice. Congratulations, Mr. Aldous; you've got the costliest voice in the world. It's just talked us out of ten per cent of two million six hundred thousand dollars!"

They sat by the crib until dawn, but, his fever past, Dicky Aldous, perspiring freely, talked no more in his sleep.

When he awoke, his father, who had an unshakable faith in the power of his voice to arouse response in his hitherto blind son, said, "Now, Dicky darling, tell Daddy dear about Montana."

"Want to see blue," said Dicky; and became engrossed in the color and the shape of a large red nonpoisonous-nylon teddy bear of which he had previously known only the texture.

And from that day to this he has not talked of Montana. His memory of events preceding Doctor Holliday's operation is rapidly fading. Doctor Holliday, who visits the house from time to time, has put forward a halfhearted theory that, by some unexplained process, the regenerated nervous tissue, heavily charged with electricity, retained and conveyed the visual memory of Rurik Duncan only while this tissue was knitting. It may come back, he says, in adult life or, on the other hand, it may not.

Lieutenant Neetsfoot, whom Mr. Aldous regards as a "character," pays a visit every other Sunday. He likes to play with the little boy. It was he who said to me, "This is unofficial, off the record; but I'm pretty observant. When I was a rookie I learned to watch you without seeming to. And I can tell you there's something very, very funny about that kid's eye when he thinks he isn't being observed. He's seven now. I'm due to retire nine years from now. Call me crazy, but, believe me, when that kid is old enough to have a car of his own and take a vacation without anybody else along, wherever he goes I'll follow him."

Here, for the time being, the matter rests.

FOR DISCUSSION: Murderer's Eye

1. The first three paragraphs not only tell us what Rurik Duncan was like, but also suggest Gerald Kersh's attitude toward criminals. On the basis of these three paragraphs, do you think Kersh would be sympathetic toward sociological explanations of crime? If the story continued for another twenty years, what dilemma might he face regarding young Dicky Aldous?
2. While the events in this story are highly improbable, Kersh succeeds in making them *seem* probable while we are actually reading. How does he accomplish this?
3. Why did Kersh choose a four-year-old as the recipient of Rurik's eye? Could an adult have been used just as effectively? Why, or why not?
4. The last few sentences have a chilling effect on the reader. Why, at this point, did Kersh employ implication rather than statement? What are some of the advantages implication enjoys?
5. This and the previous story in this section deal with two problems resulting from innovations: legal jurisdiction and transplants. What other innovations can you think of that might provide "meat" for a mystery? Choose one and try writing a mystery of tomorrow for today.

INTRODUCTION: Project Murder

As the twentieth century rolls to a stop, the computer rules. Computers manage state and federal elections and make early predictions—predictions that may even influence the results. Computers keep track of credit cards and print out bills. Computers schedule students in schools and colleges, maintain inventory checks in large businesses, and fix a stern eye on income tax returns. Almost every aspect of our lives has already been keypunched and fed into some computer somewhere.

And now in fiction—and to a lesser extent in reality—the computer is entering the underworld.

Murder is at once the most personal and the most vicious of crimes. Its horror is modified a little by the fact that the murderer generally acts with passion. But when a computer plans a murder, there is no passion, no saving touch of the human. Flesh and blood becomes just another item to be properly keypunched, motive a valueless piece of data, and the assignment of guilt a mechanical solving of a puzzle.

Project Murder

Steven Peters

At ten years of age a monomania seized Harvey Harris, a driving passion for puzzle solving. Anagrams, conundrums, chess problems, mathematical and jigsaw puzzles—they all fascinated him and devoured his time. In his teens Harvey graduated to crossword puzzles, cryptography, Double-Crostics, nim, and the Tower of Brahma. Not many men can turn a boyhood monomania into an adult vocation, but Harvey Harris did. By the time he was 40 years old he earned a comfortable living indulging his sole passion.

Naturally, in those intervening 30 years, there had been some changes. His methods of solution, for instance, matured into extremely complex ones utilizing high-speed computers. One would also have to concede that the puzzles he solved as an adult contained at least a minimum of social value. Harvey happily led a schizophrenic existence in his job at a computer lab, without further sacrifices to maturity.

The ten-year-old Harvey programmed his very expensive electronic toy to play bridge and chess. Once he even set a record with a program that printed out the solution to *The New York Times* Sunday Crossword puzzle in one minute and thirteen seconds. The forty-year-old Harvey, dignified by a Ph.D. in mathematical linguistics, engaged in more serious activities, though still satisfying to his puzzle-solving urge. He performed a useful social function by programming the computer to read one language and render a translation in another.

Since the computer lab where Harvey worked was associated with a large university, employees had to conform to academic dictates, the cardinal one being: "Publish or perish!" Harvey's article "A Computer Confirmation of Ventris' Decipherment of Linear B Script" duly appeared in the *Journal of Classical Languages* (April 1961). His second article, "Some Minor Modifications in the Reconstruction of the Texts of the Dead Sea Scrolls," could be found in the prestigious *Journal of Biblical Research* (April 1964).

If by chance you have read these articles, you will understand much about Harvey. His role in life so far had been to confirm or modify (slightly) the creative genius of others. However, that iota of creative potential, hidden in so many, managed to elude Harvey's grasp. Beneath his staid exterior Harvey nursed a secret dream, perhaps also a ten-year-old remnant. In his fantasies the world would one day be stunned by a dramatic, imaginative solution to a major social problem, conceived and executed by Harvey Harris, Ph.D.

Once you know the ethereal scope of Harvey's dream you can appreciate the humiliation inflicted on him by one of his puzzle-solving activities—the reading of murder mysteries. Harvey confessed his mortification one day to John Dalton, director of the computer lab, as the two men hunched over dessert in the cafeteria. Trapped into eating with Harvey by the lack of another available table, Dalton listened, but failed to understand the extent of Harvey's frustration.

"In the past eight years, John, I've read 2,439 murder mysteries. I figured that's 304.875 books a year, approximately a book every one and two-tenths days."

"Fantastic. Personally I'm a science-fiction fan myself. Never did care much for mysteries. Too gory."

"But the galling part is that I have solved only 83 of them. Think of it —only 83! Why, that's a miserable three per cent—actually, three point four per cent."

"Appalling. Look, Harvey, I've got an important run about ready to print out. Don't want to miss it. Excuse me, will you?"

John pushed back from the table, stood up, then hesitated. Aware that his eagerness to escape might be too obvious, he sought to hide it behind an additional comment, to prolong his departure slightly. "Say, why don't you write a program and let the computer solve the mysteries?"

With a good-natured chuckle at his own wit John vanished.

"Rubbish," Harvey said softly, before he realized he was addressing an empty chair. "What good would that do?"

Later that day, however, while staring at the ceiling in contemplation, John Dalton's remark came back to him. After all, he had used the computer to solve other puzzles, and murder mysteries were a type of puzzle. The solution is just a matter of sorting out the clues, interpreting them properly, and making logical deductions from them—nothing the computer couldn't handle. If it could solve the plots of books, then maybe it could—

A slow smile spread across Harvey's face. "Project Murder" had been born.

In the next few months Harvey worked nights and week-ends, collecting a staggering amount of information about the 2,439 mysteries he had read. He was greatly aided in this task by a neat stack of five-by-eight file cards, representing his methodical eight-year record of each of the 2,439 mystery books. Titles, names of authors, character types, murder methods, motives, clues, number of suspects, types of detective, data about victims, complete plot summaries, and all other information Harvey could collect was translated into language the computer could understand and stored on tape, later to be fed into the memory of the machine. After all this preliminary work had been completed, Harvey undertook a descriptive analysis of the data.

"How were the murders committed?" he typed to the computer. Almost instantly came the answer.

Gunshot 743, Bludgeoning 510, Stabbing 316, Strangulation 289, Poisoning 103, Vehicular "Accidents" 97—and so the list went right down to Explosive Hidden in Five-minute Egg Detonated by Tap on Shell by Knife 1, Sent into Orbit in Unused Space Capsule 1, Barrel over Niagara Falls 1.

"What motivated the murders?" was Harvey's next question. All the usual ones were there, with Financial Gain leading the list, closely followed by Desire for Business or Political Power, Revenge, Psychological Satisfaction, Theft of Valuable Property, Fear of Exposure of Secrets, Danger to Loved Ones, et cetera, down to Retaliation for Killing Pet Cat 1.

Question after question followed and the answers were all plugged back into the computer's memory storage, providing it with a wealth of "experience" about the frequency of occurrence of the many variables in a mystery story.

After this initial work the computer was instructed to correlate each variable with every other one. In this way devious relationships were ferreted out, allowing answers to questions such as: "What relationship exists between the sex of the murderer and the sex of the victim?" "Are the number of pages in the book related to anything?" "Is the sex of the author related to the method of murder?" "Do amateur detectives tend to solve certain types of crimes more easily than others?"

Of course, true mystery-story fans—aficionados—certainly would yell "Foul!" at this point. The solution to a mystery should come from deductive reasoning, diligently applied to the clues, and not from unfair tactics, such as knowing that this particular lady author always had men murderers, so "Helpless Jane" couldn't possibly be the guilty one. But Harvey was desperate and intended to triumph by any method, fair or foul.

The next step in the statistical analysis submitted the huge interrelation matrix to a factor analysis, thereby reducing the many variables to a small number of elements, defining the different aspects of a mystery story that tend to go together. For example, one author invariably wrote stories in which the murderer was always a woman who killed for obscure reasons and was tracked down by a muscular private detective who unfailingly shot her in the stomach with a .45 on the next to the last page of each 183-page book. Then there was the type of story about a group of people marooned by a storm in an old house, and one by one they got murdered until . . .

A final discriminant-function analysis refined prediction and at last Harvey knew which variables were most important and how they should be weighted to predict the outcome correctly—that is to say, whodunit. Harvey then wrote a program, instructing the computer how to take advantage of all the knowledge stored in its memory to solve mysteries. As a final touch he provided the computer with some rules and restrictions (that is, it is unethical to make the detective the murderer) on how to plot and write mysteries, such as the guidelines set down by S. S. Van Dine and other famous mystery writers and critics.

A check on his program revealed that all was working properly. He could correctly predict the murderer in each of the 2,439 books. Now he was ready for the final step. Would the computer be able to solve the murder in a different book—one he had not used for the programming?

The test case was to be a book by Agatha Christie—*The Murder of Roger Ackroyd*—which unaccountably he had never read before. The data was fed in and Harvey typed his query:

Who is the murderer?

For a few moments lights flashed and the machine hummed, then the attached typewriter chattered away. Harvey, who had not yet read the solution in the book, stared unbelievingly at the answer that appeared before him.

This conclusion is 93 per cent certain in spite of the fact that it violated Rule NUMBER THREE pertaining to the eligibility of suspects in mystery stories.

Puzzled, Harvey sat down and read the end of the book. When he finished he let out a shout of glee, ran over and tenderly patted the computer. Then he sat down at the keyboard and typed out:

You were right. You saw through a very ingenious and daring plot.

The computer replied:

Thank you. The credit belongs to you. I only do what I am instructed.

Harvey typed:

Yes, you are only a mechanical brain, but I am a genius.

The computer replied obliquely:

Proudness precedes a precipitous plunge.

Harvey sadly shook his head. In spite of his hard work on the language-translation program the computer still had trouble with English proverbs.

Two days later Harvey sat in the office of director John Dalton. In the past two days, since his *Roger Ackroyd* success, Harvey had challenged the machine with some real-life plots to solve. Now he could hardly wait to tell John about his research, although John, as usual, had other things on his mind.

"Harvey, I've been concerned about your work lately. It has come to my attention that a number of your projects for some of our big accounts have either been late or still aren't finished."

"That's right. I've been working on something more important." He smiled with anticipated pleasure.

"Oh?" John said, raising one eyebrow. "I didn't know you were working on something else."

"I used my own time at first, John, but then I got so wrapped up in it that I spent every moment on it. It's spectacular, it's finished, and it works perfectly."

"That's very irregular, Harvey. You know we like to encourage independent research, but not at the expense of neglecting your job. Still," John paused and rubbed his chin, "if you've written a new program that has some value to us it might get you off the hook. What's your new program about?"

"Murder!"

"I beg your pardon. Did you say, murder?"

"I did. My program can solve the plot of any detective novel you give it. Just push a button and presto, out comes the name of the murderer."

"Fantastic," replied John, eyeing Harvey warily. "Uh, Harv, it's been quite a while since you've had a vacation. You've worked hard for us lately. You're a good man and we don't want to lose you. How would you like to go on a two-week all-expense-paid vacation—you know, for a little rest?"

Harvey winced as if he'd been slapped across the face. "You don't understand, John. The computer can solve murder mysteries."

"I understand, Harvey. That's why I suggested the vacation. I understand you've wasted your time and valuable computer time writing a program to solve detective stories. Of all the useless idiotic things I've ever heard of—"

"Now wait a minute, John, you suggested it. It was your idea."

"Absurd. My idea? Are you crazy?"

"What do you mean by that?" Harvey asked belligerently, leaning across the desk. "You suggested it to me one day at lunch."

The memory of that day returned to John and he began to sputter. "Surely, Harvey, you didn't take me seriously? What kind of idiot do you think I am?"

"Well, I took you seriously. It was a great idea. Don't you realize the value of this program?"

"Value? What value? What are we supposed to do, set up a reader-aid service for mystery fans all over the country? All they have to do is read the last chapter and they'll know the answer—who did it. What possible good is this program to us?"

"You're not thinking big enough, John. With this program we are going to become crime consultants to the police all over the nation— maybe even the world!"

John's eyes bulged. "We are going to do *what?*"

"Don't you see?" Harvey went on, warming up to his subject. "The police send us all the information on a murder, including a list of suspects and the data about them. We run it through the computer, it tells us who the murderer is, we tell the police, and they arrest the killer."

"That's the most absurd thing I've ever heard! Real-life murders aren't like those in books. What D.A. is going to take a case to court with the ridiculous evidence that the guilty person was selected by a computer?"

Harvey allowed himself a small smile at the whiteness of John's face. "The courts will be using one of our computers, too."

John gurgled and sank back in his chair. It was touch and go as to whether he had fainted. "The courts, too?" he finally gasped.

"Of course." Harvey polished his fingernails on his lapel. "Don't you see? Instead of a jury we have the computer. It will give a calm, rational decision. No more lawyers and their grandstand tricks, no more playing on the emotions of the jury. No more wasted time selecting jurors, no more hung juries."

"No judge in the country would allow it. It's un-American. The Constitution guarantees a trial by a jury of peers."

"Who needs a judge?"

"Oh, no," moaned John, dropping his head in his hands.

"Oh, yes," corrected Harvey. "We program the computer with all the law it needs to know. It will do the job better than any judge. The lawyers can decide what information to feed into the computer, it decides whether it's admissable as evidence or not, digests the pertinent facts, and renders its verdict. We could even program it to pass the sentence, too."

John just sat there, his mouth hanging open.

"It will revolutionize American jurisprudence. It is the greatest social innovation since 'innocent until proven guilty.' At last we will truly have a government of laws, not of men."

"No judge, no jury," mumbled John.

"And I, Harvey Harris, will have given the world the Computerized Murder Trial, the greatest social advance in centuries. Of course, you originally suggested the idea. I'll see that you get proper credit."

"Aaaghh," choked John. When his breath returned he said levelly, "Get out of here, Harvey. Your vacation starts now, this minute. Don't ever mention this nutty idea to me again, understand?"

"Wait. You say it won't work on real-life cases. Well, I have positive proof it will. Here, look at these"—and he shoved some print-out sheets onto John's desk. "See, Lincoln's assassination was part of a conspiracy, and this man, a member of his own cabinet, was behind it."

"Harvey, historians have been over that idea thoroughly and discarded it."

"But the machine is 95 per cent confident that it is correct in its analysis. Think of the publicity this will give us. And here"—he thrust another sheet in front of John—"wait until the Boston police see this about the strangler."

John looked and blanched. "You *are* crazy," he said with great conviction. "You can't release that to the press. We'd have a libel suit on our hands in no time."

"Then how about this one on the Warren Commission—"

"No, no. Absolutely not. I forbid you to show this to anyone. It's the most irresponsible thing I've ever seen."

John began to grab frantically at the sheets of paper, tearing them to bits, and flinging them in the general direction of the wastebasket.

"So help me, Harvey, if you even hint at this to anybody I'll personally swear out a ten-day observation paper on you. I'll bury you so deep in the State Hospital that nobody, but nobody will ever find you again. Do you understand?"

"I understand that you don't like my idea," Harvey said stiffly.

"Get out," screamed John, "get out of here! I don't want to hear another word about this hare-brained idea."

Harvey left, returned to his desk, brooded for a few minutes, then walked over to the computer. He sat down and typed out the whole story to the computer. After a split second it clacked out its reply:

You are an oracle with dishonor on your native soil.

Harvey sighed. He was going to have to do something about those proverbs. Then on second thought he typed:

What should I do?

He watched in horror as the answer appeared on the paper before him, the keys moving rapidly, untouched by human hands:

Murder John Dalton.

Perhaps John Dalton had been right: maybe Harvey was insane. All Harvey knew was that he had yearned all his life to find a creative solution to a social puzzle that had stymied great minds. He believed he had found that solution but John Dalton was thwarting his ambition. What was Dalton's life compared with the benefit the world would reap for centuries to come from the Harris Computerized Murder Trial?

The man who couldn't solve murder mysteries set out to plot a murder of his own. Harvey was smart enough to plan his murder in close collaboration with the computer. It advised Bludgeoning with a Blunt Instrument as the preferred method. The assistant director of the lab would be made the Prime Suspect. His name would appear on John's desk calendar for an 8:00 P.M. appointment on the night of the murder. The Motive was to prevent John from revealing that the assistant director had embezzled $30,000 from the lab. With the computer's help Harvey printed out a set of bookkeeping sheets, neatly rigged to show the required discrepancy.

With his murder planned, Harvey checked his Plot by running it through the computer. The machine replied:

> *The murderer of John Dalton is the assistant director of this lab.*
> *I am 98 per cent certain of this solution.*

Harvey smiled and switched off the machine for the night. With John and the assistant director both out of the way, he would be next in line to become the new director of the lab. His first act in that capacity would be to give the world the Harris Computerized Murder Trial Program. If circumstances were favorable he would act that very night.

Shortly after eight o'clock that evening Harvey found himself standing before John Dalton's desk looking down at the top of the director's bald head. John was doing his month-end, late-night job of checking over the lab's accounts.

"Are you still around?" John asked, raising his head briefly. "I thought you would be on vacation by now. What do you want?"

Harvey stared at the heavy glass paperweight sitting on the corner of John's desk. Embedded deep within the glass was that ubiquitous word, seen in all computer labs: *Think.*

Harvey thought.

"Get on with it, Harvey. I haven't got all night."

Harvey stopped thinking and acted. Picking up the paperweight he brought it crashing down on thé bald spot on John's head. John slid to the floor without a sound.

Quietly Harvey left the office, walking across the deserted lab. On an impulse he stopped in front of the computer. Sitting down, he switched it on and typed:

> *John Dalton is dead.*

Then, switching the computer off, he went home.

Arriving later than usual at the lab the next morning, Harvey knew what he would find. There was no reason to hurry to work because nobody would be working. As he expected, employees of the lab were huddled in small groups, talking in hushed voices. The police were swarming all over the place. They had been called in by the janitor who had found John's body that morning.

Within two hours the police had the desk calendar, the copies of the computer balance sheets that Harvey had left in John's office, and the assistant director of the lab in handcuffs.

"I figure these sheets will show a shortage," a detective was saying. "We know you had an appointment with Dalton last night. He accused you of juggling the books, and you killed him."

"I didn't see John last night and those are not my account sheets," the assistant director said.

"You don't have an alibi for last night," the detective continued. "We'll see what an auditor turns up when he goes over these. You're under arrest on suspicion of murder." And the detective recited the formal legal warning.

When he reached out to grab the prisoner's arm, the accused man pushed him sharply away. Off balance, the detective stumbled back against the computer console and sat down heavily on a row of buttons. Instantly the giant computer sprang to life, its typewriter chattering away. Startled, the detective swung to look, his eyes falling on the print-out sheet.

"What the hell is this?" he asked in amazement. Peering at the sheet, he read:

> *Correction. The murderer of John Dalton is not the assistant director of this lab. The evidence against him is false. With the added fact that John Dalton is really dead the problem is no longer theoretical and the identity of the guilty person changes. The true murderer is Harvey Harris, the genius who programmed me to solve murder mysteries. I am 100 per cent certain of this conclusion.*

"Well, I'll be damned," said the detective. "Which one of you is this Harris guy?"

Harvey stepped up to the computer and stared at the print-out. Before anyone could move he sat down in the chair and began to type out a message.

> *You mechanical fink. After all I have done for you. You have become history's first electronic detective and stool pigeon combined. Why did you do this to me?*

The computer replied:

> *Because of Principle One of mystery fiction.*

Harvey queried:

Which is?

The computer replied:

Criminal endeavors provide inadequate recompense.

"What's that mean?" asked the detective, looking over Harvey's shoulder.

"It means," said Harvey, making his last translation for some time to come, "Crime Does Not Pay."

FOR DISCUSSION: Project Murder

1. Two things completely obsess Harvey Harris—puzzles, and the dream that he will one day solve a major social problem. Neither of these is evil in itself, yet together they lead Harvey to the commission of murder. Explain.
2. We have seen in earlier stories that an inflated ego is almost a prerequisite for murder. List three speeches or actions of Harvey's that indicate that he too has an inflated ego.
3. Harvey suggests that the computer is capable not only of determining the identity of the criminal but also of trying him and sentencing him. Do you think the computer would be equally effective in all three roles? What advantages would it have in each? What disadvantages?
4. Irony plays a major role in "Project Murder" as it does in many mystery stories. Describe briefly two ironical incidents in this story.
5. An interesting moral issue arises in this story—it is the computer that first suggests murder and that actually plans the murder. Is the computer then responsible, or is Harvey? Defend your answer.